Paul Siegvolk

Ruminations

The ideal American lady and other essays

Paul Siegvolk

Ruminations
The ideal American lady and other essays

ISBN/EAN: 9783337038281

Printed in Europe, USA, Canada, Australia, Japan

Cover: Foto ©Andreas Hilbeck / pixelio.de

More available books at **www.hansebooks.com**

RUMINATIONS

THE IDEAL AMERICAN LADY

AND OTHER ESSAYS

BY

PAUL SIEGVOLK

AUTHOR OF "A BUNDLE OF PAPERS," ETC.

CHEWING THE CUD OF SWEET AND BITTER FANCY.
As You Like It.

G. P. PUTNAM'S SONS

NEW YORK   LONDON
27 WEST TWENTY-THIRD STREET   24 BEDFORD STREET, STRAND

The Knickerbocker Press

1893

CONTENTS.

PROLOGUE.

Ego hæc mecum mussito.

PLAUTUS.

A BRUYÈRE says :—"A philosopher wastes his life in observing men, and wears himself out in exposing vice and folly. If he shapes his thoughts into words, it is not so much from his vanity as an author as to place entirely in its proper light some truth he has discovered, that it may make the desired impression ; . . . he demands from mankind greater and more uncommon results than empty praise, and even than rewards ; he expects them to lead better lives"—and, it might be added, perhaps happier.

Occasionally the writer, like many others, has felt (not however without serious misgivings) as if he might have something, not wholly useless, to say—to some of his fellow-men—before quitting this world. He is prone to regard any ordinary individual (especially himself) as of little importance in this life ; and to think no one entitled to much consideration for anything beyond what

I

he may do to add to our stock of knowledge, or to the comfort or pleasure of mankind, or, in other words, contribute, consciously or not, toward the intellectual development, moral expansion, or wholesome enjoyment or entertainment of at least some portion of the human race. Every man, however humble, may, and perhaps ought to, endeavor to do something in this direction. It is hardly to be expected that all efforts to this end, although earnest and sincere, will visibly produce permanently useful results. Nevertheless, out of a prodigality of offerings, some may prove beneficial ;— impracticable as it may be to proclaim, in all cases, in advance, which product holds within it a germinating seed, or what may be only an empty husk.

It is probable these pages contain nothing new to many, or essentially different from what has been better said in earlier books. Yet is it not well known that, while men generally talk much of the titles, and famil- iarly mention the names of the authors, of old books, there are in every large community a hundred who at least will skim over a new book, for one who will read honestly an old one? Moreover, of the countless books written in the remote past, only a few now popularly are read at all. How then shall the gems of thought, hidden from the common eye, in dark cabinets of elder literature, be known by a new-coming generation of desultory readers, if such jewels be not frequently brought to the light, and perhaps partially reset, so as to catch the eye, or to suit the prevailing inclination or taste of the passing day?

The human face and form vary but little from age to age ; the vicissitudes of human conduct in political, civil, commercial, or social life, throughout all known time, bear a close family resemblance ; and the discourses of meditating minds upon human conduct or worldly events, made in the course of ages past, are, to the scholar, often as repetitious as the gait of the ox in the furrow, or of the horse galloping over a familiar road. Nevertheless, changes of fashion are continually modifying personal appearance ; the perusal of the history of the events and lives of the actors of one period of time does not satisfy the desire to learn the circumstances of later occurrences —however close may be their similarity to the earlier. Neither can the unlearned be expected to find all of their literary delight in reading the thoughts of men, the lives and actions of whose contemporaries are materially obscured by lapse of time, as well as by radical changes in institutions, laws, customs, creeds, traditions, associations, morals, manners, or language.

One word more. Literature is, for the most part, mortal—fondly as genius may hope otherwise—and constantly liable to change in substance. Being largely composed from elements of transitory character, or of temporary use, it is necessarily changeable—if not wholly perishable. Not every one will agree with de Maupassant :—Il faut être, en effet, bien fou, bien audacieux, bien outrecui- dant ou bien sot, pour écrire encore aujourd'hui ! Even the few classics that defy the merciless tooth of Time gradually become only the choice morsels of a limited number of profound, elegant, or curious scholars. They are known, to the general public of miscellaneous read- ers, merely by scintillations from some brilliant name— often wholly dissociated from the text in which they originate. If more, they are relegated, for the most part, to the office of furnishing a few quotations to index-readers, or to those who retain with precision the reminiscences of youthful school-tasks, and but little else.

Indeed there is small profit in blinking this matter. After all that may be said (whether honestly or not) in a lofty way of the demands of pure literature, it is really upon the insatiable craving of the general reader for something fresh, in form or appearance—regardless of antiquity of substance—that we must rely, to keep the printing-press running, and to drive the wolf from the door of the professional author ;—saying nothing of its giving any unabashed writer his hope of a chance for a prize in the lottery of contemporary reputation, or of its help in keeping the world amused, or, it may be, in alluring the idle-minded scribbler from getting into some worse mischief than that of threshing old straw.

Perhaps, however, after all, a man may be too much overawed by the natural apprehension lest a want of essential novelty be discernible in his own purely original thoughts. Even Goethe said, to his friend Eckermann, in the seventy-seventh year of the poet's age :—"Had I earlier known how many excellent things have been in existence for hundreds of years, I would not have written a line, but would have done something else."

CONCERNING WOMEN.

I.

THE IDEAL AMERICAN LADY.

——from the all that are, took something good
To make a perfect woman.
Winter's Tale.

HE perfect "lady," although something less than an angel, must be vastly more than a merely excellent and amiable woman. The term has come to be used, among us, to express sometimes a common idea of what we fondly believe any good woman may and perhaps ought to be. Even in the popular mind, however, it seems to have outgrown somewhat its normal definition—"a well-bred woman"—and by common consent to involve the possession of the most attractive and endearing possibilities of her sex, as well as the holding in complete subjection all that may be unamiable in her nature. Although few may attain the supreme excellence of this character, her actual existence, in some form, appears to be an essential postulate

5

in the social creed which all women and most men in our country profess.

She may also be said to belong to a kind of order ; and to be distinguishable, from the mass of her sex, by some inexplicable sign, that seems to foreshadow her right of membership. There will be always about her a well-recognized, yet intangible, air of claim to be admitted to this rank. Indeed whatever may be her age, education, language, birthplace, dress, or customary ways, whensoever the proper countersign is given, the charmed circle—although apparently closed and incapable of breaking its outer line—easily opens to admit the new-comer. The members of this marvellous sisterhood seem to have been trained from the cradle—either by a kind of acolytes or by some invisible agencies presiding at their birth—and to have been so conducted, from infancy to mature girlhood or beyond, through all the cabala of their mysterious guild. By virtue of this initiation they appear always to know each other, through a sort of intuition, whenever entitled to reciprocal fellowship. Is it feasible to grasp this eidolon ;—to paint in its true colors this floating figure, that dances in the air before the eyes of us all, and may be, nay so commonly is, tinged by the hues of the media through which it is seen ?

It would be scarcely safe to claim that there is one hard outlined image of ladyhood, clear-cut, or with broad lines of demarcation, setting it apart from womanhood in general. There are many ideals in the ordinary conceptions of our people. Yet it is believed all will be found to have most of their essentials in common—however they may vary in expression of details. Apparent points of dissimilarity may indicate merely a variety of conditions, under which traits, really in common, are exhibited. Patient observation and charitable insight may enable one to find an identity of genus, widely as the species may appear to differ.

Our lexicographers have tried their trained hands upon the subject. Reference to a single one will suffice. Webster puts it, as "a term of complaisance applied to almost any well-dressed woman, but appropriately to one of refined manners and education." This vague definition is however somewhat aided by his own description of what sense he applies to this word "education," viz :—"All that series of instruction and discipline which is intended to enlighten the understanding, correct the temper, and form the manners and habits of youth, and fit them for usefulness in their future stations."

But in our ordinary talk, the word suggests, besides these general notions, certain specific affirmative qualities of individual feminine human nature. It indicates a deeply rooted, untaught self-respect and an inborn self-restraint ;—the pith of true nobleness in character. It means something usually shown by such traits as dignity, repose, ease, courtesy, affability, grace, tact, and delicacy of thought—whether in presence, manner, carriage, address, touch, look, speech, tone of voice, enunciation, or accent. United with these we imply the indefinable impress of an unobtrusive personality ;—importing, at least, a serene mind, a frank, generous, sensitive, sympathizing, amiable disposition, a noble unselfishness, a well-disciplined temper, and a tender regard for the peculiar, natural or factitious individuality of others.

A lady, too, will generally have power to inspire among men, through her ingrained, invincible modesty, a sort of gallantry of the soul; which, reacting upon herself, makes up an intercourse of quite different character from, and embraces some fascinating elements wanting in, the ordinary associating together of mere men and women.

Eve scarcely could have anticipated, in its completeness, the character of our ideal lady; since it would probably be necessary to presuppose among her associates, at least more than one man—with perhaps many women—and moreover possibly that they be disconnected from her by any recognized family tie.

The lady is the legitimate depositary of the noblest traditions and most honored customs of the best society, relating to all its intricate personal methods. These may not be taught her by any specific rule, nor any explanatory reasons for their authority be furnished to her. She absorbs them, as it were, into the very composition of her mind and heart, from the air she breathes, during her whole life. Habitudes of social refinement and courtesy are to her matters concerning which reasoning seems idle. Nature and circumstances have given her a special insight and aptitude for the demands of her position. It has cost her no apparent, or even conscious, effort to be accomplished in the complete mastery of the whole art of polite, social intercourse.

Perhaps it would be considered not extravagantly fanciful to say that, like a planet, she has an atmosphere of her own;—which must be taken into our reckoning, when we would measure her, or know her true relations with those to whom she gives light, and among whom she revolves.

In her closest intimacies with either sex, the lady will maintain a dainty reserve, which an ordinary woman cannot keep up always without awkward severity, or perhaps some ungraceful sacrifice of candor. To preserve this felicitous mean, between frankness and self-continence, is an easy accomplishment for the lady ; but a task sometimes apparently quite beyond the abilities of many lovable women. Much mingling with strangers, and wide intercourse with the social world in general, may, in due time, contribute largely to the production of a personal bearing that will gracefully baffle intrusion. But in the perfect lady an elegant awe of manner is apparently the natural offspring of some original impulse.

It has been said :—" People who, from their birth upwards, have been accustomed to deference, acquire a manner which takes that deference for granted ;—an attitude from which the element of assertion is eliminated." In the lady this graciousness of attitude is a something more than a mere conquest of habit. Whatever it may be, we easily profess to it a submissive loyalty that costs us no sacrifice of self-respect ; and we rise from bowing in homage to its empire over us, never belittled, but rather exalted. It affects us not unlike our praise of a good action. We seem to borrow a perfume from its loveliness, and to acquire a grace from our very act, when we accord it the frank recognition we feel it deserves.

There is much in this deportment of the lady that defies definition and almost escapes description. Has some patent of nobility been granted by Nature to her favorites ;—a royal franchise, by which their "art and mystery" is protected from infringement by those who

are not to the manner born ?   Look even at her gait, as
she moves to approach or walk away from you.   Who
wonders that the Roman poet, in his portraiture of the
goddesses of his mythology, made their very step, when
walking upon this earth, a trick of divinity, likely to
betray them through any disguise ?   Every one recalls
with pleasure his school-boy delight in reading that, when
Æneas met his mother, Venus, masquerading in the
woods as a huntress, her very manner of walking settled
his doubts of her identity :—

Et vera incessu patuit Dea.

"Let us, with caution," said the Father of our country,
"indulge the supposition that morality can be maintained
without religion."   Is Christian piety then a necessary
attribute of the lady ?   How can it be otherwise ?   How
else can woman have that reverence for things high and
holy, seen and unseen, here and hereafter, without which
no human being can long continue to be (except perhaps
by conscious, obvious, and painful effort of extraordinary
intellect) in true and harmonious relations with the best
social world as it now is?   A profound reverence for a
personal God, a steadfast faith in Gospel revelation, a
buoyant hope coupled with a wholesome fear, centred in
a future spiritual life and its supernatural promises, are
still the primal bases upon which all our common civilization rests.   The character we are striving to depict is
the fondling of that civilization.

Without faith, even in the leading religious dogmas
prevailing around her, woman is somewhat of an anomaly.

Without religion, she is, as it were, morally unsexed. By her nature specially imaginative and emotional, she is properly not rationalistic. To be out of harmony with the moral opinion of her neighbors and contemporaries, to be socially anarchical, unfits her for developing some of her most amiable qualities. As a motive to action, impulse is naturally as powerful with a woman as reason is with a man. Indeed a woman, by the susceptibility of her temper, and the very infirmity of some of her loveliest traits, is always liable to be dominated by a reckless will. To say the least, this proverbial force, if unchecked, may let loose her speech, or direct her conduct, to her serious detriment. Without vital and demonstrable piety, as the anchor of her soul, to stay her impulsive conduct, she may, in a storm of passion, slip her cable, and be dashed to pieces amid breakers. Perhaps this obvious remark is true of most of our race ; yet it is not to be overlooked when considering the essential rudiments of the ideal lady.

I once asked a paragon of her sex, what most distinguished the lady from other varieties of womankind ? Her answer was :—" There is a subtile, indefinable air of refinement about a true lady which is never mistaken by anybody. Be she handsome or homely this inherent quality silently asserts itself, and makes its presence known to people of all classes, as surely as the Roman lictor, with his bundle of rods, made known to all he approached, that the authority of a Cæsar was there. It is an emanation of power that exerts its mysterious influence without any objective intent, or conscious will of its possessor. Beauty will enhance this power ; but the

look and features will bear its unmistakable impress, regardless of their homeliness."

In her general intercourse with her own sex, we shall
probably find the surest test of her real nobility of
character.   Rarely, if ever, does she make enemies
among women. In the language of a lady, whose thought
has more than once guided the hand attempting this
etching :—" Neither arrogance nor servility will be noted
in her demeanor ; her self-assertion will be calm and
inoffensive, but effectual ; her apparent deference to
others will be modest, but not obsequious;—nor will it ever
be attributed to servility. She will recognize the claims
of whomsoever may be superior or inferior, giving each
her just due with a graceful and inoffensive tact." She
will have pride without haughtiness or ostentation, and
self-love without vanity or self-conceit.

In all her dealings with others, her ways are somehow
so curiously adapted to each person, that she puts them
at once in harmonious relations with herself. The
subject opens widely when one attempts to exemplify
this varying air of apparent self-abnegation, yet unconscious self-assertion or impression of individuality—so
tempered and disguised as to soothe, and never to
irritate, the personality of another. It has often tempted
poet, essayist, and artist into striving to portray or illustrate these evanescent characteristics. What a charming
cento might be made, if one would gather their various
representations of woman's multiform attitudes, as
daughter, sister, friend, lover, wife, or mother—keeping
in sole view her pure ladyhood, and its peculiar manifestations. What a book it might be ; an encyclopedia of

beauty, grace, love, truth, charity, piety in its social sense, and indeed of all kindred womanly virtues.

Is the lady a modern creation ? Is she an evolution of our Christian idea of social womanhood ? Doubtless the family intercourse of the women of the great cities of the early periods of the world (among the men and women of cultivation, refinement, political power, social authority, or public office) developed many traits of manner, many ways of thinking and acting in respect to the minor morals of their day, that neither history, literature, nor the arts have wholly preserved. Yet, with what light we have for judging—although giving due credit to woman in the pagan ages for possessing all the more robust virtues of her sex, and for many of those graces of manner and refinements of social sympathy which are by some deemed inseparable from her nature when un-perverted by bad example or imperious necessity—one well may be incredulous of her claim to fill out the exacting ideal of the lady of our day. With all her accredited tendencies towards moral perfection, is it likely she rose above the level of the social exigencies and ideas of her time ? When religious rites demanded human sacrifices, and even priestesses administered at the bloody altars, where was the tender grace that in-spires our ideal lady ? When the torture of savage beasts in the public arena, to say nothing of the open murder of their innocent human victims, and the spectacle of gladiators — " butchered to make a Roman holiday "— amused the idle hours of the women of the highest rank, one cannot believe easily, we would be very proud of the sensibility, delicacy, or even refinement of such mothers or daughters—however fully they may have satisfied the notions of their own day.

We well may ask, if their ideal of perfect womanhood was as exacting as our own. Did the gentle dignity, the softness of manner, the graceful condescension or absence of self-assertion, the clear consciousness of unasserted personal worth—never faltering or suffering anxiety lest it be not duly respected—the kindness of heart, the love of humanity, the wide charity, the sweet benevolence, the zeal for good works, the unswerving faith in the justice, mercy, and love of a Divine Father—did such blended traits of our ideal lady find full development among the most perfected women of antiquity?

Of course it is questionable whether we know enough of the more intimate social life of such remote times, to answer these questions satisfactorily. To most of our people, however, the lady is regarded as a creature of the Christian era. She represents, in the popular heart, a sort of embodiment of that idea of the exaltation of womanhood which seems to find its sublimated sanction in an image of the Holy Virgin-Mother. She is enthroned upon spiritual heights to which a barbaric or pagan conception of womanly perfection does not appear to have attained; —except possibly in the visions of the devotees of some priestly office, far removed from the common cares and concerns of mankind. Moreover she is believed to be now a practical person;—one of the specific factors of our modern civilization, a power in the republic of letters or arts, capable of a professional or business career, and a vital force in all the ordinary affairs of our social daily life.

What is the secret of that charm of manner, which is so persuasive, so compelling, so irresistible ? What gives her that sovereign deportment which seems to radiate light and warmth from her presence—so easy to recognize, so hard to describe, so tempting to imitate, yet so nearly impossible to counterfeit ? What is the seed-bud of this growth—if it be a growth ? Is there some primal essence of this finished development, some element, that dominates all the rest, and without which the other materials of the composition would be vainly brought together ? The enigma is not easy of solution. One can hope only to put forward some admiring guess, for unravelling the web of this mystery.

Perhaps it is a sort of unconscious personal equableness ;—the exquisite balance of a character, giving assurance of a well-poised physical, moral, and spiritual nature. As among men, we find a philosopher when we encounter one in whom equanimity always prevails, so of the lady in her ideal perfection, can we be sure of our model, unless in her there be this unwavering equability ?

Ladyhood, confessedly, is not wholly a matter of temperament, nor a result of mere outward circumstances. There must be some other qualities, indicating a peculiar personality. One may expect to find, in her profound self-respect, something that never wavers, nor tolerates any attempt to tarnish or slight it. So far as self-assertion may be necessary for its maintenance, the lady will quietly but firmly, perhaps unconsciously yet unmistakably, always impress you with the predominance of this cardinal idea.

Another distinguishing trait of the ideal lady, which
certainly entitles her to be esteemed a representative of
the noblest order of womanhood (as I am instructed by
one in whom the virtues of ladyhood shine with marked
brilliancy) will be her truthfulness. "Truth," says she,
"tempered with firmness, justice, mercy, and good common-sense—cardinal virtues of mind and heart—must
be the keystone of the arch, without which the graceful
fabric is but a fraud, dangerously deceptive, as a mirage
that a breath may sweep away. If there be real truthfulness in the heart, firmness will be its unconscious companion ;—but mercy no less than courage should be ever at
hand to guide its expression. It is not intended here to
portray a complacent simpleton, who would consider it
her duty to tell all she may fortuitously know of others ;
but an intelligent woman, unwilling to wound unnecessarily the feelings of the humblest person, guided by high
principles, illumined by a sense of honor, and respecting
the rights of herself, as well as those of all with whom
she may be brought in contact. Truth is the impenetra-
ble shield and armor of the lady, having something divine
in their composition, like those given to Æneas. In the
conflicts of social life, it will guard her from the vice of
retailing gossip ; while it will make her the champion,
either silent or outspoken but always formidable, of those
who, unheard and unheeding, may suffer from the insidious assaults of the sappers and miners of the army corps
of slanderers.

If we draw aside for a moment the veil of serene yet
blithesome manner, that time, training, and custom have
thrown around our subject, and look once more into the

deeper wells of her nature, we shall see a brilliant point
of light, floating in clear space, as one may see a planet
mirrored in a telescope. Call it rectitude. She is upright
in all things from the core of her heart to her finger-tips.
She never does wrong consciously, during her whole life.
She never tampers with her inbred sense of right. She
never puts her conscience to the test of mere reason —
much less of convenience. She never sets up her will
against the common religious or moral sentiment of the
day. She is conventional and modal, not so much by
calculation as by intuition. Nor can she ever be abashed,
or do anything of which she may feel ashamed. Indeed
she is wholly unconscious of personal error in the sight
of man, in any respect. And while neither arrogant nor
pharisaical, it has never occurred to her august mind,
that she could wittingly neglect a duty, trespass upon the
rights of a fellow-being, or even violate a rule of social
propriety. As she was born and grew, as she was bred
and taught, there arose and developed in her mind and
heart this exquisite moral sense ;—a clear idea of something more far-reaching, higher and broader, than any
mere rule of right and wrong, as measured by the artificial standard of a Puritan conscience—a notion of some
inexorable law of her individual and social being touching
the fitness of things, natural and artificial, human and
divine, material and spiritual, moral and religious, that
has always been her unbroken support. To such ideas
she has been constantly true ;—never, even in thought or
fancy, swerving to either side of the clear and straight
pathway before her. She mutely obeys a law of rectitude as inexorable as gravitation.

2

With all her opulence of possibilities, yet she has limitations. They are positive and exacting. Although she
does many things as matters of course, for which she
could give no satisfactory reason to the uninitiated, nevertheless there are a vast number of social acts women in
general may do lawfully sometimes, which she cannot
even think of as possible for herself. *Noblesse oblige.*
However she does not appear to be under constraint, a
slave of custom, or even excessively fastidious.

She is indeed one of those fortunate persons, to whose
placid moral and intellectual vision, as well as serene
temper, none of the things of this world appear to be out
of joint. Her gracious optimism might rank as a social
virtue. Although full of sympathy, affection, and melting
charity, yet with a conservative eye she sees broadly all
things in harmonious proportions, however obscure or
conflicting may be their immediate relations. To her
understanding, "Order is Heaven's first law." With this
key she unlocks the secrets of God's providence, and
reconciles many apparent inequalities that meet the eye
in this visible world. Hence her mind is always poised
at its proper position, seldom elated beyond the graceful
dignity of a sweet composure, or depressed below its
proper equipoise. She is never puffed up with super-
cilious pride or self-conceit ; neither can the assertion of
superiority in another humiliate her. Standing upon her
own pedestal, with envy and jealousy beneath her feet,
invidious rivalry slinks away abashed by her exquisite
dignity of bearing, her sweetness of temper, her calm
suavity, her sunny cheerfulness, her cordial affability, her
radiant and artless grace.

One peculiarity of some American women may perhaps be considered an ingredient of the character of our ideal lady. Possibly it is a native root of qualities distinguishing her from her sisters among other national types. It consists in an apparent unconsciousness, or ignoring, of any claim on the part of any other woman—by rank, birth, wealth, beauty, wit, genius, accomplishment, fame, or other consideration — to be reckoned her natural superior, in social esteem or outward recognition. She brooks no such superiors. She knows no class above her own, and no person entitled to take social precedence of herself by right. She carries this insensibly in her manner : but she wears it gracefully as the trees do their foliage, or the flowers their blossoms ; for it is a part of her nature, and not the result of either thought, effort, or policy of any kind. It is as elemental with her as for a fish to swim, or a bird to fly. Nor is she ever thrown off her balance in this respect, or forgetful of what she considers her rightful inheritance — not bought, but inherent. Perhaps this trait may explain some social phenomena that occasionally amaze a foreign visitor.

In the anarchical struggle of social conditions among the women of our large cities, the ideal equipoise we have mentioned may be severely tested, and practically does not always withstand the strain put upon it. I once knew a typical woman of lady-like refinement, well-born and bred, of whom it might be said the contact of our mingled variety of social phenomena was too much for her imperial spirit to bear. She had rather a limited love of humanity in the concrete. For the sake of protection against rude invasion of her personality she occasionally felt compelled to substitute tact or policy in lieu of her natural grace and simplicity of heart. She sacrificed some of her frankness to a fastidious decorum. In the bosom of her family, and in her own social stratum, she was natural and almost angelic. At other places, and especially in mixed society, to the observation of the few who knew her intimately, she appeared at times to be, as it were, upon stilts, and behind a mask—like some tragedy queen in a Greek play. However she could fill her rôle with success ;—looking to the common eye so simple, easy, graceful, and buoyant, that people generally believed her to be the unconsciously radiant creature she appeared to them, while they little guessed the dreary wearisomeness sometimes in her heart.

Is our ideal American lady so born, or only fashioned by human hands ? Is she purely the child of nature—or a creature of society ? There is still among us a strong, perhaps increasing, belief in the instinct of blood ;— however much we may allow for mere breeding or social education, and despite the dogmas of our political creed.

Whether the human race descended from a single pair ; or whether there were originally superior and inferior races ; or whether a celestial strain, in the far ages, mingled with human lineage, as mythologies feign ; or whether the law of evolution, tending towards perfection, among higher capabilities of the race, holds and transmits what excellence it finds ; to many it seems to be an absurdity in analogy to recognize a law of heredity in beasts, yet to deny it among mankind. The whole race, at all times, in fact, obviously has paid deference and even

homage to this law;—however much in theory nowadays it may be denied or repudiated by religious creeds
or political manifestoes.

Another kindred suggestion. We see throughout all
animated nature the production of new types approxi-
mating to perfection, and also new varieties of the higher
types. Again we find even such types becoming fresh
rivals in the struggle to attain a remoter ideal. Can we
assume that the loveliest work of nature is shut out from
the glory of this otherwise universal law? Shall dogmatic theology, or political philosophy, in their claim for
human equality prevail against common experience in
respect to a rule demonstrated even in the vegetable
world? May we not premise that, in the course of time,
nobler moral features of men and women are evolved?
When, by heroic or gentle life and conduct, one has
proved a divine right to be the *stirps* or *gens* of a new
variety of the human family, shall we not recognize the
apparent fact of transmissible nobleness? May we not
thus find the germ that grows, blossoms, and ripens into
the ideal perfect lady? It is one of nature's mysteries,
that perhaps time alone more clearly can reveal to us, as
our democratic society progresses; or when we shall
approach a golden age of social conduct, in which the
better elements of human nature may maintain a wider
predominance over the grosser, and the animal part of
us be more subordinate to the spiritual.

I know a woman who might well sit for a portrait of the
figure I strive to paint; whose opinion in the matter is
really a revelation from her own nature, coupled with the
judgment of an expert. "Ladyhood," she tells me, "is

hereditary, generally speaking ; but there can be no doubt
that a few generations of education and refinement will
tone and modify the acerbities of even the most brutal
natures. These, with a veneering of culture, may pass
current in society as ladies, and possibly there may be
ladies among them, but the probabilities are that the
majority of them are gilded images only. Even in the
savage state we may find the germ, or, so to speak, the
timber or stone, out of which to carve the genuine
figure. Among the Seminole Indians, it is said, were
found natural ladies and gentlemen. The Marquis de
Lafayette reported of this tribe of children of the forest,
that in their manner they reminded him of the old
nobility of France. With proper cultivation what might not
have been found to be their latent possibilities ? Possibly,
after many generations, the veneered people may evolve
among their class a genuine lady. I believe, however, in
original blood, yet am free to concede that of course its
admixture with a grosser strain will, with the assistance
of proper education, in process of time, 'breed out' the
common blood of the latter ;—but if the stock be not full-
blooded, the offspring will surely, as the race progresses,
occasionally 'breed back,' and here and there we shall
see the most vulgar specimens among the families which
pass current as Vere de Veres."

Does our ideal lady grow old ? Is not the sweetness of
her womanhood enveloped in an amber of apparently
continuing youth ? Does buoyant sympathy with all that
is humanly pure, good, and lovable flag with the passage of time ? Never ceasing to love, and be loved by,
her fellow-creatures, she always brings hope, joy smiles,

and brightness wherever she goes. Her youthful mien, her unvarying urbanity, her exquisitely elastic grace, and unspeakable fascination of demeanor, even the musical cadence of her speech, with her unaffected, modest assurance, whether in pose, or gesture, or in talking, listening, laughing, or sympathizing, or in directing, leading, yielding, or following ; all of these appear to endure untarnished by the deteriorating breath of time. There is at the least an airy spirit of vernal loveliness always hovering about her, that charms, soothes, and inspires like Sappho's swallow :—

Blithe angel of the perfume-breathing Spring.

As in her intercourse with the world, judicious tact— born of plain common-sense, sincerity, and simplicity— sustains her in a true relation towards all others ; so in her dealing with even inanimate things, she seems to have an unfailing sense of propriety—strong and clear, but delicate and exquisite—that informs and controls her taste and judgment. In her dress she never leans to excess in form, color, or ornament ; nor is she coarse or plain where richness and variety are suitable. She well knows there is a use of ornament that suggests, if it do not express, refinement ;—seeming to tell only half its worth, and so is wholly subordinate to its wearer or possessor. There is another sort of display of the like accessories, that is often aggressive by its iridescent gauds, and whose inharmonious variety disturbs the eye—or may even roil the temper of a neighbor. The taste of the lady of course is never at fault when choosing between them ;—or in rejecting the latter, even if the former be out of her reach.

In all her paraphernalia of wider signification, as in person and apparel, she has a dainty neatness—almost fastidiousness—that seems to exhale, from every object belonging to her, a sort of moral freshness ;—affecting our senses like the sight of early violets, whose fragrance is too distant, or confined, actually to reach us, yet which we seem to inhale, as it were, through the eyes, by some obscure sense. Amid the glare and homeliness of common things, and among a crowd of miscellaneous people, this peculiarly delicate aroma of a sacred individuality, this subdued aureole of womanly splendor, may sometimes appear not unlike an affectation of over-refinement. But in her own sphere, and with the belongings of her own special social condition about her—in her own home and among her own people—it surrounds her as her own appropriate element. However rarefied the atmosphere may appear, to persons of coarser mold and homelier associations whose lungs cannot find support in its attenuated condition, certainly she floats in it with ever sustained wing.

Among the miscellaneous rout, in Chaucer's *Canterbury Tales*, who made their famous pilgrimage from the "Tabard" in Southwark, will be remembered the Lady Prioresse Eglentine. If the poet meant to satirize her as ostentatiously fastidious, yet he paid an involuntary tribute to a minor phase of lady-like manners :—

> At mete was she wel y-taughte withalle ;
> She lette no morsel from hire lippes falle,
> Ne wette hire fingres in hire sauce depe.
> Wel coude she carie a morsel, and wel kepe,

That no drope ne fell upon hire brest.
In curtesie was sette ful moche hire lest.
Hire over lippe wiped she so clene,
That in hire cuppe was no ferthing sene
Of grese, whan she dronken hadde hire draught.

One word of another similar matter. There is still found in some circles, occasionally, an affectation of supersensitive delicacy, both physical and moral, which, being false is detestable and ridiculous, yet seems to borrow its suggestion from some of the finer traits of womankind. This simulation, however, is sure to run into absurd extravagance ; and to betray the absence of the coveted quality it slanders and travesties, by a rude imitation. The susceptibility to emotional shock, which is the natural condition of a highly organized temperament, and is ingrained in the fibre of the real lady, is not easily feigned, so as to deceive the intelligent. That good health and sound nerves, united with commonsense notions of right and wrong, are not inconsistent with real refinement of physical or moral sensibility, is constantly apparent in the loveliest class of women. But a maudlin conscience, or a morbid affectation of childish fears, a weak resolution, a nerveless flaccidity, or a masquerade of general incompetence, only betray the unlovely counterfeit.

It may not be idle to contrast some minor traits common to the lady and her counterpart, the gentleman. Being correlatives, we can hardly conceive of the practical existence of the one without the other. They are alike in some general characteristics, although varying even in these, as their natural organizations and circum-

stances differ—perhaps, however, as has been often said,
more in degree than in kind.

The idea of the gentleman seems to have originated as
soon as there was evolved a man who could live plenteously as a private citizen without the work of his own
hands. Hence the vulgar notion of the gentleman being
a man of idleness. Hardly any intelligent American,
however, would describe a lady as being a woman who
does not work. Such an one might figure as the light of
a harem—a mere toy or plaything—but not as a "lady."
Inclination to industry of some kind appears to have been
so early implanted in the habitual nature of the normal
American woman, that indolence seems associated, in the
common mind, only with one who—perhaps by new fortune—is somehow out of her true relations with the world
in general.

Possibly much of this distinction grows out of the fact
that the occupation of women is largely the management of
matters of detail ;—necessarily varied and endless. However there may be something more than this. An indus-
trious woman may carry about her, more impressively, that
indefinable charm in which a lady moves, than does an
idle one. In the latter there is a tendency of the physical
nature to dominate, and sometimes perhaps even to ob-
literate, some intellectual or spiritual feminine graces.
Indeed, it seems almost as if to be a constant doer-of-
good-works might be set down as one of the elemental
characteristics of the fine personality we are striving to
sketch.

Surmising that the production of the lady is largely the
evolution of heredity, in that respect, too, she, appears to

differ somewhat from the gentleman. A man may spring
from common ancestry and be bred among narrow social
surroundings, yet at some period of his life easily attain
the full rank of the popular idea of an American gentleman. Possibly this result is in some degree owing to the
fact that a man with even lately acquired social advantages—if he have fair intellect, with a strong tendency
towards self-perfecting by refinement in all things—may
continue, his life long, to learn and grow in this direction.
A woman of the same class, with the like relative grade
of intelligence and opportunities, usually ceases to progress, either in such mental or external accomplishment, at
a comparatively early age;—and to wear the scars of her
struggle with the world more visibly. Moreover the
necessities, as well as the opportunities, of self-education
and self-discipline, both in mind and manners, seem rather
to increase, with the growth of a man's mental stature
and participation in the affairs of the world ; till time
mellows, while practice smooths, that crudity and ruggedness, which absence of early social amenities permitted to
grow wild—unpruned and misdirected. With woman,
however, if the material chance to be naturally somewhat
coarse-grained, it does not appear generally to be capable
of so fine a polish. Friction with the world more often
betrays its natural imperfections and tends rather to
exaggerate than to conceal them. We look often in vain,
among such specimens of the sex, for that wonderful
permeating delicacy and refinement, that subordination of
self to others in all matters of interest, feeling, affection,
and duty, and that complete recognition of the obligations and limitations imposed upon natural impulse and

personal will by the dominating grace, dignity, and honor of womanhood, without which we cannot make out the full lineaments of our ideal lady.

As, according to common impression, the subtile elements of the character of the perfect lady suggest an aromatic flavor of youth, however far the subject herself may be in fact advanced beyond her prime, and there always attends her, more or less, the sweetness of womanhood with its glorious blossom ; so also it may be that the lady is more a character external—with something more of efflorescent air and seeming, as necessary qualities— than is her supposed counterpart, the gentleman. She should have for her immediate surroundings, as it were, light and color, contrast and background, to give her full effect. Like a jewel, however rare and beautiful in itself, she seems to need a setting to graduate her appearance into harmony with common persons, places, and things. The gentleman sometimes soars above the meanest circumstances, and vindicates his touch of divinity, under the trying test of misfortune, suspicion, poverty, and even squalor, by a kind of heroic halo shining through the clouds that encompass him ;—perhaps as Ulysses appeared to Nausicaa. The lady on the contrary loses so much by the absence of her kindred accessories and proper surroundings, that she may suffer, perhaps, even unconsciously, a temporary loss of dignity and power, when she is thus thrown out of her sphere, and the gracefulness of her outward equilibrium is unduly jostled.

As the lady is in some of her external aspects apparently a more artificial being than the gentleman, she has many factitious merits the like of which with him may be deemed non-essentials, or even faults. Conspicuously among such minor things might be classed her intuitive acquaintance with minute matters of social propriety and form in polite intercourse. Unlike him she will not come to know when, where, how, or from whom she learned these mysteries. She has no recollection of the time when they were unknown to her. Indeed, this knowledge belongs to her inner consciousness ; and seems to pulsate, as it were, in the veins of her mind.

The writer is not vain enough to suppose he has drawn the contour of this ideal portrait with sharp lines ; much less given the precise color, tone, or expression of its finer features, to general satisfaction. The matter is not fit for dogmatical opinion. The ramifications of its development, and the varieties of its appearance, are difficult to classify or to reduce to any single formula. Popular ideas differ essentially, as to the excellence of many apparently dissimilar types. People look at this subject from many different points of view : and even the fairest-minded are apt to be unconsciously swayed in judgment by some association of ideas with special individuals, through love, friendship, gratitude, or some other like disturbing force.

Neither should any woman suffer disparagement in her own eyes because she is unable to realize in her outward act all, or even the larger part, of what has been here suggested as the similitude of the ideal lady. However nearly in her own heart she may feel that she comes up to the highest standard, doubtless sometimes she will be painfully conscious of her failure to impress that conviction upon others. Few of us, in this brief life of vicissitudes and interruptions, develop our best possibilities.

We are all—even the most fortunate and the strongest-willed—more or less the never-manumitted slaves of what is nowadays called our personal environment. Seldom are we permitted to choose what kind of figure we shall present to the world around us. How generally, in fact, are our worldly characters, and our outward semblances, carved out for us by other hands ; or made up, first, by the social mold in which our early life is cast, and afterwards, by tyrant custom, the attrition of stronger natures, and the use the world makes of us, during all of our journey to the goal where alone all are absolutely equal.

II.

THIRD-LOVE.

There 's beggary in the love that can be reckon'd.
Antony and Cleopatra.

IRST-LOVE is an expression, upon the lips of every one, to which most persons of adult age attach some specific meaning—however inadequate that may be. Second-love, among matured men and women, is likely to continue the subject of endless thought and discussion—especially with the widowed. Not a few of these class it among their most fortunate experiences. The life and character of man or woman—at an age when little is known or felt of the capabilities of the heart, and while the impediments to what may be expected or imagined seem to be few—differ so essentially from the life and chàracter of the same persons at a later date—when through experience much is really known—that there is hardly room to doubt the frequent subsistence and absolute sincerity of a second passion of pure love. It comes after the first has exhaled in disappointment, or has lost the freshness of its memory through long irremediable separation, by death or other-wise.

But what shall be said of third-love ?   After the heart has passed through a second matured married love—an honest, thorough, all-embracing, altruistic, self-absorbing love—does a third love ever come?   If so, shall it be ranked as a passion, an affection, a sentiment, or as a delusion ?   Or is it simply an inexplicable fact, or phenomenon, that defies analysis and baffles description ?   He who avows such love perhaps ought to explain how its genuineness may be known, since it is so commonly challenged by the world whenever it is seriously asserted.

"O, sovereign power of Love ! " sang the gentle Keats. Is it an instinct, an impulse, an illusion, a magnetic suggestion, a subordination of will, an infatuation, or a mixture of some or all these—with or without something more ?   Whatever it be, all will agree with the poet it is a "power."   Love and passion when distinguishable are naturally, to some extent, the complements of each other. Yet it hardly can be questioned that the former may subsist without much of the latter.   Passion alone may assume the form of love, with no quality worthy of its name.   It may even foster some evanescent sentiment, yet through lack of endurance of essential traits be undeserving to be called love.   Where love is something more than the hey-day of the blood, it has its seed in the brain. It is also a special function of those who are still young— at least in all the tenderest feelings of the heart.   It survives as it is fed by hopes, expectations—nay even delusions.   Whether first or second, it is usually the child of sudden and involuntary impulse.   *Jam satis.*

It is not proposed to discuss here this topic with scientific precision or logical accuracy.   We treat it rather as one addressing a Court of Love, where the sympathy of the audience may be assumed and some individual experience or the imagination of the hearer may be relied upon to supply whatever of illustration or detail shall be supposed to be omitted.

First-love, then, as all the world knows, is the dawn of a sentiment, commonly although not necessarily, mingled with a latent something that is wholly new. It thrills, absorbs, dazzles, blinds yet illuminates. It purifies, elevates, and ennobles its subject, while it seems to transfigure its object. It comes usually, with an early morning's dewy freshness, at a time of life when internal experiences are few, when the feelings are spontaneous and unhackneyed ; when the blood is warm, the fancy free, and the imagination easily excited ; when the judgment is crude, and the temper rash, if not foolhardy ;—when strange fancies are playing mad pranks in the brain, and the world appears crowded with things novel or wonderful, to be coveted and enjoyed. It embraces the whole circumference of the heart, like a tight-fitting garment that cannot be shaken off at will. It asserts itself so powerfully, and shines through every disguise so vividly, it cannot easily be mistaken for anything else. Having taken possession of a vacant territory, it claims an absolute property by right divine both of discovery and primal occupation. It recognizes no superior here or hereafter. Defying ejectment it professes to limit its sway only by the incredible possibility of a death that shall be followed by annihilation of both body and soul.

Second-love is usually a tamer creature than its earlier brother. Although fierce enough, in some aspects, it is

3

commonly less spiritual, and plays less with the fancy. It is more robust and physical—although having a powerful ally in the imagination. It follows, with unequal steps, glowing in purple light, yet far behind its predecessor. It comes after the heart has been taught some hard and perhaps bitter lessons. Some of the hallucinations of youth have been swept away, and the understanding has begun to put its conclusions upon a more matter-of-fact, if not a more truthful basis. Some of the vivid fascinations, that have had their time of dazzling and misleading the temper, have vanished, leaving behind a somewhat luminous but formless vapor ;—which, however obscure it may be as a medium, usually does not transform much the object seen through it. If the red and yellow light of these fading illuminations still linger, as around a setting sun, and sometimes settle in shape of an aureole about the head of some newly discovered type of sweetest womanhood, it does not commonly—as when first-love was master of the revels—wrap the whole body of the loved object in a shining garment, or give it such an ethereal buoyancy as to make it appear incapable of touching the earth with feet of clay.

While second-love impresses the fancy more lightly (having little or no puling sentimentality about it), usually its sincere sentiment is grounded in respect and esteem, as well as in warm affection. It is a suggestion of judgment almost as much as of emotion. What it lacks of such nourishment as first-love draws from fancy, intense sensibility, novelty, or pure illusion, it may often find in a full-blossomed passionate emotion. It holds possession of the heart with the strong arm of a conqueror, who has driven out another occupant. If wise, it will not forget the fact that its right rests upon usurpation. Nor ought it ever to be quite off its guard, or wholly without a lurking subconsciousness that it stands upon the defensive. However, in a certain sense, it may be deeper and more absorbing, capable of higher effort and greater self-sacrifice, than first-love. With wider-opened eyes, greater dignity and profounder self-respect, it fully appreciates what it has found. Besides it knows how much its treasure has cost, and the full worth of what itself gives, or hazards, to prove its own honesty and sincerity or to gain and keep that of its object.

But ah, third-love ! We come back to this enigma. What shall be told of it ? Shall we begin with a challenge of sincerity in its pretensions ? After the fire has twice swept over the ground, apparently consuming every green or living thing, what can we expect will germinate and grow upon the barren stubble field ? Is the soil exhausted after its double fructification and second harvest ? Can anything but strange weeds be looked for to spring up there ; weeds, coarse and of ill savor, however gaudy in color ? Is there any aliment for pure and simple love, besides the ashes of a passion—warm, perhaps even glowing with its wonted fires, not, however, from fresh fuel or blazing embers, but—alas, ashes ; dust and ashes ? Shall we say *requiescat*—stir it not ?

By the expression third-love, no reference is intended to a merely third in number of fancied objects, but rather to that maligned semblance of love itself, which is tertiary in its stratification, and comes, if it come at all, after the grand climateric in man or woman. Shall this be called love? Must we say, with La Bruyère, "the most unnatural thing in the world is an old man in love"?

There are, indeed, some men, with so little imagination, so deficient by nature in the depth, singleness, refinement, sentiment, romance, or, if one may here use the expression, poetry of love—or else so large, catholic, and commonplace in their affection for women—that in their breadth, and perhaps consequent shallowness, of sexual sympathy, they are always open to the blandishments of the entire sex. With such persons third-love—so far as they ever have been, or are, capable of any love whatever—may perhaps pass merely as part of an endless series.

It will not be suggested here that the fidelity or honor of this special class is subject to question. Simply their scheme of life appears to be to take one wife at a time, and always to hold themselves in readiness for another; to be looked for not very long after the one has gone. It is not fair to say they prized the last one less;—but their love (according to the sense of that word in their vocabulary) for the whole sex seems to themselves more than they could give to any one woman, by whatever tie she may be possessed!

With reference to such omnivorous natures, perhaps a little light might be thrown by classifying their first-, second-, and third-love, or even more, as the ordinary accompaniment of three or more separate stages of existence, but without much difference between them. With such malleable persons, however adaptable, formality is still the governing factor of their lives, and conventionality, if not inborn, is at least second nature. To the searching analytical eye there would be visible a cool formalism, of a mild type, in their first-love, and a good deal of it, perhaps almost cruel, in their second-love. In the third, or subsequent stages, this anti-psychic characteristic would be so plain that the passional or even sentimental observer would scarcely venture to class the feeling as high as mere friendship. He would rather incline to call it a convenient association with just holy matrimony enough to cover it respectably.

Of course in these cases one may say, "matrimony" without hesitation. For in the history of the lives of such modal characters marriage is apparently the only natural state. If not always existing in fact, it is prob- ably always at hand. Indeed with them, fortunately for social well-being, the proprieties of conventionalism are thus strictly observed. Possibly however this may be sometimes not so much through reverence for the · sanctity of womanhood as because they know instinctively, or have learned by shrewd calculation, that the most profitable moral investments in this life always lie inside the lines, where adventure parts company with prudence. With this class we may leave the safe-keeping of this species of third-love ;—perhaps a conscious delusion. At the least it involves no danger to their moral constitutions, or risk of subjecting their fortunes to the caprices of senile infatuation.

Nevertheless, there appears to be occasionally among those who have preserved their vigor of body, mind, and heart, far beyond middle life, a capability, and even a yearning, for the strongest personal, sexual or psychic attachment. What less can be said of the conquered passion of Goethe, in his seventy-third year, for the charming Ulrica von Levizon?

Sometimes in men or women—with whom the finer qualities of the soul either never existed, or, from inherent infirmity, have perished early or have been overwhelmed by some lava-like irruption of disordered nature—this yearning may take on a form so physical that it were better relegated to the domain of medical science. Such cases are however abnormal and altogether exceptional.

Normally, while there may not be a passional emotion that thrills the blood like the untried impulses of youth, yet there may be between man and woman, quite late in years, a strong sentiment of affection resting more in the mind than in the heart, yet warmer, finer, and closer than is likely to exist at this time of life between persons of the same sex.

Shall one provoke the derisive laughter of those who have not yet advanced to the age when "the hey-day in the blood is tame," by calling this sentiment love? If so, perhaps it were better for them to treat it gently, and let it pass without considering it too curiously. Possibly, too, in some future age when men and women are universally charitable in guessing each other's motives, such an attachment may be popularly recognized as an aftermath, sprung from some of the richest soil of our common human nature.

What a puzzle, also, is that apparently pure love of a young woman which is sometimes ungrudgingly bestowed upon an old man! What does it find to feed upon if there be not reciprocity? To endeavor to solve this riddle one must not forget that love is an eccentric creature, with a diversity of shapes as well as of phases. The most superficial reference to the civilizations of different periods of history reminds us, by their mythology and poetry, of the almost countless variety of love's metamorphoses.

Although mere passion be one, and perhaps generally is the primordial, rootlet of human love, nevertheless, by the vicissitudes, growth, expansion, and fastidious refinement of social circumstances it has diverged into many branches widely different from this simple sprout of mere impulsive instinct. It is not indeed by any means necessary nowadays to sincere affection of the closest character between the young and the old, that there should burn the intense flame that consumed a Romeo or a Juliet. Doubtless some degree of it, at some time of life, glows in every healthy bosom. But the duration of such special exaltation of the blood long beyond early prime is the good or evil fortune of only a few.

When however the first fever has run its course and ended in nothing;—when a young woman has, by a course of flirtations, and a succession of sweethearts, learned something of the shallowness, pettiness, and selfishness of her male companions—if she be of a moderate temperament, blessed with a liberal stock of cool commonsense, coupled with a high valuation of her own worth; —she will sometimes grow weary of impertinent curiosity, and tyrannical exactions, from the young men she has taken perhaps too thoughtlessly into her confidence. She may covet a freedom in thought and action which

the genuine simplicity of her nature assures her is both
innocent and rightfully her due.   She may find that those
men of her own age, toward whom her heart inclines
tenderly and perhaps fondly, expect too much, and are
willing to yield too little.

Whenever such an one has reached this stage, abnormal
though it be, she may be ripe for the sincere adulation
of an elderly man.   She may be sought by some one who
(having passed through second-love) will give fair play to
the instinctive delicacy of her maidenly reserve, who will
not press too closely upon her innermost confidence, but
who will be willing to recognize and wait upon her individuality at a respectful distance.   In him she may believe
she has discovered an admiring lover who readily gives
much and asks very little ;—one who values every mark
of affinity from her, yet does not presume upon her favor
to endeavor to make her his bond-slave forever.   In such
an association she may find a marriage that satisfies her
heart, while her judgment approves.

Again, it is a common experience that nothing is more
grateful to the heart of many a man who has lived so
long as to be wearied with striving to cherish the broken
promises of life—and who begins to lose his hold upon
hope for their renewal here—than the sincere affection of
a young woman whose anticipations are still vivid and
whose heart is buoyant with expectations of continuing
happiness.

Of course these words are written only of such attachments as are mutually pure and honest, without the taint
of close-calculating individual selfishness on either side.
Where this latter element controls the problem, the sub-

ject may better be turned over to students of morbid moral anatomy—or perhaps to the police courts. And the sensational novelists of the day can take care of those in this category, if any, who are beyond such special jurisdictions.

The mark here aimed at is higher, and in spite of the skepticism prevalent concerning the possibility of third-love, the claim sometimes urged for the propriety of such relations—when, in good faith, assumed in the face of a carping world—may be found to be rather complimentary than otherwise to the possibilities of social life under our modern civilization.

So much for third-love. The subject is somewhat ticklish, and perhaps it would be rash to attempt to dilate more fully, or to assume to speak from the chair upon such a topic.

III.

FRIENDSHIPS BETWEEN MEN AND WOMEN.

There 's flattery in friendship.

Henry IV.

CAN honest friendship, pure and simple, subsist between man and woman? Perhaps the majority of both sexes candidly aver it to be impossible. Many women scoff at the notion of what is sometimes called platonic affection ; and most men count it a fraud or a dangerous delusion. With all such persons at the least, it may be said to be impracticable. Their own involuntary self-judgment could not be wisely or even safely gainsaid. Yet it would be too harsh to condemn all those who avow their earnest faith in such a relationship, as being either hypocrites or fanatics. The sweet romantic story of Goethe's "friend," Charlotte, Frau von Stein, alone appeals to the consciousness of too many noble-minded men and women to vilify human nature to such a degree of humiliation.

Doubtless this relation is exceptional ; and nearly always—when counted as the sole foundation for an intimacy between man and woman—is regarded, to say the least, as equivocal. Being liable to both misconstruction by others, as well as possible mischief to the parties concerned, its open expression is usually avoided by prudent people, who are conventional of necessity, or have a large practical stake in an unquestioning good opinion of their social congeners. Generally speaking, probably it is something a little beyond the range of feeling of most merely matter-of-fact people.

Indeed, whether in its mainspring it be fanciful or not, at least some degree of reciprocal idealization seems to be a necessary ingredient in the make-up of such an association. And one must look among those who, either by excess of imagination and correlative sensibility, or from a deficiency in the temperature of the blood, or both, are a little outside the normal standard of human nature, for such attachments in their full honesty, simplicity, and purity. Certainly in the song of the poet, in the talk of the artist, and in the life of the ideal philosopher, do we find the heartiest, and apparently the sincerest, recognition of such friendships. But even among the half-savage " Toueregs of the Sahara," we find a maxim :—" Friends of different sexes are for the eyes and the heart and not for the bed only as among the Arabs."

There are usually at least two impediments lying in the way of a man desiring to maintain intimate friendships with women. First, they are inclined, if they like a man well, soon to like him too much for the peace of mind of either party ; and next, women cannot look ordinarily with much complacency upon a male friend's likings for other women. They are prone to fancy, in such cases, they receive less than their proper share of his attention or regard. For, apparently, despite the dictates of their own good sense, they seem constantly disposed, by their vivifying breath, to fan the sedate embers of friendship into the glowing coals of love. Just as persistently, as in case of love itself, are they beset by the irritation of jealousy, whenever favor is shown by their friend to another woman. They dislike instinctively anything resembling a partnership or community of property where they are to have, or to be the subject of, or to furnish even the fiction of, possession. Indeed their inclination, from pure impulse or sweet will, is to be Turk-like monopolists in all cases of occupation of the domains of the heart ;—wanting the whole or none.

Lord Byron can hardly be suspected of more want of experience, touching this phase of human capability, than most men. Moreover he was likely to speak as frankly as any one about it. His diagnosis of the abnormity is at least curious. In his thirty-fourth year, writing to Lady ——, he says :—" I have always laid it down as a maxim, and found it justified by experience, that a man and a woman make far better friendships than can exist between two of the same sex ; but with this condition, that they never have made, or are to make, love with each other. Lovers may be, and indeed generally are, enemies ; but they never can be friends—because there must always be a spice of jealousy and a spice of self in all their speculations. Indeed I rather look upon love altogether as a sort of hostile transaction ; very necessary to make or break matches, and to keep the world going, but by no means a sinecure to the parties concerned."

A discriminating French writer pleads for a dual demand by male friendship. He would lay both sexes under
contribution to satisfy a full-made man's necessity in this
direction, saying :—Il faudrait donc peut-être desirer un
homme pour ami dans les grandes occasions, mais pour le
bonheur de tous les jours, il faut desirer l'amitié d'une
femme.

Whether the man or the woman, or both, be married or
single, such an intimate association between them, outside the lines of consanguinity or affinity—unless in contemplation of marriage—being beyond the ordinary groove
of social routine, generally, as already suggested, is looked
upon askance. If tolerated at all, by the self-constituted
duennas of a social circle, it is accounted something to be
at the least suspected and watched ;—even if it escape
"calumnious strokes."

Unfortunately, too, this bare suspicion—suggesting mischief and breeding secrecy or mystery—is a most effectual
prescription for generating the very evil deprecated.
As both men and women commonly, though unconciously,
judge their neighbors by themselves, it is hard, and almost
impossible for any one to suppose other human beings
to possess moral qualities or fine attributes beyond the
reach or capacity of his own individual nature. There
are some things in human nature we hardly ever can
be taught, by external observation, to comprehend.
Our self-love is constantly impelling us to interpret
all facts germane to the matter in a manner adverse
to any theory which tends to exalt the intrinsic nature
of another above the loftiest possibilities of our own.
In this wise the mass of mankind are not at all indis-

posed to deride the notion of platonic love as an unreal mockery.

Although with so many a real friendship is usually predicable only of an intimacy between persons of the same sex, nevertheless there are undoubtedly men and women who appear, to themselves if not to the world, never to reach the full measure of their moral natures, except through confidential association with persons of opposite sex. Certainly there are not a few men, of a special temperament, to whom woman in general seems to be a sort of fascination, and with whom the assurance of one or more intimate friends among women is necessary to maintain, as it were, a psychological balance of character. The corresponding condition is said to be true of some women. In such cases passional love ought by no means to be called an element essentially necessary to this relation.

The experienced Bulwer in his elaborate, but unfinished posthumous, masterpiece *The Parisians*, speaks earnestly of—"one of those cordial friendships, which, perfectly free alike from polite flirtation and platonic attachment, do sometimes spring up between persons of opposite sexes, without the slightest danger of changing its honest character into morbid sentimentality, or unlawful passion." Perhaps, among those thus spoken of, such unhallowed love, sometimes, ineffectually may come and go, yet leave an honorable friendship undisturbed.

Not only, however, is this capability for an unmixed friendship between man and woman far from being universal, but a claim for it is often asserted without its having any real existence ;—being a delusion that deceives only those who blindly fancy it to be in their possession. Hence spiritual affection is so often a sneering by-word of the incredulous. Nevertheless that it has a real subsistence in many cases, and has had from the beginning of the world, is the unshaken conviction of some of the purest and best specimens of our frail humanity. So it will doubtless endure forever ; inconceivable as it may be, and hard for definition or accurate characterization as it may be, to a majority of our race.

As Rider Haggard says, in one of his novels :—" It is that sympathy and perfect accord which is the sweet sign of the highest affection, and while it often accompanies the passions of men and women, is oftener found in its highest form in those relations from which the element of sensuality is excluded, raising it above the level of the earth. For the love, when that sympathy exists, whether between mother and son, husband and wife, or those who, while desiring it, have no hope of that relationship, is an undying love, and will endure until the night of Time has swallowed all things."

With all that may be said of this delightful relationship, however, it cannot be too clearly kept in mind that it is full of hazards from both within and without. Those who have the good fortune to inspire or reciprocate it, have need to be always on their guard both to avoid its running into that passion which, to the common eye, it so nearly resembles if it be not identical with it, and more especially to escape the calumny of that vigilance-committee, called "Society." This functionary is largely— possibly sometimes for conscious good cause—a doubter of unqualified human virtue, and by some deplorable instinct seems to have a supersensitive keenness of scent for scandal.

Probably it is safer—at least as a discreet sacrifice to our social conventionalism—to postpone (as Pope advised concerning matrimony) the indulgence of this luxury of the soul to one's ripest years. The example of the devout affection of Buffon, in his sixty-seventh year, for Madame Necker—the jilted virgin lover of Gibbon—suggests that such a time is not too late for its enjoyment. At this calm period he wrote to that exemplary woman of his own feelings toward herself in these vehement words:—
"Ah, gods! It is not a sentiment without fire; on the contrary it is a true warmth of soul, an emotion, a movement gentler than that of any other passion; it is an untroubled enjoyment, a happiness rather than a pleasure; it is a communication of existence· purer and yet more real than the sentiment of love."

With such authority in vindication of a relationship so endearing to the fancy, it may not be too much to expect that this vestal flame will perpetually survive the incredulity or the derision and the condemnation of the obtuse, the flippant, or the consciously evil-minded. Acquaintances, companions, and so-called friends are common enough among men with men, or women with women; but for perfect friendship an intimacy of the soul is essential that can only spring out of a reciprocal sympathy with that inner life and individuality which is peculiarly our own. This specialty of nature is usually guarded with so jealous a watchfulness that it is often carried in secret loneliness to the grave. Many believe it is never fully revealed except between man and

woman. If then we must concede that love of some
sort can alone be the basis of such an intimacy ; still we
may discriminate and insist that this love need not be
passional, but may be higher, and at least purely emotional and sentimental.

If Love be love for love itself alone,
If Soul-love may push Cupid from his throne,
And hold the kingdom of our hearts' desire,
To what celestial joys may we aspire !

The bloom that mantles on the hanging plum
Dissolves beneath the gardener's wanton thumb ;
But dewdrops hid within the lily's cup
The thirsty morning sun will not drink up.

Give me to rise above a lover's rôle,
To find the true nirvana of my soul
In calm delights—communion of the heart—
As mingling streams embrace and never part.

4

IV.

WOMAN SUFFRAGE IN AMERICA.

A woman impudent and mannish grown
Is not more loathed than an effeminate man
In time of action.

Troilus and Cressida.

HENEVER a radical change in the established order of society, or its methods of government, is proposed by any one, it is well to go back to first principles and see whether the proposal conflicts with those axioms and postulates in which all agree.

Society cannot be upheld in peace and security nor justice administered without a Head, and its necessary executive or ministerial subordinates. How this head shall be selected is a problem the world has wrestled with for six thousand years. For the most part this office has been held by virtue of successful usurpation, backed by force and sustained by some species of public opinion. The title to this position being always of equivocal pater-. nity, for thousands of years it was taught popularly to be regarded as based upon a divine right, perhaps the better to silence impertinent inquiry into its origin.

The necessity of this head being universally conceded, mankind have been more inclined to criticise its conduct than to question its right, generally believing that it is of little importance how the governor be selected, provided he govern wisely and mercifully.

So long as a government has been good, or even better than revolution and the necessary risk of anarchy, society has submitted and made the best of it. But often when the administration of government has become intolerable, the people (*i. e.*, the mass who are governed) have risen in their strength, thrown off the yoke at whatever sacrifice, and taken a fresh start.

No one has a positive, absolute natural right to govern any others, neither a king (by the usurpation of himself or his ancestor) nor any other governor, although made such by the choice of the majority of a people—except those individuals who personally choose him or in some manner acquiesce in or ratify his selection.

The people (neither as a body nor by the voice of a majority) have no such right to govern anybody, except those individuals who choose thus to acquiesce. No man has a right to govern me against my will. But if I find my greater advantage in submitting to the control of the law of the community, whatsoever it may be, and choose to live in it rather than to flee from it, I become a member of that community, surrender a portion of my positive rights, and submit myself to its will as expressed in its law. So also if I violate its law while witl..n its territory I subject myself to its power whether I wish or no. In such case, too, it has a control over me and has acquired by my act or sufferance a right to govern me.

Suffrage, or voting for persons for office who may make or execute the laws of the land, is not a matter of abstract individual right, but a privilege of convenience, of expediency, of law, of agreement—and may become an obligation or duty. While we live in a community it has the power to make its own laws, to which we must conform. If we do not choose to submit to and obey them our reserved right in the premises is to quit that community and leave it to the peaceable possession of those who do like it ;—and so on. So much for the positive natural right of any one, man or boy, woman or girl, to vote.

What then is the most expedient rule for a wise community to impose upon itself, in determining who shall be permitted to vote ? Pure, " universal suffrage " no one claims. All persons under a certain age (generally twenty-one), and all incompetents (lunatics, criminals, etc.), are everywhere excluded.

Where shall the line be drawn and upon what idea ? Who shall be allowed to vote, and who shall not ? Certainly all will agree that in the abstract, except for some special abnormal reason, only those capable of intelligently and honestly exercising this privilege and likely to do so should have it. The ignorant, the vicious, those under duress, and those who will not take the trouble to use the privilege honestly, or will sell it for money, probably all will admit, ought not to have a voice in the choosing of governors, or in making laws to control the rest of the community. So, also, those who by nature are unfitted for such a duty, or who by the habitudes of society are disabled from intelligent independent

action in the matter, in like manner ought to be excluded. But who shall determine which are the incompetent, and how shall we separate them from those who
are competent?

If any be foreign-born and therefore unacquainted
with our laws and customs, they are excluded (until fitted,
or adjudged to be comparatively so, by naturalization)
under a rule easily ascertained and applied. If any be
manifestly unfit, by crime or imbecility or infancy, no
one doubts how to exclude them. " Infancy " being a
variable term is fixed by common consent of mankind as
including all persons under some specific age—say from
eighteen to twenty-five. Those so excluded do not usually fret under the application of the rule, because time
soon cures the grievance, if they feel justly any there be.
Now among the remaining classes a large proportion of
persons is manifestly unfit—when taken separately. But
it would be impracticable to draw the line by law except
by classes. Let us particularize.

There are the uneducated. Some States exclude those
who cannot " read and write." This is a sound rule in the
abstract. But in the application there is much difficulty.
Many unfit persons can do both ; while many worthy ones
can do neither. There were the negroes, born and bred
in slavery ;—clearly unfit, both by their nature, habits, and
want of training. They were so large a class, and the
surrounding whites believed to be naturally so hostile in
feeling and interest as respects their claim of both political and civil rights, that it was deemed expedient (whether
wisely or not) to give the vote to this class ;—as a necessary
measure of policy, for the best interest of the whole com-

munity ; perhaps a tyrannical experiment with an insoluble problem.

There are those persons who are without property, and therefore apparently without a conscious interest in the management of the government, which is principally concerned in respect to property and its uses. Some of these are likely to abuse the privilege, and to make a class, many of whose votes will be either bought and sold, or influenced by unworthy considerations, leading to party corruption ; and so on. Surely in a perfect community this class, large as it is, ought to be excluded. But it is unsafe to exclude them as incapables, because they will gradually organize themselves into a turbulent body. Under a purely monarchical or despotic government, these may be kept in order by force, but in a republic they will be likely to make more trouble if excluded than if admitted. So that, undesirable as they are, merely from political expediency they generally have the vote.

Then, after all others are named, there are women. Common consent of mankind for six thousand years has found other occupation for all their capacity. They are as yet far behind this age in doing what they are not prevented from doing, and what as citizens they may do, if their special natural limitations do not prohibit. If they can do more than fulfil all their social duties and functions as wives, mothers, sisters, and daughters, nevertheless as a class it must be conceded they have accomplished comparatively little beyond. The trades, countless occupations, and nearly all the professions are, by law, open to them—as well as mechanics and the arts. They have not yet demonstrated their capacity to fill all these employments to an appreciable degree. Even their own apparel and ornaments are still largely the work of men.

No one complains of this, or pretends that it is their fault. It is their choice, for the most part, as far as practicable, except when necessary, to avoid such supplementary employments. To do most of these things well and successfully demands denial of pleasure, convenience, and comfort, an apprenticeship of long study and discipline, with steady and persistent application, besides severe practical training. Some women have partially tried it, and a few have succeeded in a measure. But as a sex and as a class, their instincts being wiser than their artificial and borrowed reason, recognizing their natural and social boundaries, they have not made hitherto very serious attempts to conquer all the inevitable difficulties in their path.

They are not fitted apparently by nature or habit to be political citizens, even if wholly left to themselves. As a class they would fail as a useful factor in government if brought in competition with, and subject to the influences of the sex which is their superior in force, and likewise in persistent fraud, and chicanery in general.

If admitted to the exercise of the duty or privilege of suffrage, they would add one more capricious element to the many now existing, which (being only disturbing forces, it has been found impracticable to exclude, and have been admitted only from expediency to prevent some greater mischief to the community) are in fact simply tolerated as necessary evils, and suffered as an unavoidable nuisance.

The opinions of prominent men are often quoted in favor of woman suffrage. In a matter of this kind no man's mere opinion is of any special value. It is not unlikely his whole notion of woman is an imaginary ideal, or is derived from his knowledge of some individual, such as his mother, wife, sister, daughter, or sweetheart, without any thorough knowledge or thought of the sex as a class, or of its history. The experience of the human race may be appealed to when abstract argument fails to convince either way; but simple individual opinion on such a subject as an argument, is little better than rubbish.

The experiment in Wyoming and other sparse communities is no more valuable than if it had been tried on board the " Mayflower." They are equally remote in their conditions from the circumstances of the large cities of America, which now control the politics of this country.

It is nonsensical to endeavor to make it appear that, as a community-governing-person, woman occupies a status the same as that of man. Whoever assumes to exercise political power, by his very assumption pledges himself, at whatever inconvenience, to bear political burdens, unless for special individual reasons he be excused—as a favor. He must fight if he expect to vote. The majority controls by virtue of superior power, active or in reserve.

Voting is disguised war. The guns, the marches, the toil, the sweat, the privation, and the suffering are just behind the ballot-box. The battle is here to the strong. True the weak accompany the army and live under its protection; but they follow in the rear as non-combatants, with the commissary and medical departments. They care for the hungry, the sick, and wounded. They are none the less useful, none the less necessary, in their proper places. But reverse the order of position or of movement, and there would be first chaos among them, and next annihilation. Is it not obvious then, that it would be unwise statesmanship voluntarily to add another element of weakness where so many now unavoidably exist ?

Woman is by nature emotional, and swiftly obeys her will and inclination, when she can lawfully do so. Man is by nature more logical, practically governed by his intellect and actual interest, present or remote. Self-discipline and voluntary resistance to his impulses are generally believed by him to be necessary to his fair development and ultimate success in pursuit of his personal aims in life. She lives in the present ; and by flattery, simulation, appeals to her emotional nature, and other arts, is more easily led or betrayed to her own destruction. He is commonly conceited, selfish, cruel, grasping, ambitious, and aims at power ; striving by force or fraud to subdue others. He shrewdly waives present advantage, calculating " the long result of Time " to make up any deficiency and to acccomplish his schemes of self-aggrandizement.

Amid the collision of these powerful forces of man's nature contending against each other, justice is wrought out, in a rough way, and ultimately prevails to some extent. But every disturbing ingredient, every unnecessary or equivocal factor, in the problem, further delays the progress of right, the establishment of just laws, and the fair government of a political community.

Woman in refined communities, generally, is physically incapable of the relative duties and burdens that the exercise of this franchise would devolve upon her. Whoever asserts a right in this world must be prepared to maintain it in some manner by force. If she had the privilege of voting she would soon lose the practical use of it through fraud or violence. She could not maintain it by reason of her want of physical strength to defend it.

All " rights," so-called practically, in the last analysis, rest upon force. There are no classes in society (except those recognized as incompetents and incapables) who hold their "rights" by favor and by the protection of the stronger. If they are not the wards of society they must be prepared to contend by the strong arm, as its guardians and masters. But a refined woman cannot bear ordinarily the trial and fatigue of such a brutal conflict. She could not endure the physical burden of upholding such citizenship. She was born or bred for other duties than politics, and instinctively knows she has a higher, a more radical and further reaching mission than that of making laws to regulate civil rights and obligations, or even of filling offices.

Moreover, if the scheme of giving woman the ballot were adopted and it were put into successful operation for two or three generations—which period at least would be required to adapt society to the change, so that woman could have the practical benefit of it (for so strong are the habits of society that it would take more than forty years to give her any real advantage in the use of it)—what would be the inevitable result? One is forced to answer ;— nothing less than the moral unsexing of woman. The

chief amenity and consolation of the weariness and emp-
tiness of life in this petty world would be gone. If the
dreams of utopian female enthusiasts were realized, and
even paradise were so re-established, it would be at best
but such a paradise as there was before Eve came into it.
More probably it would be pandemonium, with only the
difference that the lesser demons would have the upper
hand in misrule. At its best it would be a "society"
without "family" (as we understand that term) or "property";—a world not worth living in.

And after all were done as sought for, it could accomplish nothing whatever for the benefit of woman herself,
in respect to her political condition. It would add in
fact merely (as has been said) another impracticable factor to the already difficult problem—how to produce a
wise and equitable government that shall sustain and pro-
mote the progress of civil society;—a problem as yet very,
very far from solution. Besides, at the same time, it would
necessarily take away, or at least paralyze for most good
results, one of the chief supports and most conservative
influences which now uphold all that is pure, sweet, and
lovable in our present social system. Woman becoming
self-assertive and aggressive, the rival of man in his
ambitions and selfishness, would forfeit or lose the
deference he now gratefully accords to her.*

* The following is cut from a contemporary Boston newspaper:
" Courtesy in the Boston horse-car is a lost art. It has been crushed
out by the hand-to-hand struggle for existence, where room for twenty
serves for fourscore. The most courteous gentleman becomes a social
savage the moment he steps upon the platform. ' Pay your fare and
fight your passage,' is the received motto, It 's a question of the

She would no longer have the privileges, now joyfully awarded to her as a dependent. She would be compelled to contend for her acquired rights. Society, however, would suffer most by being deprived of that graciousness which grows out of the social intercourse of the sexes, as now regulated by the law of reciprocal dependence, in the manner nature and history have unmistakingly willed it to be.

Finally as woman's friend, and also as a friend of humanity, I would entreat her (when ambitious and discontented) to remember the homely fable of the dog and the shadow ; and never to let go her present firm hold upon man and society in a frantic anxiety to grasp the illusory image of " woman suffrage."

survival of the fittest in its most barbaric form. In one ride from Scollay Square to Charlestown a woman stood with a child in her arms the entire distance, and nearly every seat occupied by men."

V.

WORDS ABOUT WOMAN.

Who is 't can read a woman ?
Cymbeline.

Her Childlike Nature.

EARLY a century and a half ago—before the present "emancipation" of woman was accomplished—Lord Chesterfield wrote to his son, as most readers will remember :—"I will let you into certain arcana that will be very useful for you to know, but which you must, with the utmost care, conceal, and never seem to know. Women, then, are only children of a larger growth. . . . For solid reasoning, good sense, I never, in my life, knew one that had it, or who reasoned or acted consequentially for four and twenty hours together. . . . But these are secrets which you must keep inviolably, if you would not, like Orpheus, be torn to pieces by the whole sex." What portion, if any, of these traits of our greater grandames has been transmitted to the present liberated generation ? Shall we suffer the fate of Orpheus if we tell ?

Woman, as a subject for generalization, has been from time immemorial a fascinating but bewildering puzzle to civilized men. Virgil calls her *varium et mutabile semper.* Pope says she is " a contradiction "—" at heart a rake "—has but two ruling passions, " the love of pleasure and the love of sway." Then he gives it up —quoting with approbation his friend Martha Blount's saying :— " Most women have no character at all." Byron says she is " false " as " an epitaph." Otway, with Helen and Cleopatra in his eye, calls her " destructive " and worse. Schopenhauer's venomous malice need not be referred to. Scott tells us she is " a ministering angel " ; Lowell, that when " perfected " she is " earth's noblest thing." And so on. One might quote hackneyed phrases endlessly, and yet find only confusion of ideas. Possibly, however, no small share of this masculine muddle comes from the overlooking of a physiological condition that is so obvious it is not seen at all by her censors ! Michelet alone seems fully to comprehend her complexity and perhaps irresponsibility. It would be idle to be dogmatic on the subject.

Aside from the temptation to be satirical or sarcastic, the fatuity of man's judgment in this matter appears to be of, at least, twofold origin. First there is an incapacity of some men—who are perchance destitute of feminality —to comprehend, by sympathetic insight, either the intricate complexity, or the spirituality, or the evanescent traits of a woman's nature. Second, others, who are too sentimental and perhaps also deficient in virility, attempt to characterize the whole sex by a generalization deduced from the too few striking examples best known to themselves, either historically or through personal observation. Exceptional characters are an unsafe basis for generalization, or even for wide speculation, concerning human nature in either man or woman. The method is easy and alluring, but the result is unsafe for practical purposes. Doubtless the writer will be thought to make some worse mistake than either class referred to. At the least, however, in this imperfect, one-sided sketch, he will endeavor to keep on familiar ground and to be not unjust—even in attempting to deal with a supposed chameleon.

Probably it will be not unsafe to say that women, in many of their foibles, as in some of their lesser virtues, generally seem to incline to resemble children more closely than most men do. Perhaps this tendency is a still lingering result of their traditional and habitual, real or apparent, subordination to men in the more important affairs of life—ever since, in a state of savagery, they were accustomed to be captured, or sold as chattels, and compelled to be wives or slaves, or both, of their conquerors. Not that all men are superior to them in intellectual attributes—very far from it—but they widely differ. Their mental characters for the most part are not naturally or habitually quite judicial, dispassionate, or impersonal, according to the masculine ideal standard of what is becoming to the judgment of a high order of matured intellectual manhood. Instinct, insight, and intuition are prone to be restive under scientific opposition. For instance, in personal controversy concerning matters of opinion, however ready to argue in a reasonable way (which is not always) they—like ordinary children and indeed like too many men—are, by inclination, for the most part, apparently, loth to be convicted of a serious error, if they happen to be involved in one. In their hearts they are apt to suspect the motives of an antagonist ; and sometimes will find it hard even to believe in the honesty of those who seriously differ with them in their cherished views. When in such debate facts or sound arguments fail them—as will sometimes occur, when they chance to be in the wrong—if pressed too hardly by an inconsiderate adversary, are not they prone often (again not unlike some very young men) to lapse even into personal censure, secret or expressed ? Or if utterly routed, are not they moved, sometimes strongly, like children, to whimper, possibly even to sulk ? Do they expect to gain the apparent advantage of victory, through some concession of an adversary's magnanimity ? The world seems to be of that opinion.

Another not uncommon trait of women, although perhaps both amiable and commendable, may yet be said to be childlike, in some of its aspects. They prefer immediateness, and dread circumlocution, or even preamble. If you desire to hold, or even to excite, their attention, come to the point at once. Indeed in all dealings with them, as with children, it is better to avoid every form of circumlocution, disguise, or indirection. If you would be popular with them, or wish to preserve, as well as to deserve, their esteem, be always frank and simple—never ironical or sarcastic. To begin with, if you deal in satire or ridicule, they will not understand you ordinarily. When they perceive your drift, they will suspect you probably of desiring to make them appear ridiculous.

This—like most men and all children—they cannot for-
give easily. Besides soon they will be afraid of you, and
in the end dislike you altogether ;—perhaps even imagining you a monster of ill-nature, bad intentions, and insincerity. For, although imaginative, they despise untruth,
in others, even in a jest.

Most women proverbially take as little interest in an
abstract proposition as do children. In the mass, they
usually care almost nothing for the mere general principles
of thought. They are not ordinarily zealous, or of long-
enduring patience, in a search for the primal seeds of
philosophic thinking. They want to know the facts, the
incidents, and especially the actors, as well as the direct
aspect of specific matters, as they have been, or are now.
They must have all things—except mysteries—as it were,
in concrete form. In questions of judgment they do not
usually ask for the raw materials, out of which an independent opinion may be formed upon any novel subject.
They prefer perhaps, like children or common men, to
know what you think about it. If you would instruct,
persuade, or influence their judgment or conduct, against
their will, even in general matters, never seek to do so
with a maxim. You might as well try to produce a musical sound with a logarithm. Give them an illustration
from some vivid fact, or, better, some personal incident.
But beware of relying upon unfamiliar postulates or
axioms to sustain your statement or opinion. Indeed a
woman is strongly inclined to contemn and resent an
aphorism ; unless perchance it be in full accord with her
present convictions. When uttered to demolish her side
of a controversy, it seems to her, usually, palpably ab-

5

surd, and wholly fails of its purpose, however apposite you may consider it ;—more especially, if you call it logically conclusive. It operates somewhat like a random shot, or perhaps not unlike a spent-ball. Either it will fail to hit the mark, and she will not heed it at all ; or, if it happen to strike—its direct, or projectile, force being lost—its irregular, or rotary, motion will survive, only to tear and irritate, by a ragged wound.

Again women are supposed to resemble children in their general way of meeting opposition to their wishes. It is often said they do not, ordinarily—as men ought to, and sometimes think they do—appeal directly to the reason of their opponents, or even elaborately urge expediency. They seem to think it quite enough to show personal convenience or desirableness. Indeed, as a rule, when excited, they appear to abhor altogether what men call pure ratiocination. Perhaps this is so, for the reason, that what they wish for seems to themselves to be so plainly fit and self-evident, as not to require argument with a person of sense, and should be granted as a matter of course. In fact the king-bolt of a large part of the favorite methods of feminine demonstration is this little phrase—"of course." Lacking sometimes the power of sheer strength to overcome a determined masculine resistance, in order to carry a coveted point—as for instance, commonly, in domestic intercourse—her childlike nature, while in good humor, will incline her to cajolery or to caressing. But, if an evil temper be aroused in her, perhaps it may drive her occasionally to—shall it be said ?—threats, insult ; or mayhap—when tormented beyond saintly endurance—even to ill-suppressed malediction—in cases where her early moral education has been too much neglected ! Failing, however, in these gentle or malign expedients, like children again, she may shed tears to show how harshly you are dealing with her, and how mercilessly you are exercising a tyrannical advantage of your ill-natured, superior power in opposition to her reasonable wishes. For, generally speaking, as with children, whenever a man successfully resists a woman's will, through some latent law of her nature, an impression is left upon her mind that he is either cowardly or cruel, or both. In fact cruelty and cowardice appear to her to be precisely the words to represent that gratuitous abuse of superior power a man seems to her to be exercising— or of that advantage of accidental opportunity of which he is meanly availing himself—when he wholly prohibits what she earnestly and innocently wishes to enjoy.

Childhood's extreme sensitiveness to undeserved praise or blame seems naturally to survive longer in woman than in man. Although less conceited, and no more (perhaps less) susceptible to flattery, when adroitly administered, than are most men, women are said to be more habitually covetous of general approbation and admiration. They fade and wither more easily than men when they lose the verbally expressed good-will of others. Men are often so strong in their self-reliance, they can defy even an adverse noisy public opinion, without detriment to their self-respect ; but women cannot, with equanimity, except in rare instances, face a frowning world— be it right or wrong in its displeasure. For alas, an unprotected woman's character is commonly so susceptible to slander—from a rival or a coward—so difficult, when breathed upon, to be vindicated and restored beyond suspicion ! Men usually appear to have also stronger and clearer abstract notions of mere right and wrong, apart from conventional *dicta* or religious dogmas, to sustain their self-love. Indeed, some look up to an ideal far above received opinion, and grow almost sublime in their efforts, despite obloquy, to reach it ; while most women, who chance to find themselves on the wrong side of conventional rules, are liable to lose even their self-respect, and perhaps to retrograde in real character, if not in actual conduct. So children—even when well grown —are often demoralized, and proverbially become incorrigible, through bad treatment, arising out of the ill-advised or excessive suspicion or disapprobation of those in practical authority over them.

Again, nothing has been more commonly noted, by harsh and exacting men, than the apparent likeness of many women to children, in their usually accredited craving for forbidden things. The impulse of self-will being strong in the nature of each, the suggestion of things prohibited has been supposed to provoke an appetite for what is denied. Perhaps they find a fascinating pleasure in the consciousness or exercise of power to overcome obstacles to inclination in their path. A recognition of this similarity of disposition is the motive of many a nursery tale—just as it appears to crop out, in myth or history, as an instinctive trait of our earliest mother.

Women are also said to resemble children somewhat in respect to their unsatisfied wants. Almost every woman appears to be constantly craving something—a little, or more than a little—beyond her immediate ability to reach it, without the assistance of some other person ;—something she desires above everything else. Whoever shall carry her nearest to it, or bring to her the largest portion of what she so covets ; whoever shall most quickly enable her to possess it, with the least expenditure of force or material, on her part, with the smallest sacrifice of her pride or self-love, and with the least concession by, or cost to, her, of what she values—whether she seek it for power or pleasure—usually soonest will win her alliance and friendship—perhaps her affection, or even love.

In their fondness for dress, trinkets, and finery, women are usually supposed to possess, in common with boys, an enduring trait ; which the latter, however, first outgrow, and, if they become real men, soon discard entirely. A man's vain pride in symbolical gewgaws—emblematical of power, or public distinction—depends upon another principle.

Some claim to have discovered also in woman a specially juvenile and unmanlike tendency to spontaneous prejudices or antipathies, and inexplicable instantaneous personal likes or dislikes : *Ignoramus.*

Women and children are not troubled generally, as are most men, by the common bugbear of inconsistency. They are disposed to follow unhesitatingly the bold lead of Emerson—a man of feminine intellect—in this matter. Not only do they appear sometimes to exercise their conceded prerogative of changing expressed opinions at will, but they are said to be able to act in two opposite characters at the same time without wincing ! A single instance may illustrate :—To be the petted and responsive darling of an uxorious husband, seems to involve a disqualification for playing the rôle of a tyrant or a scold. Yet there is sometimes seen a woman high-bred, beautiful, lovable—and to the world perhaps always amiable—who, with unconscious incongruity, can claim and accept, when allowed, all the privileges, immunities, and endearments of a minion, yet be able to exercise, at the same time, the ugly attributes of the other characters mentioned.

One word more. Like children, too, women, from their mere simplicity and honesty of character, are usually credulous, seldom skeptical ; not easily surprised by effects without apparent causes ; but inclined to be speculative among chances ; having faith in their good luck, and confident of favorable results, with little question of why or wherefore.

Let us stop. If Chesterfield be deemed correct in his analysis of femininity, and these supposed attributes of our remote grandmothers survive, enough has been said to emphasize his wonderful discovery. Probably too much has been uttered to be forgiven by the woman-like men or man-like women, who fancy they represent the respective sexes, if any such shall condescend to hear it. It would be rash to ask woman, however metamorphosed, to look at man's judgment or opinion concerning herself, from a masculine standpoint. Indeed, it would involve a contradiction of all that has been said here, even to expect it.

WOMEN AS RELIGIONISTS.

It is a well recognized peculiarity of women that, irrespective of mere emotionalness—whether she be naturally possessed of more spiritual insight than man or not—at least her understanding is usually ready to accept, without much question, the abstruser formularies of dogmatic theology. She yields somewhat easily to the suggestion of supernatural agencies. Her nature, so inherently, is inclined to religion, as a system of faith and worship— beyond and indeed quite outside of morality or virtue— that she acquiesces kindly in its most absolute creeds, and readily adopts all of its mystic symbols. Man—though easily terrorized by superstition—is naturally more skeptical, if not indifferent. Ordinarily his understanding or reason somehow first must be convinced, before he can be said thoroughly, to believe any doctrine ;—however much, through his passions or temperament or training, or from motives of policy, he may yield to it. If the matter be outside of his common experience, his real judgment, if disciplined, usually demands explicit evidence and extraordinary proofs of its verity ;—although such tangible proofs may not be always necessary to induce him to conform to established custom in religious matters.

As in other affairs, he is sometimes indifferent, and perhaps more often a creature of habit—consulting his own ease, or prudently avoiding disadvantageous collisions with the religious methods of the community in which he dwells. But whenever you seek his active partisanship, or ask him to change or adopt some cardinal moral or practical rule of his life, or endeavor to bind his conscience by some mysterious rite, you must at least furnish him a positive motive of personal benefit in his worldly affairs, or convince his understanding and show him some apparently logical process through which he may find such a mental conviction as he is capable of having.

With woman there appears to be a difference. Some accredit her with more intuition or insight. However this may be, at least she accomplishes her intellectual processes, as it were, *per saltum*. She sees the point at which she wishes to arrive ; she shuts her eyes, perhaps opens her mouth—and—*presto*, she is there !

Let us furnish an instance or two by way of illustration of what is meant. Here is a brief minute of a conversation once had with a devout woman of much ability and education, upon the dogma of the Trinity —a subject which it is understood most theological scholars concede to be undemonstrable to the ordinary understanding.

She : It is a marvel to my mind that men should higgle so much about comprehending this vital article of our faith, when it is so easily illustrated.

Myself : Madam, you amaze me. I thought learned theologians were agreed it is a mystery—a metaphysical idea beyond ordinary comprehension, and certainly inexplicable to the external senses—one that must be taken, if at all, by credence purely, or at least unassisted by logical demonstration.

She : Why, by no means. Here, in this little triplet of clover leaves is a complete illustration. Look at it. The three leaves are combined in one stalk, and the one stalk is three leaves. Could anything be more simple ?

Myself : Nothing, if satisfactory. Does that elucidation wholly satisfy your mind as to an identity, a personality, triple in essence ?

She : Perfectly.

Upon another occasion, in a talk with a woman of unusual intelligence—the wife of a clergyman—about wrong-doing, confession, repentance from evil, and the difficulty of reconciling with common reason how religious faith can compensate for moral delinquency ; how one, having erred, confessed, and repented, can keep on erring and repenting, yet come out right at last by virtue of mere repentance, as is sometimes taught from a pulpit.

She : I cannot perceive any difficulty whatever. It astonishes me that men make such a pother about being good Christians. Why, the whole system of Christianity is summed up in three words—justification by faith.

Myself : May I ask you to explain what specific meaning you attach to those words ?

She : Certainly. If you believe in the teachings of our Saviour—no matter at how late a period, or after whatever extent of sinning—all is forgiven ; and you will reap the reward of everlasting happiness. The only thing to be apprehended is delay—lest you defer the matter until it shall be too late.

Myself : When will it be too late ? Must not one—instead of sinning and repenting—avoid wrong altogether, or else suffer consequent punishment ?

She : Not at all. That is the doctrine of what you call natural religion. At the best it is mere deism. Christianity is immeasurably beyond that. Your tenets would save only the righteous ; but Christianity was given us to save sinners. No matter though you have been immersed in wickedness, if you once believe, you will be saved—as, of course, thenceforth you strive to sin no more.

Myself : Thanks.

MEN AND WOMEN.

The common talk about an imaginary, absolute "equality" of man and woman is wholly misleading. They might be accounted exactly equal in many of the qualities which they possess in common ; and yet—by reason of the dissimilarity of some, or the possession or the absence of others, quite as essential—be found so different in entirety as not to be susceptible of the notion of profitable comparison at all. In fact, the suggestion of a bald equality does injustice to both. It is a coarse, rudimentary, and indiscriminating view of the matter, suitable only to a people recently emerging from savagery ;—a sort of gross reaction of opinion, against that long slavery of woman, which has been the natural outcrop and survival of the instinctive tyranny and brutality of the stronger, prevalent among barbarous and warlike nations. The peculiar mental and moral characteristics of woman—difficult as they may be to formulate in words, when taking the sex as a unit—are as well recognized and as easily discriminable from those of man, by our common consciousness, as are the outlines of her bodily conformation, or the exigencies of her physical nature. The closer the scrutiny and keener the eye of the observer, the more obvious become the distinctively peculiar mental and moral traits of either sex.

They are as much unlike in some respects as they are alike in others. And there is no apparent evidence of any design, in their respective creation, that by force of artificial training they should be brought to resemble each other more closely, either in mind, body, or temperament. As barbarism recedes, and educational refinement advances, the more man and woman are found to differ in essentials. Nature seems to have settled this matter by a law that cannot be disregarded with impunity. As either sex approaches a uniformity with the other, it deteriorates in its best peculiarities. The almost universal verdict of mankind is that a man who succeeds in making himself resemble a woman, impairs, to some extent, those qualities which make him most respected by both sexes ; and that as a woman approximates in resemblance to a man, she diminishes, to say the least, her claim to be considered what a true woman ought to be. In short, both reason and experience seem to indicate that woman can contribute best her proper quota to the progressive civilization of the world, by cultivating and energizing those faculties of power and skill, and those amiable and virtuous traits of her nature, wherein she most differs from man. She can accomplish best her natural mission by turning her attention away from all attempts to rival him in such characteristics as she may most resemble him. For it is easy to perceive that the whole world moves forward most steadily, when the least force is wasted by the rivalry of coincident powers. The greatest momentum is acquired by the reciprocal co-operation, through special adaptation, of such forces as are natural allies. And although the progress of the woman of our day, in some departments of art, science, scholarship, artisanship and even of common labor, has been immense, and the horizon of her capability is still far from being reached ; yet there is a steady accumulation of proof of the rule that difference from, and not similarity to, man's work, is the test of excellence in the result of her well-chosen labors. In fact, the resemblance of woman to man is only in gross. Her distinguishing traits, instead of disappearing, become more marked in proportion as civilized society begins to discountenance war, and to progress, through the gates of commerce—haply, at no very distant day, free commerce—towards permanent peace ; and as the gentler peculiarities of human nature continue to develop, and harden into habits of personal, moral, intellectual, and physical refinement.

The better the cultivation of the higher faculties of the masculine intellect, the more judicial, colorless, and impersonal it becomes in its dealings with human affairs. With woman, however, mental acquisition, cultivation, and exercise—developing her special tendencies towards the imaginative and the emotional—while they broaden her comprehension, and sharpen her intellectual vision, give a keener edge to her power of analyzation, heighten her faculty of appreciation, refine her feelings to a more acute sensibility, yet rarely do they appear to lead her intellect up to the dry atmosphere of the absolute, or carry it far aloof from the warm precincts of the personal and sympathetic. It almost truthfully might be said, generally, that in woman the judicial faculty seldom grows and never ripens. Man, for the most part, creates and shapes the thought of the world. Woman can illustrate and embellish whatever she touches. Man can find his intellectual ideals in a conception of the abstract, and, by an induction of general principles, form a comprehensive grouping of vast varieties, having some common germ or *radix*. Women in general are less scientific, cling more closely to the particular, and are liable to lose their way—in clouds of fancy, or the vacuities of an undisciplined imagination—when the logical clue (as may easily happen) slips from their gentle grasp.

Let a highly intellectual and attractive man talk with an average woman about matters purely general, and, ordinarily, she will appear to follow him, so long as she can see the speaker, or hear his voice ;—although too often she will be thinking only of him. As he goes outside of himself, and soars into the abstract, her feet begin to miss the ground, and she begs to be set down again. So long as she can make a personal application of what is said, her intellectual sympathy is active ; but so soon as that fascinating process becomes impracticable, her mind is likely to go wandering amid the tangles of an intricate maze, while her apparent attention is retained only by her admiration of the demi-god of her fancy, whom she begins to worship, as he utters harmonious sounds that convey to her mind no specific meaning.

Let a real poet read his higher musings to an intellectually cultivated man, and the sympathetic hearer probably will say :—" Yes, I appreciate fully your pictured thought. I recognize those types or emblems ; they are true to nature, and I feel the everlasting brotherhood of the human soul. Your arrows strike at the heart of the mystery of many embarrassing varieties. By the torch-light of your genius, I now see the continuity of countless things that formerly seemed to me discordant and frag-mentary." And so on. Read the same work to a woman of similar grade of cultivated capacity, and very likely she will say :—"Whom do you mean to personify? Did that really happen to you? Do you mean me?" or something of like import.

Indeed, as has been often said, this difference of intellect between man and woman appears to be wholly one of kind, rather than of degree; where-fore comparisons upon any other basis are liable to induce more mischief, than advantage, toward whole-some and practical views of this seemingly intricate matter.

Possibly what may be called the wrong-headedness of those who talk so earnestly of a supposed equality of the sexes arises, as has been suggested, from their seeing the manifestations of power in a few women who have mas-culine intellects, and contrasting such productions with the efforts of men they know, who have only feminine brains ;—for, in spite of what often is said speculatively to the contrary, there is obviously and practically recog-nized a real and radical distinction, as of sex, in intellect. But such cases of masculine women are strictly abnormal, and really illustrate only an exception. However, these fugitive suggestions are designed to touch but a single phase of the profound and ineffaceable distinction Nature has made between the essential and elemental characteristics, both intellectual and moral, of man and woman.

CIVIL RIGHTS OF WOMEN.

To the eye of anxious, thoughtful forecast, it sometimes seems as if the popular ideas of our day, pitching headlong toward the legal emancipation of woman from all male right of control of her person or property—and the consequent disappearance of the universal, time-honored relation of dependence and support between the sexes— might ultimately leave but little practical ground for the fact of legal marriage to rest upon, beyond the uncertain basis of love, passion, or the desire for offspring. The possibility of such a result—remote as it may be—suggests the notion that, in this movement, possibly we are not rising higher in the scale of civilization. Perhaps we are sinking backward, nearer an older condition of some of the race in this respect ;—sometimes, perhaps figuratively, called barbarism. The notion of social independence—although a contradiction in terms—is attractive to the imagination, especially with the young and inexperienced ;—but practically it does not appear to wear well, in ordinary human intercourse.

There would be nothing wonderful in this aspect of the tendency of this self-called reform, even if it shall prove to be accurately characterized by what has been said. It could hardly be deemed singular, to Americans in this respect. How many of our proposed reforms, and "modern improvements" in social ideas, morals, and manners, consist chiefly in repeating the trial of experiments many times exploded ; or in attempting to break down, as useless or tyrannical (because not comprehended, or because misunderstood, by reason of ignoring their history and purpose) ideas or habits which have perhaps cost centuries of sacrifice and self-denial, thousands of lives and millions of treasure, to establish and ingrain with the mental and moral fibre of socialized human nature !

As society moves onward in its march toward refinement, and toward higher, nobler, and purer aims of enjoyment, the relations of men and women to each other obviously must become more artificial, complex, and intricate ;—with larger capacity for ensuring reciprocal happiness and varied delights. Social interdependence, although it involve some loss of natural liberty, on either side, is yet conducive to reciprocal enjoyment, and should supersede the natural tendency to covet isolated freedom. Secondary and relative ideas steadily become more important in social esteem than those purely primary or individual. In attempting to sweep away, as immaterial or fraudulent rubbish, the legal and social fictions, that lie at the artificial and secular foundation of the marriage institution—as it has stood for thousands of years—hasty, one-ideaed reformers are often little aware of the fragile condition of the superstructure they may leave, and how liable it may be to topple, and some day fall headlong.

When, however, the reformer's work is done ; when women shall have exploded the hallowed legal fiction that the husband is the head-of-the-family ; when, as a natural consequence of a nominal divided sovereignty—with equality in all power and authority between husband and wife—rebellion and license shall become the chronic condition of children, within every household ; when the policy of law, aiming at a unity of interest, by an identity of person and property, in married couples, shall be among forgotten things ; when even the natural pride of founding and perpetuating a family name, with its accumulation of traditions, nobleness, refinements, and amenities—one of the strongest peculiar motives in the human breast, as well as one of the greatest factors, when judiciously employed, in civilizing and moralizing mankind—shall have dwindled or perished, what can we have as a substitute ? While the assaults of advanced thinkers are apparently weakening our faith in the sublime consolations of a hereafter-life ; while the pressure of the complicated and bewildering problems, cares, and troubles of this superactive condition of our modern world—upheaving political strata, and demolishing social landmarks—is too great for the over-anxious minds of many, even among the strongest, it would be a pity if any wholesome stimulant to the pride of nobleness in this life should be taken away, or seriously diminished. If the fabric of society, as now constituted, be really in danger, we should at least pause long enough to find assurance of something worthy to replace it, before its foundations shall be seriously impaired.

Perhaps the most appalling consequence now apparent, of this confounding of the nature of man and woman, which threatens the peace and order of families as well as of modern civil society itself, is the impending possibility of the extension of full citizen-suffrage to all women. By one of the strangest perversities of human endeavor, this stupendous change is strenuously urged upon the ground of its inevitably purifying tendency ! It appears to be a necessary moral equipment of the idealistic reformer of

6

our time, that he shall be either blind to the dominant instincts and impulses of human nature, or that he shall wilfully ignore their forces in his more daring speculative projects. In the consideration of this matter, the omnipotence for evil of at least one human passion seems to be left wholly out of view.

Hitherto the greatest common danger to which the purity of the exercise of the elective franchise, in large complex and growing communities, has been exposed in a free country, confessedly has been always the power of money. The advocates of " universal " woman-suffrage appear to overlook the fact that the influence of money for tempting men into political corruption may be far less in force than a well-known power of infatuation, which brooks no rival in its appetite for treason and stratagems—to say nothing of " spoils "—as history too sorrowfully proves. When Paris was a divine arbitrator, he refused both power and glory in order to accept Helen's beauty as an insuperable bribe for his judicial corruption. Since proverbially Love conquers all things, and in his court—as now in politics—almost every wrong is right if it be successful, let those who most honor womanhood beware. A mistake in enlarging the area of suffrage is one of those political blunders most nearly impossible to rectify. The history of American politics proves this conclusively.

As George Savile (Marquis of Halifax) wisely said :— " Women have more strength in their looks than we have in our laws, and more power by their tears than we have by our arguments." The question then comes to this : Are statesmen prepared to add one more uncontrollable, and perhaps unscrupulous, element to the already apparently insoluble problem of pure elections, in large and complex communities? At present this suggestion may seem to savor of superabundant precaution—or at least of want of faith in the infallibility of American womanhood. But what student of history can shut his eyes to the hazards involved by this untried experiment in democracy in our compacted cities, when party-spirit may be running high and when ambition for individual aggrandizement may be more secure even than now, in the reckless, unhallowed, employment of the means of achieving the possession of power and place?

One argument in favor of absolute woman-suffrage—as a right despite inexpediency—most often urged as conclusive, runs thus :—Women are taxed ; it is an American axiom that taxation necessitates the recognition of a right of representation ; representation can be secured only by suffrage of the person taxed ; wherefore women have a moral as well as political—and should be no longer debarred from a legal—right to vote in the same manner as men. It would be difficult to find more mistakes and fallacies in any single plausible proposition. First, women are not taxed—although the property some own is sometimes taxed, in the same manner as that of corporations, trustees, guardians, executors, infants, and lunatics. If a right to vote necessarily resulted from the fact of paying taxes on property owned or possessed by every one, then all the above classes would be entitled alike to the ballot. Besides if voting be a right, chiefly growing out of the fact of a burden of taxation imposed upon property, comparatively few women would share it. Moreover, it would seem that in justice this voting power should be also proportioned, in some manner and to some extent, to the amount of taxes paid. This would give control of the government to the rich ; and the mere ballot would lose its value to others.

A singular paradox, however, seems to control this movement. Woman is, by public opinion, apparently supposed to show her best intellectual title to suffrage by her good sense in not wishing for it. There is a latent intuition among the average citizens of the sex, that seems to tell the wisest of them they would surely lose more than they could possibly gain by exercising such a function ; that they would both add to their public obligations and impair their social privileges by the possession of it. Besides, being conservative, by nature and habit, they hesitate by instinct to enter a vortex which would begin by turning upside down a primal basis of order in society that has prevailed since our first parents met in Paradise, and might lead to social chaos or worse.

Threatening, therefore, as the aspect of this question may sometimes appear, it is not worth while ever to despair. In the long run, human nature, in its upper as well as lower traits, is sure to be self-vindicated. Human life, whether social or individual, is proverbially full of extraordinary mutations. While a few, whether well or ill-advised, are striving to lift up the many, the mass, through sloth or love of pleasure, or the mad thirst for notoriety, or the power of selfish or enthusiastic leaders, are continually exposed to being pushed in a downward direction. But all trust, in their hearts, that error is for but a day—truth for all time. The misfortune of all this, however, is still sustained by ourselves. It lies chiefly in the fact, that oftentimes one or more generations—through such experiments—must suffer, and to some extent waste their existence, by being cut off from that comfort and joy in life which otherwise might easily be obtained. Meanwhile the noisy enthusiasts of the community are making a false *éclat* for themselves, by destroying holy temples and battering into pieces divine images, whose purpose and beauty they cannot see. Like savages they mistake them for something of evil import, fit only to be demolished. Before the renaissance comes, however, the defrauded contemporaries of the false reformer are beyond the reach of its amenities. Truth survives, but the victims of error have perished miserably.

TOUCHES OF NATURE.

Man is a strange animal, and makes strange use
Of his own nature.

BYRON.

SPECIAL HUMAN NATURE.

THE adage that human nature is always the same—even when individually considered—seems to involve a serious fallacy. However true it may be in general, it is misleading, if not for the most part false, in the sense it is popularly understood. The essential elements of our common human nature are indeed substantially identical in every age and clime of the world. Yet the practical revelations of that nature, as they appear to ordinary observation, are so far dependent upon traditionary rights, privileges, customs, and duties—upon temporary motives, social circumstances, and general environment—that, both in impulse and in action, it at least appears to be radically variable. Indeed men's conduct, in matters involving a vital moral principle, at one period of history will be found to be sometimes precisely the reverse of what it has been, under an apparently similar condition or emergency, in the same civil society, at an earlier date. Yet at each time, contemporaneously it may be regarded as equally fit, just, and honorable.

This paradoxical fact is sometimes quite puzzling, or indeed shocking, to the astute or inquisitive youthful mind. Neither public nor private teachers can be too careful to avoid shaking the foundations of adolescent conscience by openly or covertly confounding the intrinsically good or bad—right or wrong, proper or improper, just or unjust—with that which only conventionally, factitiously, or even accidentally may be so regarded from time to time.

Moreover, we talk glibly of what we call human nature, as if it were a specific identity, susceptible of being measured, or reckoned like a fixed quantity ; but it would help us more, in comprehending the social and political enigmas of daily life, if we would bear in mind more frequently how far its very character, as often suggested, may be radically transformed by circumstances.

Strange as it may appear, there are in fact certain definable phases of human nature that always should be considered separately, when we pass judgment upon, or forecast, the conduct of men or communities.

First, there is a species of local human nature, which is full of special traits, resulting apparently from mere place of birth or education, local habits and interests. Then, beyond mere individuals, there is a kind of social human nature, which is developed by association and greatly modifies merely individual characteristics. Again, there is what may be called a national human nature, which owes its growth to the exercise of one's love of his

native or perhaps his adopted country, and his sympathy
with the passions or interests of his immediate fellow-men
in their political capacity. Finally, there seems to be even
an international human nature, which crops out in the
patriotic pride we feel for our own country, its particular
interests, advantages, and power, above the rest of the
habitable globe, whenever, in peace or war, we come in
contact, or contrast ourselves, with men or communities,
identified with the soil, climate, laws, customs, passions,
or interests of other nations.

WORRY ; OR, THE TRET OF FRET.

It is a familiar observation that no ordinary bad habit
of mind is more unwise or useless than self-worrying.
The matters usually causing this kind of mental disquietude, if at all practical, concern either others or one's
self. If they affect others, a man can do only his duty
as he comprehends it. This being found and done, it is
common philosophy to be content and accept the result
as inevitable, without regrets, longings, or self-reproach
for shortcomings. If, however, the troublesome matters
concern only one's self, there is still less cause for this
fruitless discontent. At least one should reflect of how
little importance such matters are, for the most part, in
the economy of the universe—whether they be done well
or ill, or not done at all—and how insignificant in a large
view, and to every one else, is anything that pertains to
one's self, and how wasteful even of self-staying power is
all idle fretting about them.

Probably the open secret of this habit—so persistent in spite of its being so contrary to reason—is that the things worried about are seen in such undue proportions, because they are too near the mind. Like any small object very close to the eye, they obscure other things a little distant and take on a consequence they do not deserve. When we are in a deep valley, a mole-hill may hide a distant mountain. When time, or the occurrence of some other matter of greater interest, has adapted us to the trouble before us—so that it more nearly assumes its true significance—our anxiety diminishes or ceases altogether. But if we act while under such a mental disturbance we are liable to act foolishly. Undue anxiety is the ordinary vice of a shallow nature and implies poverty in the possession of patience.

One available method, of putting down this tendency to unreasonable fretting over personal disappointment or apprehended evil, is to recall how many of our dearest friends have more real cause to worry than ourselves. While thus discovering that we are comparatively happy, we may be stirred to act somewhat in relieving their troubles. And as nearly all worry comes from excessive egoism, we can sometimes find its best cure in active altruism. That is the preacher's view.

This teasing plague of the mind is so little in accordance with common-sense that it is matter of wonder it prevails so frequently among reasonable people. For example, there is the commonly exaggerated fear of one's own death. If this were confined to those who, from consciousness of their mortal sins, are fearful of wrath to come, the dread of the day of reckoning would be natural enough, and perhaps wholesome. Or if the germ of this apprehension were merely a shrinking from common pain and suffering—as the necessary accompaniment of the passage from life to death—or from the agony of separation from all those we hold dear, one might understand that such ideas were pertinent to our instinct of self-preservation, and necessary in nature's economy for preserving the race.

Of course nature revolts at the idea of death, so long as health, strength, and the normal conditions of continuing life prevail. But what is gained by a painful anxiety lest death should overtake one unexpectedly? It seems as unwise as it is useless. After proper precaution against rationally probable disaster, all further anxiety is idle and works against the end desired. It really unfits one to meet any mischance when it shall occur, inasmuch as it takes away both the spontaneity of confidence, and that fertility of resource in trouble which is largely the outcome of a determination to achieve success in our undertakings.

When a man is not in expectation of anything worse than his present condition, and is at least hopeful of a happier life than the one he is called on to give up, it seems unphilosophical, to say the least, that he should tremble and grieve at the suggestion of the approach of the end of the inferior condition. At the proper time, as Bacon says, it is as natural for a man to die as for a child to be born. This time may be deferred for years, or it may be briefly limited by a thousand accidental circumstances. It can hardly be supposed that one who looks confidently forward to a career of endless enjoyment among immortals can dread his translation to such a sublime and attractive state of existence. Nay, this suggestion would seem to be an impeachment of his steadfastness in such religious faith. But if one believe that with death ends all that consciousness which is associated with the body and the life here (an opinion possibly more common among thoughtful men than is known or even suspected by those who have not of late rigidly scrutinized some of their neighbor's real convictions) why should a man trouble himself with what he cannot prevent happening, and which when it does occur will leave him without a pain or a regret, or even a memory?

Obviously there can be no real sense of loss to one who will know it not. Why should one fear what he can never realize? If death itself were a protracted transitional process, it might justify all our habitual dread of it. But it is neither short like life, nor endless like eternity. It is not even brief, like an instant of time. Death is in itself merely a word, descriptive of a conceivable something. The essential idea of it is, however, nothing but a fact to be known only to others. It is and always must be quite beyond the reach of our own personal consciousness here.

An illustration has led away from the theme. The habit deprecated is that common infirmity of worrying over ordinary past or anticipated ills, small as well as great.

There are, as already suggested, two familiar ways of meeting unpleasant coming events. The one is apparently as wise as the other is silly. They seem, however, to be, quite frequently, the choice of temperament, rather than of reason. The vicious way, however, may be overcome by self-discipline, as it is merely the result of a mischievous propensity, which grows apace, unless subdued, or subjected to reason.

I once knew intimately a man of this evil temper, who, by his friends, was said to be, like many others, continually looking on the dark side of things. His present enjoyment was usually clouded by fear of coming evil. When misfortune actually overtook him or his friends, he was liable to the reproach of insensibility. But—like cowards who are said to die many deaths—he had really gone through with all the agony of suffering from the mischief incurred many times before it had actually happened! Instead of hanging "between a smile and a tear," he was always on the side of the tear, but so accustomed to the element that he was seldom in danger of being overwhelmed by it. In fact, by continually keeping the tone of his mind and heart in one lugubrious strain, he had lost all spontaneity—even of grief—and had apparently become either devoid of, or callous to, all natural feeling.

This man's wife was his opposite in all these things. She was not, however, frivolous or even light-hearted. Although she appeared like a stream of sunshine, diffusing cheerfulness wherever she went, yet one who knew her thoroughly might have found no lack of innate sadness in her nature. Nevertheless—perhaps from the very breadth and profoundness of her character—she never anticipated misfortune, or dwelt upon past calamity ; but resolutely accepted things as they happened. Consequently she was always natural and spontaneous, fresh in her impulses, genuine and hearty in her sympathies. She wept with those who wept, and laughed with those who laughed ;—ever appearing bright and happy, or otherwise, as the passing hour permitted.

Every act of the mind, we are taught, costs an expenditure of nerve force—a loss of so much power—to be supplied by retaxing the recuperative resources of our nature. It is a draft upon a capital far from inexhaustible, and of easily definable limits. In this view it is painful to reflect how prodigal we are of our vital inheritance, and how much of it we waste by sheer bad self-management.

While one constant drain upon our reservoir is the common habit of fretting over the irreparable or the inevitable, another like foolish extravagance, in the way of dissipating brain or spirit power, lies in that impertinent curiosity which—through imaginative speculation, or by silly consultations with absurd mountebanks and oracles of many different forms—strives to penetrate the supposititious mysteries of the inscrutable. Sometimes more preposterous than this inquest itself is a habit of helplessly deploring uncertain, though possible, evils, which a morbid fancy, so stimulated, will suggest.

Indeed it has seemed not unfrequently to some as if even religion itself—designed divinely as it is to be the great consoler of the bruised spirit in its most trying afflictions—had been perverted often into an engine of immense proportions for mischief, through this very waste of the power to act, and to suffer in the real business of life. We lose greatly, it is feared, by occupying so much of our thoughts and time with reference to that future state of which necessarily—from our limited powers and the scantiness of Revelation—we know so little, in comparison with its infiniteness, as to count for almost absolutely nothing. It would not be irrational to believe that perhaps the days of this world might be happier, and its work better done, if more of its temporary residents would ponder—as some already do—the absolute gain of making a profitable use of the present;—with only a judicious, and far less anxious, forecast of the remote and unsearchable future.

THE PHILOSOPHY OF SELF-INDULGENCE.

The love of ease—or, as one might say, laziness—and the love of luxury are instincts born with most men. By the energetic and the wise, a full gratification of such desires—however easily attainable—is usually deferred, through some higher or better impulse, until their indulgence may be allowed, without prejudice to more lofty purposes or to the valid claims of others. But with the ordinary mind, whatever will regale an appetite is generally grasped as soon as it comes within reach, and is used without stint. Like most of the tendencies, good or bad, of our common nature, also, this inclination to yield to these desires grows merely by involuntary encouragement, or even by simple sufferance.

However, an actual giving way to the pleasures of ordinary self-gratification, and perhaps of pampering our inclination in that direction, often seems, to ourselves, to be only relative and not absolute. That which at one period of life, or in one circle of society, or to one individual, or among people of one generation, may be

reckoned extravagant sloth, or wasteful luxury, at another time or place, or with a different social group, or by
another person, may indeed appear to be almost a
necessity.

Yet only a few are controlled by an honest, thoughtful
judgment herein ; or compel themselves to live according
to a special standard of their real approval. We are all,
more or less (as every one knows), creatures of custom,
even in those matters which most nearly and chiefly concern our very selves. Sometimes we seducingly call this
weak surrender to self-indulgence, a progress toward
some more perfect state of being—as it were, a mortal
Nirvana ; but in truth it is often only the disguised
atrophy of all natural bent of the mind toward superior
things.

Nevertheless, not only through an amiable concession
to the contagion of custom, or to the allurement of social
sympathy in pleasure, do we abandon our Spartan ideals,
but also by a selfishness-in-idleness we sink into the mire
of slothful ease, and dwarf our capacity for something
better. In general American society, however, most
virile people are constantly busy. Idleness among us is
also exceptionally deteriorating, as a method of life.
Whoever would be wholly idle must be practically
isolated.

Few men or women of the common stamp—not wholly
limp or flaccid in temperament—are fit to live either idle
or alone. Even household cares are better than none.
While being the head of a family has a constant tendency
to warm the heart and to expand its sympathies, it is a
common observation that the fact of living apart, even in

city-life, works in the opposite direction. Both men and women are liable to deteriorate in this way. They are prone to become selfish in proportion as they are withdrawn, and become exempt, from the minute concerns and responsibilities of domesticity. If they have no business duties or affairs to counteract such belittling influences as empty egoism begets, their pathway in life becomes exceedingly narrow, and shut in from any broad view of the great or profound interests of their fellow-creatures. A sagacious man said of such an one :—"He carries his world and his family under his hat."

Many of this sort find nothing to do besides feeding, clothing, and amusing themselves ;—which last not uncommonly they do largely by finding fault with the doings, or fancied shortcomings, of their better-employed neighbors. Almost unavoidably they become fastidious, exacting, discontented, censorious, and illiberal, or unjust in all their social opinions. Each one revolves in a small orbit, while a very imperfectly developed *ego* is its axial centre. This is sometimes true of the upright or wholly well-meaning. But if there be any whose natural inclinations are evil, this "devil's workshop"—selfishness-in-idleness—by a paradox of its own, will easily turn out engines of mischief sufficient to put the most quiet neighborhood in an uproar, or to set a whole community by the ears.

Social life, by its interchangeable vicissitudes, is fertile enough in petty discomforts, yet it has a thousand vents for their escape. But individual loneliness commonly tends both to corrode and debase the temper, for want of either sympathy or social distractions. Probably it is not too much to claim, as among the stronger incentives to the formation of family-life, the fact that it affords the charms of privacy and seclusion, without the terrors and deteriorations that attend a life of isolation from the business and sympathies of the common world.

It is needless to say how poor our most coveted pleasures become, when not subordinate to intellectual restraint and guidance. Whether we eat, drink, walk, travel, play, laugh, read, or talk, it is a great gain if we may enjoy · rationally, and not simply gratify a simple inclination or an animal instinct. In the ordinary matter of eating and drinking, a large portion of men, without stopping to taste, merely devour their food in order to satisfy a craving appetite. The Roman glutton had more sense in his method ;—gross as it was. To feed delicately, or with discrimination — mingling pleasant conversation with deliberation at table—is the habit of comparatively few, in our country in the daily routine of their active lives, even among those who have full opportunity of choice. The same trite observation is true of other physical, as well as mental or social, enjoyments of the passing hour.

The longer one lives, the more thoroughly he must become satisfied that the tongue, acting merely as an organ of taste, is an indiscreet, if not wholly untrustworthy door-keeper of the stomach. As every child knows, many deadly poisons are sweet, and the most dangerous waters may not only look innocent, but sometimes relish as refreshingly, as if drawn from the purest spring. The police-duties entrusted to the tongue alone are often badly performed. Even the teeth do this work much better.

7

The Bohemian—so-called—having both imagination and susceptibility, with an exaggerated love of common self-indulgence—is usually a malcontent in any well-regulated community. He is constantly bumping his sensitive skull against his artificial limitations. He opposes what is generally deemed good for the greater number, and prefers what is best, in his opinion, for the very small class of which he is a self-elected member. The Philistine contrarily—being realistic in temperament, matter-of-fact in mental nature, and objective in all things—sees his boundaries. Knowing them to be morally impassable, with cool tact and astute policy he makes a graceful concession to social necessity. He kisses the chain he is compelled to wear and easily keeps himself within the bounds society prescribes for him ;—sometimes making a profit, as well as a convenience, of an artificial virtue. Although each may be a mere voluptuary, after his kind, yet the latter will fatten while the first may starve.

Restraint, moderation — *ne quid nimis*—and even method in pleasures have countless other, and more estimable, advantages over headlong self-indulgence. The enjoyment of life may be also much enhanced by a habit of constantly recognizing and acknowledging present good. It is wise, when not suffering any immediate grievance, to inhale the joy of every pleasant breath in life—however intermittent they be—as it passes ; instead of putting off our attention to its full recognition, until a consummation of the event of the hour. Perhaps too it is well to strive to keep constantly before the mind the idea that, whenever we are really happy, nothing is, will, or can be more beautiful, good, or desirable, than what is then within our own immediate control.

HAPPINESS.

Although by common opinion earthly happiness con-sists chiefly in self-content, it obviously varies in degree from the somnolent sloth of the lowest animal to the triumphant satisfaction of a conquering hero who has saved his country from impending ruin, or an ecstatic parting soul reaching out to receive the proffered embrace of eternal bliss. The larger a man's capacity for intellec-tual or spiritual enjoyment, the more difficult it will be for him to satisfy the demands of his nature and to attain that self-complacency which is essential to his complete felicity.

This may be a too purely abstract view of the matter. Perhaps in order to be quite trustworthy it ought to be supplemented by a suggestion of the personal traits of evenness of temper and what is known as a naturally cheerful disposition.

But to all methods of attaining continuing happiness, of a high order, by personal effort some other specific things are essential. The first in importance is, that one should have a purpose in life, adapted to one's nature and circumstances ;—with due recognition of one's limi-tations, as well as capabilities and obligations. One must have also a clear self-approval of one's own aims and conduct. This involves bravery as a necessary element ;— a courage that says to a man's self, *nil time nisi male facere.* The rest may be summed up, as a preacher would say, in the expression, the discharge of duty ;—that is obedience to, and compliance with, the laws of God, Nature, and society, as well as the performance of what obligations a man owes specially to himself.

Most of the unhappiness of life, however, comes from an inability to discover, or a neglect to recognize, the truth that only by obedience to law in its universal sense —far higher than custom or statute—and not by the following of will or inclination, shall we find the true clue that alone can guide us unharmed through the devious or intricate ways and among the vicissitudes of our mortal career.

Radically different as they are, yet often, in common speech, and even in our thoughts, are happiness and pleasure confounded. Writers are not wanting who contend for their absolute identity. Happiness, however, is more sober, while pleasure is more exhilarating. Pleasure usually springs from the concentration of the attention and faculties of mind or body, or both, for the time being, upon a single purpose or object, which is immediate and specific. Happiness, in a liberal sense, grows out of content with things generally that influence us ;—involving usually a more comprehensive survey of surroundings and a more calm spirit. Happiness, as its verbal root appears to indicate, rests much on good fortune. It implies conscious satisfaction with one's condition, full approval of the present, absence of hopeless regret for the past, or of apprehension of evil for the future. It is quiet, equable, and but little agitated by undue expectation. Pleasure on the contrary is full of anticipation. It is joyous, though with interruptions of disquietude. It feeds largely upon hope—centring its ventures a good deal in the future. Pleasure belongs more to a sensitive temperament, to the body, and to the passions. It is stormy, too, and apparently comes and goes oftentimes as it were, in waves, great or small, of irregular succession.

Happiness seems to grow up gradually in the mind, yet is dependent for its sure poise upon that equanimous temperament called a happy disposition, as its unconscious centre. The heart, as the seat of enjoyment, of course plays the largest part in both pleasure and happiness—standing between the mind and the animal nature. Happiness often finds its accomplishment in present ease and leisure, or in contemplation, or in the orderly discharge of duty, or in the conferring of pleasure upon others. Pleasure delights us through exhilarating occupation ;— as by excelling in games of physical strength, skill, or chance, and by what pleases the sense, or amuses or distracts the mind from care or thought. Although both are inclined to nourish selfishness, still pleasure is more reckless of others' rights. While happiness often includes pleasure, yet pleasure seldom, merely in itself, involves true happiness.

Who is happy ? Perhaps almost every one might be, if outward circumstances and inward self-conduct alone could produce happiness at will. Yet nearly all are supposed to be more or less miserable. The really happy man or woman is said to be almost exceptional. The truth seems to be, that it is not always an affair of the will, even where there is no cause for discontent. Men of the finest capacities of reason and imagination, in apparent health, have often found life, even without adverse circumstances, almost insupportable. It would be hazarding little to say that some of the most wretched lives have been those of men and women possessed of superior intellectual endowments with most other worldly advantages.

We all recognize a phase of the understanding, distinguishable from the reasoning powers, or imagination, generally called common-sense, also a species of physico-moral temperament, usually characterized as animal spirits. When these are combined in one person, we have what is called a happy disposition. This equable kind of nature finds its happiness as a matter of course. It does not forecast evil, it expects everything to be as it should be. If the past prove otherwise, it wastes no energy over what it regards as having been inevitable.

This is not like the happiness that comes from the exercise of either religion or philosophy, nor even from a self-gratulation over the performance of duty, or the practice of virtue in self-denial. Neither does it resemble the pleasure growing out of the achievement of the objects of ambition with a successful appeal to the plaudits of the world. Nor is it like the happiness that sometimes accompanies the possession of power, or the practical exercise of commanding intellect.

Perhaps if we would look for the verification of what, in the common sentiment of mankind, is reckoned ordinary happiness, we shall be more likely to find it unalloyed as we descend, rather than as we rise, in the social scale. Contentment absolute, irrespective of the extent or character of what is possessed, seems to be the sole recognized key to the treasure. "Happy as a king," or as "a lord," although a childish phrase (meaning idleness and freedom from want or care) shows in what direction the common mind idealizes. It could, however, only apply to brief periods or moments, and not to material parts of a lifetime, even if it were as true as supposed by those who utter the thoughtless words. " Happy as a fool," would be a much truer expression of the realization of what is commonly understood by the term happy, when thus applied.

It would be deplorable indeed, if it were true, that ignorance monopolizes the happiness of the world, or if old Matthew Prior rightly had said :

> From ignorance our comfort flows ;
> Those only wretched are the wise.

If so, then verily would it be folly to be wise, as Gray also puts it in his familiar paradox.

The young are happy in their insensibility to the inevitable sorrow that is in store for them. As they cannot foresee, therefore they naturally hope, and live buoyed up by cheerful expectation, happy in their pleasures. The older are not so blind. Guided by experience, observation, and reflection, they anticipate too accurately what may happen. Although not sustained by an eyeless hope, yet through calculation, they more accurately forecast the future, and calmly prepare to meet its obstacles. This is wisdom for them. But it might be disastrous if the young could see clearly what is often so plain to their elders. Not yet knowing how to meet it, they certainly would lose some of their courageous energy. Perhaps they might incline early to a despondency that would check the advance of the race, or at least put a stop to some of the best work going on in the world.

OUR ILLUSIONS.

Who does not know that most of the varying views we entertain of actual things in this life, or of possibilities in a future, owe much of their contrariety as well as of their charm to the influence of the illusions we accept or cherish? To their power too we must attribute the larger part of the inconsistencies of conduct or opinion scattered so liberally through our lives. These hallucinations are inwoven with our mental and moral fibre, and closely attendant upon our incipient growth of mind or enlargement of mental vision. We are all overcharged with the illusions of self-delusion. It is not easy to say how much we are indebted, for our intellectual headway through life, to a natural expansion of the understanding, and how much to a mere sloughing off, as time advances, of the deceptions which self-love, influential circumstances, or other chance-teachers, may have practised involuntarily upon the ingenuous credulity of our youth.

During early years our life is full of petty misapprehension. We are prone to take everything upon trust, or to assume that appearances, as we purblindly interpret them, are real and true. As we grow we largely delude ourselves by our own hasty misconceptions. This private hoard of error is also liberally enhanced by the mistaken policy of unwise instructors, or the officious suggestion of ignorant or ill-advised friends and acquaintances. The mind being not quite capable of comprehending the full

truth in many matters, yet curious and eager for explanation of seeming phenomena, the readiest fiction at hand
is commonly furnished to us. We take it too greedily to
question it closely.

As the understanding matures (and many ordinary
illusions, having played their part, lose their utility in the
economy of nature) we begin to purge the soul of rubbish
and to endeavor to sweep away the drift-wood or impuri-
ties that obstruct or roil the broadening stream of our
intellectual life. Often however our misconceptions are
endeared to us by some of the sweetest associations of
happy days in a guileless childhood. We part from these
with painful reluctance, and they very often leave an
aching void in the sentimental part of our nature never to
be filled. The delusions of our judgment are more obstinate, and, however, thoroughly unmasked, quit us still
more unwillingly.

We may, however, and many do, fill their vacant places
with the more virile fibre of tested truth. This process
continues, in the liberal and fecund mind, throughout life,
until we have long passed our grand climacteric, and
sometimes even until sterile old age creeps on apace.
How far we shall have gone during a normal life, in this
endless progress of finding out verity, will of course depend more especially upon each man's self. The space
will be measured by his opportunities, his labor in sincerity, his courage, earnestness, or enthusiasm, his independence of popular opinion, and his self-sacrifice in
searching for reality—at the expense of convenience or
comfort—and in facing absolute fact, however repulsive
or cruel it may appear to be,

Happy the man, in a certain inferior sense, whose body lives only while his pleasing illusions continue. Unhappy indeed is he who outlives them all without finding a solid basis of philosophic truth, upon which, in the serenity of a disillusioned soul, he may calmly contemplate, in a large way, the candid austerity of Nature and the eternal fitness of things.

But our illusions by no means continue the same. They change with our time of life. Those of childhood, youth, manhood, maturity, middle age, declining years, and old age, are commonly no less complete, the one than the other. Yet is each usually unlike the other in many conditions ; sometimes in their tenacity of endurance, oftentimes in their power to influence the temper, the passions, the will, or the judgment. Generally, however, they are special and peculiar ; as well as adapted to each stage of our existence. They are usually born with, or nourished by, the events, interests, passions, or sympathies of the particular period of life through which we are passing.

Besides, the unquestioned faith of one period, when dissolved, is usually counted a folly during another, even by the same person. More especially, however, is this true when we sit in judgment upon the conduct of others. For instance : an old man smiles loftily at the exaggerated importance a young man attaches to some petty triumph of the hour ; while the young man laughs knowingly when he sees an octogenarian infatuated by the measured caresses of a simulated youthful affection. Literature finds its largest commodity in illustration of the more frequent, as well as the profounder, illusions of life. It shows through its prismatic glass how they arise, color, and fade in regular succession from infancy to age.

The delusions of civil society—even more deep-seated and enduring than those of individuals—furnish ample food for the genius of the liberal-minded historian. They affect alike nations, communities, parties, families. They appear as superstitions, fetiches, shibboleths, political hallucinations, or traditional fascinations, that long defy even the demonstration of common-sense to dispel them. The divine right of kings, witchcraft, and countless political tricks and devices that have had their day of deluding mankind, each in turn, illustrate the adage of Oxenstierna: —with how little wisdom the world is governed. In the early history of a people these delusions seem to be commonly necessary in order to form a bond of fellowship and to compel a coherence of the body politic. However, as any civil community advances in intelligence, unity, homogeneousness, and independence, it gradually shuffles them off, just as individuals do their personal illusions, during their growth from infancy to maturity.

Most of us pass, as is sadly proverbial, through the last gate, opening the way that leads rapidly toward senility, with a loss of most of the delicious illusions that once charmed our youthful mind, and have oftentimes continued to hallow our human nature, even until middle life was wellnigh spent. Yet do we also sometimes carry late in our journey, closely clinging to us, some bitter superstition or dogmatic delusion, we have never had either the leisure, the strength of will, the clearness of judgment, or the moral courage to wrestle with so effectually as entirely to shake off its insidious embrace.

When, however, old age shall come upon us in full mastery, our remnant of life will be calm and content or unquiet and worried, in proportion as we have, or have not, at last got anchored in a sea where truth has taken the place of painful delusion;—where the shores of time are plainly seen, and no mirage of either beauty or horror longer cheats the vision. Happy will it be for us if then we are able to discriminate between what may and what may not be known to our human intelligence; and the unknowable, the unsearchable, and the unthinkable shall have lost their power to distract or madden us, with doubt or fear, or even to fill us with an arrogant assumption of possessing faculties of infinite comprehension. Then we may compensate ourselves for the deprivation of those delights of fancy which regaled the eager appetite of our early days, and for the decay of those mistaken faiths which may have even sustained the enthusiasm of maturer years, by laying the sweet solace to our calm souls that, however little may be the residuum of real knowledge we actually possess, at the least, we can no longer be deceived or alarmed by those who are as ignorant as ourselves.

Good-Luck.

It is a common observation that many of the obstacles to our cherished purposes are crushed by the mere grasp of courageous endeavor. Weak natures go to the wall by letting " I dare not," wait upon " I would." It seems silly to say simply, if you wish a thing done, and it be not wrong :—" Do it." Yet it is a familiar experience that the desirable things in this life often are thus accomplished, by those bravely resolved, in the face of apparent impracticability.

It is a trite observation that strong natures have confidence in luck. They seem even to overcome ill-fortune merely by their courage and energy. To a hesitating mind it is astonishing to note how the obstacles encountered will appear to recede, and how obscurity will clarify itself, before the onward pressure of a determined and hopeful will. Hope is always the natural ally of the normal body or mind. Vague doubts and vacillations of purpose are common symptoms of mental infirmity —whether it be natural weakness, or the growth of a vicious habit, or the result of a morbid disturbance of physical equilibrium.

The vigorous will, by an inspiration or law of its nature, always expects to succeed. Although we cannot foretell the future, with certainty, yet we may reason toward it, with some probability, or shrewdly divine it, with faith and hopefulness. While we are doing all in our power to ensure the accomplishment of our purpose, it is also a necessary ingredient of true courage to cherish a faith that the result must be as we would have it. The very state of mind, thus begotten or nourished, is not unfrequently itself the most important factor in achieving success.

The weak are always marvelling how strong natures reach their ends with such apparent celerity and ease. They themselves waste time, and lose energy in apprehension of failure. Vibrating between rashness and cowardice, they often bear all the fatigue of bolder effort, yet miss the prize by their vacillation. Fearing to risk, as the proverb runs, they fail to win. Acting at length, but impetuously—when spurred by shame of their cowardice, or by some exterior propelling motive, or by some headlong rashness of blind impulse—they strike at random. Taking more blows than they give, they often sink under inglorious defeat, disheartened by their imaginary ill-luck.

It is an instinct of great natures also to be bold and even prodigal in the choice of means. Having their eye fixed upon an end, they rapidly select the best auxiliaries;—not always closely counting even the cost. They favor alliance with the strong. They select their agents, by sympathetic intuitions of their nature, from among the intelligent, the skilful, the courageous, the hopeful, the ambitious, the energetic, the determined, the capable. Conscious of innate superiority they have not that fear of comparison and rivalry—that jealousy and envy of their abettors—which is a common infirmity of petty minds. A sovereign or leader, of powerful cast of intellect, with energetic will, thus aims to draw about him, by natural affinity, as counsellors, ministers, or lieutenants, men of large measure and virile strength. Weaker men, when chance has put them in commanding position—jealous of others' fame—are afraid to expose their own littleness to a humiliating contrast or an overshadowing, by calling around them men of capacity, energy, and courage, or dominating will.

Despite the common outcry against the inevitable inequality of conditions in life, there appears to be a kind of book-keeping accompanying the favorable chances of Fortune. It seems as if notwithstanding her

fabled blindness, she sometimes kept a strict account
with her beneficiaries. She appears to make her gifts
the means of opportunity of good or ill, according as
the recipients of her favor are proved deserving or otherwise. When a brave man, however humble, sets a definite
aim before him, apprentices himself to the elementary
methods of something worth doing, devotes his time,
labor, and zeal to the training, disciplining, and adapting
of his mind and hand to the work he is about to under-
take, until he has acquired that hability in his occupation,
which nothing but study, experience, and familiarity can
give ; and then—by the added moral momentum of this
protracted effort—devotes himself (with living faith in
the result he aims at) to hard work, skilfully and persistently applied, he is on the high-road to what the hasty
observer of only the last stage of the process calls good-
luck. These things are axiomatic with both pagan and
Christian men—ancient or modern. *Audentes fortuna
juvat.* To him that has, more is given. And so on. If
a wise man encounter good-luck, he will make of it a kind
of provision against the accidents of ill-luck ;—so that
good-fortune commonly seems to attend him to the end.

But when a man will wholly trust to luck, and not to
himself, even if it come he cannot husband it. For want
of the habit of prudence, and also because he has usually
allowed himself to become necessitous, he lays his hand
upon the largess of chance as if it were his due, and he
were bound to scatter it in extravagance. So it is soon
gone, leaving him poorer than before. Every stroke of
his good-luck may carry him farther into the morasses
of life, until at last he sinks in despair. Unless, when

some violent stroke of calamity shall perchance overtake him, before the divine spark of energy is extinct within him (as will sometimes happen) he rally and reverse his methods of life. While profiting by that wisdom of fools, experience, he may make amends for his folly through supreme privation or self-sacrificing effort in a new direction—until he has achieved fortune. In fine, it is proverbial that the diligent, self-denying man will at least overtake good-luck ; while ill-luck commonly pursues the slothful and improvident lover of ease, present comfort, and pleasure. For it is well known that good-luck is, for the most part, only another name for well-used opportunity.

HOPEFULNESS.

It is a lesson of an old philosophy that the charm of man's existence lies more in what seems than in what is. Imagination and fancy furnish the staple of our greatest pleasures. Illusion dominates even practical human affairs. Hope plays a conspicuous, if not the chief, part in the drama of life. "A hopeless person," says Berkeley, "is one who deserts himself." Indeed it goes without saying that life ceases to be desirable when this fairy goes out of it, or hides herself. For then joy—which is as it were the blossom, as hope seems the bud, of human happiness—may no longer be looked for to show us its rosy hues. As poor Coleridge lamented, in his sixtieth year :—

> Where no hope is, life 's a warning,
> That only serves to make us grieve
> When we are old.

Morally, as well as physically, we know we are contrived inscrutably. Bare and hard though it would be,
yet existence alone might content us if we were merely
animals. Our composite human nature, however, fills us
with ideals and longings that must somehow be satisfied
—or we must hope for a satisfaction—else these cravings
of our spiritual hunger make us more wretched than can
the pangs of physical starvation. Bodily pain, if unchecked, usually soon runs its course into stupor, if not
to entire insensibility. But mental anguish can grow in
intensity, even by simply feeding upon itself ;—and, unless alleviated by hope, may become intolerable, and
seek its cessation even by voluntary death.

In the conduct of life, both mental and moral hygiene
demand of us constant watchfulness of ourselves. Our
happiness here lies so much within our own control, that
proverbially a large part of human misery is the result of
vicious, self-taught, or indulged habits of body and mind.
Indeed most of the signal events of our lives affect us
vitally or superficially, for good or ill, according as we
educate ourselves to allow, or not, their influence to have
much or little sway over our after-conduct.

Generally speaking, one may say, the experiences of
this life are thrice tasted—first, in the anticipation or apprehension, second, in the actual fact, and third, in the
retrospect. The first and last are to a large extent what,
by our temperament, religion, or philosophy we choose to
make them. Of the "fact," we are not always masters. If
it be pleasant, we may give ourselves up to it consciously,
and enjoy it heartily in its consummation. If it be painful, we may still bear it with patient resignation, and ex-

tract a moral from its bitterness;—often learning how to avoid a like ill in future, and finding perhaps some comfort in the lesson. We may also make it a starting-point for a new onward and upward movement not otherwise opened to our view, chasten the retrospect into soothing melancholy, and sometimes taste the sweet uses of adversity. But out of the first—anticipation—by sheer habit of mind, we may make or mar the largest part of our mental or moral fortunes;—just in proportion as we cultivate hopefulness, and courage, or give way to cowardice or idle apprehension.

It is so obvious that groundless distrust of the future in any enterprise is not only useless, but positively tends to disable us for reaching what we strive after, that the permission of it to influence us can be set down as only the result of a depraved condition of mind. By nature it seems we should be cheerful and hopeful. It is by this theory and impulse alone that the young world moves on. For while hope energizes, fear paralyzes.

Although some are constituted so fortunately that the former is always in the ascendant without any effort to keep it so, yet there are others—too many indeed—who are not full-eyed, but myopic, and need a constant self-watchfulness to keep the torch of hope blazing. It is worth all the trouble it costs. Nay, one of the lesser advantages of encouraging a disposition to take the cheerful view is that we spare ourselves the useless mischief of twice tasting the bitterness of things disagreeable. For by idle forecasting merely possible evil, we infuse the hemlock into the cup of many of our real joys;—while also depriving ourselves of the luxury of pleasing anticipations.

Proverbial and even axiomatic as are these suggestions, so much are we influenced by temperament or obstinate habit, that they usually slip out of the memory when most needed for our encouragement, to sustain us either in our real afflictions, or when a strange consciousness of the apparent worthlessness of life seems sometimes unbidden to come over us like a pall. The best tonic for keeping the heart constantly sweet and sound, through all its vagaries, is to have some large, congenial, and worthy purpose always before the mind ;—with a determined will to accomplish it. Then the song of Hope will commonly be heard in the air. For :—

> Work, without hope, draws nectar in a sieve,
> And work, without hope, cannot live.

JUDGING MEN.

When we are forming opinions concerning our contemporaries—whether canvassing their characters, motives, or conduct—as every one knows, we cannot be too carefully discriminative in adopting a standard, or laying down rules by which to measure and determine their real merits or relative position toward each other. There are no fixed, general or special, formulas by which all may be rightly judged. It is hard to scrutinize our neighbor's conduct from his own stand-point. Every man being, to some extent, the creature of circumstances—internal as well as external—each will be more or less successful as he overcomes the adverse, or avails himself of the easy, conditions of his life. Besides while many, who are favored by fortune, have the good sense to accumulate the gifts of chance, others, thinking the stream will continue to flow always, seize and consume only the pleasures of the day—taking no care for the morrow.

Easy success in life, from whatever cause, has a constant tendency to make men arrogant and intolerant toward others, without their being conscious of their differing from ordinary men in this respect. Nothing in experience, however, makes a fair-minded, noble man so disposed to be liberal and charitable toward others, as his own personal hardship or sufferings by misfortune. Success through great personal effort by such an one, or the overcoming of obstacles seemingly insuperable, usually produces a character alive with sympathy for those who are struggling with like difficulties or making a manly fight against odds. Easy success, on the contrary, commonly puffs up an ordinary man with conceit, and fills him with such a vain sense of his own importance, that sometimes it is difficult to award simple justice to his real merits.

Indeed in forming honest and sound opinions of many of those whom the world and themselves deem successful men, it is necessary sometimes to take charitably into consideration this fact—of their success without personal effort or signal ability. It is better to make a large allowance to accident, for some of their shallow manifestations of folly and arrogance ;—which may be merely a kind of parasitic growth, and not native to, or inherent in the root of, their character.

However fairly we may intend to judge of our neighbor's capacity, disposition, or actions, of course we insensibly analyze them by, and compare them with, what we believe we know of ourselves. Every man's expressed opinion of another, in this respect, is liable to become, to some extent, an involuntary autobiographical betrayal of his own character. It is worth much or little, not merely from his opportunity of observation and intended impartiality of judgment, but, more largely, from his sympathetic appreciation, or insight, whether natural or acquired by self-study. This is dependent, not simply upon the fulness and ripeness of his capacity, but rather upon the degree of his own self-knowledge—mental, moral, and practical. In abstract matters opinion may be colorless and impartial ; but in the notions we form of our fellow-men, or of practical matters, it is rarely true that our own views are not fashioned closely after our real or ideal selves and our own affairs. By such guiding or misleading lights—almost always unconsciously, too, influenced, if not controlled, by prevailing popular opinion—do we grope our way amid the labyrinthine recesses of other men's characters or motives.

Men, whose natures are narrow, and only objective, or purely matter-of-fact, whose social sympathies are feeble, or who are deficient in imagination—lacking either moral or mental insight—or who, by limited intercourse with mankind, have little knowledge of the ways of men and their modes of thinking and acting, who have lived isolated and apart from general intercourse with the active world, and whose external experience has been confined to a small routine of daily cares or duties, are prone to be harsh and severe—nay, very often bitter and apparently malignant—in their judgment of the lives or characters, motives and actions, of those of more liberal natures or more widely varied vicissitudes of conduct.

On the other hand, men of larger mould, who have participated in important affairs, public or private, whose natures are composite and many-sided—with minds original, creative, fertile, and versatile—whose imaginations are vivid and expansive, whose fancies are lively, whose sympathies are warm, excitable, broad, or penetrating (such men as Shakespeare, Bacon, Goethe) appreciate the great variety and almost infinite complexity of human nature. They recognize good mixed with bad, make large allowance for seeming inconsistencies, are prone to hear not only " both " but all sides of any story —especially one affecting the conduct of another suspected or accused of ill-doing—and are wisely liberal or comprehensively charitable. They seldom condemn another unheard, or upon partial statements, or merely by ordinary circumstantial evidence, or without an opportunity for his own full, unconstrained, and personal explanation.

Puritan Philosophy.

It is too common in these pleasure-loving days to rail thoughtlessly at the ascetic intolerance of our Puritanism during its primal history. Its extravagances had obvious defences. Where all honest men vividly realized, as a truth beyond decent question, that the soul of a man may exist independently of his body, that it is immortal, and that any departure from prevailing Christian dogmas

is sin—involving punishment by keenest torture of endless duration—while the avoidance of such sin ensures
eternal happiness and immeasurable joy, what wonder
if large-hearted and noble-minded men were commonly
reckless of the means to be employed for accomplishing
their magnificent purpose of evangelizing the human race.
Was it not worth the sacrifice of all the petty pleasures of
this ephemeral existence to escape temptation and secure
everlasting bliss ?

Even if it were a mistake to lose our temporary gratifi-
cations here through superabundant caution, and though
such deprivation should prove to have been really needless, what would such trifling considerations weigh in the
balance against an assurance of perpetual enjoyment
hereafter ? And how could men of superior capacity—
the born leaders of their people—calmly and idly look
upon their fellow-men violating the precepts of Christianity (as then recognized and understood by their community) when it was so clear, to these responsible makers
and executors of the supreme law of the land, that such
heedless sinners were unquestionably bringing upon their
immortal souls the irrevocable doom of endless torment,
as the inevitable price to be paid for a few fleeting grati-
fications of the senses, passions, or inclinations of a miserable, depraved, and despicable body ?

No wonder they doubted the professed faith of any
light-minded man of the world (no matter how attentive
to mere outward religious ceremonials) that could not
easily be reconciled with his apparent indifference to
such pending infinite disaster. Their cardinal error lay,
as is now acknowledged, in their contempt for human

nature, and their hatred of some of its instincts as they
understood them.

The atmosphere grows clearer nowadays. Men's
eyes are opened more widely. Less inclined to purblind-
ness from too much straining of the sight in an endeavor
to catch a glimpse of the invisible future, they see the
tangible present more distinctly—and perhaps with a
more just perspective.

A truer philosophy of normal life is the offspring of
rational hope, courageous joy, and unquestioning cheerfulness. This leads one neither to mourn over the past
nor to shudder at the future, but innocently to reap the
harvest or gather the fruits of present existence, and to
enjoy the fulness thereof. It welcomes spontaneity and
revels in freshness. It finds no need to analyze imaginary conditions or morbid emotions in its endeavors to
convince a reluctant proselyte of the existence of some
obscure happiness he cannot conceive.

But our Puritanical philosophy—in its severest phases
—seems to have been the reverse of all this. It was
always counting its imaginary beads—apparently in order
to keep its conscience lively. Although it sometimes
looked helplessly into the past, with a sigh of regret for
pleasures missed, yet it leaped beyond the present or
near future, and lost all the elasticity of mere appreciative hope by seeking to adapt men to a remotely possible
condition of things immeasurably beyond the scope of
their capacity or even adequate conception. As Heine
says:—"Its secret was the deification of suffering."

When this unnatural process of dealing with the facts
of life stumbles against some insuperable obstacle; when

this kind of philosophy teaches the anxious soul to put questions for which no satisfactory solution is found ; or when from the nature of things the questioning spirit meets only a hollow echo or a silent rebuff—the inquiry recoils, like an awkward boomerang springing back upon its holder.

The prospective punishment threatened, by these Puritans of the early type, to recalcitrant followers was fiendishly harsh ; but the promised rewards offered here to devotees were little better. Some of the lines even in Longfellow's famous *Psalm of Life*—although said by the author to have been written for self-consolation in despondency—appear to be tinctured with something of this Puritanical spirit, and give voice to a weary soul striving to keep itself miserable according to a supposed divine law. The prospect mapped out before a perfect man is not joy, nor even content ; but alas ! a task of sober toil during his too conscious march to the grave ! Nothing is offered but the poor consolation that his footprints can lead others, who may be shipwrecked on life's solemn main, to trudge on with hope, like ourselves, of —waiting forever—for what ? We listen long and profoundly. No satisfactory answer comes—but the boomerang flies back again.

FAVORS.

It is hard enough to earn money by joyless labor— done merely for the sake of the money. It is harder still either to keep it (that is, to invest it so as not to make losses) or to spend it judiciously—not wastefully nor foolishly—when one has acquired more than enough to satisfy one's current needs. But the most difficult of all modes of dealing with money is to give it away wisely. The problem is to give so as to be least morally hurtful to the giver, and so as neither to make ingrates, encourage laziness, cultivate pauperism, nor to wound the self-love of worthy recipients of pecuniary or other material favor—and at the same time to arouse neither envy nor resentment in others.

The commonest check to the good impulses of one who loves to give, or in anywise to help another, is, of course, ingratitude. It is a pity this is true. One ought to extend a helping hand to the needy, we are told, in whatever degree, at least according to one's superfluity, without the stimulus of an expectation of gratefulness from the receiver. We are taught to do so simply and purely in obedience to that lofty, natural or civilized instinct—which is the gentle command, whether divine or human, of a kind nature—that "Asian ideal of unknown antiquity," to do unto others as we would they should, under like circumstances, do unto us.

When gifts are unremitting, forgetfulness of kindness is a common infirmity of preoccupied minds, as well as of shallow or selfish natures. As much as misery itself, it is apt to dwarf and enfeeble, perhaps wholly demoralize, the finer faculties, mental as well as moral. Sometimes, too, the recipiency of unmerited favor has such a paralyzing effect upon the sensibilities of ordinary people, that it deadens their inward self-respect, and even checks the common outward desire, or look, for respect from others.

Once in a while this failure, or tardiness, to acknowledge the obligation of favor, assumes a humorous aspect.

When a beneficiary returns after a long absence to thank you for past favors he has thoughtlessly neglected to acknowledge, you may be reasonably sure his quickened memory has a politic impulse. His sudden access of thankfulness is a prelude to a supplication for some additional help, such as a fresh gift of money—nominally disguised as a loan payable at his convenience.

It is sometimes a nice matter to deal properly, either in bestowing or receiving favors, even among ordinary friends and acquaintances. Among kindred where love and affection sincerely prevail, or with those who are held in bonds of true friendship and consequent intimacy and mutual good understanding, there is little difficulty. Instinctive good impulses, tempered by polite custom, appear to regulate the subject pleasantly enough. But among the hundreds, classed sometimes as our friends and again as mere acquaintances, there is no small embarrassment. If I accept a favor pressed upon me from a mere fugitive acquaintance, it is very likely to be soon followed by an application for a pecuniary loan, never to be repaid ; or perhaps for the use of my supposed personal influence in some quarter where I would not exercise it, or to gain a purpose which I deem questionable in itself or unsuitable for me to advance, or where perhaps the applicant himself is undeserving of what he seeks to obtain.

It seems as if some unconscious dread of such a result were the prompting motive of many persons to reciprocate as soon as possible any favor bestowed. Doubtless too, it is a spectral suspicion of the prevalence of this kind of apprehension that makes a sensitive person feel so annoyed, and perhaps even insulted, upon finding a favor or token of pure esteem, admiration or incipient affection —as yet perhaps not thoroughly recognized—returned either in kind or too quickly.

The sensation experienced at such times is not unlike that felt upon having a proffered gift rejected, or, when unavoidably received, sent back to the giver. It comes upon one more like a rebuff than a cordial recognition of intended kindness or compliment. Sometimes, however, necessarily it is resorted to as a protection against intrusion. Perhaps, it may be said, these are not native traits of our common humanity ; but rather derivative ones. They have grown out of a complex, or, sometimes, too refined social condition. They are a species of defensive outworks occasionally necessary to ward off the approach of designing social impertinence.

THE SPECULATIVE PHILOSOPHER.

The actual working of the social relations of man with man must always continue to be a complex and embarrassing study. His general conduct, as a social being, is the resultant of such innumerable and diverse forces, latent as well as open, that the study of maxims, rules, and formulas alone, without practical experience—by dealing with generalities and omitting exceptions—tends, by false or imperfect ideas, to mislead the most sincere and earnest student or comprehensive thinker.

For discreet and effectual participation in the transactions of men (whether in social life, in business, or in public affairs), also for wisdom in forming opinions of human character or actions, nothing can compensate for the want of a practical personal acquaintance with human nature, as it is manifested by both individuals and communities, great or small, in their ordinary actual movements. It is often observed, that the merely speculative philosopher, or closet-thinker—like a poet or novelist of the library—falls into many practical errors, and often misses the mark aimed at. He errs in some of his profoundest studies and calculations, or shrewdest forecasts, from mere ignorance, or from mistaken notions of the common motives, impulses, and methods of action of men both in their daily pursuits and in their general affairs.

He is prone to regard man too much as a logical creature, who is quick to perceive his own real interest— remote as well as immediate. He fancies him to be swift to follow his convictions concerning what leads to his own advantage, when made obvious to his unobstructed vision, either by his own observation and reflection, or through being pointed out to him by another. Such a schoolman innocently assumes, like other idealistic dreamers, that every man, not under external restraint, is a free, mental as well as moral, agent. He perceives nothing, in man's will at least, to impede his voluntary choice of the obvious, readiest, and most effectual means available for him to accomplish the desirable end he has in view.

What a mistake ! Whosoever has observed and closely studied the nature and ways of his fellow-men, by long, actual intercourse with them, well knows that logic, like consistency, is to be computed among the weaker of the dynamics of common life. Many may be convinced, but few will become, or remain persuaded. Association, friendship, prejudice, passion, habit, indolence, accidental circumstances of trivial moment, present convenience or comfort, personal peculiarities—natural or acquired, physical, mental or moral—love of ease or pleasure, and a thousand other factitious obstacles, as everybody knows, will often stand in the way of reasonable action. Like the hungry cat, that craved the fish but dreaded the water, a man will also sometimes almost starve in the midst of abundance for mere want of decision to choose, or courage to change, his course, or for lack of strength or will to thwart present convenience, by following either his mental or moral convictions concerning what is clearly best and most desirable for him to do or to avoid.

Whoever, therefore, would guide individual or social conduct, or control either public opinion or common thought, in civil or social affairs, must begin by expecting but little consistency or logical coherence in men's doings under any circumstances. He must make always a liberal allowance for inexplicable deflections from the straight line, that reason may indicate to a rational man to be the direct road to his true and permanent interest, or that even conscience shall tell him it is his duty to pursue.

ADVICE.

Advice, although good, concerning our personal conduct, when opposed to our inclination, is not unlike a nauseous curative drug offered to a sick man. It is proverbially easier to give than to take—however greatly it may be needed. The chief obstacle, however, in the way of

sound advice being well received, is generally a simple incapacity to take it. Unsought advice is commonly repelled
as impertinent. It is regarded as too cheap for utility.
It is presumed to have cost the donor nothing, and to be
the mere flippancy of a meddler. Even judicious advice
—especially from a superior—by its tone of authority,
sometimes, seems like an unwelcome command. At the
best it inclines to arouse irritation, as if it impaired our
liberty of conduct. It seems to put us, as it were, under
some kind of obligation to follow it, or at least to appear
to do so, despite our indifference or disapproval.

Likewise, when a man seeks counsel of another, unless
he have in his mind, in his temper, or in his culture, the
conditions necessary to enable him to comprehend, appreciate, and assimilate good advice, it will be a pearl
thrown away, when given to him. It is therefore often a
misfortune, rather than a fault, with many, that timely
words of wisdom so commonly pass unheeded.

A person suffering such a disability is not unlike a patient,
under medical treatment, whose constitutional *stamina* are
too feeble to bear the application of the remedies proper
to expel, or suppress, the cause of his diseased condition. In such cases, some preliminary palliative may be
necessary, until mere rest from irritability or exhaustion
shall have restored the body to such a degree of strength
that medicine can aid nature, without too great disturbance of unbalanced or enfeebled functions. But above
all, the prosperity of advice is generally dependent upon
a thorough assurance that disinterested good-will, and
honest intention, prompt one's adviser.

A few simple rules might make advice more palatable,

and less ineffectual. First the adviser should be well assured he is free from all unavowed personal motive of selfish interest, or even inclination, and that he sincerely wishes well to the person he would counsel. Besides, he ought to learn specifically all the important facts of the case in hand, from the real party interested, with their special bearings—viewed from that person's individual stand-point. Next he should weigh all such facts and views, fairly, with due care and forecast, from his own point-of-view. Then he should compare the two sets of views, if they differ, as well as ponder all their resulting considerations, as best he may. Finally he should strive to put himself, as it were, in the very shoes of the one seeking his counsel, and to offer then, sympathetically, only his best judgment. When thus sugar-coated, quite a bitter pill may be swallowed, by one needing it—with but little resistance and sometimes with real benefit, if not gratitude.

Social Isolation.

Philosophers smile contemptuously at the fondness of people for a crowd, and for their slavish reciprocal dependence upon each other to amuse and entertain them, as well as to guide them in their thoughts, opinions, or actions. Yet the basis of this tendency is in the love of our fellow-men ; and is the corner-stone of the human side of Christianity. Being founded in simple and honest human nature, it works harmoniously with other like tendencies toward an equilibrium in self-conduct and self-estimate, according to the measure of the strength of each individual.

Isolation, by self-concentration and the exclusion of a relative, or even intrinsic, view of the rights and deserts of others, necessarily begets in us self-conceit, exaggeration of the merits of our own selves or belongings, and a consequent, if not additional, underestimate of the value of other people.

Association and familiar intercourse with our fellow-men, on the contrary, induce toleration of, and liberality toward, the opinions, manners, conduct, and characters of others. We afford them a chance to give their own version of the matters within their special cognizance, or peculiarly affecting themselves. In this manner we become able to hear with their ears, to see with their eyes, what concerns them, and to sympathize practically with their special emotions. By such means too, we can better contemplate them and their surroundings in their true character and relation toward each other, giving each credit for what is his due—instead of blindly or superciliously condemning them for folly, or wrong-doing, without charity, or even a hearing. We can thus, also, far more readily, regulate our views of our own relative position toward them, than if we had stood apart—

> in a shroud
> Of thoughts which were not their thoughts.

Nevertheless, we cannot get always, easily, ourselves into a true relative position in such matters, merely by force of nature or by the chance of common circumstances. Some men are born with an overbearing instinct for solitude, and some, by the evolution of unusual circumstances, come in middle life to find themselves standing

9

alone, although naturally social, and loving their kind. It becomes every one then, closely to study either his own nature or his peculiar individual history, or both, in this regard, and—if he would keep mind and heart sound and savory—to beware of drifting away from the tonic influence that comes from heartily mixing with mankind in general. At least as a matter of moral regimen in his self-treatment, one inclined to solitariness should cultivate and strive to keep up a lively interest in all human affairs ; modestly following the sympathetic suggestion of old Terence :—*Homo sum*, etc.

MENTAL BALANCE.

Generally speaking, one may reckon safely the degree of his health of body or mind, according to his ability to see or feel the common, every-day things around him in their true and just relative proportions. When, therefore—through honest introspection—he shall find himself inclined unduly either to exaggerate or belittle any ordinary present matter or passing event, or such as is usually coming, he may count that circumstance as evidence of a loss of at least somewhat of his mental equilibrium. The lying scale gives false weight. Indeed, this suggestion indicates to the close observer a common practical, and not unfair, test of the condition of the mental sanity possessed by most persons we chance to meet in ordinary social intercourse.

Even in the best ordered lives there will sometimes come strange moments, of short or long duration—a sort of collapse of hope or zest for anything in life—when men will pause and say to themselves, with something of the querulousness of despondency—*cui bono?* What advantage is there in anything? This may happen even without apparent cause. But when a great man suddenly drops dead in the midst of active and noble usefulness to his race, when a grand purpose is frustrated by some trivial accident, or when, by some unexpected event, the result of years of patient, painful labor is swept away, amazement seems, for the time, to paralyze hope and almost to unsettle the serenest judgment. It leaves only a stolid indifference in place of the natural spring and joyousness of healthy life.

As respects the mental dissatisfaction—sometimes approaching despair—that so often overwhelms the youthful aspirant for learning, power, fame, or the intelligent good-will of mankind, little need be said. This is merely a symptom that Nature is working out in him a theory of intellectual expansion, and may perhaps be likened to what are called the " growing pains " of a young body.

Failure too will embitter, sometimes, the soul of the envious or vain, so as to unhinge reason. There is no sharper or more unscrupulous tooth than the malice of the unsuccessful. When failure is not only conscious but deserved and frankly self-confessed, it may become more amiable. But then, perhaps, the prospect of oblivion will be its only coveted respite from inward regret, and the mortification arising from outward neglect.

LANGUAGE.

The words we use betray involuntarily the temper of the mind at the time we employ them. The calm, clear, honest mind finds nouns and verbs most useful in expressing its ideas. It philosophically and dispassionately lays open to the common eye all it would unfold. It is in no hurry to accomplish its end, and approaches its climax by a gradual movement. When, however, passion or excitement (especially with superficial knowledge and partial views) prevails—as they are prone to do when the subject is too big or unfamiliar for the mind that strives to hold or express it—it is observed often, the speaker inclines to adjectives, descriptive participles, and mere expletives, accompanied by emphasis, exaggeration, or hyperbole. These are the natural outcome of a super-heated mental condition ; and almost inevitably obscure the more valuable distinctive particulars of the subject in hand.

The cold, impartial, reasoning talker prefers simplicity of statement. Trusting to the merit of his thought, he is liable to be even careless of the dress it wears, except so far as to make it explicit and presentable. He desires neither to attract, or distract, attention by the mere external garb of his ideas. The passionate writer, on the contrary—especially if invention lag—hunts throughout his vocabulary for extravagant terms, and for pictorial or inflammatory words. His imagination is fired, he inflames his reader, his effects are vivid and intense. Yet, except on occasions of vital moment, as when life or fortune is at stake, they are transitory. They leave but little residuum worth preserving in the memory, besides, perhaps, a merely overwrought beauty of diction.

When a theme is worn hopelessly threadbare, this extravagance of ornament may be sometimes a merit—if something must be said. But when a fact or thought is fresh, worth telling, and deserving of preservation as an addition to, or as a comparison with, our stock of valuables, the simpler and plainer the language used, the better for the prosperity of the idea.

By some unconscious process, when such a thing is done by a strong hand, the severity of style becomes a lucid channel, in which the idea floats so naturally, the hearer, almost unconsciously, is taken captive at once. As Webster superbly says :—" The costly ornaments and studied contrivances of speech shock and disgust men, when their own lives, and the fate of their wives, their children, and their country hang on the decision of the hour. Then words have lost their power, rhetoric is vain, and all elaborate oratory contemptible."

BORES.

To a busy man in a large city, during business hours, the importance of economizing time can hardly be over-estimated. Every minute wasted by himself, or taken idly from him by another, costs him at least some extra exertion ; but more often actual loss of opportunity, or fatal delay, in vital affairs. His most exasperating foeman is an idle man, who visits him at his place of business in the crowded part of the day, and thus thoughtlessly robs him of his most precious and very limited possession.

In social intercourse inopportunity may be as distressing as petty iteration is tiresome. The enemy may come in the shape of a city-man-of-leisure, who will sit an hour and talk of pictures, books, travel or amusements, not seeing that every word he utters is a torment to his victim, and that the idea uppermost in the mind of his listener is how to find some pretext for forcibly expelling the intruder. Mayhap the visitor is some chance acquaintance one has met very sociably during their recent summer vacation, and who is now passing leisurely through the town, but stopping for a little chat over past enjoyments. Or, perchance, it is some favorite relative from the country, who makes an annual trip to the metropolis and has left all care and concern about his own affairs, with all notion of the value of time, behind him. The antagonistic moods, in which they now meet, sometimes put them at such reciprocal disadvantage that they seldom afterwards can endure complacently the sight of each other.' Amiability and congeniality sink rapidly to the freezing-point. Only some extraordinary event in after-days can restore the lost warmth. A tacit misunderstanding thus begotten may disrupt forever the harmony of all their sympathies.

In some form this is a very old notion. Yet in our day—when limited hours of work, distance between home and shop, and the rapidity or multiplicity of complications in business or practical duties, have so greatly increased the strain thus put upon the attention of both commercial and scholarly men—what was once a delightful interlude, or, at most, merely a petty annoyance, has become a real affliction. Not unfrequently it exposes the thoughtless cause of it to the severe secret animadversion of even a most patient or charitably disposed sufferer.

FASTIDIOUSNESS.

Fastidiousness may not be a vice or a misfortune, but certainly it is an impediment to some persons. Perhaps, however, it is not always an unmixed evil ; nor, in some communities, a source of serious vexation. Among our people, however, it is commonly reckoned a superfluous embarrassment, and a source of real annoyance. It tends to destroy equability, and the possibility of repose, by putting and keeping one constantly in a frame of mind that is expecting too much. With all present drawbacks to the hope of a condition of ideal perfection in any of our surroundings—public or private, social or individual, common or peculiar—it demands the charity of a wide toleration to discover even general laws working smoothly, where so many things in our daily lives are apparently at cross purposes.

Fastidiousness is not a native American trait, nor has it yet become an acclimated one. Whatsoever we may seem to have of it has been transplanted immethodically from an older civilization into ours. Perhaps it has come to some few individuals among us by a mysterious law of heredity, from the refined nature of some ancestor, near or remote, who has lived in a society where social per-fectibility, and a realization of the visions of ideality, were far more approximately possible than with us. For it lies deeper than method or manner. It has its root in the genius and conscience of the individual.

For at least a century to come, and perhaps longer, we must be content to take our lot, social and political, in the rough. Everything of a public or private nature, and almost everything that touches us merely as individuals, is now in a transitional state. Repose, without apathy, is almost unknown among us. Uneasiness is our normal condition. Quiet and stillness are classed among undesirable conditions, like sloth or death. Restlessness is deemed a virtue, and counted upon as an indication of moral or intellectual activity and ambition for excellence. The subsidence, and orderly settlement of the disturbing elements of social and political life, are delayed indefinitely, by their constantly changing, augmenting or diminishing in character, quality or number :—

> Double, double toil and trouble ;
> Fire, burn ; and cauldron bubble.

Success in Life.

What we call success in life—especially as respects wealth—is attained more often through narrowness of views and limited capacity, than by comprehensiveness of mind, liberality of opinion, or a large sympathy with human affairs. In common practical business the man of contracted range of vision, by his singleness of purpose with pertinacity of endeavor, will ordinarily accomplish what misses the grasp of his larger-minded neighbor. To the first it is easy to limit himself to attempting but few things—obvious, or at least practicable—and to doing only one thing at a time. Such a rule appears to be indispensible to personal success. With the man of larger mould, however, nothing short of necessity, or a self-dominating will, can confine his efforts to those few and narrow lines that thus surely lead on to individual fortune.

In youth the imperfection of vision, the limited experience and the very deficiencies of immaturity, added to the enthusiasm of our young blood, usually keep the eye of the mind riveted upon few objects of permanent desire. When the will is strong enough to conspire, such influences push us on to achieve our undertakings. But when the zest of a fresh pursuit begins to wane ; when our minds, if liberal by nature, expand and grow with time and experience ; when our moral prospect broadens as we mount the hill of life ; when the darling projects of early days—by contrast and relationship—are shown to be but toys or baubles ; when the once few objects of life have multiplied to be many ; when we are able to compare ourselves and our aims, with our predecessors and the grand achievements of heroic men ; then, indeed, it demands all the strength of a disciplined nature—and even sometimes the sharp spur of necessity, backed by a determined will—to resist the temptation to scatter our forces, and, by wasting our energy upon a multitude of projects, to end in accomplishing none of them.

It was a wise old Greek myth that made Misfortune gleefully reply, to the question once put to her :— " Whither are you going ? "—" Ah ! I am about to visit the man of many trades ! "   •

CONFESSION OF IGNORANCE.

For some people it is very difficult, and seems almost impossible to say :—" I don't know." This painful effort, which it costs to confess ignorance—whether naturally so designed or not—often, however, acts as a wonderful stimulus to prick the ordinary mind to study and acquire knowledge of matters that commonly interest mankind. It is not so much that the large possession of general information exalts one above the common man, but rather that to know many things saves one from the humiliation of confessing ignorance of what it is presumed, by our companions, we ought to know.

Yet many are, both in mind and body, too fond of slothful ease and idle self-indulgence—too prone to listen to the lulling voice of that step-mother of ignorance, procrastination—to take the trouble to satisfy the natural desire of even a normal mind to know what is worth knowing, or what is commonly expected to be known in ordinary intercourse with the world. For such people it is far easier to say :—" I guess "—a proper expression, sometimes derisively miscalled American, meaning merely " I conjecture "—without any other basis than idle fancy for their vague supposition.

When a man is truly recognized as being well-informed upon many subjects, of course he may safely be so frank as to avow his ignorance of some. But if one knows little or nothing of a topic that happens to be under social discussion, he will not unfrequently furnish you with a supposition to explain the most embarrassing phenomenon. Indeed, with this kind of character, when thoroughly unscientific and undisciplined, his conjecture is usually quite out of proportion, even to his opportunity of acquiring real knowledge. As in other human affairs, however, it is far better, even for one's social credit, as our primers teach us, to be honest and confess ignorance of what we do not know. Looking also merely from the lowest point of view—if we have no better motive—a sense of shame may thenceforth at least drive us to giving a little more time and labor to wiping away the clouded surface of our neglected minds—thus saving ourselves from future mortification under like circumstances.

A RULING PASSION.

Aside from the insurmountable circumstances that control our lives—or "the divinity that shapes our ends" —more men are led through life by an inclination and passion of some sort, than are self-moved by their mere will or intellect, in the accomplishment of character. The latter faculties are, for the most part, exercised by ordinary men merely as the means of attaining some temporary possession or some ephemeral heart's desire, rather than to achieve such permanent good as their sober judgment approves. Only a few lofty souls are guided by pure reason alone in the whole conduct of their lives. Such sublime men, although too frequently mal-treated by their contemporaries, are likely, however, to leave their work—when allowed to be done according to their designs—ultimately to be appreciated by the race, and themselves sometimes to be classed as god-like.

They form strong attachments among the pure and the just, and exalt friendship to something almost divine. Profoundly does Hamlet say to his friend Horatio :—

> Give me that man
> That is not passion's slave, and I will wear him
> In my heart's core, ay, in my heart of heart,
> As I do thee.

But even among higher natures, generally speaking, love of power leads the most strong, love of fame the more sympathetic—the noble lovers of their race—love of wealth the ordinary. Meanwhile love of pleasure—sometimes innocent, sometimes debasing—dominates the character of a great many who possess ample abilities to achieve either power, fame, or wealth, but who prefer what they regard as philosophic ease, or what may in fact be enervating luxury, or even degrading vice. Early inclination also—natural or artificial—when long fostered, has very much to do in determining the choice of paths in life by some men. But on the whole, and in the long run—although often unknown to us until too late to change—some ruling passion or inclination of mind or heart (despite the tyranny of circumstances) either elects or materially shapes our chief purposes, and our persistent ways of life.

Dread of Censure.

Our most amiable traits are constantly liable to betray us into error. Love of the good opinion of our neighbors is accounted one of the most precious elements of human nature. Yet, so fickle and ill-grounded is popular applause, that they who strive merely to win, are almost sure to deserve to lose it, by sacrificing, or at least maiming, their own natural sense of good or evil in the struggle. The endeavor to avoid blame would seem to be a motive so lovable that it must always secure admiration. Nevertheless it is usually regarded as the companion of weakness, if not of sheer pusillanimity ; likely often to mislead the over-anxious into the very slough of unpopularity he wishes especially to eschew.

No man of practical talent or positive character, who

is (as such generally must be) a man of industry and action—and one necessarily taking sides upon all questions of immature or growing opinion concerning the current matters of his time—can escape a frequent exposure to ridicule or even reproach. Such are the human weapons naturally used in the battle of life, both by those who have no better implements of warfare, as well as by those who know how much the notice and sympathy of numbers may be provoked by the employment of these stimulants to attention. With many, the yielding to this dread of reproach or ridicule is often an easy method of reconciling themselves to their indulgence of a selfish indolence, when put under the prickings of the spur of duty. By this cowardly means too, some can soothe even their excited vanity or longing, jealousy or envy, when unprofitably stirred by seeing another do what they perhaps could not do or dare not attempt. Their love of ease persuades them to omit the effort. By such inaction, they hope to escape at least the mortification of derision or obloquy. They accept a negative compensation of inglorious peace for the loss, real or imaginary, of the spoils of war.

SELF-KNOWLEDGE.

Besides what we may gain by inner self-study, truly to know either ourselves or others, we must change our point of view—as it were, getting outside of ourselves and making our observations externally. Only when we thus honestly compare ourselves with others, do we approach a correct self-estimate. The stand-point of self commonly blinds us when judging ourselves, as well as bewilders us when we judge others,

The sum and effect of the study of many others give us a better ideal standard of measurement, by which to test either our own short-comings, or to guage the degree of any special merit we ourselves possess. We may too well know our own peculiar weaknesses or deficiencies, but we seldom properly can measure our own strength or capacity, except by some comparison based upon observation and close study of the doings of other men, in their actual work—or perhaps even by collaboration with them.

This spice of knowledge of comparative human nature cannot be acquired by any mere reading concerning the lives and deeds of other men. Books alone will not suffice. They furnish outlines, but the vivifying motive, and the details of the picture, are generally somehow wanting. Only a small residuum of the real workings of any life, however open and public, goes into a book. In the case of most men, what is known to the world in general, of even their vital movements, is like a mere point of candle-light in a dark mine. Generally, practical life (involving daily intercourse among men) with its novel suggestions and endless comparisons, is a much higher school for real self-knowledge, than even the closest lonely self-contemplation.

SUPERIORITY.

There appear to be, at the least, three conspicuously separate, open roads for a man to pursue who wishes to excel the common mass of his race. One class of men will strive to accomplish great ends merely in order to win the applause or favorable opinion of his fellow-creatures. Another order finds its greatest gratification in excelling, chiefly because its members are thereby put in the possession of coveted power, or afforded the pleasure of exercising it, over other men. Still another class may be said in large measure to love excellence in itself, for its own sake, and in order to be happy—through an imperiality of their nature—by pursuing and achieving superiority, either as a matter of course, or from a dominating sense of duty to their fellow-men, regardless even of recognition of their greatness or of what a prating world may say of them.

Each of these three great divisions of men appears to be moved, in greater or less degree, by a common or like impulse. Yet while this grandest class of characters may grow where sheer egotism is absent—despite the most untoward circumstances,—the others are usually nourished by some form of selfishness ; either by the expectation of a gratification of their vanity, or by zeal for applause, or by some of the lower intellectual motives. These, it is suspected, compose the more numerous body of famous men. The other class is more rare, yet it has furnished nearly all of the great surviving lights, in the pathway of invention, discovery, science, learning, knowledge, wisdom, and human advancement, across the track of past centuries.

INCONSISTENCY.

Apart from that order of men, like Emerson, whose intellect is always undergoing a process of germination, and is fecund in fresh growths from infancy until long past middle age—men whose increasing intelligence, with a more commanding point of view, renders a change of opinion a necessary ingredient of mental honesty—there is a much humbler part of mankind with many of whom apparent inconsistency is unavoidable. This variableness arises, not so much from any want of fairness as from downright frankness. Instead of being an indication of insincerity on their part, it is rather a manifestation of the superficialness of their mental or moral nature, and the weather-vane-like fickleness of their instant attitude and outlook.

With some men, expression of opinion as well as mode of conduct are almost wholly dependent upon the particular mood of temper or frame of mind—however temporary or fugitive—in which they happen to be when called upon to speak or act. Both their reason and understanding—if the intellect of such persons be susceptible of such a division—are governed by their general temperament or disposition, except when that force is thrown out of gear by some momentary passion or inclination. What appears to them at one time prudent and proper, at another—with no material change of person or circumstances—seems rash and unsuitable.

Yet are they, on each occasion, quite honest and sincere. They are variable in their opinions by a law of their nature without suspecting it. The very axis of all their revolutions of thought and conduct is itself naturally shifty and inconstant. A friend suggests that this class of persons are, however, usually at least consistent in refusing to look at a matter from any point of view except what may be, for the time being, their own. If this be

true it is doubtless something of a virtue, because unreasoning obstinacy is the chief main-stay of weak minds.

CUSTOMARY RELIGION.

Many men among us appear to treat most of their religious observances as they do their ordinary clothing.
They seem to put on religion as a habit, and wear it as a
matter of course, without question or consideration.
They care to see only that it shall not look singular,
although, perhaps, it may sometimes shine with some new-
ness of lustre, a little more than usual on a holy-day.

Here, they naturally wear the apparel customary to
civilization. Had such men been bred among barbarians
they would have been easily pagans. They would have
worn also garments made from the skins of beasts ; perhaps little more than a girdle—possibly only a scrap of
Fuegian fur—or whatever might chance to be the custom
of their country. So had they been brought up in other
civilized society they might well have been Buddhists,
Mohammedans—or perhaps even Mormons. Indeed they
would have accepted readily the dogmas and complied
with the tenets of such so-called prevailing religion. They
would have conformed to its rites and ceremonies—with
the like complacency and with as little question, solicitude
or anxiety—as they now do to Christianity.

By an easy habit of mind they instinctively relegate all responsibility in such matters to the care and management of a
priesthood, or its representative or equivalent—whatsoever
shape it may happen to wear—and turn their whole attention to the practical affairs of this life. Indeed they seem

10

to think that, were it otherwise, this world might stop moving onward, and simply go to pieces, for want of unremitting attention to their sublunary affairs.

SNOBBERY.

The poorest, and least profitable investment a man can make, in his personal scheme of social conduct, is the sacrifice of anything good in himself to snobbery. There is no trick, in the game of daily life, for which one lays down so much and takes up so little as the round of the tuft-hunter. The entire fabric of his fortune is based upon a delusion, involving an underestimate of himself, and an exaggerated, if not wholly mistaken, valuation of the importance and the good will of others toward him. Snobbishness is the Pharisaism of manners. It is a social false pretence that usually makes a man or woman the dupe of his or her own servile hypocrisy.

It is fostered, if not born, of the self-deceptive notion, that one may gain favor, innocently, of a real or supposed superior by voluntary humiliation. In truth it begets little beside contempt, where it expects good will, if not favor. It makes one a pack-horse to carry the burdens of an imperious master, without any substantial reward of provender. The priests of Baal who minister at the altar where such votive sacrifices are offered, live by the altar. They devour the offerings, while secretly sneering, or at best smiling with pity, at the abasement and genuflexions of the voluntary victims of a paltry cheat. A single spark of manly independence would consume the whole gossamer contrivance and dispel the illusion.

Popular Delusion.

It is a mortifying affliction for a sensitive man to be obliged to dwell in a community where some common delusion concerning vital matters—such as touch life and death, morals and law—prevails, but in which he cannot honestly participate. You may be compelled to appear either a hypocrite or an enigma—or else possibly a pariah —to the moral sense of many of your neighbors or associates, and perhaps even of your friends. For, ultimately, your skepticism or disbelief will be found out—however well-guarded and unobtrusive your incredulity may be— and your reputation for integrity, perhaps for common honesty, will suffer, if it be not wholly undermined and destroyed.

Nothing short of the grave is so relentless as blind and undemonstrable moral or religious conviction. More especially is this true, where such conviction does not rest at all upon facts, evidence, or reason, but draws its entire aliment from family tradition, early training, childish association, personal assumption, or external popular opinion. To doubt the thoroughness or rationality of such conviction is to insult its possessor. To invite an argument, or to offer a reason, against such conviction, is very likely to expose one's self to ridicule or obloquy, if not to ostracism, persecution, or social contempt.

Insanity.

Why do insane people so commonly rush to self-destruction ? By what juggle of morbid imagination is life led to take away life ? Is it nature's shortest cut to relief from insupportable agony? Does it require unclouded reason to preserve that calm equanimity without which life may lose its charm, and the natural love of life lapse from being merely :—

weary, stale, flat and unprofitable,

until it becomes a condition of unbearable torment? Or is desire for suicide the natural tendency of life, whenever the understanding, for any cause, fails to exert itself toward self-preservation?

Is it not rather because the absence of reason in a man (or its logical or illogical working from false premises or assumptions) throws the machinery of life out of gear? Something seems to put him out of all sound and true relations with common things and with his fellow-men, so that his strange isolation becomes morally intolerable. Possibly, it is nature's merciless method of discarding what has became hopelessly useless in the economy of the social world. A too brutal suggestion! At least, however, it is better to think of, as a theory, than the sneer of the pessimist, who finds in this human enigma a case where extremes meet—because both reason and unreason alike point to the worthlessness of life.

PROCRASTINATION.

Procrastination, though a privilege of old age, is a vice in the young and a crime in a man who is in the full maturity of his powers. The wilful procrastinator is, however, subject to a constant intermittent fever of remorse. His special sin is ever and anon arising, like a spectre,

before his mind, to reproach him for neglect of lost opportunity. Relief comes to him only from his continually
recurring promises of reform. He bristles with good
resolutions, perennial but ephemeral. Always he is going
to begin soon. This covenant with himself becomes a
real, nay, the chief source of consolation to him for his
neglect. He never performs the compact, yet he fancies
he intends to do so, at some time. The elation of spirits,
caused by his worthy resolve, operates either as a counter-
irritant, or a sedative. It allays his compunctious self-
reproach for laziness, vacillation, and consequently
growing infirmity of will, so long as he remains under the
temporary spell and soothing influence of his brittle promise of doing better in future. The exhilaration subsides,
memory stumbles, and delay rules. Then another spasm
of regret brings on an access of hurry, which, as everybody knows, is the twin brother of procrastination, and
its rival in making mental disturbance and bad work.

SOCIAL TEMPER.

It happens, not unfrequently, that men of eminence—
especially in a professional career—who have been ascet-
ics, solitary and perhaps habitually morose, all their lives,
as they approach old age, become social, genial, and
generally companionable. It appears as if, in the prime
of life, they had found enough of social fellowship in their
ambitions and business affairs ; or in their real conflicts
or co-operations with men—or in work, studies, ideas, or
abstractions—and had disdained to waste their precious
hours in petty social distractions.

However, as time has loosened their grip upon the means of achieving the great ends of life first set before themselves, they seem to soften towards humanity in particular. As their hearts now begin to lean again toward childhood, they can find something lovable in concrete human nature, and can pick up a few grains of real happiness, in mere friendly, or even cordial, association with other men. Especially do such men incline to cordiality with their juniors, whom they have, through life, been accustomed to reckon greatly their inferiors in intellectual stature or accomplishments, and to snub, or ignore except as mere counters in the game of life.

SELF-ESTIMATION.

While it may be better in most cases that our self-estimate should be accurate and just, if possible, yet in guiding our conduct it is safer sometimes to pitch our moral self-valuation a little above, as it is wiser to drop our mental self-esteem a little below even what appears correct to our own eyes. Perhaps we ought to allow, as it were, somewhat for a refraction of intellectual light in the latter case, and as much for a sort of attraction of gravitation in the former. An over-estimate of our moral worth—consistently maintained, without priggish self-conceit—will not unfrequently make up for something of its deficiency in fact, by first assuming, as is said, a virtue not originally possessed. In this respect the character, with due humility, may grow sometimes up to the high ideal, which, in self-flattery, we have claimed to be the real bloom of its native quality. A lofty sense of intrinsic

personal merit may—if rigidly restrained from ostentation—thus become a fructifying element of better things
to come. So much wiser is it, as the preacher tells us, to
look up and not down, in the practical conduct of life,
and to endeavor to acquire, by habit, whatever elements
of nobleness may be lacking in our native composition.

MENTAL INDOLENCE.

Mental indolence in men is merely a bad habit arising
from injudicious self-indulgence. Yet it is often comparative merely, and dependent upon degrees of natural
nimbleness of intellect—upon the amount of fertility,
quickness, and versatility of mind each one possesses.
What is, in fact, inexcusable sloth in one man, may be
real activity in another. There are many men whose
minds are eager, rapacious, and, as it were, omnivorous.
There are others, with like inducements, who are sluggish,
receptive of but few ideas at a time, and who must hold
these a long time under observation in order fully to possess them. Some men will analyze a thought, adjust it to
their own preconceptions, deduce another from it, and
perhaps even formulate a third arising out of this process
of assimilation, while other men are simply deliberating
whether it be worth while to give common hospitality to
the idea first suggested.

RETALIATION.

For some natures it is easier to return good for evil,
than merely to check a feeling of resentment, and preserve equanimity. The latter method of meeting aggressive

wilful injury is simple rectitude. It is based on self-respect or pride of character, implies subjection of passion or temper, and is largely intellectual. The former may find support in gratification of the feeling that such conduct pours coals of fire on the head of the offender. It surely is a mode of gratifying the feeling of resentment ; and is not unfrequently a mark rather of temper than of charity or love. Indeed, it is sometimes a cunning mode of sting-ing an enemy by disguised retaliation for suffered wrong.

TOLERATION.

Toleration, or liberality of sentiment toward a depar-ture from strictness of moral rectitude, or toward an unsound opinion, may be a virtue or a vice, accordingly as our judgment proceeds from a high or low standard of morality or intelligence in ourselves. If a bad man be tolerant towards a wrong-doer, possibly he is seeking merely to justify himself. But if a good man be chari-table toward evil, or those who are responsible for its mischief, such toleration or liberality will usually spring out of the kindness of his heart or the breadth of his understanding, or perhaps from both.

GIVING OFFENCE.

Beware of badinage or equivocal pleasantries with stupid people. There are men to whom it is dangerous to give offence—however trivial—even accidentally. Their penetration into the character and motives of others is so dull, they must be treated as we treat dumb animals, whose invincible dislike we often incur without knowing it—with no power of reconciliation. To apologize to them for levity is full of difficulty and embarrassment. To explain to them our innocent drollery or inadvertence, or misdirected good will, is impossible.

RESPECT OF MANKIND.

Sympathy and kindness easily beget friendship among congenial people. Even love may be inspired generally by coaxing and gentle assiduity. But, as a rule, respect from the mass of mankind—I say nothing of esteem— must be compelled. Power and energy of will, whether openly exercised or tacitly recognized, always command respect. Perhaps, because an element of fear is also in-volved.

MENTAL VARIETY.

Some striking characteristic trait predominates over all others in almost every one. It is plainly visible in very early youth. So far from its being true—as once was a favorite theory—that all men are naturally alike, it is a common experience to find (even in the same family, where all are subject to substantially an identical environ-ment) an idler, a dreamer, a poet, a philosopher, a mechanic, a thinker, and a lover-of-action purely—or one who is content with nothing but wild adventure.

PASSING EVENTS.

The signal events of our lives often affect us more deeply afterwards, than while they are occurring. Sometimes the suddenness of the shock seems to stun us and benumb our faculties. At other times the mind feels itself incapable of grasping what has recently happened, or of comprehending it with its most important bearings. Long afterwards—when our mental and moral equilibrium is restored—we know it better.

Troubles of the Brain.

Work and love are two panaceas for mental suffering, that have saved more lives from shipwreck than any other alleviations. The first belongs properly to man, and the other to woman ; but they are often interchanged. Perhaps this is because in some men the womanly nature, and in some women the manly nature, is originally the stronger or comes to predominate, by habit.

Self-Control.

Self-restraint is the first law, or lesson, of civilization. It should be taught to the infant in the cradle, and practised even on the death-bed. Men, women, and children are fitted for personal association together, only in proportion as they are proficient in their submissiveness in this social obligation. This proposition is just as true as its correlative, that self-defence is the first law of nature. We must each reconcile them as we can.

Opinions.

Men and women have mere understanding, much alike. Man has judgment, while woman has tact and intuition,

Man thinks, woman ruminates ; man reasons, woman guesses ; man deduces, woman divines.

COURAGE.

There is a courage of passion—like that of animals at bay when their life is assailed. But there is a higher intellectual courage of the will and reason that stands up for right—personal or general—at all times when a champion is needed.

EVERY-DAY TALK.

The plain highway of talk.
Merchant of Venice.

TRUTH.

AT this period of the world a full-grown man's intellectual and moral development—in respect to his just relation to the past, present or future, and as to what pithily might be called the conduct of his soul, involving not merely his understanding but also all his mental and moral faculties as well as his spiritual nature—lies not so much in learning merely what others know, as it does in unlearning what he has been mistaught involuntarily—or in stripping off and discarding what might be said to be the traditionary husks of his environment. Until he is able to discover how much of the body of laws and customs, civil and social, prevailing among the members of the society in which he lives, is local and temporary—or purely artificial and arbitrary, or rooted in mere superstition, or drawn from mistaken analogies, or grown up out of ignorance, groundless assumption, and baseless imagining—he cannot be free to choose between the true and the false, or to act independently and according to nature and right reason,

For many men, even when bold and strong, it is the
work of a life-time to emancipate themselves from the
shackles of erroneous patrimonial ideas. Few ever actually
attain the full enjoyment of real freedom of soul in a
broad and comprehensive way. Those who believe they
do so are compelled sometimes to hide from the world's
too close scrutiny the liberty of opinion they secretly
enjoy—lest they call upon their heads a fate not unlike
that of the historic martyrs to this right of private
judgment. The vast majority of mankind, knowing
nothing better, die slaves to prejudice, or common
opinion, and are buried in the manacles in which they
were born.

In moments of depression, or partial mental obscuration,
men have been led sometimes almost to doubt whether
the unflinching, unlimited, indiscriminate, reckless pursuit
of what we call "truth" be really an unmixed good.
How small a portion of the human family are fitted by
cultivation, training and occupation, or even moral elevation, to receive or to be trusted freely with it in its nakedness ! Presented, as it usually is, in a fragmentary condition, it often rudely discrowns the regency of some strong
predilection or illusion, some favorite habit, some petted
and indulged personal peculiarity, some loved association,
or, what is often more powerful, some controlling passion
or interest. Error, despite its hideous mien, when it has
become endeared to us by familiarity of association, has
also frequently a sort of well-known infatuating fascination, growing out of its very character for danger-breed-
ing and even its forbiddenness. Then, too, so far as the
immediate eye can see, the prevalence of what some of the

wisest believe to be "truth" necessarily involves serious mischief—or, at least, the destruction of a present tolerable condition of things, without offering us a better, or even a passably good substitute.

The only consolatory refuge in our dilemma lies in the assumption that truth is for all time ; that our present misfortune is to be reckoned as absolutely nothing in a contrast with the broad claims of countless future æons yet in store for the teeming human race ; that truth alone is imperishable ; and that all things in conflict with it must pass away—useful or tolerable in their day only as humble stepping-stones to firmer ground and higher things. This, however, is a hard doctrine to teach contemporary mankind, nearly all of whom live only for themselves and the things of their day—not caring to sacrifice their interests or even their pleasures for the sake of an unborn race, that shall spring out of an incalculable future.

And indeed it does seem sometimes to many as if—when the alleged discovery of some moral truth threatens to take away the established safeguards or amenities of this life—it might be time to stop and wait for the race to grow up to the already proffered new ideas, before more of the like nature shall be evolved. Should such a state of social chaos supervene, it may cost too much blood and treasure to reconstruct a systematic happy social life again.

The bold adventures of our day into the void of agnosticism, or into the obscure sea of natural religion with its fathomless psychology, or into the civil chaos of socialism, suggest these dangers ahead. But they will not be heeded.

The pursuit after truth—once hedged and made dangerous by kings and popes with their convenient dungeons, tortures, and assassinations—now goes comparatively unchallenged in many communities either by superstition or force, or legal or social proscription. Hence its discoverers, real or pretended, travail and wander widely, often seeming, however, to cry out " Lo here ! " and " Lo there ! " when the new-found city of delight is only a mirage. But time, we may be assured, will cure all this—however much it may destroy, in its path, of our possessions as well as of ourselves.

Every age of the world has, in some degree, its own peculiar idea of what is the reality of things in this life ; what are appearances only ; what is the significance of life and of ourselves, as well as of our relations to each other, and to those who have gone before and those who shall follow ;—why we were born, live, err, struggle, enjoy, suffer, hope or despair, and die. Yet each age, if times past may be separated into definite periods, differs in vital substance from its predecessor—largely rejecting as folly, what once popularly had prevailed, meanwhile passing for both truth and wisdom.

Few men too are so entirely steadfast—amid all the fluctuations of opinion that history or even the apparent demonstrations of the present day exhibit—as to have no misgivings whatever. They are liable to be troubled sometimes with doubt lest, while struggling to emancipate mankind from error, they shall be themselves, in turn, after all, the unwary victims of some moral delusion. Much as it has been the fashion, among our pulpit-teachers, to deride that significant expression, it was doubtless the echo of some wild and hopeless cry—forever before and since reverberating in the desolate chambers of many a human heart—when that obstinate Roman vice-governor asked:— "What is truth?" It consoles us very little to be told that, some millions of years hence, the human race may grow to such a moral stature as to be able to know and to comprehend it. Like the dying statesman we "want the fact—the fact"; and we want it now.

Queries About Beauty.

Beauty is truth, truth beauty.

Keats.

Since the earliest recognition of æsthetic philosophy, human ingenuity has been agog to tell us what is the essence of the beautiful. Grossly speaking we appear to grasp the beautiful, as a property of matter, by only two of our senses. But Taste puts in a claim as a faculty for perceiving a world of beauty beyond the explorations of eye or ear. What then is such beauty? Lord Jeffrey in his famous essay gives us what he calls " rather explanations of the word than definitions of the thing it signifies," by saying it is that "property in objects by which they are recommended to the power or faculty of taste— the reverse of ugliness—the primary or more general objects of admiration." He then takes more than twenty quarto pages of fine print to prove that he does not mean anything by what he has said—but that beauty is entirely dependent upon association. If this indeed were all, and beauty dwelt only in "objects," we might well trust the eye and ear—aided perhaps by memory—to comprehend the whole of it.

But few are willing to believe the domain of the beautiful is limited by form, color, and sound, without reference to imagination and judgment. For what, then, should we call the ideas in poetry and art that appeal to our intangible sense of the beautiful, and thrill, warm, soothe, elevate, or, in any manner, stir the passions?* Does beauty exist in the soul? Has the mind two or more senses—like those of the body—that perceive ideals of beauty, as the eye and ear perceive objects? If mind be simply an attribute of an animal body, have dumb animals a faculty of taste to some degree? Even a well-bred horse will sometime seem to enjoy the prospect of a beautiful landscape. But if mind be more than a peculiar property of some combination of living matter, if imagination be in some sense an independent power, then what such faculties alone perceive as truly may be said to exist, as the objects which we know and realize only through our physical organs.

Yet, after all, what is beauty? Is it a thing or is it an illusion—a personal impression not reducible to any infallible standard? Is it simply a product of associations, and therefore diverse as circumstances about which men cannot be expected to agree? Or is it something perfect in itself, but only for the most part imperfectly perceived? Is not a colorless crystal sphere, when seen in a clear light, beautiful to every human eye? Are not some simple musical sounds so universally recognized as beautiful that even most dumb animals, really or feignedly, are touched and moved by them? Was there ever a human

11

being—not blind—who did not, at some time in his life, think a rainbow beautiful ?

Socrates is said to have argued, that beauty arises out of our sense of fitness and adaptation, and that it is impossible a thing beautiful for its color should also be beautiful for its sound. Yet there may be an affinity between sight and hearing unperceived by the ordinary exercise of our faculties. A friend once told me of his being waked from a dream of walking through a gallery of grand and exquisitely beautiful statuary, by the sounds of a fine serenade under his window. Leibnitz, we are informed, insisted that our appreciation of the beautiful arises out of a desire of the mind for perfection in everything it contemplates. An ingenious and learned contemporary fancies he has discovered that beauty is founded in morality ; and that nothing false or wrong in human life can be beautiful. Others seem to think none but the imaginative have any native notion of real beauty. As one puts it :—" The white light of truth, in traversing the many-sided transparent soul of the poet, is refracted into iris-hued poetry." For what is the essence of poetry beyond verbal expression in suggestion of the beautiful? Let us digress to answer briefly.

Of course the basis of poetry—as of all pure literature —is thought ; or the intellectual evolution of æsthetic truth. As Coleridge says, the antithesis of poetry is science, not merely prose. In its essence it is rather an idealization of concrete fact or an imaginative embodiment of abstract truth. Such fact is not ascertained by scientific discovery ; nor is such truth deduced by a logical process on the part of the poet. They come to him out of his intense love of the beautiful and strong desire for perfection in everything. He arrives at poetic truth by some creative, or reproductive, power of intuition, insight, or clairvoyance of his mind and heart ; through his imagination or fancy, his feelings or passions. The expression of poetry in verse is—like music—somewhat an affair of the senses but chiefly a matter of form ; yet by virtue of its cadence and rhyme this form is so inextricably mingled with its substance as to become a necessary part of it, in its perfect state. Its effect upon reader or hearer is not only mental and psychological, but also physical and magnetic. Proper expression of poetry involves the possession and exercise of the power of invention and the faculty of taste ;—a musical ear, a facility in the use of imagery or metaphor, together with the employment of rhythmical and appropriate language. The charm of poetic diction, like the magic of poetic thought, is difficult to define ; but they are twin factors in the production of what all the world calls poetry.

Goethe said to Eckermann :—" I cannot help laughing at the æsthetic folk who torment themselves in endeavoring, by some abstract words, to reduce to a conception that inexpressible thing to which we give the name of beauty. Beauty is a primeval phenomenon which itself never makes its appearance, but the reflection of which is visible in a thousand different utterances of the creative mind, and is as various as nature herself."

So we come back to our starting-point—as much in the dark as ever ! We shake our heads, with wise significance, and conclude, with Goethe, that beauty is a " primeval phenomenon " the essence of which is inexplicable.

Of Beauty, what can art or science know ?
Its essence in the matter or the mind ?
Is this a trick of sense, a raree-show,
Or something that the soul itself must find ?

Is it a primal force of human life,
A light auroral on a trackless sea—
Beyond the scope of analytic strife
Refulgent—an eternal verity ?

The gliding of a bird aloft in air,
The circlets in a pool a pebble makes,
The water sparkling mid the billows, where
The sun shines and the tossing wave-crest breaks ;

The motion of a full-sailed ship at sea,
The hissing of the frothy waves on rocks,
The twisting breakers on the distant lee,
The surf that splinters with tumultuous shocks ;

The imaged mountains, clouds and leaves, in lakes,
The sighs of strains æolian from trees,
A radiance the moon in summer takes,
A star that glitters in the wintry breeze ;

The myriad charming colors, shapes, and sounds,
Kind Nature fills this teeming world withal,
Not these, O Beauty, thy enchaining bounds :
Thy deeps most answer to our spirit's call.

Imagination, fancy, thought, and care
Evoke thy infinite variety ;
Thou hast no limit in the earth or air,
Thy treasures boundless as eternity.

A HINT ABOUT POETRY.

Perhaps after Sidney, Milton, Shelley, Goethe, Schopenhauer, and so many others have discoursed almost
exhaustively about the art of poetry, it may be thought
idle—at least for the unprofessional—to talk further. But
like love, poetry being an idealization of fact, the subject
is always near us, and never wholly tiresome to everybody—however superficially, or even iterantly, one may
speak of it.

If one might be allowed to judge from the effusions
now prevalent in newspapers and magazines, it would
seem our early Colonial notion, that rhymic versification
is the only essential element of distinction between poetry
and prose, has survived to our day ;—not merely as a
juvenile delusion, but as a wide popular faith. When to
this persuasion is added the advanced idea, now current,
that elliptical incoherence is the quintessence of poetical
excellence, it may be well for some of us to resume our
horn-books, and, by going back to first principles, to have
a fresh reckoning of the matter.

Schopenhauer says:—"Metre and rhyme are fetters ; but
likewise a garment which the poet throws about him, and
under which he is allowed to speak as he otherwise could
not ; this is what delights us." But what formulas are
essential to poetry, pure and simple ? If poetical inven-

tion, imaginative ideas and passionate emotions be clearly
and handsomely expressed, by fit words, suitable incidents, and congruous imagery, are they the less poetical,
because they lack rhyme and metre ?

Shall not a man, being possessed of the genius of a poet,
communicate his poetical conceptions to the world,
although (as Wordsworth says) he lack the accomplishment of verse ? Ought mere melody or numbers longer
to be deemed the only element that is indispensably necessary to the popular notion of genuine poetry ?

Could such mere expressions, as "winged words" or
"laughing water," be other than poetical, without the
factitious aid of metrical feet ? Does the cardinal distinction between poetry and prose or science rest at all in
blank or rhymic versification ? Is such outward clothing
absolutely material to poetic thought, or is it chiefly valuable as a charming, world-loved accessory—that ought
not to be abused by using it as a lure for vacuity or a
mask for disguising bald fact ? If one's thoughts and
even images be wholly commonplace or matter of fact—
or merely rudimentary, vague, evanescent, or simply incomprehensible to both author and reader—shall the
witchery of melody or the art of versification, however
consummate of themselves, be held competent, through a
popular hallucination, to transform such productions into
poetry ? If beautiful or terrible ideas, incidents, images,
situations, emotions and fancies, clearly conceived and
coherently expressed in words appropriate to excite the
imagination, or electrify the feelings, be written in the
form of prose, it would seem they ought not, for that
reason alone, to appear any the less poetical, even to the

ordinary mind—or to be relegated to the lower plane of eloquence or mere rhetoric. Our English version of the Hebrew Bible furnishes too plain a contradiction to such a view ; either with or without its rhythmical dress.

If honest prose be mellifluous in language and melodious in cadence, or even if the same ideas be expressed in harmonious verse, doubtless we may derive the more pleasure from reading them aloud. And perhaps too, there is even a sort of ear of the mind that can catch— through eye or memory—the melody of rhythmically-expressed thought, without even the aid of vocal sound. But does not such pleasure, thus given, come wholly from the ear, either outward or inward ? Is not this charm the trick of a sense more than half physical, like the involuntary motion of foot or hand on hearing the concord of familiar sounds ? Does it necessarily, of itself, involve the existence of intrinsic poetical merit in what is heard ? Does it really hit the poetic sense, or appeal to intuition or spiritual insight ?

Possibly indeed, poetry ought always to be read aloud, in order to give us full assurance that we gather all its sense and beauty—of sound as well as of meaning. Nevertheless, may not one whose thoughts are intrinsically poetical still hopefully give them to the world as poetry —without dread of the critic, or of sinning against any inexorable law of belles lettres—although he be wholly incapable of verse, and even lack the achievement of melody in his prose diction ?

Indeed would it not be more like fair dealing with the reading public if merely passional, or simply chaotic, versifiers—except as confessed song-writers—would more

frequently discard poetical forms altogether? Even if
this test should prove sometimes to be suicidal to the
author's fame, perhaps his experimental readers would
suffer less from confusion of ideas, or enforced vacuity
of mind.

One other suggestion. May it not happen (through a
more widely popular recognition of the apparent fact of
musical versification not being an absolutely necessary
element of the soul of poetry) that common authors—
who have none or but a scanty allowance of the poetical
faculty, either natural or acquired—can be brought to
perceive that a talent for metrical composition is but a
small part of the substance of the real poet's equipment?
Who does not know that bare prosaic ideas are too often
made even absurd by putting them into rhymic verse—
however respectable, as commonplaces, they might be,
when methodically expressed without metre and rhyme?
In other words, does not a too popular impression that
rhyme and metre are the supreme vital forces in poetic
composition work evil in two ways;—first, by keeping back
from full expression many who have the vision divine,
without the rhymer's art, and next, by bringing forward
into deceitful prominence, crowds of impotent poetasters,
whom the world would very willingly and profitably let
die?

None will gainsay the added charms Milton found in
" soft Lydian airs," or Wordsworth in " wisdom," when
" married to immortal verse." Doubtless too—as already
suggested—there is a natural as well as traditional affinity
between poetry and music—while the magic of song is a
force that outstrips calculation. But a miscegenation of

prosaic or chaotic ideas with harmonious sounds, however pleasing it may be to the undiscriminating ear, ought not to be allowed to confuse forever the too lenient popular mind, concerning the high lineage and noble office of pure and true poetry—without at least a continual protest.

ANCESTORS.

Paradoxical though it be, however inconsistent or even incomprehensible the dogmas of social usage or opinion may sometimes appear, it seldom happens that they are without a solid basis of good sense and real merit, growing out of both utility and fitness. Especially is this true where they have been long maintained and are of substantially universal acceptance. To many—among the unthinking or flippant of speech—it appears to be the mere arrogant efflorescence of an indisputable special possession when those born of distinguished ancestors make a claim of merit, attaching to their own persons, merely out of this circumstance. They are told it is based merely upon a common good opinion, toward which they have in no wise contributed, and the existence whereof depends wholly upon the past, in which they could not participate. Yet this hasty and superficial view has never made great headway in the social world.

Much color as it may seem to have in reason, it overlooks too many obvious facts to depreciate seriously the advantage, and real value to society itself, of upholding the prestige of ancestral good repute. But in the sideglance here taken at this topic, all specific or direct influence of the laws of heredity, the marvels of pedigree or of the amenities of high-breeding, is left purposely out of view.

Perhaps the strongest trait of youth—and the one earliest to influence and spur both intellectual and moral faculties to exertion—is that of instinctive, unconscious imitation. Most valuable, to the ingenuous and aspiring mind, is a close companionship of, and easy opportunity to feed a natural admiration with good models. Where a young person has, upon his coming forward in the world, a social background, for character, of illustrious and highly cultivated remote ancestors or immediate progenitors, he is the more readily influenced, almost unconsciously, to imitate the excellence of what is, by association, so near and dear to him. Even with those who are called "hard cases" this fact acts generally, at least, as a sort of counter-irritant to any innate latent depravity. None but those less fortunate in this respect can tell also how much the well-born save, or how little they necessarily waste, of mental or moral energy, by not having to grope about helplessly, during the early years of their studies, in a dim, intellectual twilight. They are spared from pursuing with vacillating purpose, either half-formed or ill-constructed patterns or designs held up for their imitation, or pursuit, by ignorant teachers.

Few only of us in America have the right kind of instructors, in ourselves or others, at the right moment in early life. Hitherto, most men among us, who have themselves achieved excellence or celebrity, have struggled with early adversity, and have been substantially, and even elementarily, self-taught. They owed their opportunities of real education largely to accidental circumstances or supreme necessity and hard self-effort, but seldom to well-chosen, judiciously directed, outward, early intellectual training, association, and example.

Myriads of men live and die obscurely—leading broken lives and with very little advantage to themselves or their race—who justly might have obtained renown by adding greatly to the world's stock of knowledge and to its moral headway, but for the want of two elements of true or at least of rapid success in life. First, they have lacked an early start, in the right direction, to arouse energy and desire to excel in noble conduct ; next, they have failed for want of persistent push in pursuit of valuable aims. Many of this large body have had no distinguished ancestors, the influence of whose good repute could have supplied directly, at least, one of these deficiencies. The other might have followed naturally from healthy, well-directed ambition. Such men were not generally, indeed, moulded from that material of which renowned ancestors are made in the first instance. Doubtless, they were deficient in the original energy and the fiery nature required to make the Rudolphs or Napoleons of a new line of sovereigns. Yet many of them—now lost to mankind— might well have swelled the ranks of that great second class, by whom most of the useful work of this world is accomplished—besides perhaps tasting the supreme happiness of a better managed life.

In painful contrast, however, to these general observations, is the commonly recognized fact, that, from some obscure cause, parental conspicuousness—when derived only from the possession of wealth, or mere power of place, in American life—so often demoralizes or deteriorates the succeeding generation, and unfits it for noble life.* It must perhaps be conceded that, in our new communities, transmitted ancestral distinction is too often the means of weakening the motives for personal exertion among the offspring of distinguished families. Although it may polish the manners, just as surely it seems to enervate the brain. Nevertheless, as our society grows older—and our well-born, leisure-loving class shall increase in numbers —the necessity of self-exertion, to keep in honored position among so many darlings of fortune, will become more pressing, and may furnish a more urgent stimulus to the rising generation among them for earning, themselves, the laurels they so greatly desire to wear.

Gossip and Autobiography.

A love of personal gossip is inborn with the common mass of people. It seems, however, to be most fascinating to those who find but little of what is substantial in the outer world of things within their reach, and less within themselves, that is interesting to their tastes or inclinations. Tattling busy-bodies of this class, who cannot restrain their impertinent curiosity and meddling impertinence, are well typified by the man in the familiar play who, when told to mind his own business, meekly said there was "so little of it" he had an abundance of leisure for the affairs of other people.

In a large city this fondness for gossip usually finds so much of absorbing interest in the petty, social vicissitudes of many conspicuous people, that it is less apt to meddle in the private affairs of an immediate neighbor. Hence city-people are sometimes called selfish and unsocial. In smaller towns and villages the dwellers are much more "sociable," as they call it. This expression, however, usually means, in homely phrase, that every man's finger is constantly in every other man's pie.

Our instinctive appetite for private details of other individual lives is doubtless the chief cause of the insatiable popular demand for autobiographical memoirs, and letters of men and women of distinction. Our interest in the lives of ordinary people, of whom but little is comtemporaneously known, usually ceases when they die. They are soon forgotten—except where we hold some personal relation to them, or they are closely connected with our family history, or some event or scene in which we feel a special concern. Where, however, men or women, by their lives, actions, writings, or speech, have once excited the sympathy, admiration, romantic interest, or even ill-will of contemporary mankind in general, they continue long in memory to survive their mortal existence.

Each new detail of their private lives, like every personal anecdote of them, forms a sort of nucleus for fresh interest—tending to excite a kind of second-handed curiosity and a desire for more. These *memorabilia* pass from one person to another, quite as often by speech as by writing. As each narrator adds or alters a little—from defective memory or lively imagination, or zeal to make a good story—the tale grows by what it feeds upon, until the fable is often more widely popular, and better known, than the true history.

Later, another class, chiefly composed of writers, take up the heterogeneous mass, and strive, by analytical criticism or sifting of evidence, to deduce what is probable, if not certain, as well as to discard what is inconsistent and apparently fictitious. This process itself makes endless talk and more curiosity—stimulating the natural hunger for more minute biographical details. The result is a general impression in the popular mind that the truth in such matters lies at the bottom of the well, if anywhere, and only by constant diving—whether by experts or volunteers—one can hope to find it. This notion brings forward many divers and more bidders for what is brought up from these depths.

To these circumstances may be added the fact—of which none are ignorant—that men are seldom able to speak frankly or colorlessly when discoursing of themselves. There is always something concealed—often from modesty or even more creditable motives, such as sparing the feelings or good fame of contemporaries. But perhaps not seldom this suppression of fact comes through a desire to appear well, or to avoid increasing the importance of others. Besides, in self-portraiture, generally some rainbow tints are added involuntarily from self-delusion to the picture, that heighten its effect.

Some will have it, that, as a rule, men cannot possibly speak the whole unvarnished truth, when themselves form the subject of comment. However this may be, from some or all of the causes mentioned (and others that easily suggest themselves, to both the good and ill-natured) there is no book so eagerly read, or likely so long to remain among our household favorites, as one which purports to contain matter of sincere, artless, full, literal, uncolored, autobiographical details (even of persons of little public distinction) having no apparent effect in view in its composition, beyond an honest narration of unadorned facts.

Such frank memorials as the plain common-sense sketch of the early life of Dr. Franklin, written by himself, or even the Dutch-like painting, of the morbid egoism and fevered thirst for fame, of that unhappy little savage, Marie Bashkirtseff, will continue to find innumerable readers—at least until human nature is changed, or that special civilizing of their simple human nature which gave them conspicuousness is wholly outgrown, or has become otherwise obsolete.

Doing Nothing.

Until lately this specialty has been accounted among Americans, fortunately, as one of the lost arts. To be idle, like a stone or a dozing animal, may be possible for a stupid person, whose highest aspiration is only to sleep and feed. But for a man of good health and sound mind to have neither an object in view beyond the pleasure of the hour, nor any aim or stake in the future, and to be wholly content with all things as they are, in our transitional social condition, is not easy.

Never to be eager or excited or deeply interested about what shall be done or omitted in public affairs—meanwhile keeping clear of all reformatory schemes : to be able to turn a deaf ear to all solicitations that one shall come before the public, however unostentatiously, in good works : to resist even the allurements of vanity and a natural love for the expressed good-will of our neighbors and acquaintances, or the world at large : to disdain the blandishments of committeemen and trustees, who are forever prowling about among the quiet nooks of social life—where men who love their ease are prone to congregate—seeking whom they may trepan into their seductive coils and enslave to hard labor, for the remnant of life : to repress the promptings of a warm heart, a generous liberal, charitable, mankind-loving disposition : to close one's eyes to the multitudinous accidents, wants, and miseries that are constantly bringing those one loves or esteems into temporary trouble—out of which one can, without very great sacrifice, lift them up to light-heartedness and content : to give one's self wholly to one's love of following one's own idle wish, and doing or omitting to do only as one pleases with one's own time and resources for mere pleasurable dalliance—regardless of the inward promptings of one's *daimon :* to live forgetful of others, and in the enjoyment of undisturbed appreciation of stagnant self, and of one's own imaginary virtues, or cloying pleasures : to ignore what others are pleased to call the claims of society upon our exertions : to forget what might trouble one in a remembrance of the appalling spectres of things that ought to be done, while philosophically, and with shiftless composure, putting off, until a distant receding to-morrow, that which the good of others, or the orderly administration of affairs entrusted to our care, demands to be done to-day : to shirk gracefully, or—with an affectionate and bewildering complaisance—to shove off from our own shoulders, and cause to sit with an attractive lightness upon the shoulders of our neighbor, those burdens of care, duty, labor, anxiety, privation, annoyance, loss, expense and other sacrifices, which are our own, by birthright or other necessity, or perhaps by a self-imposed obligation—possibly as the bitter compensation for the sweet juice you have already extracted from some nut you volunteered to take as a whole, yet reject, now that you have enjoyed all you found, easily extracted, purely enjoyable, succulent and tooth- some, contained in it :—these are brief hints of some of the things necessary to be done by most of us, who would do nothing.

It is indeed no trivial task, for a live man, long to per- sonate the fiction of a *cadaver* without becoming a real one. You might as well expect a running mill to stop moving, while the water is falling upon its wheel, as look among us for idleness in a well-constituted man. You may cease to fill the hopper with grain, but the mill-stones will continue to go around. And if they find nothing better to grind, they will wear out themselves. The only way of arresting the motion is to break the connection, and to take off the power.

If a real vital man would do nothing and be happy in American life he must benumb his mental faculties, he must harden his heart, he must isolate himself from the sympathies of his race, he must cherish selfishness as his chief good, resign himself to the complete domination of his lower nature, and perhaps dwell chiefly down in the slough of merely physical pleasures—until satiety shall so narrow the border-line between life and death, that he is scarcely conscious which side of it he would prefer, if he had the energy to make a choice, unless indeed (as the moralist would say) by some happy convulsion of his re-

bellious and outraged nature (before his second youth has
passed) he shall have broken away from his thraldom,
and, with thrice-armed resolution, risen to an upper air.
Exchanging thus soul-eating selfishness for a larger life,
he may attain perchance a better outlook for the real
enjoyment of existence.

A Peep at Fine Art.

When Guido sent to Rome his famous picture of St.
Michael, painted for the Church of the Capuchins, he
wrote to the Pope's steward these words :—"I wish I
had the wings of an angel, to have ascended into Paradise, and there to have beheld the forms of beatified
spirits, from which I might have copied my Archangel ;
but not being able to mount so high, and it being vain for
me to search for his resemblance here below, I was forced
to make an introspection into my own mind, and to have
recourse to that idea of beauty which I had formed in my
imagination, for a prototype."

To the uninstructed observer, there seem to be at the
least two leading methods by which the artistic instinct
moves in the direction of self-development, and a realization of its inclination and aims. The one is chiefly
imaginative—the other is much more matter-of-fact. The
first prevails where the artist clearly conceives an ideal,
and works confidently toward producing it. Although,
while to his imagination the thing prefigured may constantly become more perfected in mass and outline as
well as in detail, it may yet, in execution, steadily recede
from his grasp as he strives to approach it. The other

method is common where the artist sees some work of man he considers fit for imitation—in whole or in part or by modification—or some object in nature he hopes to represent, in some of its aspects, precisely as it appears to his actual eye, complete in all its parts.

The first, poet-like, moving from within, seems to be inspired by an instinctive love of abstract beauty or fitness ; and strives to reproduce in actual form, color, or composition, or all combined, some phases of a representation of a genuine and pure conception, unembarrassed by accidental or transitory accessories. The other is impelled from without, and appears to seek a reproduction —perhaps even with microscopic fidelity—of some actual and material object, in such seemingly palpable form that the bodily sense can almost grasp it as a tangible thing. He appeals only to the understanding and the practical senses—unlike the former—leaving little or nothing to the cognizance of mere imagination, spiritual insight, or perhaps even to the finer æsthetic sense, of a spectator.

In the beginning this latter one has the larger crowd of sincere admirers. His work strikes the understanding or common-sense of appreciation of the present multitude. It takes hold at once of the attention and interest of the ordinary mind. It reaches its highest credit and popularity within a limited period. Artists of this class, however, having found the limit of their naturalistic domain, —as interpreters of nature—can only repeat themselves, or perhaps vary the stamp of individuality in their works by changing immaterial circumstances, or by departing arbitrarily from fact at the risk of violating artistic truth. When they begin to call upon their inward resources, they are prone to mistake conceit or fancy—or memory of fact—for real imagination, and, as their work progresses—not having the clew of truth—it unavoidably runs by exaggeration towards the bizarre or, at least, the incoherent, and perhaps the grotesque. Instead of drawing, as it were, from an inexhaustible original spring, or even a pure stream, they recompose old materials upon the theory of imitation or reconstruction, but not of recreation and reproduction. They are constantly stumbling against the impassable barriers of their limited territory—without ever overleaping them, or passing into the indefinite region of an ideal, beyond their natural limits. If they sometimes seem to attempt such a feat, it is only to lose themselves in an apparent *terra incognita.*

But true art has no recognized bound to its field of vision—though it has many limitations to its power or means of reproducing its ideals of nature. It projects into the indefinite upon lines starting from a real centre ; and, so far as it may go, one step prepares the way for another, while its progress is always toward perfection. Even when it betrays how much it is unavoidably hampered, by its vehicle and method, or by the feebleness of human capacity to overcome its intrinsic impediments, it suggests to the mind some perfection beyond the reach of art. It leaves the intelligence of those who rightly see the depth and suggested insight of its works, to supplement what the pictorial, or plastic, or other art cannot specifically attain.

If one could speak with the tongue of an artist, he might perhaps venture to point, for illustration of this common laic hint, to the recognized early, or progressive,

works of the best periods of Greek art, as an accomplished
result of the purer method ; and to the marvellous imitation, or the grotesque extravagance, of some Japanese
decorations, for an extreme, though natural, consequence
of the other.

A WELL-ROUNDED LIFE.

All the world agrees with Cicero that it is most sweet
—toward the close of his career and during a cheerful
old age—for a man to be able to rejoice in the soothing
recollection of a life well-spent.

From this point of vision it might be a pleasant, as well
as a profitable task, for a well-equipped, philosophical
poet of our time to portray an ideal, introspective autobiography ; composed of the inner, or spiritual life as well
as the cardinal experiences, of a man, brought up among
and living philosophically through the vicissitudes of our
empirical and immethodical American society.

Beginning with humble circumstances, he could emerge
into larger intercourse with the world by slow degrees, yet
always feeling within himself the *mens divinior* and the
impulse to find out what was best for him to do in order
to justify the fact of his creation. He might be shown
discharging with fidelity the duties of life, and developing
his faculties to the fullest extent commensurate with his
circumstances, and accomplishing the best discovered
purpose of human existence, by doing the greatest amount
of good to and for others of his race—whether contemporaneous or future—consistently with a fair enjoyment
of life for himself.

It should not be a vague abstraction, nor a tale of improbable virtues, nor the portrait of a smug or of a prig. It ought to be the vertebrated story of a man of at least average capacity, with all the vagaries in temper and passion of our mixed genealogies in his blood, and with mind and heart swayed by the multifarious, irregular influences that, in our crude but nascent civilization, most men among us encounter. Yet, by force of character, natural or acquired, and by a large leaven of common-sense and natural piety, he might, in the end, find out the right, redeeming himself from error, and keeping on in growth of wisdom and the busy practice of good conduct, as he ripens in years. In some of these excursions, the diffusive verbosity of Wordsworth's *Prelude*, despite its lofty poetry and descriptive eloquence, might perhaps teach the writer something to avoid.

First, there would be his childhood, with its time of unconscious impressions and mute wonder. Second, would appear his early youth when, dissatisfied with his haphazard teachers, he was groping his anxious way, amid the darkness and pitfalls that beset the path of the beginning of all irregular self-education—before the instinct of a wise eclecticism is much developed.

Third, would come out the category of his audacious opinions, or rather fragmentary views, largely made up from imperfect knowledge and irregular models, with misconception of the entirety of their significance ; his bold questioning of matters settled as fate, and his implicit confidence in the permanence of things ephemeral, or already waning to decay ; his defiant distrust of authority as it stands in the way of his pleasures, his aims or his ideal work ; and his blind and tame obedience to the commands of arrogant assumption ; or his acquiescence in ill-founded popular faiths. Then again, one might see his dismay and revulsion of feeling, as human nature discloses its deformity, or his chosen gods fall from their pedestals, or his seeming monumental land-marks, of right and wrong, crumble away—all these things breeding in his soul a paralyzing doubt whether, in truth, there be anything but—"what is not."

Fourth, might be shown his ripening judgment and broadened love of his fellow-men despite their frailties, as his own middle age comes on ; his growing comprehensiveness ; his recognition of some eternal fixed principles, of truth and religion, growing out of a conception of absolute necessity—founded upon the intrinsic nature and fitness of things ; his feeling that the ground is becoming solid and firm beneath his feet ;—and then his mental and moral march onward and upward, as he co-operates with other men, in consciously fulfilling the grander purpose of life.

Fifth, he would come to the borders of old age ; when, before infirmity overtakes him, his field of view has so widened that he embraces, in the scope of his mental, moral, and spiritual vision, the whole world, its history and its people ; when he sloughs off the priggishness that grows out of easy success in life, but the individual, though insignificant in himself, has become of importance in his own eyes, while considered as a component element of the race ; when he sees how all things—even the apparently trivial—have their uses ; when, acquiescing in the general harmony of the universe, he finally accepts, with composure, the fact of a gradual dwindling of his powers or faculties, and, loosening his grasp of things temporal, he complacently sinks back again into the vast obscure of eternity ; to make way, in this mundane arena, for the crowding, onward procession of humanity, that carries upon its banner gleaming above all others in brightness, one inscription :—

The individual withers, and the world is more and more.

NOVELS.

There are obviously at least four great facts, moral, social, and physical facts—of the human race—the experience or history of which is always especially interesting to mankind in general. In the ideal world—represented by fiction, poetry, painting, music or sculpture—they stand out with significant prominence. Birth, love, marriage, and death are the staple of nearly all story, or imaginative or emotional fiction, in letters or art ; and appeal to the widest curiosity and sympathy.

The romantic tales—whether true or feigned—that appear to take the strongest and most lasting hold upon the popular mind (aside from some rather accidental ones that typify in concrete form some popular sentiment or modernize some deep-seated tradition) are those that begin with the passion of love, and end with the fact of marriage.

Since biography or history—made up of whole lives of men and women singly, or together—composes a large part of the common resources of the discursive, omnivorous reader (such as feeds so plenteously upon fictitious story) it is rather strange that writers of novels do not more often push their adventures farther into the later and remoter ways of life of their characters. With some readers, a true picture of married life, written from the same stand-point as the romantic novel, well might interest greatly. Can it be true that the modern novelist is willing to teach the narrow lesson that with marriage the romance of life ends, and only the hard prosaic reality remains ? Wherever such more thorough and complete books have been well written, they usually have laid hold upon and kept the attention of mankind for very long periods. Mayhap with the novel-writer it is easier to cater to the taste of the younger readers. And perhaps the passion of young love (when it is the substance of a story) appeals to a larger light-reading constituency than do any other of the common dynamics of human life. Possibly, too, the capacity to tell a tale, embracing the whole, or even the maturity, of a life, involves greater imaginative and reasoning powers, higher culture, broader experience, more comprehensiveness—and possibly, besides, a special genius for fathoming the mysteries of, and finding the secret clue to, the complexities of the later part of a human existence—than does the composition of a story, which is but an episode in a life, or only a half-developed career. The opulent and unabashed genius of Balzac demonstrates what excellence may be achieved in this direction.

In a romance or novel—except in archaic reproduction—generally that writer finds most success, immediate and perhaps permanent, who makes his hero reflect the essential undertone of the current day and hour in respect to feeling, opinion, thought, and human conduct. The very hour always has its typical hero in the common mind, either in fact or fancy. This comes perhaps from no special or intrinsic merit in the ideal man ; but rather because he is the creature of the exigencies of the time, or sometimes because he comes to us in due season to satisfy an intelligent want. It is not unlike the case of the breaking out of a new, but necessary, word for our common vocabulary. Besides, from a special point of observation, such a hero seems, for the time, to be the best that may be had. And then, as all surrounding things appear to lead in one direction, that is perhaps the easiest way for the writer to go. Hence many things work for the success of such a tale. If the type be worth preserving, it will endure, like other natural products ;—either in its singleness for a long period of time, or as part of the rudimentary traits of some new product in the future.

The Dramatic Faculty.

The dramatic faculty is possessed more commonly than generally is supposed. It is manifested very often by children in the facility with which they compose stories of fictitious persons and events. In early youth, necessarily, self-experience and self-consciousness play an insignificant part in human nature. Where, however, the youthful mind is imaginative, and leans toward the picturesque—inasmuch as it works almost wholly outside— it usually borrows its material chiefly from reading and superficial sight-seeing, or what is very commonly heard or known. Yet such productions are far more genuine

and truly dramatic than when, as sometimes happens—
through injudicious parental treatment of ephemeral pre-
cocity—the little brain is morbidly sentimental, or gives
itself up to formulating the results of its own petty
morbid introspection.

By cultivation and encouragement, this faculty sometimes may become a source of great mental and perhaps
social pleasure ;—even if it never mature to such a degree
as to add anything to literature. For those whose well-
conditioned dispositions lead them to love human nature,
and to be deeply interested in human actions, what can
furnish a more pleasing, interesting, varied or endless
occupation (merely by musing if not by writing) than
the sincere study of other people—the feigned reproduction of their dispositions, motives, intelligence, actions, and
general conduct ;—not from our own but from the special
point of vision of such people themselves ? That is the
essence of the genuine dramatic method.

When a genius of the stamp of Byron—morbid, introspective, and egotistic — creates a mimic world with
angels, devils, and men, each, as often has been said, has
a strong family resemblance, and if not Byron himself,
is thoroughly Byronic. But when a catholic and universal mind, like Shakespeare, peoples the earth or the air,
the more we study his creatures—their vicissitudes and
their conduct—the more we are inclined to listen to the
conjecture that their author had no special individuality.
Some profound critics seem to think he held the whole
world in solution in the alembic of his imagination. Being
a microcosm in himself, he could divine the thoughts and
probable actions of others from their separate individual

stand-point ; and thus reproduce their conduct objectively—so that the common eye can see such persons as they move and breathe like living beings.

This is the true mental creativeness of normal genius ; not to copy with partial hand the lineaments of our own special and perhaps distorted features, but rather to sit inside the mind and heart of another, who may be a typical specimen of some phase of human nature ; to feel and think as that one does in the nakedness of his own soul ; and then to represent by an outward form some of his actions as he is likely to make them — varied by all the mingled motives and external forces that shape his special individuality of conduct. Look, for instance, at the marvellous effect with which Shakespeare—following the meteor-like trail of " Marlowe's mighty line "— wrought out, with a bold hand, his historical plays.

The frequent exercise of this faculty (without intent of authorship) as a mere personal discipline, might supply sometimes a good practical antidote—if kindly employed in the catholic manner suggested—to that morbid condition of mind which is too commonly begotten (among the over-scholarly and the excessively reflecting) by a habit of continual self-introspection, and a consequent growth of exaggerated self-consciousness.

WASTE OF TIME.

It is deplorable that, during our brief lives—with so much to be learned and done, with such capability of strengthening or rendering joyously effective our intellectual and moral powers by judicious study or timely training and exercise—despite immemorial teaching, we should waste so large a portion of our petty span of time. We store the memory with rubbish, stale the vividness of attention with vain repetitions, and allow the vigor of our faculties to wane instead of expanding—from sheer lack of energetic will, of systematic discipline, and methodical endeavor. In our school-days most of us are careless spendthrifts in this way. In later years few are able to overcome habits so acquired, leading in the same direction.

During how many weary hours of youth also do we tax our strength in acquiring that which for nearly all beneficial purposes is wholly valueless. Usually it is even a burden to carry, until through indolence or other neglect, it slips from our shoulders. It .would be quite enough, of idle sacrifice, if our acquisitions of useless knowledge were limited to those errors and false notions which sometimes furnish the key to correct ideas, by setting us to the work of close thinking, or by making us ashamed of our ignorance or misinformation—through comparison of ideas with those of our more advanced, or more fortunately instructed associates. However, there is sometimes a consolation in the reflection that much of what we find to be worthless this year—and, for that reason, now to be discarded—was, last year, even a little in advance of us. It has become insignificant only because it has been, as it were, merely a ladder reaching to something beyond, which we could not formerly see, and which might never have seen at all, had we not attained our new and higher stand-point. Our ideals grow with our acquisitions,

Considering the shortness of life—and how much a willing hand may find to do—one wonders at the habitual state of mind that so commonly welcomes any diversion merely in order " to kill time." Some men always find so much more mental employment at hand than can well be disposed of, they never know what is meant by having time hang heavily upon their hands. Neither have they any desire to kill it. It dies long before it becomes a burden. Yet doubtless this kind of murder is the chief occupation of too many capable of better things. By beginning early in life they become expert in the slaughter.

The art of life was well expounded, from this point of view, the other day, in a conversation overheard of two gilded, or rather lacquered, youths—already more than sated with frivolous pleasures. After some despondent talk of the nothingness of existence, one of them concluded the requiem of his philosophy, by saying :—" Well what is life, after all, but a constant struggle to kill time ; —and to avoid the public alms-house ? "

EXAGGERATION.

A common vice in ordinary conversation, as well as in written speech, is the often reprobated habit of making recklessly exaggerated statements of facts or circumstances. Its long affiliation with coarse and cheap American humor has given it a currency among us beyond its deserts—if any merit it really has. There is much to be said against it—even as a stale device of provincial buffoonery or coarse waggery. There is so little to recommend it—except perhaps as a wand in the hand of

a genius like Rabelais—one is inclined to wonder that it
has not been long ago banished utterly—at the least,
from all well-bred social intercourse.

To practise it (without specific design or as a vehicle
for humor) usually betrays a frivolous disposition, an
irregular imagination, or a slovenly inattention to important details. It indicates an almost reckless disregard
of moral accuracy, and a carelessness of the effect of
language upon another—which, to say the least, are
traits by no means respectful to one's auditors. Again,
although it may not even suggest the notion of a wilful
perversion of actual fact or any intent harmfully to
deceive another; yet it insensibly begets—when one is
accustomed to hear this sort of talk—a habit in hearers
of giving but little attention to such a speaker's statements. It dissociates all seriousness from what he may
say ; and finally men regard him as a common laugher,
who cannot take himself seriously and whose speech does
not deserve ordinary notice. Moreover it produces a
bewildering effect upon the general listener, which is
quite incompatible either with a serious interest in, or a
care to remember, what is thus said. And in the end it
is likely to cheat the speaker—however humorous—of
more than half his due, because of his common discredit
as a narrator, or reporter.

Perhaps it is sometimes not inexcusable in an earnest
advocate or a real humorist, whose reputation for good
sense is unclouded ;—who seeks to produce an immediate
effect and is not supposed to be limited by an obligation
to speak with impartial accuracy. Nevertheless its frequent use tends, in most cases, to destroy capability for

judicial impartiality, where such faculty exists—precisely as a contrary habit of conscientious accuracy of statement usually runs with fairness of judgment. When Rufus Choate—who habitually revelled in hyperbole—was asked to accept a judicial office, he declined emphatically, saying shrewdly :—" It would destroy my power of exaggeration."

CRITICISM.

As this word indicates by its origin, criticism is discrimination and judgment—not mere censoriousness, or even petty fault-finding, as the vulgar impression sometimes assumes. Sound criticism is analysis, exposition, and comparison. The good or bad in art or letters appears involuntarily by this operation. All else in it —that is good—is mere illustration from a true point of view.

Unfortunately, however, the more profound the study, or the more elaborate the analysis and exposition, the less likely it is to catch the popular ear. The easy, flashy, empirical criticism—that which tickles the sense of the superficial, and economizes attention and thought in the hearer—the hasty, the inconsiderate, the ill-natured, the witty, the arrogant, the flippant, and the pedantic comments are much in vogue at all times.

False criticism has its motives and its formulas, that save time and labor for itself. Its apparent spirit is to exhibit the erudition, the sagacity, or the superior potential capacity of the critic. Two of its favorite methods are to show first, what a particular work of art or letters is not, and next, to dwarf it by ill-natured comparison with some widely different work, or with something not attempted by the work in hand.

The intellectual world in general is, of course, deeply interested in cherishing the growth of good literature—even more so than in the suppression of that which is bad. The latter contains in itself the germs of its own destruction. The office of good criticism is not to discourage intelligent effort, but rather—so far as it honestly can—to point out merits, while not misleading by suppressing faults. When kindly sought, this golden mean is easy to find.

The chief business of the true critic is first of all to consider a work of art from the special stand-point of the artist himself. This view should temper and qualify at least all the critic's judgments. This is his lowest point of observation ; but it should fill his mind with a real sense of appreciation of what has been attempted, and soften his heart with mercy towards every honest, earnest effort. In this spirit he should mount the judgment-seat and begin his survey of the field into which the new-comer has entered. When by comparison he has given it the relative character it deserves, he may with sounder discretion analyze it and expound, praise, condemn, or illustrate what it has done or omitted, well or ill—in short what it has accomplished in the direction of its own aim.

Learned, honest, faithful, impartial criticism, though a subordinate, is a noble ally of true art. The artist is foolish in his own case, and an enemy to art in general, who deprecates it. No man can ordinarily see his own work as the world will see it—or even as it really is. The idea, or conception of it, may be his own—possibly true, grand or beautiful, and nearly perfect—yet the truthfulness of his mode of treating its expression, and the success or failure of his particular mode of development of it to the sense of others, may be something far beyond the scope of his own judgment to determine. Hence the fair-minded, intelligent, well-equipped, honest critic is always the author's or artist's best friend. Nevertheless, as La Bruyère says :—" Criticism is often not a science, but a trade, requiring more health than intelligence, more industry than capacity, and more practice than genius."

Generation of Ideas.

Although some men possess so perfect a combination of the higher intellectual powers that they breed great or brilliant thoughts in solitude and silence, yet it is rare to find minds really so hermaphroditic. With many the exercise of walking or riding seems to have a marvellous effect in stimulating a capacity for such spontaneous conceptions. Usually, however, the generating of new ideas —aside from the provocation of unusual events—comes more from the contact of mind with mind, in speech or reading. Embryonic germs are always afloat in fertile brains, waiting the chances of fructification. Many of these however unhappily perish in their barren singleness. Like the flowers of the field they need the fecundating dust, or pollen, of other minds to impart to them the capacity to blossom and grow into fruit. For this reason it is probably so common to find men who talk much better than they write.

By some such process of ideation come most of the infinite varieties of vivid thought, imagination, or fancy that instruct and delight the world in the wide department of belles lettres. Thus, also, as it were, by the ladder of other men's minds, we may sometimes climb to heights we had not else conceived to be attainable. By this method too we may grope clairvoyantly our way into the future ;—formulating the possible from the known, until at length we can even imagine something of the Great-Hereafter. From this consociation of intellect with intellect, often comes that fine enthusiasm, or inward-light, which springs up unbidden in some minds, and goes by the name of spiritual insight. Sometimes it seems as if one only held up a torch, while another found the way ; —so little indeed may we claim pure originality for some of our most striking conceptions.

The reverse of such minds Charles Lamb in his often quoted *Imperfect Sympathies* characterized as "Caledonian" saying :— " The brain of a true Caledonian (if I am not mistaken) is constituted on quite a different plan. His Minerva is born in panoply. . . . You cannot cry ' halves' to anything that he finds."

Knowledge.

It is a disheartening reflection that we cannot know absolutely that anything really is—or in other words, that our knowledge of things is limited to what merely appears to be. Intrinsically to us, Kantean science proposes to teach that, so far as we can know, nothing actually exists. Things simply seem to be, in proportion as we are capable of apprehending an appearance of them through our limited faculties ; everything we suppose we know depending upon ourselves for its existence. If one be blind, to him there is no color. If one be deaf, to him there is no sound. If one cannot taste, to him there is no sweet, bitter nor sour. All is illusion—mere cerebral phantasmagoria, or nothing ! The like infirmity awaits us in higher matters. None but the pure can know what "the pure in heart" may see. If a man, by gross abuse of his original simplicity of nature, be sullied, one of his surest punishments is that he becomes a confirmed doubter of, and never again can know in himself, the charitable sweetness of temperament, and the serene joys, of the pure. He unavoidably will account them all as delusions—phantoms of the brain—and look upon the innocent believers in them as dupes. One may thus imbrute nearly every one of his finer faculties.

Important then it is, even in this view alone, that we follow the preacher and keep ourselves fresh and clean, preserving all our capabilities in their vigor and perfection ; besides so guarding and cultivating our delicately appreciative powers of body, mind, and spirit, that we may thereby feel, see, and know, constantly—so far as it is given us to know at all—more and more ; and not lose our share of the higher enjoyments of life through imprudent abuse of our capacity for seizing them.

In this vein the bee said to the spider (before Matthew Arnold was born) in Swift's *Battle of the Books* :—
"The difference is, that instead of dirt and poison, we have rather chose to fill our hives with honey and wax ; thus furnishing mankind with the two noblest of things, which are, sweetness and light."

PROFESSIONAL GLORY. •

Lawyers and physicians are commonly prone to the
lauding of their respective professions as the noblest occupations of men. They pronounce them well adapted to
satisfying the most worthy ambition of any one, and well
deserving all the zeal and love they can give to this object
of their affection. One, who closes his eyes, when hearing them talk of these things—especially, when they are
inspiring their juniors or haranguing the public—might
fancy that, with all the world before them, at the pleasure
of their will, they had chosen, highly and nobly, their
occupations. Indeed one easily could suppose them to
be pure philanthropists, who had selected their lot chiefly
in order to do their utmost to serve or benefit the human
race ; and that a zeal and love for their calling had
swallowed up every other desire.

Doubtless with some this ebullition of sentiment is profoundly sincere. For such men would find their highest
ambition in being benefactors of the race, in whatsoever
place in the ranks of active life chance or choice might
cast their fortune. Many others by the contagion of
sympathy, and from absence of free-will, may be alike
honest, so far as they know themselves. Yet it is not unfrequently observed that when, by chance, one of the
magnates of these professions has attained a pecuniary
fortune, at whatever period of life, he is generally
quite ready to drop out of the field of his labors, and
quit it, as easily as if he had been all the while simply
running a race, and had reached the goal he always had
in view.

Hurry and Haste.

Easily as they are distinguishable, hurry and haste are often confounded. Haste implies quickness but not confusion, or lack of clear purpose, or choice of means. It involves directness as well as celerity of action. Haste presupposes deliberate plan, clear method and rapid execution. It is swift in despatch of business, because its outline of action is determined, and the brain leads the hand in all it does. It is usually the mark of a strong mind, with clear purpose, and vigorous intent to accomplish the end in view. It is meritorious in most human affairs.

Hurry, on the other hand, is a vice to be avoided. It is action without plan or clear conception of the object to be attained. It is doubtful in the choice of means to be employed. Instead of being a method of carrying into effect a well-devised scheme by direct effort, its plan is either confused or extemporized. It involves irregularity and delay in the conduct of business. It is a vice of young, inexperienced, weak, or little minds.

Haste goes straight to the end in view : hurry doubles its track and wastes time or opportunity, or both. Haste is a trait of a strong-man-armed who is terribly in earnest. Hurry, on the contrary, implies want of imagination or memory, and acts upon the shiftless impulse of the moment—plan and execution going hand in hand and stumbling over each other. It is like a swift runner who trips up his own heels. In times of sudden emergency it is a common infirmity—avoidable only by the cool, the wise, or the experienced. As a matter of self-conduct in most affairs, wherever practicable, a prudent man will set his face as a flint against it.

BORROWING BOOKS.

It is a more than bad manners to keep a borrowed book an unreasonable length of time. It is demoralizing to the borrower, unfair to the lender. When a sense of shame compels you to return the loan, you feel as if you were making a reluctant gift. The apparent loss mortifies you, and insensibly you make the owner semi-conscious that he is ungraciously depriving you of something you are scarcely able to spare. Your long possession has seemed to give you a sort of property-right in his goods. You induce him to feel as if you had been his gratuitous depository for his own benefit ; or perhaps worse, as if you had a claim upon his courtesy to allow you to retain his property indefinitely—even if you have not earned a right to enforce a sort of bailee's lien upon it for storage ! You make him ashamed to receive it back again ; while you put your own self-respect out of balance, and often leave it permanently in a somewhat damaged condition. All of this deplorable state of things, as you well know, is the result of your own carelessness, and neglect of prompt performance of a plain duty—to say nothing of your childish ingratitude for a favor you have not deserved.

All reference to a well-known habit of " conveying " books from public places, such as libraries, hotels, and clubs, is purposely omitted. In such cases the sense of shame having become extinct there is nothing left but to call the police.

GEMS OF THOUGHT.

How often a bright thought, a sound judgment, a sagacious opinion, a wise saying, a brilliant metaphor, or a happy expression passes without apparent appreciation, until some accident, or some inferior accessory, brings it into popular repute. Connoisseurs, critics, and experts are but a few, among the great multitude that make up the world of readers and talkers about books.

With the many, it is not the brilliancy, or purity alone, of a jewel that wins approbation. It is more commonly the fashion of the day, or the setting of the gem, that attracts the attention of the generality of mankind, or excites their cupidity, and makes them covet its possession.

So in books, many are the things witty, profound, brilliant, or beautiful, that sleep unnoticed by the mass until chance, or perhaps some adroit purloiner of other men's goods, takes them from their dull surroundings and arrays them in attractive accessories. Then they become familiar to the ear, and known as household words.

MAXIMS AND PROVERBS.

Maxims and proverbs, like many apparent analogies, unless taken in a very general sense, are often useless, or misleading, or both. If a statement of a rule of conduct be so loose and comprehensive, as to be universal, it is almost unavoidably a palpable truism. If, however, it be sufficiently definite with specific limitations, to be of practical utility, although true in some sense, it is likely, when taken literally, to contain as much falsehood as truth.

Their value consists in formulating principles or ideas of general acceptance—not so much to fix an unvarying specific rule, as to draw a line, or make a fixed point of departure, for distinct truths beyond. For obviously in all matters of opinion, as in science, it abbreviates discussion, and helps toward reaching truth in the particular, to have, as a starting-point, something that is conceded by all to be true, in the general.

SHORTNESS OF LIFE.

Few people come to the full measure of the fair duration of human life. Some do, indeed, survive even four score years or more ; yet how many of their early contemporaries such persons outlive. Often they see fall by the wayside their companions, whose chances of long life were once apparently as good as—nay, often better than, their own. The majority of mankind, however, do not in fact die in the ordinary course of nature, or from unavoidable disease. Far the greater number either come to death from accidental causes, or bring death upon themselves by some act of imprudence—or perhaps unconscious personal recklessness—which might apologetically be called involuntary suicide.

BOOKS.

It is too common a mistake to count acquaintance with books as learning or its equivalent. It is an old observation that a man's knowledge consists only in that which he has taken into his mind by assimilation, and not merely by crude possession. Memorizing is simply the first step. Books are well called the tools of learning. To know them is not in itself knowledge, but to know how to use them may lead up to it. Miscellaneous books, however, are often of little use in this respect. A majority of those generally read without method are simply useful to amuse the idle, or soothe the weary. Too many books now-a-days are chiefly occupied with profitless criticism, or idle history of, or gossip about other books, and their writers' vagaries.

WAYS OF THOUGHT.

There are divers ways by which a man may satisfy his mind in the pursuit of truth upon any subject. One instructive method is, after carefully canvassing different errors concerning the matter in hand, to contrast one error with another. The true line may be suggested sometimes by the point of crossing in the devious ways that lead astray. Often again the verity of the true path seemingly may be determined by comparing it (when believed to be ascertained) with others that have been proved to be false. Thus, by the foil of error, truth will be made often to shine with a brighter light.

RECOGNIZED GREATNESS.

Among the earliest balking impressions forced upon the attention of an ambitious youth is the suspicion that fame generally too hardly is earned and too slowly accorded,

As he studies history, visits cities, or walks the great art galleries of the world (where are gathered the emblems of the deeds, or the figures, of heroes) one of the first lessons taught him is that with rare exceptions—such as of a few persons pre-eminent in art or poetry—they appear to be men much past middle life. Next, he discovers that those who are, by universal estimate, accounted great, have already died. Finally, he learns that even these were not so esteemed, generally, until after death had silenced envy, rivalry, and detraction, among their contemporaries.

IDEAS.

Men's ideas appear to be greatly dependent upon the quantity or condition of the blood in the brain. When that blood is sluggish there is little or no thought—lazy dreams swarming in the imagination or flitting through the fancy. When there is too much of this blood, the ideas are correspondingly gorged, crowded, or confused. But when the circulation is lively and regular there is a happy flow of clear and, generally, pleasant thoughts.

THE PAST.

Unwise as it may be to look mournfully, or much any way, into the past of our lives, at the least, we may note our wasted opportunities, in matters in respect to which there is still time in the present, or may be in the future, to supply deficiencies, or yet to do what we may have left regretfully undone. So, too, may we cherish hope, that—like sleep—is a " balm of hurt minds."

AMUSEMENT.

For a man who is himself without either enthusiasm or any vagrant impulses, it seems often laughable to look on and see how large a part of the world—when removed from the necessary cares of a struggle for existence—is actually hard, if not painfully at work merely for self-amusement. Yet what worse torment can be suggested to the ordinarily intelligent man than enforced idleness? Even the common prison convict proverbially pines and grows mad, or dies under it.

LABOR.

True life must be built up, or grow, and develop by discipline, and by work. Where it involves neither, it may bring joy or doom, but it hardly deserves the name of human-life. It is inconsecutive, casual, and little better than an animal existence. Work is the only human amends for the loss of Eden.

SHREDS OF CHARACTER.

There is a kind of character in thy life,
That, to the observer, doth thy history
Fully unfold.
Measure for Measure.

A Painter's Tale.

ANY years ago I was living entirely alone. My pecuniary tide was at a low ebb. I was hourly tormenting myself about ways and means—how to raise the wind—how to pay my landlord.

.   .   .   .   .   .

I was residing in the city of New York—a poor painter in a very poor way. I was out at the elbows, very hard pressed with duns of many sorts, and had scraped together simply money enough to buy a rectangular piece of canvas, two feet by three. I was kept alive by the charity of a stout old woman who had long maintained a huckster's stall in Fulton Market. She allowed me to have daily a few boiled potatoes and a little bread —the remainder of her own frugal meal. I slept upon my overcoat and a rough travelling shawl, thrown upon the floor in my studio.

This studio deserves a slight description. It was in the basement of a large building adjoining Trinity Church-yard, accessible from both Broadway and Thames street. The light was quite feeble. I was obliged, in the darker hours of the day, as well as by night, to supplement it by tallow candles—which a grocer's boy kindly furnished me, upon credit, for my first week or two, with the promise of double pay in future. I had worked for many days upon my canvas, much embarrassed by the struggling light of my new studio—having been accustomed to better things.

I had sketched in outline an allegorical subject—something about Faith feeding Hope and Despair, while the latter two were fighting over their eleemosynary diet. It had become a mass of figures busily engaged in some absorbing occupation ; but somehow I could not make the composition tell its story—if any it had to tell. It had, however, at least one peculiarity common to many allegorical works of attempted high art. It suggested to the inquisitive observer the familiar dialogue between the managerial showman and the rustic visitor :—" Which is the monkey, and which is the polar bear ? "—" Just vich you please, my dear ; you pays your money, and you has your choice." However, I was not a mere beginner. I had been painting with great enthusiasm, labor, and patience, for several years—having begun when a mere stripling — and at different times had been rewarded with some private, though intermittent success. Yet hitherto I had not challenged really either public attention, or the malignity of critical connoisseurs, or even the amiable jealousy of fellow-artists.

But I was enthusiastic and ambitious to the verge of romance. This painting was designed to be my *chef d'œuvre ;* and I wrestled over its difficulties—by night as by day—with a Sisyphean incessancy. The achievements of the demi-gods of pictorial art warmed my imagination and sustained my hand. I could throw a good deal of verisimilitude into the expression of the face of my figure of Despair—drawing inspiration doubtless from the feelings that often overcame me while laboring with it. I had detected a gleam of light in the eyes of the grocer's boy when he brought me my candles that I endeavored to transfer to the looks of my figure of Hope. But although both of these subjects were unsatisfactory, neither of them gave me one half the trouble I had with Faith.

She continued vague and unsubstantial. Despite my zeal to give her body and form, she seemed to come out of some mythical world, where a body may be too unreal to cast a shadow, and perhaps even a voice cannot provoke an echo.

My market-woman, despite all the ruggedness becoming to her occupation, had a fine motherly face, and clearly looked upon me as a forlorn child, who might grow some day to be a man of note. An almost saintly smile used to come over her countenance when I told her I soon would be able to repay her kindness. She would tell me not to bother over that matter but to work away with all my strength, and some day she would ask the privilege of coming to look at my pictures. Yet, do what I could, that ineffable smile was too much for my brush. I could not afford to hire models. To guide me, I was forced to rely upon others' sketches, memory of

actual life, and what is sometimes called in art "inspiration"—oftentimes, by the way, as I then began to
think, a poor affair for either artist or poet without
"whiskey" to set it going. I tried in vain to give to my
phantom of Faith the sweet, self-sustaining look of
my dear old preserver. It would not stick upon the
canvas.

One evening, regardless of the flight of time, I had sat
late at my work. Perhaps it was near midnight. The
bells of old Trinity were ringing out more hours than I
had patience to count. I was fretted and distressed with
the slow progress of my picture. If it was to be of any
benefit to me, I must have it ready to send, and take its
chances for the exhibition of the National Academy of
Design, in a fortnight. Yet it lacked much to convey my
idea or to be what I well knew it ought to be, or even
what I felt I had, at times within me, the power to make
it. Faith had deserted me ; Hope was slipping from my
grasp, and Despair was already tempting me to abase my
art to a mere mechanical trade.

While in this quandary—nervous and exceedingly
excitable, for starvation was staring me in the face, indeed almost had me in its merciless gripe—I was suddenly startled and aroused by a gentle but firm tap, loud and
single, at my only door. Who could this be ? Who, at
this time ? I opened the door cautiously, rather apprehensive of something hostile. In front of it stood a well-
dressed gentleman, some sixty years of age, who asked
me, with a very polite accent, if I were an artist who
painted portraits ? Upon my rather eager reply in the
affirmative, without being invited he walked unhesitatingly

into my humble studio, and, taking the only vacant chair, asked me to paint him as he sat.

I made no answer. A horrid sense of formication ran all over me. I began to shiver like one partly encased in snow. Somehow I seemed to believe my proffered sitter was dead, and that he had just come out of the neighboring churchyard ! It appeared to me perfectly natural he should have done so. My boyish terror of the dead and my dread of being a visitor of their resting-place at midnight, had never been outgrown. Unlike Goethe—who is said systematically to have laughed and braved it out of himself in early life—I had nourished rather my childish apprehension, in such matters, until I had become matured as a man. It still clung to me with a tenacity not unlike the octopan clasp of a New-England-bred conscience. I could not pass even at this age through a graveyard without my heart thumping, my knees inclined to knock and my teeth to chatter.

Here, now, I had my pet horror in the concrete—as one might say, its essence double distilled. I fidgeted about the room a little—moved a bench—turned " Faith, Hope, and Despair " to the wall and resumed my seat, facing my lively *cadaver*, but saying not a word. Indeed I could not—I believed—utter a syllable. What should I do ? The wicks were burning long in my candles. From the movement of the air in the room, they sputtered desperately, making the light flicker in a most exasperating, and, as I fancied, spectre-like way. I felt as if my head were made of wood. My mouth was dry as a potsherd, and I was completely tongue-tied. The suspense was becoming awful.

14

After this dismal state of things had continued for some moments—which to me seemed hours—my mysterious stranger opened the way himself. He briefly told his story. He was indeed dead—and had been buried—as I had more than suspected. He could not have shaken easily my conviction on that subject; little as this fact commended him to my good graces.

He had been a physician of great wealth, a member of a family of prominent social condition in the city, and had died recently quite suddenly. A great affliction to his widow and children was added to their natural bereavement by the circumstance that they had not even a photographic likeness of him. He desired me to paint his picture as he sat, and carry it to his family, who would be glad to recompense me handsomely for it. His name was well known to me, although I had never seen him before. I could not—and perceived no reason to—doubt the truth of his simple story.

Immediately I set myself at work. He looked, talked, and moved as if in full life; and yet all the while I was conscious he was quite dead, and, although a visitant to it, did not now belong to this breathing world. However, it did not, even yet, appear to me in the least odd, that he and I should be there together or thus engaged. I soon forgot my embarrassment over " Faith, Hope, and Despair," and in my zeal over my newly-found task even lost all care for the proverbially inscrutable discretion of the notorious "hanging committee" of the Academy. An unusual power and felicity seemed to nerve my hand, quicken my eye, and guide my brush. Although my canvas itself was the palimpsest of more than one rejected

picture, the memory of such failures did not discourage
me. I painted rapidly—with a will and enthusiasm born
of the weird mystery of the hour. Mine was not a case
of "youth at the prow and pleasure at the helm," but
rather of starvation at home and plenty ahead. In two
hours the work was done, just as my last candle was gut-
tering into winding-sheets and sending up an unearthly
glare of waning, palpitating light, while its last companion had already subsided into a greasy, sulphuretted car-
bon-like vapor, emitting an odor at least suggestive of the
archaic atmosphere of lost souls.

As I put down my palette and brush my sitter arose,
looked at the painting, and expressed himself as highly
gratified. Saying I should see him again (*horresco
referens*) with a gracious bow he departed. I laid down
upon my hard bed—little less downy in fact than Othello's
metaphorical "flinty and steel couch of war"—quite
exhausted, and soon was soundly asleep. I was lost even
to the last ray of sub-consciousness, and, as I now understand it, without even the semblance of a dream.

When I awoke it was quite late in the morning. The
sun was bright and fighting its intrepid way through the
dingy panes of my window which, though small, faced to
the southeast. I arose quickly, a good deal dazed. I fancied I had been disturbed by a species of nightmare, born
of fasting and exhaustion, as I recalled the startling incidents of my improbable adventure. I did not at first
doubt it was a dream, pure and simple. I rubbed my
smarting eyes again and again, while gazing, with a singular feeling of the unreality of everything around me, at
the still fresh painting upon my easel. There it was surely ;

the size of life—a head and shoulders ; good in color, natural in position and expression. In spite of an enforced modest appreciation of my own artistic powers, I felt compelled to acknowledge it an excellent piece of workmanship. I tried to criticise it severely. It was neither cold, hard nor raw in color, stiff in outline, nor ungraceful in posture. On the contrary, my first impressions were reassured. It was graceful, gentle, glowing with kindness, and seemed almost able to breathe and speak ; nay, seemingly inclined to do so, but resting under a sweet and dignified self-restraint.

I dressed rapidly—the exigencies of my toilet being few and simple—and hurried impatiently, with my prize, into the narrow street beside my room, where I hoped to get a better light. Here, although my opportunity for seeing the picture favorably was still very imperfect, again I was charmed with the results of my night's work. There was no dream about all this. It was reality indeed, of a very satisfactory sort. I felt quite hungry, but restrained my appetite, with a single dry crust of bread, and went forthwith to seek a frame-maker, who had befriended me more than once in my sorest needs.

He kindly mounted the picture, of which he readily recognized the likeness. Finding me with apparently such good opportunities he freely gave me credit for a plain, rich frame, sufficiently large, and well modelled and moulded, to give full effect to the painting. I wrapped up my still moist treasure very carefully, and about eleven o'clock in the day I went up-town to ascertain the residence of the family of the defunct.

I had been so well directed by my ghostly visitor I

found the house without difficulty. I was ushered by a liveried servant into a rather large and plain, but well furnished reception-room, where, after a brief interval, the widow, who was a benevolent-looking lady of some forty summers, dressed in deep mourning, came to meet me. I asked her, in a somewhat rapid and excited manner, if she were a judge of human nature and could keep a secret, and were not afraid to hear the story of a stranger, which I alleged, in rather a mysterious way, affected her interests, but was marvellous, beyond ordinary belief. If she were afraid of me she might have others present ; yet I preferred to tell what I had to say to herself quite alone.

At first she put on rather a curious expression, somewhat between a smile of incredulity and a look of rigid firmness. I perceived at once she thought I was mad. Nor was I surprised at her inference. She was about to place her hand upon a bell when I begged her not to misunderstand me, for I was wholly in my senses, and she need have no apprehension of me. Moreover, to reassure her, I offered to begin my story at the end.

Upon this she hesitated and looked scrutinizingly at my countenance while I unwrapped my picture, and, the light being good, she had a fair chance to see it to advantage. She uttered a faint shriek and settled down upon a chair, with her eyes fixed upon the painting, as if she had no will or power to remove them. Thus we sat for what seemed nearly half an hour ;—I holding the portrait and she gazing at the face of her lost husband.

It afterwards came to my knowledge that she had made every effort in vain to get a likeness of him, who had been in life so dear to herself and her children ;—without even the least hope of success. Two or three eminent artists of the city had essayed to do the work from description, and others from personal acquaintance with the deceased. The results were all failures of the worst sort—exaggerating peculiarities of features and expression, making fearful caricatures of a singularly difficult subject—and had been rejected with ill-disguised horror.

After a while the lady recovered her composure, and wondered how I had done this extraordinary thing. The likeness was indeed marvellous ; while the favorite posture and most loved expression of face had been accurately preserved. Of course she supposed it had been wrought out from memory, or at least from hearsay. I assured her I had known nothing of her husband beyond a remembrance of an honored name—and even that had passed out of my mind until the night before. When her astonishment had had full vent, and she had become completely puzzled, and had abandoned all hope of conjecture, I begged her to hear quietly my whole story, and then I would leave the picture with her. She might make what inquiries about myself she thought proper, and, when she was entirely satisfied, the painting was her own, and my compensation was wholly subject to her pleasure.

I told my story from beginning to end without a pause or interruption. She listened with all the eagerness of a Desdemona—although not prompted by any interest in myself, beyond the tale as it affected her own family affairs. Again and again big tears rolled down her cheeks despite all effort at self-restraint, and I could not fail to see here was a truly bereaved wife, whose tender heart still clung to its lost darling. By some instinct—I cannot well define and would be ashamed to characterize— I felt assured my fortune was made—that I had gained a friend by whose aid I should climb up and out of the pit of poverty, and be set upon the high road to prosperity. I was yet quite a young man, and this kind-hearted woman already seemed to feel a degree of sympathy for me, such as is seldom found except between a mother and a son.

After a pause of some minutes—during which she seemed irresolute, as if doubtful in what way to make me understand her feelings—in order to give her ample time for reflection before committing herself, I arose abruptly, saying that, as I was an entire stranger to her and my story was on its face incredible, I would beg leave to go, and would ask permission to call upon her again after she had taken time to reassure herself and make such inquiry concerning me as she thought fit. One thing alone I requested—that the supernatural part of my narrative should remain forever a secret between ourselves.

Somehow she had gotten an idea that I was destitute and nearly starving. With a degree of delicacy that was hardly necessary in dealing with a famished man, she accepted my proposal to quit her, adding with a gracious and maternal smile, that as I was leaving a valuable work with a stranger, at least I need not hesitate to receive from her a trifle, on account of it, until she could see me again.

Placing a twenty-dollar gold piece in my hand, she asked my address, and I left her. Oh, that coin! With what a miser's grip I clutched it. I blushed like a boy, with alternate shame and gratification, as I held it up to my own wondering eyes. I was half inclined to throw it away at one moment—and the next I pressed it to my lips, as if I had been a Midas. A hungry Midas I was indeed ; but almost a fool in my excitement.

As common-sense, however, soon crept up from my empty stomach and demolished the sentimental nonsense swarming in my brain, I made my way directly to a restaurant, in what is now lower Broadway, kept by an Italian named Bardotti. Here I had a breakfast just after mid-day that might have satisfied a shipwrecked gourmet who had not snuffed the savor of a hissing gridiron for a month.

My next visit was to a tailor's shop, where ready-made clothes were furnished. There I purchased a coat that made me look perhaps less like the typical artist of that day, but certainly rather more conventional. After this decoration I strolled about the crowded streets for some hours—enjoying the sunshine and the sight of the pretty female shoppers and promenaders, until I began once more to realize that life was before me, and :—

> Hope told a flattering tale,
> That Joy would soon return.

A night's sound sleep in a clean bed at a good hotel, and an ample breakfast the next day, filled the blood-vessels of my brain, and I felt once more that I could paint. My ambition and consciousness of power rose rapidly. In the latter part of the day I returned to my dingy studio, where I found a note from my last bene-factress desiring to see me. I called without delay. I was received again graciously, and paid a handsome price for my picture. The amount is an artist's secret. Torture could not wring it from me.

Suffice it to say it was ample to set me agoing in a good studio, with proper paraphernalia. My old friends, the market-woman and the grocer's boy, shared my good luck. I was promised favorable notice by my new-found friend, and in a very short time I had several portraits under way. Soon a flattering description of one of my pictures appeared in a leading newspaper, and business began rapidly and copiously to flow in upon me. It got whispered abroad that I had—or pretended to have—some preternatural gift or assistance, and could—if not raise, at least —paint the dead from an imperfect sketch or verbal description—or even less !

This reputation resulted in many orders, some quite absurd in their demands or expectations, and not a few very lucrative in their consequences. By some chance or inspiration—diabolical or otherwise—I did achieve often what was really marvellous and passed for supernatural success. Whether my courage imparted skill, or collusion with the rambling tenant of a charnel-house guided my hand, or the easy faith of my patrons supplied my deficiencies, I am disinclined further now to suggest. Enough to say, the public was satisfied, and I was amply paid.

This course of events continued for a long time. Years of prosperity passed on. I became famous. I grew rich, and consequently fashionable ;—without a resort to the "salting" of a gold mine, or even the stale sybaritic trick of going into bankruptcy and living upon a wife's collusive income. I gave up all my noble aspirations for high art. I devoted myself to pure money-making with inordinate greed. I turned my back, with a miser's disdain, upon the Academy of Design, and let the friendly dust gather upon my allegory of " Faith, Hope, and Despair." The leading painters of the city sneered loftily at my good fortune. But every open sneer brought me one or more additional orders for portraits ; and I demurely, with inward exultation, pocketed the affront.

Yet there was a heavy drawback to all my apparent glory and princely fortune. I was single, solitary, and heart-hungry almost to desperation. I had little fondness for male friendships, but woman was my idol. I fell in love repeatedly, and as often fled conscience-stricken from the several objects of my attachment.

I felt I was a doomed man and unfit for the intimate association of marriage with a confiding and sensitive mate. I lived in a cloud and walked in a vain shadow. The cause of all this was the most wonderful part of my career. Strange to tell, I never was really quite alone ! My dead sitter was always my companion—more constant than my shadow. By day or by night, in daylight or in darkness, whenever I opened my eyes, he stood or sat beside me. All speech had left him ; in other respects he never changed. He seemed to have some diabolical hold upon me as the founder of my fortune, and to claim me as his own. He had made me all I was. My society was apparently the penalty I was compelled to pay him for my unconscious league with the Powers of Darkness.

There was no ransom permissible, and release was hopeless while my life lasted. My blood curdles now as I think of it. Needless to say, I tried many a ruse to escape him, but with no success. He would not go, and

I could not elude him. He wearied me beyond my power of expression. He was invisible to others, but to me he seemed always even " sensible to feeling as to sight."

It would lead me far beyond the scope of this sketch were I to attempt even an outline of the vicissitudes of my strange life as I climbed the ladder of notoriety and wealth. At some future day I may reveal the incidents of this by-play with my ghostly companion before I was finally rid of him.

. . . . . .

One summer night I was sitting alone—except for the presence of my tormentor—at a very late hour, reading some book of Hume, the well-known Spiritualist. I began to fancy, from some of his more obscure observations, the writer must have had an experience not unlike my own.

I grew very intent in my study of the phenomenon then oppressing me, and had not observed that a gaslight was dangerously near the curtains of my window. A sudden gust of wind brought them in contact with the blaze. In an instant I was in the midst of fire.

I rushed furiously at the hanging drapery, but too late. The flames were already out of my reach. I inhaled the fire and smoke. Inwardly, as well as externally, I was being burned alive. I shouted " Fire ! " and strove to get out of the room ; but blinded as well as choked, I could not find the door. Presently I heard an unearthly clatter in the street below, and almost in a second a monstrous jet of water drenched me to the skin. My next recall of consciousness was the sense of my being put upon a mattress in front of my old studio in Chapel Street, New

Haven, and told to lie still until I could be placed in a carriage and taken to a hospital.

By degrees I realized a painful fact, that everyone around me had known for some hours. I had been sitting beside my window and had fallen asleep there. The curtains had taken fire, and my rude awakening from a long trance was due to the fireman's hosepipe, that so hastily brought all the airy belongings of my castle of happiness and misery to a watery grave. And so, by the ordeal of fire and water, I escaped the clutches of the evil one. My fabled life of avarice ended in a pyre of smoke and ashes. Yet I never forgot its moral, so well expressed by Allston :—" The love of gain never made a painter, but it has marred many."

METROPOLITAN PREACHERS.

In our large cities those who attend places of public worship from curiosity, chiefly in pursuit of pulpit eloquence, are inclined to become fastidious, if not hypercritical. Naturally hard to please, they seek the kind of speaking that best suits their particular temperament or taste, rather than their dogmatic belief. To such observers there are apparently certain broad distinctions in the manner, as well as in the essential traits of city clergymen, by which, in view of a nice sense of fitness to such special individual needs, some of them may be roughly classified. Without attempting to embrace all who are conspicuous either by their adaption to the demands of their particular congregations, or by their general efficiency in satisfying the function of their high office, it may not be unprofitable—from the point of view suggested—to outline two or three of the leading types that arrest popular attention—indicating merely the genus—leaving the reader to collate the species that may be classified under each head.

First in rank—of those now referred to—as nearest in spirit at least to the example of the Divine Master, is the Enthusiast. He may or not have talent, learning, eloquence, rhetoric, or a superior manner ; but at least he has sincerity, earnestness, singleness of purpose, forgetfulness of self, love of his fellow-men, devoutness, and, above all, entire, unwavering, unshakable faith in the miraculous birth, vicarious mission, works, and resurrection of the Saviour, as well as in an almost literal interpretation of all the startling promises and menaces of divine Revelation. Beyond this he is under a vivid, never-faltering conviction that he has been called himself specially to be wholly a man of God, and as such devoutly to give his time, without stint, together with all his strength and capacity for labor, to expounding and illustrating, both by precept and by the example of his daily life, the divine theory of eternal salvation to men ; and to persuading them to live this life only in such manner as shall more assuredly win for them the glorious and immeasurable reward that awaits the saints in the endless life to come.

Next in the order of merit might be put what may be called the Formalist. This term would represent a very large class. Such an one never offends propriety, or trenches upon received opinion, inside or outside of established theological dogmas. The most devout never flutter at his daring, nor would the lukewarm or the careless ever be stirred by any moral magnetism, or any impulsive sympathy on his part. Coldly correct and classically dull, he furnishes such an element in the composition of divine worship as the wooden idol does to the undoubting pagan—a spiritual director who receives all his inspiration from those he is supposed to inspire, and a reflector that shines only by a borrowed light. He has no fire within. It is not the case of a flame that has merely subsided or gone out. None has ever burned or really glowed.

He has come into the profession as a man grows up to be a clerk in a mercantile business. He began life with a plan made by his family sponsors for him, and his easygoing, tractable nature has kept him within its lines as contentedly as is the ox in his transit from the pasture to the plow or back again. He reads, prays, and preaches with precision and good taste ; he never offends a prejudice, touches a nerve, or gives a pain. He is always in the line and never straggles. Indeed, all his duties are performed with scrupulous exactness. Possessed of the genius of commonplace and the soul of propriety, he is respectable and respected. Indeed, he may be relied upon always, and upon all occasions, to do the right thing at the right time and in the right manner.

The rich cultivate and the poor fear and unwittingly worship him. He is one of those who "live of the sacrifice," and are "partakers of the altar." He makes no enemies. He is honored and made the recipient of all worldly comforts by his followers in the most gracious way, because they inwardly congratulate themselves (for the most part unconsciously) that they are doing good deeds, and paying tribute to God and religion by bestowing benefactions upon a genuine vicegerent of the Almighty. This comes to be so much a matter of course, and the good understanding between pastor and parishioner is so perfect, that in things spiritual and things moral—so far as outward manifestations may go—he is practically their conscience-keeper and their priestly master.

Beloved however as he is in a formal way by his own people, he has but little attraction for others outside his fold. He is part of a socio-spiritual organization, and he is interesting—to those who contemplate him inquisitively from without—only as the visible organ of a useful combination, or social machine. He never provokes the understanding, stirs the blood, startles the conscience, fires the imagination, wakes the passions, rouses the fears, or exalts the hopes of a stranger. His mission does not invade alien territory. His limitations confine him to his own country, and his own people. With them he lives and dies. When he is gathered to his fathers with due pomp and honor, another, as nearly like him as may be found, takes up and fills the same official round of duties and labors.

After the Formalist next in importance among the masters of the dynamics of visible piety—or outward religious observance—comes one who, with due reverence, (for want of a better word of characterization) may be styled the Actor. He is both mimetic and dramatic. He has a part to fill, and he knows his cue "without a prompter"—for he is a born player. He may be earnest or not, commonplace or not, but at all times and in all places he has a rôle to play, and he plays it *secundum artem.* If he plays ill he descends in the social scale until he reaches his level, and his audience comes up from the hedges and ditches, delighted to see him in his bravery. But if he rise to the grand manner that his theme can and ought to inspire, if he have eloquence and sense, voice and rhetoric, besides personal magnetism, and that vast appreciation of self which makes the stamen of the hero, and this shall be coupled with the practical sagacity that keeps turned away, from public sight, the side that shows how much of it may be unfounded self-conceit ; if he shall have all these, and, in the prime of his manhood or even the efflorescence of a glorious youth, shall have captured that protean witch, success, then you have a man who thrills the world—a man whom men are proud to follow—a man who is deemed fit even to glorify God.

True, there will be some Diogenes-like critics who, in their ragged pride, disdain to follow the crowd, and whose eyes penetrate beneath royal purple and see nothing but meagre bones. Still they are few and far between, and their shrill voice of disapprobation is lost in the swarming murmur of half-suppressed applause ;—as the hum of myriad insects sometimes drowns the harsher cricket's cry in our summer meadows. He is the hero of popular applause, and he lives by inhaling the incense he makes to arise from the sacred altar, with the fire of his own eloquence and theatrical action.

After these great figures comes a herd of many stripes ;— of lesser importance, though harder to classify. There is the Common-routine preacher, who year by year follows the same method or formulas ; preaches only what has the stamp of authority upon its very letter ; who conducts all his round of business with exact formality, and with endless repetition unvarying as the sun, and moves as if an automaton. He does not suggest the idea that he has any special personality or any hearty sympathies in common with his race. He is not unlike the Formalist in many things, but moves on a lower plain, and within a narrower circle.

Then there is the Rough-and-ready parson, who is easily an iconoclast without knowing it. Possessed of vulgar manifest self-conceit, and intrinsically ignorant of what most of his profession regard as essential to his sacred office, he is not unlike the fabled "bull in a crockery shop," and smashes things generally, with no capacity to mend them. Indeed, he has but little appreciation of the mischief he does in up-setting beliefs, destroying convictions and vulgarizing things that centuries of hallowed association have made dear to the human heart and consecrated to the noblest feelings of our nature. He is a "cheap fellow"! But he draws a gaping crowd, who believe him sincere—as perhaps he is—and foolishly esteem him to be a man of genius—a man of the people, and one who will soar sometimes beyond the common restraints of propriety, only to snatch a grace from some higher and holier law of his own gifted being!

Besides there is the Charlatan, pure and simple, who believes nothing, and who loves none but himself, and who :—

Plays such fantastic tricks before high heaven
As make the angels weep.

After him there come varying kinds, not worth while here to signalize by special mention, in this limited cate-

15

gory ;—to say nothing of the great class of pure, simple, holy men, who by their learning, piety, wisdom, and spotless lives ennoble human nature and glorify their calling.

A Melancholy Man's Devices.

There is a kind of heart-ache that occasionally seems to come over some men, without any tangible cause. It is rather a negative condition, except for a yearning or heart-hunger that is not uncommonly its attendant. Be it spleen, or vapors, or hypochondria, or simple sadness, it is all-powerful in mental—and perhaps moral—repression. It leads one to doubt the value of all human endeavor, and to ask, of even virtue itself, *cui bono ?*—with no satisfactory, or at least no comforting, answer. This low state of feeling—stagnation of blood and apathy of brain— sometimes tends to desperate acts, such as reckless gaming, intoxication, debauchery, or even suicide. It can overcome the strongest man, if he be emotional, imaginative, and moody by nature as well as solitary or isolated by habit, and prone to :—

Chewing the cud of griefe and paine.

It is truly a morbid state, that should be dealt with rather as a disease than as a wilful offence against the laws of cheerful social propriety. How may it be warded off, or conquered when it has taken hold of one ?

Many find consolation in their religion ; and, by prayer or confession or both, are enabled to lean upon the Strong Arm, and to cast their burden upon that support. To some, however, this mode of relief appears to be denied. Others seek by love, affection, or benevolence to warm the chilled current of their souls. Although ordinarily irrational, and powerless for self-surrender to a conviction of the judgment, it may yield sometimes to force of will—when this can be invoked—except so far as it may be purely physical. In that case the black choler first must be subdued, by drugs or change of air, or more.

My friend Tristis is, and has been from birth, a melancholist. Possibly he suffers, in his late generation, for an abuse of nature by some remote ancestor. He is a scholarly man, of independent fortune, fastidious in his tastes, and a sincere lover of mankind. He tries to bear his vicarious punishment—if such it be—manfully, and to mitigate its severity with a practical philosophy. Recently he told me that, after testing many expedients, he had formulated a few plain rules for his self-conduct ; to which he could turn and yield, as to a command, when the demon of melancholy took possession of him. " For," said he, " it is a fact, that I sometimes suffer a sort of paralysis of will, and without such artificial aids I am almost powerless to take the first step toward my disenthralment. By these means, however, it is frequently practicable for me to dispel these evil humors—as the physicians of the last century used to call them."

A few of these formulas have been here copied from his note-book, as possibly useful to his fellow-sufferers, if any there be, of like affliction :

I.—Ascertain, by careful survey and rigid self-examination, the actual extent of your discomfort, also how far your apparent troubles are real and how far imaginary.

As a criterion of this write them down, one by one, honestly, and without color or exaggeration. You may thus the better estimate their importance or insignificance ;

II.—Determine, with judicial fairness, and unsparing impartiality, how far the evils you suffer may be a just punishment (which you ought to bear without complaint) for your personal violation or neglect of some natural law, whether physical, intellectual, moral, or social ;

III.—Consider how many of your acquaintances, whose circumstances and condition you know—who may be quite as worthy of the smiles of good-fortune as yourself —are suffering from ills of greater magnitude than your own ; or how far you have reason to rejoice that, in any respect, your lot is easier and happier than theirs. If you are inclined to envy any one for his placidity of temper, remember that many who seem to be thoroughly self-contained, are like streams in no danger of overflowing their banks, simply because—their sources being feeble and their waters shallow—they have so little to hold. The sympathies of such people also usually are limited to themselves ;

IV.—As a means of finding diversion, or restoring a normal state of mind, and bringing cheerfulness out of gloom, try some of the suggestions now to be named ;—

1.—Write out, with detail, your most troublesome thoughts or reflections, in a terse style—in order to see how far they will bear such a statement. Having revised them carefully and honestly, read them critically again and again, pruning severely—and then burn them.

2.—Select some familiar topic of thought or opinion, respecting which you differ essentially from the community in which you are living ; write down your peculiar views, without mincing phrases, but severely testing their conformity to written reason; revise, read—and burn them as the last.

3.—Visit places of public amusement, galleries of pictures, libraries, or museums of curiosities; try to find some desultory distraction, by casually seeing busy men, and observing current things, or by reading, superficially and miscellaneously, the lighter literature of the day.

4.—Take up some interesting old or odd book that may arouse and keep your attention amused; continue to read it so long only as it is absorbing or very agreeable.

5.—Seek the society of those whose tastes are thoroughly congenial. By conversation, or by pleasure excursion, or some other general amusement, get you outside of yourself, and aloof from your broodings, as widely and quickly as you may.

6.—Go into the open air—driving, riding, sailing, walking, or the like ; but never alone.

7.—Begin some severe work, either of business or amateurship ; endeavor to give it your whole mind.

8.—So soon as you find yourself strongly interested, in any occupation that involves no egoity, give your full strength to it. Nay, do not hesitate to commit yourself to the execution of what you have undertaken, so far, that your self-respect, or love of the good opinion of your fellow-men, will make you ashamed to leave it unfinished.

9.—Alternate upon these rules, when practicable—as either one becomes irksome—until your fevered self-consciousness has acquired a normal pulse ; then resume your real life-work.

" By these simple devices," said my friend Tristis, " I can sometimes attest the merit of the well-known remedy prescribed, in somewhat similar cases, by Lady Macbeth's physician."

The Thirteenth Man in the Omnibus.

The common New York City omnibus was constructed so as to seat and carry twelve persons inside—certainly not more. When only twelve, of normal size, sit squarely on the seats, each one may ride with some degree of comfort. With these conditions, he may escape generally having his toes crushed, his shins kicked, his shoes soiled, or his trousers daubed with mud or dust by his neighbor. But this paradisiacal state is disturbed often by the wilful intrusion of the thirteenth man.

Shall I attempt to portray him? He is known pretty well, and perhaps the picture will be recognized by others, if not by himself. Sometimes he may be seen standing at the corner of a street, lying in wait for the " 'bus." He is never known to walk towards its starting-place, or to wait for the next stage, lest he might be confounded with the " twelve " by getting inside before the seats are filled. No ; he is nothing if not odd. His very hat never sits squarely upon his head like the hat of a gentleman. It is either elevated in front like a sophomore's, or depressed on one side as if he had just come from a cheap spree in the Bowery, or as if he were troubled with some obtrusive "bump " that kept his hat awry. If by chance he gets a seat inside the omnibus, he must cross his legs and wipe the mud from his ill-shod feet upon your trousers or your wife's dress.

Did he invent the vice of sitting cross-legged in a
public vehicle? Do savages ever sit in this manner when
in close company? I have never been able to imagine
what special human sin this ingenious mode of annoyance
was meant to punish. It has been suggested that it might
be this man's pantomimic protest against sitting at all.
The saddest commentary upon this vice of our hero is,
that by a mysterious magnetism of awkwardness and
ill-breeding he has betrayed into imitation of it some
men whose early education has been less neglected than
his own.

Sometimes, as he gets into the "'bus," he carries in his
hand or mouth the stump of a half-burned, extinct cigar,
which fills the atmosphere with a rank and sickening odor.
Frequently his well-worn black clothes reek with noisome
exhalations of stale pipe-smoke. Shall I finish his picture?

I see him now in my mind's eye. I am riding down-
town this morning in a Fifth Avenue omnibus. I have
just handed up my fare, and, taking my seat, have sur-
rendered myself to a sweet half hour of reverie. I disdain
to spoil my eyes, or waste my time by newspaper reading.
I dream ; and thus save my half hour for better things,
as I fancy.

The stage is full. "Twelve inside." The driver does
not seem to get along. He is constantly stopping or turning his horses to the sidewalk, right or left. You wonder
what is the matter. You begin to think the whole town
is striving to get a ride down with you in that particular
"'bus." At every street corner we linger or stop. Suddenly the door is pulled open with a jerk, and our enemy
leaps in. He sees the seats are filled ; but he does not

hesitate. There is always room for him. Indeed, his spirit rises with the occasion. He becomes pertinacious as he is offensive. He tramples upon more than one pair of feet in his struggle to reach the middle of the convey-ance. The passengers patiently submit to the intrusion, with that quiet good nature with which Americans usually suffer imposition, and public invasion of good manners or petty social rights. They seem to feel they can "stand it" if he can.

His mode of paying his fare evolves a climax of be-wildering impertinence. In order to have the free use of one hand, to pass his money to the box or driver, he grasps his cane or umbrella with the other hand by which he holds the rail or pendent strap. By this means he loses control of the lower end of his stick, which thereby be-comes an automatic instrument of torture, menacing your face and eyes in quite a savage way. Indeed, his apparant unconsciousness that he is a nuisance really approaches the innocence of a wild animal.

He appears to be a pet of the driver. Some thoughtless people wonder the drivers of omnibuses or street-cars should feel so charitably disposed toward the human family in general, as sometimes to take up even a crowd of extra passengers when all seats are filled. Short-sighted simpletons! Do you not see the pith of it? The more passengers, beyond the complement of the "'bus," or car, the more uncounted perquisites available for an ill-requited profession.

To return to our black sheep. Look where he stands. As he grows tired he grasps the straps on either side in order to steady himself. His attitude now appears to be

a cunningly devised mode of tormenting his fellow-pas-
sengers. Either elbow of our nondescript just reaches
the hat of your opposite neighbor or yourself. With each
jolt of the vehicle, by a little dexterity of movement—or
the want of it—he can knock their•hats over the eyes of
two persons at a time; and by a slight shifting of his position he can frequently bring down even four hats by a
single spasmodic lunge.

When he is fresh, as in the morning, and can hold his
own weight, he falls however, into his more natural posture. Would you know what that may be? Did you
ever observe one of the supposed descendants of the "lost
tribes" who once inhabited some parts of Chatham street,
dreamily waiting for a passing rustic? He is apparently
in a comatose state. His abdomen is drawn in ; his body
is bent like a section of a hoop ; his eyes are cast down ;
while both his hands are thrust deeply into his trouser's
pockets.

But I am weary of the subject, and stop by commending
the thirteenth man in the omnibus to curiosity-hunters, as
a fungous growth of humanity, nursed by the over-virtuous
forbearance of a suffering public.

A MISERABLE MAN.

Miser was a tall gaunt man of nearly seventy. His
hair was thin, and, like his beard, dry, loose, and iron-
gray. His face was seamed with wrinkles, his eyes dull
but sly and cunning. He stooped a good deal when
standing or walking. There was a little appearance of
feebleness or shambling in his gait. This might have

been the result of years, but seemed rather an involuntary and necessary betrayal of what might be called his furtiveness of character.

I had known him many years, but my acquaintance with his personal history was slight. He was formerly a practising lawyer in the city of New York, where I had met him. His class of cases had led him chiefly into the Courts, at a time when much of the business of the legal profession of the city was small in importance. Suits for slander, libel, assault and battery, and trespass were then far more frequent in the old courts of record than nowadays. As this kind of "practice" gradually fell into a sort of disrepute, and such legal affairs as are transacted almost wholly in an office became more engrossing and lucrative to him, he had been heard less of in public.

He was neither a good speaker nor a sound thinker. He could address neither a jury nor a court well or effectively. He was, however, a shrewd practising attorney—wonderfully versed in fees and costs, in petty devices and crafty expedients. By great diligence and thrift he had accumulated a good deal of money. He had indeed kept all he got. He had sagaciously invested his savings, and now he was rich by the chances of the times—although he had been only a working lawyer

I overtook him one morning going down-town. We walked together and I purposely set him talking. His easiest theme was himself. In fact that person had always been the central figure in all his serious views of life. His chief maxim had been, and still was : *Proximus sum, egomet mihi.* He was childless, a widower, and past the hope of safely marrying again.

He did not relish the subject of family affection, when our talk drifted in that direction. His discourse was indeed melancholy, and mostly disheartening. He had, as he confessed, lived, struggled, and toiled solely for himself. Business cares and the searching out of ways and means to possess wealth had, until within a few years past, occupied all his thoughts and busied all his time. Now he had more accumulated money in his possession than he could use fairly for himself during the possible remnant of his life. He had no longer any need of attending to business for lucre, nor had he any remaining love for work. Neither had he now—strange to say—a greed for money-getting, sufficiently absorbing to make him forgetful of his morbid consciousness of self-worthlessness. His desire to amass wealth was gone. This latter failure involved, in his view, the utterly stale unprofitableness of all else besides. He had worn out the one string in his harp of life, and, singularly, had survived even avarice. His loud lament to me was, that " he had nothing to do ! "

I reminded him that he had known many celebrities of the Bar, and had seen much of what had now passed away—the reminiscences of which would doubtless entertain and instruct those just coming before the public in his profession. Then why not at least amuse himself writing gossipy sketches—biographical or incidental—of those he had familiarly known ; also of what events he had seen or participated in, or of what had occurred generally in his time—among judges, lawyers, and suitors since gone to their long account ; or of celebrated causes—their scenes, events, trials, arguments and so on ?

He might perhaps live over again and re-enjoy his happiest days.

"Ah!" he said, with a despairing sigh, "who would read them?" I replied encouragingly,—"The young—those advancing in the profession; indeed, probably the public in general." He might illustrate a principle, embalm a good example, inculcate some wise precept—never stale, but always to be kept fresh and green—by striking illustration before the rising generation.

"Alas!" said he, with a tone of voice lower down in hypochondriacal depths than before, "I don't know these people and I take no interest in them. The truth is, I have no longer any zest for life. My contemporaries and friends have all retired from this mortal stage, and I am left standing alone—awkwardly waiting for the curtain to drop. Not even my surviving relatives interest my sympathies. They could not hide from me—were they to make the attempt, which they do not—the fact that they are looking forward eagerly to my welcome demise and the joyous cutting up of my estate!"

Not finding any encouragement, I was forced to recognize a case of atrophy of the heart and to cease my endeavors to resurrect this moral *cadaver*. It was dried up!

An Unlucky Man's Story.

We had known each other long. Our opportunities for getting on in life had not been dissimilar. While however I was running always close to the wind, luck seemed to wait upon my friend Felix, and easily to fill

his sails. Once I ventured to ask him why he was favored so much more, and how he had compassed so much
more of the substantial goods of life than myself. He
frankly answered :—" I too sometimes have been disposed to think you the more unfortunate, but upon fuller
reflection I doubt it.

" The reason why Fortune seems to have distributed
her favors so unequally I suspect to be that I have taken
more care to fortify against evil chances than yourself.
Were I to count even my mere pecuniary losses, I believe
I could show a heavier black list than you. But very
early in my practical life I began to make up, and set
aside, what a stockbroker would call a 'margin,' for
misfortune.

" As in my conduct I believe I have endeavored to
pursue what I supposed to be a just course—without being elevated by praise or depressed by blame, letting the
elevation of the one be a set-off as it were against the
depression of the other—so in like manner I strove
always to keep in mind the obvious truth that, owing to
a difference of surroundings, inequality of results, from
equal human effort, is a normal condition of things, and
naturally to be expected. In effect I was ever mindful
that, in order to be well provided against the assaults of
ill-fortune, one should accept an excess of good luck as
something to be put aside, and kept in reserve, to make
up the deficiency likely to result from the next bad turn.
Thus (if you will pardon my priggishness) I would say I
avoided, by discipline, both dejection and the pride of
prosperity—easily keeping steadily on in the even tenor
of my way.

"To illustrate : if I were to draw a prize in a lottery I would not say to my friends : 'Lo, here is a boon of Providence, let us spend it in merriment and extravagance.' On the contrary I would say to myself : 'This year the tree bears a double burden of fruit, another year it may be barren—I simply have my next crop in advance.' I also made it a rule, whenever bad luck touched me, to renew, and, as far as practicable, even redouble my exertions, merely in order to disperse the vapors of despondency ;—so that in the end ill-luck, no less than its opposite, often resulted in a material advantage to myself."

This surprising statement led me to say :—"How then did you avoid the inevitable consequences of this line of conduct? By natural sequence it seems you should have become a thorough miser, but I do not find you have made any headway toward sordidness." He rejoined :—"Not only as a matter of principle, and from inclination or taste, but also as a part of my plan and policy in the conduct of life, I have always lived expensively. I have spent a great deal of my income in gratifying the tastes of those around me—not forgetting (if I may say it) to give liberally to those who needed and desired my practical sympathy. Such conduct, besides tending surely to keep the heart open to charity, checks the tendency to grow miserly."

Our conversational episode having ended abruptly, I was awakened to the melancholy discovery that my state of hand-to-mouth impecuniosity had not come by chance, so much as by my own wilful improvidence.

A MEAN MAN.

A mean man is one who spends no money for himself but his own, and uses no property not belonging to him. He never borrows what he does not intend to repay. Neither is he lavish or even liberal in giving or loaning another's goods. He was a mean man of whom it was said :—" He got rich by minding his own business." He has no stomach for superfluities, and is therefore called niggardly. With him enough is as good as a feast. More than sufficient is not only wasteful extravagance, but a burdensome annoyance.

When I was a little boy I was taken by my mother to supper at the house of a Quaker. There being no servant waiting at the table, and, seeing that an aged Friend who sat beside me was not served with the chipped beef, I timidly volunteered to offer him the plate. Imagine my terror when he turned, and, fixing his mildly severe blue eyes upon me, said with deliberation, but so loudly and distinctly as to attract the attention of the whole table to my indiscretion :—" Thou seest I have cheese." Unquestionably in the outside world he would be called a mean man.

The mean man is content to be just. True, he gives and takes like other men—among his equals. But if he bestow charity, or benefactions, it will be upon those who need aid and who try to help themselves. He is intolerant of drones and spendthrifts.

A mean man is one who has not acquired the art of being esteemed a man of great liberality, either by plundering the public and giving to charity, or from the circumstance of parting with a small, near advantage, in the sure expectation of reaping a large remote personal reward. He neither can rob the few to give to the many ; nor the reverse. He has not the adroitness to throw away one card, in the game of life, in order to ensure the retaking of two—while posing as a model of disinterested benevolence.

He lacks the necessary imagination and recklessness (even if he had the inclination) to make a rogue. Although heartily despised by the thoughtless and the improvident, at the least always he will be rightfully esteemed honest ; for his motto, in all his dealings, is to owe no man anything and to render unto every one his due.

Unfortunately for his peace of mind, he is inclined to expect that others, in their dealings with himself, will do likewise. Hence even his friends call him an "exact" man; while to the eye of the world, that likes to reap where it has not sown, he always appears to be a mean man.

It was said of the late Duke of Bedford :—" Having begun life as a very poor man, he had contracted the habit of close attention to details of expenditure, and this habit passed with superficial observers for stinginess. He had the liveliest dislike of being cheated or overcharged, and he insisted on knowing the application of every disbursement he was called on to make. But when these requirements were satisfied, there were no bounds to his liberality, and where charitable giving was concerned he preferred that it should be anonymous."

A Man on Horseback.

He was a long, lean, yellowish-gray man. His hair, skin, and dress were each buff and gray intermingled,

His horse, lean as himself—long and rawboned—was a dingy sorrel. The man's legs dangled and the horse's legs sprawled. I laughed aloud when I saw these figures in the distance ahead of me. When I came up with him, while I was trying to keep my countenance, he saluted me, and we soon fell into a hap-hazard conversation. He talked much at random, as if thinking aloud ; scarcely heeding what I might say, even in answer to some of his rather impertinent questions. He seemed most happy when indulging in loose speculations uttered in a fierce declamatory style. I could but look and listen, with no little wonder at what manner of man this might be, whom I had thus encountered one early winter morning while riding in the city park. He professed to be a citizen ; having lately come here to live from some distant country town.

As we returned and were approaching the Fifth Avenue exit of the park, just as the sun was rising, he suddenly wheeled his horse a little nearer to my own, and looking off toward some newly-built and rather elegant dwelling-houses, near the park gate, of which I had previously spoken as well-designed, he exclaimed (as if addressing the buildings) with startling abruptness :—
" But what is there in this life anyway ? Nothing ! What is the use of living ? None—except to fit ourselves for the next world. This is but a stepping-stone to an hereafter. Why, man knows nothing. What does a man know ? I would like to have any gentleman tell me what man knows." This was delivered in a very high key—almost a yell. " True, we are told by the scientific that sound is produced by the vibration of the air.

16

But how does it produce it? That is the question. So they say these rocks are held together by molecular attraction? But what is that? Who has seen it? Man knows only what he sees. Bah! There is nothing in what he does see. Man knows one thing, and that is all knows. He knows the way to salvation. Good morning!"

This was the last I ever saw or heard of my mysterious equestrian companion. I often afterwards looked for him; but he seemed to have accomplished his mission toward me, and then to have vanished into the air, never to reappear.

THE WIDOW.

I saw her in a city railroad car. My attention was first drawn to her wedding-rings. She wore five upon one finger. As she held up her thin hands, I began involuntarily to count the epochs of her life;—very much as you would attempt to determine the age of a cow by the rings upon her horns. My guesses about her personal history grew very amusing—to myself. She seemed to be a person possessing great vitality, but not of the kind which belongs to people who give it to others. She was rather of that class who absorb the vitality of their neighbors.

I return to the rings. They were unlike in their degrees of thickness and apparently in their ages. The one lowest on the finger, or nearest the palm of the hand, was lightest; the next stronger and less worn, and so on till the last, which was still quite thick, fresh, and nearly new. Sometimes, as her eyes fell upon them, she, with her other hand, would press them back;—as if perhaps to assure herself there was still room for more.

She could not have been far from forty-five years of age; but her brow was smooth and serene, without a mark of care or anxiety, and indeed was indicative of a promise of constant youth. Her neck was slender, her face thin and her figure neither angular nor quite plump ; but something midway between. Her hair was a glossy, pure black, her complexion that of a brunette, but clear and healthy, her teeth small, regular, and well preserved, yet looked sharp and decidedly rodential. Indeed her thin face, vulpine jaw, and glittering teeth suggested that she might become dangerous to a man whenever she should set her head in his way. Her dress was mostly of simple black, with a little vigorous white rigidly peeping out here and there ;—as it were protesting against absolute widowhood, and giving her a rather determined appearance—as if she had " business " before her.

She had moreover throughout a kind of self-satisfied, yet withal a hungry look, as though to say : " I have done much to be sure, but I would like to do more ; "—and, as if she thought it fully as blessed for others to give, as for her to receive. In fine the impression she made was not altogether pleasant ; and being myself a single young man —sometimes called a good-looking fellow—an undefined dread seized me, such as appears to thrill and startle the fowls of a barnyard, while the shadow of a hovering hawk falls among them. When she left the car her very dress seemed to rustle aggressively ;—but I felt better after she had gone.

CONFIDENCES.

I once knew a woman who seemed insensibly to inspire —even in those who became only slightly acquainted with her—the conviction that she was always heartily in full sympathy with them.

It was a common circumstance with her to be made the recipient—often unwillingly on her part and never sought for by her—of the confidential disclosure of personal secret experiences by her casual associates, as well as by her more intimate friends.

As a matter of fact she had less than ordinary heartfelt interest in those who thus confided in her; but somehow, through her large mental capacity—combining imagination with knowledge of the world—she so readily divined and thoroughly comprehended what was revealed to her, without too circumstantial detail of matters painful to recount, that she seemed unavoidably to win these unreserved confidences of others.

As a curious phenomenon I used to study her manner in order to penetrate this mystery; and, aside from her wonderful moral intuition, I observed that she never asked a question or betrayed surprise. By this means she left the impression of a total absence of personal curiosity (a vulgar trait pretty sure to extinguish the warm gush of confidential revelations) and an apparently full anticipatory consciousness of all that was either told or suppressed;—without inquisitively waiting to hear, or stopping to conjecture, whether there was more to be disclosed.

Moreover she impressed those who thus talked with her as one placing implicit faith in what was said; and yet as being one from whom it was not only useless but unfair to attempt to conceal anything.

In respect to the use made by her of this extraordinary knowledge and information, a good deal of watchfulness enables me also to say that she never betrayed a confidence or repeated gossip. Though always full to exuberance of talk about circumstances and things, she seldom or never mentioned a person or personal events, or common hearsay about either.

A Beautiful Woman.

She was a " Beauty," both within and without. Nature seemed to have enjoyed her own handiwork, and had inspired this lovely model with a joyous spirit of apparently unending youth. The boundless elasticity and freshness of a magnetic temperament made her appear, both to herself and others, always young. Indeed, to be consistent, she ought never to have grown in years.

After she had passed forty-five she was an embodied anachronism. Her person—although still exquisitely fair —no longer quite harmonized with the soul she possessed. While in joyfulness of manner she remained a bright girl, she startled the eye by appearing as a gray-haired grandmother. She moved triumphantly through life's troubles, always gay and brilliant, careless of the shadows of the past, and radiant as a butterfly, flitting from one object to another in unbroken summer sunshine. When death took her at threescore she had not languished or faded, as other mortals do, for even in her shroud she was as surpassingly beautiful as she had been in her prime of health and juvenile loveliness.

A Shy Man.

He was as timid in his intercourse with the world, as a little maiden. In character he was not unlike those eggs we sometimes find—with no lime in their shell—which take something of the shape of whatever touches them. He appeared to have no moral vertebræ. He shrank from both public gaze and private scrutiny. His sub-consciousness seemed to be the outer covering, instead of inner core, of his personality. Being morbidly super-sensitive to the possibility of a refusal or a rebuff—while he constantly gave freely of his money, personal attention, and even influence, such as it was, to benefit others—he seldom accepted and never asked a favor for himself. Throughout life he courted obscurity, as a favorite, and found her a not unwilling mistress. "Blessed are they," said he, "of whom the world expects nothing, for theirs is the jewel of real independence."

A Moral Vagabond.

Though an accomplished scholar and accustomed to society ; having good social position, with large acquaintance among both men and women ; himself of exceptionally clever conversational powers, of agreeable manners, pleasing personal appearance and easy address ; yet he was a bore. Why was he a failure ? He had no earnestness or purpose in life. He seemed to be incapable of accomplishing or even of having any definite aim. His sentiments and opinions were fragmentary, or for the most part at war with the settled axioms of the society in which he moved. Indeed, he belonged nowhere. He was too insignificant to be a power, when standing alone, and he was no part of anything. He was simply himself —clever enough—but passed for a social idiot, and a moral vagabond !

SOCIAL HINTS AND STUDIES.

O vitæ philosophia dux ! . . . . Tu urbes peperisti ; tu dissipatos homines in societatem convocasti.

CICERO.

SOCIETY.

AN, when contemplated individually, and man, when considered socially—or as a part of that human aggregation commonly called society—appears to be (both by outward manifestation and by inward character) of two widely different natures—at the least in many important particulars. A man, regarded as a separate being, may be said to be a specific product of nature, modified, from the ideal possibilities of his race, by the law and evolution of heredity, by the impulses, traits, and restraints of his peculiar identity, by the accidents and opportunities of his personal, social, political, or legal surroundings, and by the exercise of his own will and faculties ;—subject, however, to the natural results of all these circumstances when combined.

But how shall we analyze or define society—civil society, associated humanity, " the world "—an organization founded, in the beginning, upon the wants and fears

247

of mankind, but grown by development and accretion into something so artificial that it has changed or swallowed up much of what is purely natural in human intercourse? What is it not? The family, the neighborhood, the voluntary association, the corporation, the community, the town, the country, the state, the nation, the whole inhabited universe—all are its forms or elements. Man, in his relations with his Maker, with his immediate neighbor, with himself, each individual may somewhat understand—at least after his own fashion. But who can comprehend the boundless and innumerable traits, or factitious ingredients, of society? What are the sources or the limits of its powers, its laws, its rights, its duties? Who made them? By what authority do they exist? Consent? Acquiescence? Contract? Usurpation? Force? What is the proof of the essence of their obligation? Who but itself, or its viceroys, in the last analysis, decides upon the extent, validity or effect of its self-constituted sovereign will and power?

In most Christian communities there is but little serious popular discussion, among happy well-regulated circles, as to any of these matters in the abstract; and men generally find greater personal advantage, in practically interpreting them to suit their special local or communal needs and interests, than by questioning any prevailing opinion concerning their origin or authority. Nevertheless there are some bases of society, never to be lost sight of, and to which it is often not unprofitable to appeal;—especially whenever private interests, disguised as public rights, claim to enter the domain of unjustifiable usurpation. Among its recognized immutable foundations are prominently first, a common human nature, with its instinctive struggle for self-preservation — usually called selfishness — qualified by personal affection, love of the general good-will of others, and sometimes by a conscientious, or expedient, notion of duty to a neighbor or even an alien ; and next, the necessity of making large concessions to the mere claim of our neighbors in general, in order to live peaceably with or near them.

Again, besides religion, there are the acquired materials of the composition of society—the maxims, formulas, tendencies, restraints, and limitations, which a concourse of ages has stamped upon it, with an indelible brand, as rules and characteristics for its continued inheritance and transmission. To these may be added the obligations of its history, and the domination of its policy, its laws, its precedents, its customs ;—to say nothing of its unbounded power (and sometimes shameless tyranny) frequently exercised over some natural rights of an individual or of a class, evolved from its assumption of a so-called "police-power" and general political sovereignty. Nor can we lay out of our calculation the influences—open or secret, avowed or denied—of communities themselves interacting upon each other in their relative political, social, or natural functions. Then, over all, in our reckoning we must take into the account society's consciousness of the reason of its existence, its traditionary instinct of self-preservation at all hazards, and the need that, in order to perpetuate itself, it shall appear to its own members—if not to all mankind—to strive to accomplish the object for which it was originally, or gradually, self-established. To this end also certain other large definite purposes, always, at the least nominally, must be kept clearly in view.

Suffice it to name some of these purposes :—to make the government of society appear to be administered (so far as may be practicable) in such manner as to benefit all and to injure none materially—certainly not unnecessarily—also to establish justice among all ; to restrain the strong from trespassing upon, or neutralizing, the rights or privileges of, the weak ; to keep the ministers of all public functions ever mindful of the axiom that fidelity to trust is the only purpose of, or excuse for, their holding office ; to avoid the natural tendency of political power to use its strength, for the continuous benefit of its possessors—by the oppression of those from whom it indirectly derives the very means of thus selfishly perpetuating itself ; and finally to raise the means for only just and necessary expenses of its due administration, by equal taxation ;—doing this latter always in such manner as to procure the largest public revenue with the least private inconvenience or partiality among those who, directly or indirectly, bear its burdens.

Perhaps too it may not be inapposite here, in this little peep at the skeleton of society, to advert—parenthetically at least—to the common observation that associated humanity not seldom keeps a special conscience, or recognizes rules of right and wrong, and regulates its actions by a standard of virtue (or the want of it) that individual human nature would blush to own. For we all know that officers of secular corporations, vestrymen of religious societies, members of voluntary associations, or even high public functionaries (in their conglomerate capacity) will not unfrequently advocate measures, and act upon principles, which, as merely private men, they would not hesitate to hold up (as they ought) to the execration of mankind.

GREAT FORTUNES IN AMERICA.

Perhaps the least objectionable, if not the wisest, testament ever made, contained the bequest by a penniless father to his able-bodied son. "I give to my beloved son, John, one thousand pounds sterling," said the dying man. "Why! what does that mean?" inquired his amazed solicitor—either having no sense of humor, or not expecting a jest at such a moment—"you have not a tithe of a thousand pounds in the world."

"No matter for that," replied the philosopher; "it is my will that he should have it;—and I wish him to work and earn it."

There was, I am sure, no quarrelling over this legacy. They who got less, and the cousins-german who were left out altogether, did not employ attorneys—hungry for "fat contentions and litigious fees"—at champertous rates of per centage, to dispute the soundness of mind of the testator, or to prove an undue influence, exercised by John over a doting father, *in extremis.* No jealous heart-burnings were excited, among the disinherited next-of-kin, over any supposed inequality of favor. The meanest poor-relation could admit that John got his just deserts; and no more or less. As chief legatee he would not be called upon to divide with other beneficiaries. Neither

would the residuary legatees complain of a senile infatuation. In short, the most cynical would approve this
just disposition of the testator's bounty—without a cavil.

How much better for John, than if he had been left a
pecuniary fortune in hand ; relying upon which he might
have abandoned his school-books, and set up himself as
a young man of society ;—with nothing to do besides
spending money, and perhaps making a fool of himself,
conspicuously.

To a sensitive man, the controversies possible to arise
in these days over the division of his estate, after his
death, would seem enough to deter him from desiring to
accumulate much beyond a provision for the real wants
—present and prospective—of his immediate family and
himself. An aged farmer, in his dying hours, was observed to be suffering some keen mental anguish. When
asked what troubled him, he replied that he was fancy-
ing how he might suffer if he should be tempted to peep
out from some loop-hole of the next world, and could
see what shameless quarrels his sons were having in the
division of his farm. When the great Rachel, at the
height of her fame, was playing at a Broadway theatre,
in some critical situation, she held her audience in breath-
less wonder, before she spoke a word. A friend felt a
great curiosity to know precisely what contending feelings, evolved by the circumstances, had given her the
almost superhuman expression of face, figure, and attitude, that had so electrified all who saw her. She
frankly confessed to him she was not thinking at all of
her part in the play ; but, at the moment referred to,
there had flashed into her mind a notion of what havoc

the vultures among her family surely would make of her property as soon as she was in her grave.

When a virtuous man, of moderate means, composes his limbs for the exit from this world, he safely may suppose his memory will be respected as much as it deserves. But what frightful chimeras nowadays must haunt the death-bed of a man who successfully has given his life-long strength—laborious days and sleepless nights—to amassing a vast fortune ! If he have imagination, ever so little, the roots of his hair probably will be excited somewhat at such a time. But if he have much clairvoyant power of forecast, how vivid may be his apprehensions of what will follow his demise ! First a hasty autopsy— to search for symptoms of mental unsoundness, or perhaps traces of foul play by those who have watched tenderly his exhaling spirit—set on foot by some of his relatives who have had least sympathy with him during his life. Perhaps even his grave will be desecrated— after a decent Christian burial—to find some possible idiosyncrasy in his remains that shall furnish ground for speculative conjecture to additional surgical specialists ; —egged on probably by ghoulish lawyers.

Next may come the scandalous legal controversies over his will and the disposal of his estate—however judicious —all scattered by newspapers over the land ;—horrible suspicions arising from the conflict of experts in physical and mental dissection ; an exposure of every foible in his conduct or character, and then a calcium light thrown upon every equivocal detail of the privacy of his whole career—long after all surrounding circumstances are forgotten, and there is no living witness to give an honest clue to the villainous travesties of his motives, or to the incoherent and disunited facts, that crop out in the misty recollections, or fancies, of his rivals or enemies ;—to say nothing of the diabolical innuendos of traditional gossip, the paternity of which is lost among weird shadows.

Finally, after the public has been made sick to loathing, by this foul feast of harpies, and it would seem as if the unfortunate Dives might be permitted at least to keep his body in the tomb—if even that be not stolen by another set of freebooters—suddenly may appear, as if coming out of the air, like Macbeth's witches, a countless flock of impromptu widows ;—each claiming her life-interest in a third of his landed estate, yet willing—for love and peace sake—to abate proportionately her claims, provided that, together, they may have the whole of it ! Surely to such a death-bed vision the fate of Midas must seem Elysian in the comparison.

Shakespeare's Henry IV., seems to have felt the pangs of dying more excruciatingly from something not unlike such a view, when he broke out upon his sons :—

> See, sons, what things you are !
> How quickly nature runs into revolt
> When gold becomes her object !
> For this the foolish, over-careful fathers
> Have broke their sleep with thoughts, their brains with care,
> Their bones with industry ;
> For this they have engrossed and piled up
> The cankered heaps of strange-achieved gold ;
> For this they have been thoughtful to invest
> Their sons with arts, and martial exercises ;
> When, like the bee, tolling from every flower
> The virtuous sweets ;

> Our thighs packed with wax, our mouths with honey,
> We bring it to the hive ; and, like the bees,
> Are murdered for our pains.

What can compensate a man for so shocking an abuse of his labors and his memory ? Has he been upon a false scent all his life ? Was the mainspring of his life-long exertions an illusion—a fictitious and wholly misplaced ideal ? With the best of motives, and with the most self-denying sacrifice of much that could have made his life lovely—and at least might have made him a participant in the bounty of his own fortune, or have given him some taste of the happiness of self-enjoyment—has not his career been a failure, his prospective castle in the air a tower of Babel, full of the confusion of babbling tongues ? Even if his will shall be respected, and

> Large was his bounty and his soul sincere,

yet perhaps he has made a crowd of ingrates, who will dishonor his name by riotous living, and who will be hostile to the spirit of the republican society to which he owed allegiance, and by means of which he gained his great wealth ? If they do not provoke envy and malice among the less fortunate, by foolish ostentation of riches, may they not furnish an unedifying example in other ways to the great mass of the rising generation, who must toil and spin, or starve ?

It would, however, be wantonly wrong, even to insinuate that all who are partakers of munificent testamentary bounty bring discredit upon inherited wealth. Our land is dotted over with too many magnificent temples of religion, palaces of art, academies of learning, schools of the useful arts, hospitals of charity, and caravansaries of timely aid and improvement to both the helpless and self-helpful—founded or supported by the wisdom and benevolence of those who were born rich—to leave a doubt concerning the existence of innumerable exceptions. Still they are none the less exceptional ;—although the names of such benefactors will endure the more honored, so long as human nature continues to appreciate a good deed or a worthy motive. Yet it must be conceded that the general tendency of inherited wealth in this country seems to be to make men and women over self-indulgent ; and to put a conspicuous class of our citizens a good deal out of harmony with American ideas.

Why is it then, that a man still "heapeth up riches" not knowing "who shall gather them ?" There is indeed a good deal of exciting pleasure to some in the mere chase for money. Nay, there is a secret satisfaction in having more than enough for the present, or even the emergencies of accident, sickness, and old age. As Horace says :—

> suave est ex magno tollere acervo.

The "big pile" has its fascinations. To some others —perhaps a large number—it is an immense gratification to have the means of satisfying the benevolent sympathies of heart and soul—feeling and pride—for those near and dear, as well as toward struggling humanity in the world at large. Besides, with still others, there is the lust of avarice, that clasps a man's whole moral and intellectual nature in its gripe, and transforms him into a monster that craves to raven all that may be gotten. But these are not all. Nor do they fairly exemplify the general rule under which so many great fortunes are accumulated in America. Other ruling motives are notoriously prevalent. Many hope now, as men did in former days, under a different political and social system, to found a family, and to ennoble their posterity by putting their children in the possession of transmitted wealth.

Some of the evils of our present condition appear to have their root in traditional or foreign ideas, sentiments, or prejudices, which are not in harmony with the sounder growth of social agencies among us. Such notions are sometimes, as it were, part of an obsolete system, the framework of which, by reason of its solidity, has outlasted the use for which it was originally contrived or adopted. Not a little of this state of things is perhaps due to the fact that the social thought and manners of this country have been nourished so long by the literature of foreign peoples ;—in the absence of a strong original, native body of American letters. It is the flattering hope of some, however, that the recognition of the right of literary property (which is really the kernel of our new copyright law) in time may work a radical change, in this respect, in the intellectual food of the great mass of the American people.

Modern society was feudal in its origin ;—chiefs and clans, kings, nobles, and serfs. The commons were a later growth. The old order of society rested, in the last analysis, upon the assumed divine right of kings to govern, and was sustained by the hereditary power—political, social, and proprietary— of great families. But the feudal system is

17

dead, root and branch, beyond possible resuscitation. Changeable personal property — and not inalienable estates—now constitutes the mass of the wealth of the world. The feudal spirit (however pleasing to the memory or imagination of an infatuated few) like the age of chivalry—which was its best embodiment—is gone, never to return. The French Revolution as a political and social evangel—despite its horrors—and commerce with its new wings, given by steam and electricity, have changed all that. The social power of wealth has passed from the hands of a few pampered favorites of fortune into the hands of the many-headed people. There is no longer a rallying of the many to strengthen the hands of great traditionary families. On the contrary the once insignificant common people have gradually grown, and learned to combine, organize, and co-operate, so as to defy or destroy the power of the one supreme man, and his hereditary adherents. Kingship, as a historical symbol, may survive in some societies, near akin to our own ; but, as a self-sustaining power, or as a representative head of hereditary family power irrespective of popular opinion or will, it is merely a traditionary illusion—a feudal phantom.

Where, then, as a civic factor, or as a basis of social prestige, shall we put family pride ? Family pride, when based upon blood and breeding—upon the recognition of a nobility of nature proved by deeds of heroism, self-sacrifice, and the exploits of magnanimity or genius—is a touch of divinity. It is a voice of nature, the recognition of which time cannot subdue in the human heart. The distinction thus earned—and naturally awarded to superior blood or race—so far as it is transmissible, may be left to shift for itself, without wealth ;—except such as its inheritors may gather with their own hands. But, among us, mere wealth no longer can ennoble ; nor family prestige now be established and continued by money alone.

One source of hindrance to the proper development of the fundamental elements of our society, as already suggested, lies in the fact that our young men and women, who are farthest removed from the struggle for existence—and from whom the most fairly might be expected —often contribute least to the growth and improvement of social ideas in a legitimate direction. In many respects however they are blameless. Their parents foolishly have pampered their natural indolence, and nursed their inclination to extravagance ; at the same time quenching the spirit of independence and self-reliance born within them. Such parents, in many cases, in early life having passed through a Spartan discipline of poverty and privation— perhaps the stimulus, if not the source of all their virtues, or at least of their success in life—they think themselves serving the highest purpose of their existence, by giving their children an easy time, and enervating them into mere seekers after temporary and debilitating pleasure, or saunterers through life.

Ease is well, and social pleasure is better—our lives would be juiceless and tasteless without them both—but ease is consistent with such reasonable labor as delights the liberal mind ; and pleasure may be had by seeking something besides dissipation or wholly frivolous amusement. Ordinarily the manly spirit does not survive long a loss of individual personal merit, or of the pride of personal independence.

Indeed it is one of the social eccentricities of our day, that in many instances a father, from his early manhood —misled by some effete traditionary influence—is really so far as it were a voluntary serf for his family, that a large part of his own moral and intellectual nature never has fair play. He may become little better than a machine to make and store money for the sake of transmitting it to those who under our social system are generally liable to be demoralized by the expectation of wealth, if not made mischievous members of our society by too easy a possession of it.

Would it not be better for the race, if when a capable man-child is well-fitted, at the expense of his parents, for the battle of life, he should go forth into the world and win his spurs for himself? That is the true method of recognizing the inevitable rule of evolution, toward a better state of individual manhood and of society;—called the survival of the fittest. This old-fashioned notion may sound harshly to some effeminate ears. It would, however, be misinterpreted and misapplied if it tended to take away a helping hand when needed by the weak or unfortunate, or to withdraw benevolence, kindness and sympathy from those whom nature or chance has classed among the incapables. Yet whatever system discourages the spirit of self-help and virile independence among the rising generation, saps the very foundation of our democratic society.

American Politics.

Although our political system has safely passed one centennial climacteric, it is in fact—when its career is contrasted with the rise, duration, or fall of historic nations—yet in comparative infancy. The amalgamation of all the incoherent parts of a league of *quasi*-independent civil communities into a nation—preserving the autonomy of so many varying individual so-called States (whether ripening to any extent or only in premature blossom) which yet profess allegiance (or absolutely yield it) to the sovereignty of a Union over all of them— has proved itself to be a problem of a vast number of changeable and embarrassing factors in the art of public government. Perhaps more centuries, at least, of absence of fatal civil convulsion must elapse before all the threatening forces involved can be adjusted, or its comparatively permanent safety can be assured, with any real probability. Meanwhile, if the government survive there must be much dangerous friction and rough work ;—involving, often necessarily, monstrous injustice and exquisite tyranny to many—whether States, communities, or individuals.

There appear to be now, however, at least three conspicuously great human or personified powers diligently at work striving to direct and utilize the energies, possessions and opportunities of this marvellously active, miscellaneous, and indefinitely multiplying and increasing people. They may be rudely classified as the thinker or scholar, the politician, and the statesman.

The First seems to be endeavoring to find a way of working out the scheme and purpose of this imposing Union through an honest conflict-of-opinion—having faith that in the end truth, or at least the true policy of this nascent nation, will prevail. The Second power—

standing nearer the mere masses of the people, and feeling beat in his veins the blood of an irrepressible, if not tyrannical, organized, apparent majority of that people, also partaking of their selfishness as well as short-sightedness—cherishes and represents local enterprise and special individual or class interests. He naturally cares but little for the general or ideal good of the whole country. He is prone to shape legislation through a mere conflict-of-interests—often practically doing great mischief and evolving rank injustice by disputing established principles, denying facts, iterating lies, and bargaining for a distribution of partial or private advantages, to the prejudice of the ultimate good of the people. The Third power—having some of the acquired sagacity of the second, but less reckless selfishness, coupled with much of the superior intelligence of the first—stands practically upon a higher plane than either. With a broader outlook he endeavors—though not always successfully—to put the nation in its proper relation to the whole civilized world ;—while having due regard to all the local and individual needs and interests of his own country.

Having no apprehension of foreign foes to minimize the importance of our local affairs, or to teach us a necessity of economizing our resources, the Politician has, for the present—as during a large part of the past history of the Union he has had—greatly the upper hand. American politics hitherto have been too much if not chiefly the outgrowth—or crazy patch-work—of an increasing conflict of local interests. Through the want, until recently, of general education—of a broad, scientific, catholic, and accurate kind—concerning political econ-

omy, among our leading public men ; through the mingling with our native population of so many foreigners,
who were born under, and habituated to, widely different
political or social systems ; and through the shifting
character and domicile of the masses of people congre-
gating in the great cities ; our public opinion has been
controlled largely by appeals to passion, prejudice, short-
sighted self-interest, avarice, or ignorance. As Burke
says :—" When the leaders strive to make themselves
bidders at an auction of popularity . . . they will
become flatterers instead of legislators—the instruments,
not the guides, of the people."

The Politician, sinking to the level of his meanest
work, himself steadily has deteriorated, until—from his
point of vision or blindness—the notion of honor has
evaporated into words, morality has become obsolete,
and the habit of deception in political controversy or personal ambition, has made fraud, peculation, bribery, or
forgery a common method of his tribe.

The Thinker, by his scholarship, thinking, and writing,
lifts a few—especially among the better educated of the
rising generation—up to his high stand-point, and, with
devotion to and faith in the progress of humanity, still
hopes unflinchingly and looks for a purer and better state
of things.

The Statesman watches the changes and growth of
popular opinion and enlightenment (although it be, to the
impatient, apparently as slow as the movement of a glacier)
bides his time ; occasionally fixes a landmark that he
trusts may stand forever ; bears frequent defeat with
philosophic composure ; sets up again his guide-posts

when they are knocked down ; and, as his own life-time wears away, passes on the watchwords of reform and progress to younger men. Meanwhile, patiently but confidently he asks mankind to await the fuller development and more rightful direction of the now incalculable forces of this mighty democratic empire.

Hitherto the excessive resources of our country—both in the prodigality of nature and in the energy and genius of our people, added to their inborn patient submissiveness to the law of the land, however established—have enabled us to overcome, for the time, almost unconsciously, some of the necessary consequences of absolutely vicious legislation.

The success of self-favoring class-interests, appears, however, to have begotten in many a sort of judicial blindness. Ignoring the instinctive love of fair play—a fair field and no favor—that lives in the blood of our native people, they have overlooked the rights of the innumerable silent classes, and are the dupes of a temporary triumph over the underlying laws of human society. Sooner or later, however, moral justice always vindicates herself when her laws have been violated. The recipients of governmental favor may flatter a government for a while in its apparent security ; but the end is usually nearest when aggressive injustice appears to be at its acme. The great French Revolution taught mankind a lesson of prudence in oppression, that, however temporarily unheeded, never will be forgotten wholly by the unsleeping among ourselves.

As the interests of the American people grow more complex and vast, the temptations of those who are strong in wealth and political power to exercise oppression increase by opportunity. The unanticipated defects of an artificial, and somewhat improvised, system of government press more heavily upon some individuals or classes and involve much unforeseen injustice. Meanwhile, there is an increasing consciousness among the invincible masses of untrained men, that with them—as a " despotic democracy "—especially rests the ultimate power to dictate the law, and to prescribe its inexorable formularies. The temptation is strong to favor their own peculiar interests exclusively, regardless, at least to a great extent, of the rights and privileges of others. All of these things tend to make the problem—not merely of administering, but even of preserving and perpetuating our peculiar republican form of government—a study for the anxious intellectual man. It is no easy task for the gifted, learned, wise, and patriotic. It demands of those who temporarily hold official power a sincere vow—as they are often reminded—both to wield that power with moderation and to keep a far look into the future consequences of whatever policy or practical measures they shall sanctify and perpetuate by the authority of established law.

To the contemplation of some of our more prosperous citizens, the past appears to be only a history of colossal legitimate natural growth ;—the present serene and the future full of magnificent promise for the human race. This may be true and correct from a single aspect. But what shall be the development or vicissitudes of the great political and social dynamos—embodying local selfish interests and now at work beneath our feet especially in our great cities, or in national affairs—no sagacious man can estimate with clearness of vision or placidity of temper :—unless indeed he be either selfishly indifferent to the fortunes of his country and his race, or possess an unflinching faith in the utopian doctrine that Providence charitably governs the political affairs of mankind, irrespective of their voluntary choice, or of human effort in the direction of wise statesmanship.

AMERICAN SOCIAL RESTLESSNESS.

While there is about us, almost everywhere, a fierce desire of the common mass of people to lessen the burden of their physical conditions, *per fas et nefas*—to procure, for the least possible labor, the largest compensation at the expense of those who happen, for the time being, to be possessed of the greater part of the accumulated wealth of the world—a state of things, in some of its phases, euphemistically called " the conflict between labor and capital " —there appears also to be a dearth of contentment in the social life of a majority of those who, in easy circumstances, occupy our large cities.

Most of these—who can choose their hourly occupation, or give themselves up to idleness—appear to find their chief satisfaction of living in some novel subject of excitement which shall keep them constantly in motion. They are usually amid a turmoil or in a whirl. Men who are by chance, or successful venture, beyond the stress of a daily struggle for more. comfortable subsistence, are striving eagerly to reach some fanciful goal, or to accomplish some vain purpose, whose real underlying significance they generally misunderstand—if any substance be involved in it. They find actual pleasure sometimes in the mere pursuit of a social phantasm. Their choice of it is blind and headlong, while they are apparently quite careless of its intrinsic worthlessness.

Few of them seem to act in such matters from any original impulse. Most are either led or driven—many willingly, some unconsciously, unaware of what they are doing or why they do it. Yet they are uneasy. The charming sobriety of intellectual contentment no longer seems to be the aim of intelligent men or women among them. Their religion or philosophy is relegated to only a few hours of a single day of the week, whenever either of these have any recognition at all ;—which is not always. Political duty is shirked as vulgar, laborious, or vain. Pleasure, amusement, especially novelty and exhilaration, or the supposed means of obtaining these, seem to be the subject of all their daily thoughts. The demon of unrest dominates them. Vain-glory, covetousness, envy, jealousy, rivalry, detraction, often usurp the place of moral repose and domestic virtues of the milder sort ; while class-strife and social ambition fill up the measure of activity in the lives of many, born capable of, or fortuned for, better things.

Among some of our rising social classes few, while in health, seem to ask themselves concerning any of their doings—*quo tendit ?* They push on resolutely, like a man upon a treadmill. They act as if they must give all their time and attention to something, which appears to them to be moving ahead—but is really revolving in a mere circle—with constant effort and endless repetition.

In this vain pursuit, fired by the intoxicating fumes of a fancied social equality, men and women sometimes thrust themselves amid special surroundings, for which they not only have no fitness, but are, both by nature and circumstances almost disqualified. They find themselves unexpectedly in an atmosphere where they see others gliding about with grace and ease, but in which they can only flounder by continuing effort. The air is thin and their heavy weights overtax its buoyancy.

Knowing nothing which does not show itself upon the surface, they naturally take for granted everything they encounter must be what to them it appears to be. With these superficial views they are apt to imagine they may do what they suppose they see others doing. They are prone to believe the actions of those they would imitate are artificial and not spontaneous. They do not know how much of good social conduct is the prompting of a second nature—a matter of heredity and automatic individual impulse, arising out of a perfected system of minor morals which has been the growth of ages. What some people do, in their intercourse with and bearing towards the world, unconsciously and without effort, others strive to copy with but a feeble resemblance. Even this poor effect is reached by manifest exertion, often attended with a painful anxiety lest they shall fail in the attempt and their own unreality be discovered. Such a state of mind, like a bad conscience, is necessarily full of apprehension, doubt, and consequent nervous restlessness.

When a set of people are seen thus striving to appear what they consciously are not—whether it be by a simulation of education, breeding, social position, or even of wealth—any one knowing what vultures are tearing their hearts, must pity them. Nothing however is more pleasing to a lover of mankind than to see the easy intercourse of well-bred people, assured of their social standing—not under-valuing the good opinion of the world, but knowing they deservedly have it, and that it comes unsolicited. Lifted above the temptation to make a false pretence of what they do not possess, they are not in hourly fear lest some borrowed prestige shall vanish, because they may choose to be natural, frank, honest, simple, straightforward, plain-spoken, or communicative. Their movements —airy and long maintained—remind one of the beautiful sweep, billowy undulations, and poising on snowy wings, of sea-gulls, skimming along an ocean shore ; while another class, who would fain imitate them, more resemble the forced motions through the air of some awkward domestic fowl, overweighted for aërial navigation.

And yet, although this unhappy class of people try to deceive themselves, they delude no one else. It is suspected, too, that they not uncommonly suffer—as has been already suggested—the pangs peculiar to those who are both conscious of a fraud, and in fear of its detection. Perhaps not all see these things in their naked deformity. Many indeed do not care to look so closely. Yet there are enough to whom mere masks are not disguises ; and who are always willing to keep the social idiot—who, shutting his own eyes, feigns to believe his neighbor does not see—uneasy and incapable of repose, while constantly apprehensive lest he shall be detected in his masquerade and exposed to that ridicule he so terribly dreads.

These allusions, however, touch only a single phase of the condition of social disquietude that pervades many of our more fortunate circles. Tranquillity has grown almost obsolete, as a social virtue. There seems to be among some of our most prosperous classes an unsatisfied desire for something unattainable and indefinable. They chase some phantom of delight that eludes pursuit, like a will-o'-the-wisp. When riches are secured, and the coveted joys of idleness are exhausted, the absence of any profound or even real purpose or value in life makes it grow oppressive. Failing to find continuity in the chain of human existence ; looking upon each individual as merely a disconnected link, and society as a mass of disintegrated fragments ; they feel with Marcellus :—

Something is rotten in the State.

Indeed the very pleasures of an unchecked profusion of wealth have severe limitations. Heaping up riches for spendthrift heirs, or cormorant will-breakers, grows wearisome. When Heliogabalus has had his swim in a pond of aromatic wine, and finished his feast garnished with the brains of six hundred or more ostriches ; or when Caligula has sated his crazy thirst with pearls dissolved in vinegar ; what next ? Such pleasures pall. Society is bored with its own luxury ; and the outlook is toward vacancy. Its more energetic members traverse remote seas, chase the sun around the globe, skim over the surface of other countries old and new, tempt domestic disaster by foreign alliances, participate in social phantasmagoria alien to their own history, association, or habits, and fancy they are enjoying life. In fact they are only drowning, by incongruous noise, the deep cry in their hearts for something earnest and real;—something that shall ultimately weld their class into such a sympa-

thetic unity with the race—such a proud nationality of
feeling and such an unspeakable consciousness of high
social destiny—as is the natural birthright of the leaders
of a great people that is opportuned to lead the way for
the whole world in an experimental civilization.

Who shall analyze or define this uneasiness, this craving hunger, this unsatisfied want, so obvious among the
body of our wealthy society? Is there not here a dull,
but persistent longing for something in the social basis
that shall smack more of worldly perpetuity?—some
greater stake in the family or the State? It appears to
be a tedious round of life that so many successive generations of men and women should be going continuously
over the same path—leading nowhere! Until near our
own time a social pride in the prosperity, growth, and
prospective greatness, of our country, has done much to
satisfy this moral and intellectual craving for some living
interest in the future of the vast world before us. But
now the *Demos* is rapidly learning, through self-organi-
zation, not only its unlimited power and irresponsibility,
but also a sagacious method of prostrating political
parties in abasement at its feet. Large classes, although
fortunate perhaps through inherited wealth or learned
education—and not without public spirit or political ambition—are still morally disqualified to

> crook the pregnant hinges of the knee
> Where thrift may follow fawning.

They are therefore put out of practical control of
the destinies of the republic. These latter seem to
find but little spur for their ambition, and less satis-

faction for their pride, in the vague contemplation of a future they cannot foresee. They—for the most part —lack the martyr-like spirit of self-sacrifice to endeavor to direct it. Higher social life seems to have become merely a kaleidoscopic changing—a shuffling of the same, or like, bits of artificial unmeaning color. It does not appear to move forward or upward. Although it has its varieties, is it not too commonly harlequin-like or grotesque ?

What is the worth of a society, and what is the significance of its life, if it must be without method, and continue without improving growth ? How can there be either of these among us, when the family institution— the very soul of civilization—instead of crystalizing (through recognized heredity, continuous social affinity, or perpetuated power or wealth) is constantly undergoing an alternating process of disintegration and new re-formation—without continuity or progressive reform? These are hints of some of the quandaries that disturb the bosom of our society. How shall we find a clew to guide the way through this labyrinthine maze ?

RIGHT AND WRONG.

When inclined to do what is contrary to the interests, opinions, or wishes of our fellow-men, how shall we determine, in nice matters, what is right or what is wrong ? Apart from Scriptural command or precept—which in so many complex cases itself appears vague or equivocal— where shall we find a specific, authoritative, infallible, guide ? Shall we rely upon our own moral sense or conscience ? This may not be always a safe arbiter for all, because so many delude themselves with the notion that, in private conduct, each one is, as it were, a special and peculiar law unto himself. The uncertainty that we encounter in searching for a universal and inflexible law inclines the superficial to doubt even the existence of any valid rule whatever.

How far too is conscience itself the creature of education, utility, convenience, custom, or habit—inspired by a commonly prevailing opinion of the age and country we live in ? How far is it the child of cowardice ;—the offspring of apprehension of punishment, here or hereafter, for doing forbidden, or omitting commanded, things ? If it were a divine and absolute umpire would it speak to man with so uncertain a sound or in so many diverse voices throughout different countries or periods of the world's history ? How can we rank as infallible such an apparent changeling ? If what is commonly reputed right alone be right, and what is so reputed wrong be wrong intrinsically—and not merely from custom or convenience —why does conscience so often seem to interchange them, according to the mutations of climate, civilization, historical emergency, social policy or popular opinion ? If we consult our own sense of justice—to determine for ourselves how *honeste vivere, alterum non laedere, suum cuique tribuere*—are we not still, consciously or not, almost wholly dependent upon contemporary public opinion ; when estimating in what essentially consists such living honorably, harming no other one, and rendering unto every other one his due ? So also if we attempt ourselves to apply the more subtile golden rule to our own conduct,

18

where is the guarantee for impartiality ; when suitor, advocate, and judge are one and the same person ?

Is conscience then simply a convenient regulator—adopted by common consent, only because supposed to be necessary for the well-being of a particular community ? Is it merely an artificial rule of local social conduct? If there were only one human being could he never do wrong ? Would there be no moral code ? If none, then how can the dictate of conscience be said to exist as the original, inborn law—latent or obvious—of an individual ?

If, however, we dive into the depths of our own purely egoistic, inner, moral consciousness ; or even if we give ourselves up wholly to the study of what is the chief good of man (both individually and socially) and of what ought to be done or omitted in order to conform to a code springing out of the natural fitness of things—when re-regarded only in their essential nature, stripped of all factitious circumstances, and independent of the fluctuating, contrived, opinions of the world around us—although we may hope to find a rule that shall never vary, but always be consistent with itself, yet in many matters of grave moment, we may nevertheless run counter, not only to the best judgment of our companions, but even to the penal mandate of the law of the land !

In order to formulate a definition of right as opposed to wrong (broad enough to embrace everything proper to be included, according to the popular judgment of some of our modern communities) it would seem almost as though one must use such latitude, or narrowness of expression, as to adopt unqualifiedly whatever is locally or temporarily suitable or convenient to present demands—whether through usage or expediency—in the opinion of those who, for the time being, have the power, legal or social, to enforce it ! Such a postulate would be apt to stagger any ingenuous, inquisitive mind—if not permanently to unsettle whatever fixed principles there might be in it.

In fact we are, for the most part, born and bred in communities where canons of intrinsic right and wrong are confounded too commonly with such rules as are made to suit a supposed expediency, by the arbitrary will or conventional opinion of those around us. They often have also the sanction of an equal weight of a large public judgment ; and, from our childhood—when, it is commonly observed, the deepest and most lasting impressions are made upon our moral nature—we are not seldom taught that the natural and the artificial, in morals, are founded upon the same principle, are of equal validity, and have the same binding force upon us. Thus tutored, in our own individual civilized conscience, we cannot always discriminate fairly. To illustrate :—that still small voice pipes in the same strain when it checks the arm about to be raised against a brother, as when it covers with confusion a New England boy whose childish glee betrays him into whistling on a Sabbath day !

What then shall we do to be safe, yet preserve our liberty of mind and body ? In the exercise of a right of private judgment (in such matters as virtue and vice, right and wrong,) if we regard our own comfort, it behooves us to beware of going contrary to commonly received opinion. In all overt acts at the least we must take cognizance of law, written or unwritten—whether it be formulated by expression or merely slumber in the conscious bosom of society—lest we be sent to jail or to coventry ; according as we infringe the law of the land, or violate the dogmas of social opinion.

To keep ourselves entirely secure, the rule of prudence for an ordinary man, in his conduct through life in most communities, would seem to be reduced to the formula of doing or omitting what his Bible commands and his good sense teaches, to be right or wrong ;—provided, however, it be not otherwise ordered or compelled by law or opinion ! For while we live in this world, society will be always stronger than any one man. And if one shall make war upon society—no matter if he be right in the absolute or before God—the victory will be always on the side of the heavy battalions ;—at the least during his lifetime. Future ages may indeed canonize his memory, for his noble daring to be free ; but himself, neverthe-less, will perish ignominiously. Society must have peace —even at the cost of human sacrifices ! A windmill may look to a man like an absurd adversary ; but despite its awkwardness, its long arms will smite, with powerful blows, him who shall oppose it.

Nevertheless, even if we were compelled to concede conscience—as too commonly understood—to be a mere thing of custom and of artificial mould, yet there must be, behind it, or at its very foundation, some divine instinct in our human nature—higher and broader than the notion of convenience—that always has prompted mankind to set up some ideal standard of right and wrong. Through this, in the long progress of time, the way ultimately must be cleared to a positive, infallible rule of pure justice and rectitude. For instance : can any man—unless he be abnormally base by nature, or artificially self-brutified— injure voluntarily another's right without feeling a lump in his throat, or a qualm of moral dyspepsia? From whatever origin it may spring, or whatsoever may be its composition—whether or not it be " the oracle of God " —shall not every true man say :—" Thank Heaven, I have a conscience ? Pity for the man who believes he is without one ! "

DOMESTIC PEACE.

It is pleasant, for even a cynic, to look upon the members of a harmonious family circle. Without factitious aid, they appear to be able to make their own happiness. It seems to pervade their atmosphere ;— spreading far and widely, like some sweet and powerful perfume. The social influence of such a group continually broadens, carrying its amiable attributes with it. However small or feeble the beginning, if it have nobleness and refinement at its centre, it surely will become great and strong in the affection and esteem of a world of neighbors and acquaintances. All of this is easily practicable, without either the possession of wealth, or power —or even the luck of good fortune.

Yet, in these days of social ambition, anarchical social strife, and intense intellectual activity, the majority of mankind are engaged busily in ways that tend to make such felicity quite exceptional. Husband and wife, father and son, brother and sister—not content to dwell happily together—seek different and incongruous ideals. With contrary aims, and respecting no past, they are incapable of forecasting their future. With hearts perhaps too shallow for reverence to take root in them, they wander or rush in opposite directions. Each expends his or her surplus energy upon what is often a mere chimera of the hour ;—when by co-operation they might attain substantial results, and, perhaps, unconsciously, obtain possession of the very object of their now futile pursuit. On the contrary, following the dictates of self-conceit and perverse self-will—reckless of the happiness of others—they not uncommonly push headlong upon experimental courses, too often only to work out the punishment of their folly.

One of the surest foundations for the permanence of family harmony and cordial co-operation is a mutual respect for each individual's personality, and an absence of, or an unbroken restraint upon, all desire to invade, or ever to spy out the innermost self-hood of each other. For no human intercourse can long endure, with mutual esteem and respect, unless there be some reserve on both sides. We should never be able to take for granted that we wholly know, and are in the fullest possible confidence of, another. We must always withhold something, on each side, in order to keep our special individuality sacred and inviolable. The homely adage that "too much familiarity breeds contempt"—although probably pointed at the relation between unequals—contains the seed-bud of these suggestions. Generally, even among equals, it may be said, when we give up ourselves to each other quite unreservedly, satiety, at the least, is not far away.

Nevertheless, in an intimate intercourse, we ought always to feel that we are progressing ; that, although we do not know all, we are constantly learning more and more of something inexhaustible. It is well to believe that, even if we shall never reach the end, we are not standing still. As soon as progress ends retreat is likely to begin ; while indifference or worse—nay, even separation, secret or avowed, is not long in following. Perhaps, like asymptotes, we should be continually approaching nearer to each other, but—though the lines of our spiritual intercourse be continued indefinitely—never absolutely meet, or become co-incident, so as to merge in literal unity.

Few mortals—especially if they be of highly sensitive organization—can long dwell together in harmony, unless they thoroughly understand each other's general character, natural or acquired. They must exercise habitually toward each other not only some reserve, but also very great—nay, in some cases, almost superhuman—forbearance. Many fail from expecting too much ; some from even exacting too much ; more, however, from yielding or forbearing too little.

In the marital relation such failures are lamentably conspicuous. Although it is proverbially impracticable to ascertain with certainty the real direct cause, in most cases, of such domestic infelicity—inasmuch as both parties are bound naturally to secresy—yet the general verdict is that there are usually abundant faults on both sides. However impartial one may feel disposed to be in such matters, the solution of the problem is necessarily difficult by reason of the confused and imperfect data commonly furnished. Doubtless, however, a fine analysis would disclose the fact that, in ordinary cases, this social misery arises, not so much from wilful misconduct of either party (too commonly suspected) as, from some innate incompatibility of temperament, loosened from judicious self-restraint.

On the other hand, it seems strange to the mere looker-on, that such very antagonistic characters, as we sometimes see quite happy in their conjugal state, should have been ever put in so close relationship. Indeed, it is not uncommon for husband and wife, of amiable and matter-of-fact natures, to be so blind to their latent incongruousness, as, in their loving intercourse, even to prefigure to themselves a supreme bliss they shall realize, as disembodied spirits, in a future state ; when, alas ! in truth, if they really could see each other, in pure essence with all delusive alloy of mortal life purged away, probably they would shrink from each other with mutual aversion ; —if they did not fly instantly apart with reciprocal repulsion !

EDUCATION.

As has been said often, and seldom heeded, a preliminary step to the practical education of any man—whether for general usefulness or to do anything in particular— ought to be to find out his tendencies and capabilities, his inaptitudes and impediments, in the matter of the acquirement of any branch of knowledge, or in the practical use of it.

It would be hard to overestimate how much is embraced in that thread-bare word—education. To bring

up. Few men, women or children, for either themselves
or others, comprehend it. Fewer still fully achieve it.
It involves the entire make-up and career of life, almost
from the cradle; first, the specific nature of any particular man, then the life-ends to be aimed at by him,
and last the means of his attaining them. A man's whole
complex nature must be fairly contemplated—intellectual,
moral, and physical. The purely spiritual we now leave
out of view.

The essence of education is confessedly artificial training. Learning and wisdom come later. The object to
be kept in view should be, by giving each part of this
triple nature of man its due share of discipline in due
order—to fit the whole character for the business of
working out its potential destiny.

To cultivate, develop, and exercise in true proportion
each of these three parts of man's composition, yet to
neglect neither; to make their growth harmonize, and to
let them so work together as to carry out the purposes of
an intelligent, methodical, far-seeing, consistent will; and
thereby to accomplish its purpose, so far as is permitted
to such capacity as one has; this would be indeed to
educate a man.

How shall this be done? The chief means of real
education are three: 1st, instruction through another;
2d, thought and reflection, or education of one's self;
3d, the lessons of personal experience in practical affairs.
Obviously they must be used and applied in different
proportions at different times of life. In early youth the
degree of instruction should be greatest; next, self-education, or discipline, and last, practical experience. In

second youth—perhaps from the age of twenty to thirty
or somewhat later—a man acquires less wisdom from the
instruction of actual methodical teachers, and more from
the conversation of men, or the writing of profound and
learned masters ; but now he derives the most solid part
of his intellectual accretion, or growth, from a process of
self-education, by means of his thoughts and reflections
based upon the gathered resources of his mind, drawn
from without as well as within.   For at this period he
begins to acquire wisdom from his own observation of
external facts, and from his own experience in his dealings with his fellow-men—both individually and as rep-
resenting the society of which he is gradually becoming
a substantial part.

After thirty or perhaps forty—until advanced beyond
middle life—he gains less either by the teachings of
others, or from the process of mere self-education.   Now
he derives much more wisdom from his practical dealings
with human affairs and the deductions of his judgment
from the knowledge thus acquired.   This puts to the test
all his acquirements from every source.

Now if ever he lays aside his false doctrines, his traditions, his arbitrary dogmas, his delusions, his impractical
theories, his imperfect judgments, that have been biased
by social surroundings, or by his own temperament, passions, prejudice, or favor.   If he has true intellectual
growth, he now rises into a clearer atmosphere.   He reasons more fairly ; he escapes more illusion, as imagination and fancy are held in check.   He learns the sublime
peace that hovers over intellectual patience.   Hasty conclusions from imperfect or inadequate data or premises

are no longer swift to dazzle, mislead, or betray him into folly. He learns to know his comparative weakness or strength as he measures himself intellectually with other men, past or contemporary.

He comprehends the elements of human power, individual, social, or political. He gives due weight to moral considerations. He understands men. His practical calculations do not longer miscarry, from reckoning men as mere mechanical figures or scientific machines. He appreciates what is meant by weight of character. He perceives that sentiment, thought, and opinion are influential in the world in proportion as they are backed by a man who is recognized as faithful, true, consistent, independent, liberal and unselfish. But he no longer looks for the triumph of abstract truth, unaided by persistent, hard, earnest work to illustrate its practical utility. Indeed he now may become a real live working factor in the composition of the society that surrounds him, and the State that upholds his civil or political rights and measures his obligations to the world, of which he is a part.

MONASTERIES.

Can Christianity be held responsible for the theory of conduct of the unfortunates who resort to these religious houses as hiding-places, in order to skulk from or shirk the duties and burdens of practical life? The Saviour taught especially severe lessons of what in our day is called altruism; but these institutions sometimes, for some inmates, have been made the hotbeds of a stagnant egoism. The virile tonic and practical piety contained

in Longfellow's *Psalm of Life* (however unsatisfactory)
are far more wholesome aliment for a living soul than the
sweet opiates of Thomas à Kempis—or Chancellor Gerson.

Pushed to extremes, some of the doctrines of Christianity—when considered separately—might seem to
lead on the one hand to a real sacrifice of one's self to the
uttermost, as well as all of one's worldly possessions, for
the good of one's neighbor.   On the other hand, by mini-
mizing the business of this world to an almost insignificant
item, they apparently suggest, to some minds, the notion
of giving up all of our care and all of our thoughts while
here, to the affairs of ourselves in a world to come.   Both
versions would be too extravagant in practice.   The latter
apparently is a desertion of the post of immediate duty.
The first would involve a needless, and perhaps mischievous martyrdom, detrimental to, if not destructive of, the
true interest of all concerned in the functions of our
mortal lives ; including even the demoralized recipients of
such misplaced bounty.

The monastery appears to have been used by some as
a sort of hospital for diseased souls.   Many such invalid
spirits were, by their possessors, perhaps too rashly, deemed
incurable, through ordinary methods—such as the health-
breeding exercise of social usages, and an orderly discharge of the common functions of civilized life.   When
thus resorted to by men in bodily health the cloister
becomes, in effect, a living mausoleum for the bodies of
moral suicides.

It is proposed to speak of these institutions now, only
in their character of asylums for disappointed lives ;—we
omit here all other views of their establishment (whether,

from obvious or recondite motives of policy or piety on the part of the Roman Church, made seminaries of learning or auxiliaries of religion, and charity toward the sick and the poor) as well as all observation upon any grosser abuses alleged to have been made sometimes of them by corrupt inmates.

The relief suggested, nay even prescribed, by nature, for embarrassing misfortune—exaggerated passion, morbid self-mismanagement, or even undeserved obloquy and similar human calamity—lies immeasurably in one word —action. A man so afflicted may far better say to himself in the forcible, though unpoetical, language of Tennyson, speaking for one inclining to despondency :—

I myself must mix with action, lest I wither by despair.

When life seems least attractive to us, is it not then, more than ever—for the sake of example, for the sake of the divine spark within us, for the sake of an honest performance of the obligations we religiously owe to ourselves as well as to all men, or at least to the race, and indeed toward countless exacting circumstances around us—is it not our natural duty, even at some risk, to live actively? That indeed is the very precept of Christianity ;—as is well illustrated by the essence of the severe parable of the slothful and unprofitable slave.

It has been common to defend the too ascetic use made of these pious communities—for the purpose referred to —upon the sentimental side of the matter. Men talk as though there were some special merit in abandoning the innocent pleasures of this world, and in taking on a sap-

less life of abnegation of all worldly happiness. But
those very persons—for whom our sympathies are invoked
by such a view—are usually led in this direction by mere
pusillanimity, in thus running away from the battle of
life. Not unfrequently too they are so moved merely by
an exaggerated self-pity, or a yearning for the pity of
others. They sometimes madly propose to find a cure
for erroneous inclination—or involuntary. brooding over
unmerited affliction, or morbid moral growth and abnormal evil-development—by nourishing some other perhaps
more vicious tendency, or by feeding a smouldering flame
with slow combustibles. At the best they often seek to
escape the natural penalties of a misguided life, and to
find absolution, for voluntary error, through inanition.

As a recognized sanctuary and asylum, or place of
refuge for those guilty of crime against civil or social
law, where such persons were exempt outlaws of society
—inasmuch as suicide was believed to be impious and
wholly forbidden—perhaps, (as voluntary jails,) they
may have had their uses and excuses for some such
inmates. But why should merely timid, or despondent,
souls seek to propitiate in this manner a Creator supposed
to be personally offended? Why desert the plain
demands of society, as well as of their nature, to dream
away, in effeminate vacuity, the duration of a life given
for human reciprocity of active, well-doing, and consequent enjoyment of the real pleasures of human existence?—Is the God of Christianity a reflex of humanity,
in so bad a phase, as to look with favor upon slothful
adulation from men playing the rôle of cowards, or
yielding to an unmanly despair?

RELIGION, AS THE BASIS OF SOCIETY.

Based, as our civil and political condition now universally is, upon the fixed belief in a personal God and our
own soul's future existence—with all the Christian consequences of their relationship—it would be difficult for
us even to conceive what our social life might be, without
these fundamental ideas and their essential dogmas.

Faith in a system of future rewards or punishments for
well or ill doing here—which shall hereafter supply the
deficiencies of this mortal state in such matters—is so
deeply imbedded in the convictions of the common mind,
that ordinary men, now, act and suffer with a degree of
fortitude, patience, and elasticity we can hardly imagine
them capable of, without such a conviction.

Would an instinctive love of virtue, a natural sense of
justice, the restraints of civil or social law, and the love
of the good opinion of their fellow-men, long withhold
mankind from lapsing into a condition of moral, and perhaps physical savagery, if it were commonly understood
that this life is all we shall have, anywhere, of a conscious
existence ?

At this period of the world's social development only
a learned and thoughtful few, of those living among us,
appear to have such unqualified confidence in the completeness of the laws of nature—supplemented by those
of man—as to believe that, in all cases of wrong-doing,
we shall have due punishment here, in ourselves, or at
least in our posterity. What shall we say, however, of
the apparent lack of compensation anywhere, for those
wretched victims of involuntary suffering, whose calam-

ities befall them, without their fault, and oftentimes while in the discharge of sacred or self-denying duty? Moreover, with the general body of mankind, the expectation of avoiding detection of evil conduct, while this life endures, would be, apparently, equivalent to an avoidance of all punishment whatever, unless it shall be inflicted at some time hereafter, when all shall be known and escape be impossible.

Besides how many crimes against the well-being of society are recognized to be beyond the reach of human law, even when they are discovered. Nay, how many grievous sins are more than tolerated by social opinion. What attitude would a merely moral system, with no sanction beyond the grave, hold toward such offences, in the eyes of those who might fear neither the vengeance of nature, or any Nemesis whatever in this earthly life?

Inasmuch however as our entire social fabric, from time immemorial, has been founded upon the notion of a Divine personal supervision of individual human conduct perhaps it would be a blind, or at least rash, estimate of the untried capabilities of human nature, for us to say *ex cathedra*, that humanity can never attain to such a recognition of the eternal fitness of natural justice, as to be entrusted with an emancipation from reliance upon a hope of future reward, and from restraint by a fear of future punishment — without irreparable detriment to general social well-being.

Naturally men believe that state of things which they assume has always existed must be necessary. Consequently most people, among us, are of opinion that a disbelief in our future existence would necessarily involve the rushing into a ruinous indulgence in every excess or vice of which unrestrained man is capable. Undoubtedly this would be largely the first result of sudden total infidelity of a whole people, who had been habituated to the threats and promises of our Divine religion. For, as Erdmann, in his *History of Philosophy*, well says :—" The breaking of the chains of slavery is not by itself enough to confer freedom."

Yet there have been in the past, and now are, numerous individual men, just and honest, by a law of their own nature. They find more happiness in virtue than in vice—in moderation than in excess—and are so unhappily constituted, that, for themselves, a belief in supernatural religion seems to be impossible. It cannot be certain that in the lapse of future ages their numbers may not be greatly multiplied. Perhaps, too, it would not detract from the sublimity, or grace, of our own Gospel Revelation, if we might be permitted to hope that, at the least, in some remote day, its threats and promises would cease to be regarded, by so many, as necessary chiefly in order to prevent the wickedness of the great mass of men, toward either themselves or each other.

Teaching Backward.

One of the many bad consequences of the incalculably useful invention of the art of printing—and the consequently inevitable multiplication of mere books to supply the demands of universal *quasi*-education is that— by reason of excessive, injudicious, desultory reading of literature in youth—we are taught words, opinions, or

19

thoughts, before we learn things, facts, or events. Books of "elegant extracts," "wit and wisdom," or "beauties," debauch the minds of many misguided readers. By this reversed process of self-instruction—or rather misinstruction—ideas are often wrenched from their natural belongings. They are set afloat through the memory and mind, dislocated and disassociated from their context, as well as from the tangible realities out of which they grow, and of which they are designed to be only the immediate interpretation. Their actual significance being thus sometimes quite distorted, a fruitful result of mental misleading—frequently of life-long endurance—necessarily follows.

Perhaps, from this prolific source, too, springs the deplorable fact that so large a portion of modern belles-lettres productions—catering to a popular appetite for sciolism in letters—consists of books drawn from books ; —instead of being deduced from Nature herself, or real observation or experience in human affairs, with genuine opinion or idealization from fresh verity. For sometimes threadbare rhetoric, artificial imagery, or criticism of criticism usurp the function of scientific information, knowledge of mankind, and human affairs, or fine observation of the actual forms and processes of nature. In short the fruit appears to anticipate the maturity of the flower ;—resulting in blight or deformity. Hence are so many authors, and so few classics—or books bringing permanent addition to the stock of good literature.

The true method, either of imparting or acquiring information and knowledge, in science, literature, or art (outside of the realm of mere imagination and fancy)

—particularly with the young pupil, as every one ought to remember—is, to set real things before the growing mind. This should be done either by objects, or statements of fact about objects, or events, or characters, and by teaching it to think about them as actualities ;—substantially what is now called "object-teaching." When one, thus instructed, wishes to formulate and express his own ideas—self-formed upon any subject—or to deduce a derived knowledge through comparison of the ingredients of his real information, he may then begin to read arguments and opinions about the matter to be so considered.

This latter procedure ought to be quite a secondary process. In this manner one may be taught to value opinion when read only in proportion as it is true, verifiable, and clearly expressed. Also the mind will, by this means, escape being the slave of popular authority, or inclined to value words more than things, or names of authors more than their works. For one of the mastering literary sins of our day is a tendency to talk in print about what one knows nothing, except what has been picked up, as it were by chance, in writings of the thoughts, opinions, or mere random speech, of others.

This species of intellectual vice comes largely of indolence and conceit, either in teacher, or pupil, or both, and is prone to discourage real learning and well-grounded self-reliance. Object-teaching—as opposed to parrot teaching—always should be the first step in early and even late education. Human nature, society, and history, rather than criticisms and book-reviews, should be the.food of the hungry literary aspirant. It is well to let one get fully possessed of facts—either from general reliable sources of knowledge or from personal observation—before he attempts to deduce or express ideas ; otherwise they will necessarily be purely second-handed and probably inconsistent.

Indeed, books about other books, and books of criticism concerning writings not well-mastered or not read at all—or books of mere literary or ethical opinion—should be almost prohibited to the young student. In short, this wretched process of word-teaching, that unduly exalts mere books—more especially in the domain of pure literature—overcharges the memory with words without specific or accurate meaning, tends to emasculate the brain, to take away its independence or elasticity, and to stunt its growth. At the same time, it works toward a condition of mental somnolence, if not of atrophy itself. Most truly, as was wisely said, of bare book-mongering, long ago :—

> Small have continual plodders ever won,
> Save base authority from other's books.

POINT OF VIEW.

Must we agree with Marcus Aurelius that everything is dependent upon " opinion ";—that, not what is, but what commonly seems to be, controls the world ? It is hard to govern our conduct by the mere experience of others, however many, when that conflicts with our own judgment, will, or inclination. We always incline to suspect the cases are not parallel, and that ours is somehow peculiar. We wish to try the question anew, and make up a judgment for ourselves—blindly overlooking the risk of partiality to our own inclination impairing our decision.

The world has little respect for pragmatical individual opinion—but a profound regard for its own. " No man is as wise as all men," is an accepted apothegm, the adoption of which at least perhaps correctly is attributed to the sagacity of Talleyrand. *Vox populi, vox dei* is an adage of unknown age, or origin, but very widely popular.

Wherein then lies the secret of that prodigy, called Public Opinion—which seems to be the autocrat of the nineteenth century? How does it happen that the voice of many ordinary men should so often appear to evince a greater sagacity, in practical affairs, than that of any one wise man? How does the whole become better than any of its parts? Does it not come—if it come at all—from a multiplication of observations from many different points of view? When we look upon events, the mind's eye of an individual is ordinarily confined to a single point of observation. In rare cases perhaps he may have capacity, learning, experience, imagination, acquired or natural insight, to enable him to look from outside of himself, and, as it were, to divine what may be seen from some other point of view than his own.

However even all of this kind of adventitious help is often liable by prejudice or interest, to many chances of error or misconception. But when, with due humility, we candidly and without prejudgment, take counsel of others—be they wise or not—we can get at least the benefit of their several special stand-points in looking at a matter. We now also change the perspective. We can discern—differently from what was before apparent to our limited observation—the juxtaposition and relation of things to each other. Besides we can see thus many things otherwise obscured as it were by shadows, or actually hidden by intervening objects, before. We should not necessarily adopt their judgment as sound— else we might merely exchange one uncertain element in a problem for another, where both may be fallacious. But even if our own opinion be, most likely, substantially correct, or most surely the better one, we may still use the calculation of another to test the accuracy of, or perhaps to correct some subordinate deflection from the true line in our own.

In current practical matters—public, ethical, or social —each man ordinarily looks from his special point of vision and sees, usually, only a single side of anything; a consideration of vast moment sometimes, when canvassing his individual opinions. Many men, however, may see separately many sides of the same object, matter, or event ;—if, as generally happens, it have many sides. By degrees, when these views are all gradually brought together, by comparison, into some kind of harmony, they make a public opinion. Usually, for immediate purposes, it is therefore wiser than the individual, unaided, opinion of almost any one separate man.

True each man's judgment is likely to be colored and disturbed by his individual interests, passions, or other peculiarities—or to be limited or distorted by imperfect vision or opportunity. Yet when the opinions of a great number are brought together, (although of comparatively little value when taken separately) immaterial elements seem naturally to drop out, or neutralize each other, and the residuum is probably in most cases a more just estimate of any matter under consideration, than could be obtained ordinarily by a single person. Inconvenient therefore as it may be, to tyrants and self-willed people (generally speaking, at least) the old truth remains that, " in the multitude of counsellors there is safety," for the management of many practical affairs, of public as well as of private concern.

The colossal strides, of late years, made by modern science, in pursuit of truth, by the study of comparative religions, jurisprudence, politics, philosophy, morality, and sociology, furnish a further illustration of the hints shadowed forth in these suggestions.

SOCIAL APPEARANCES.

Happy the man who is so constituted by nature, so disciplined by habit, or so surrounded by association, that in social matters he is never over-tempted to do obviously, or to say aloud, anything uncommon ! Formal society keeps a species of secret police, constantly watching the doings of its own members, and appears determined, by severe intimidation (or, if necessary, by extreme punishment) to keep them all in apparent uniformity.

Social despotism, however, does not usually pretend to look very deeply into motives, or even closely to scrutinize all actual conduct. But it is apt to be merciless in its judgment upon what it sees fit to regard as equivocal, or worse, in appearances. The outside of the platter, at least, must be kept clean at all hazards. Social laws are sometimes unhappily so obscure in their terms, or hung at such a Draconian height, that it is not easy to read them, or if read to understand their precise meaning. Yet all are supposed to know them, and mere ignorance of even their most arbitrary formulas seldom excuses any one.

It is frequently safe, in some circles, to be pretty bad in fact—or at least suspected of being so—if outward conformity to social exactions be complete. But it is very dangerous to appear in anywise irregular, however good the motive, or unexceptionable, or even excellent, the real conduct. Although it may be conceded the enforcement of the extreme penalties of the social code is not alway impartial, in respect to persons.

There is one curious anomaly of unwritten social law in general, deserving of mention in this connection. The higher the caste of society, the less scrupulously it seems to take cognizance of mere facts in social conduct, and the more weight it seems to attach to any appearance of evil. Yet as we descend in the social scale a different rule will be found to prevail. Here even equivocal appearances are either wholly overlooked, or supposed to be innocent ; while known facts (however secluded from the general, public eye) will burn into the social memory, beyond any chance of effacement even by the charitable sponge of time.

The popular rules of social right or wrong are nowadays rigid ;—but few exceptions being admitted. Such rules are sometimes unreasonable, ethically obscure, and

even contradictory or at least inconsistent, as well as
fruitfully minute in their several provisions touching
common social intercourse ;—judging chiefly however,
as has been said, by outward appearances. Yet usually
they are construed so as often to leave individual misconduct, when unobtrusive, severely alone. At the
same time society holds all of its members to a strict observance of its rites, form, or ceremonies. It looks upon
a disregard of any of its common tenets as an insidious assault upon its very power and prestige. Indeed, it
cares little or nothing for any mere person, but everything for itself.

Unlike our municipal law, the social code has no merciful maxims—not even *in favorem vitæ.* Nor does it
often presume innocence, and wait until guilt shall be
established. On the contrary it usually assumes the
guilt, upon accusation, and condemns in advance. It
distrusts personal asseveration or even direct proof of
innocence—where appearances are of bad or doubtful
import. Indeed, its highest test of verity is one-sided
or circumstantial evidence, wherever the theory of guilt
will plausibly explain appearances. Whenever it becomes important to preconsider how one's social conduct will look in the eyes of the world—something of
course not worth considering where a principle or a duty
is at stake—it is well for him, who would escape
calumny, to bear in mind that society will surely put the
worst probable constructions upon whatever he may do ;
—if it be in any respect susceptible of a double significance. Hence too has grown up a habit, among some
frank and honest but politic people, never to do a thing,

or even make an observation, liable to misconstruction
—unless in obedience to an imperative dictate of either
a practical necessity or of some grand purpose.

OBLIGATION TO POSTERITY.

The careless light-heartedness of happy human nature
—however fortunate for us in other respects—tends to
make us unconscious of the obligation we are under to
the myriads of human beings who have toiled or suffered
heretofore in order to bring into the common stock of
civilization, the precious comforts and amenities we
enjoy, without price and as freely as the air, of land and
sea, we breath. Yet a moment's reflection will stagger
the narrowest or dullest understanding, when it contemplates a contrast of the present condition of things with
our possible situation, if we were the mere beginners of
our race ! What can be more unanswerable to the liberal
mind, than the statement that we ought in some way to
recognize, and to be willing in some measure to repay,
somehow, the debt we owe to those who have contributed
so much to our present happiness ?

The question is : How can we do it ? Our benefactors are gone—where nothing can touch them further.
Yet obviously one generation is but a link in the endless
chain of human life. Although we borrow of the past,
surely we may repay to the future. The world's knowledge
and wisdom were not amassed in a day. What we have
of them has been a slow accretion of " the long result of
time "—line upon line, precept upon precept, here a
little, and there a little. No two men are alike in all

things—not even in essentials. Every man has his peculiarities of mental, moral, and physical structure, surrounding, and opportunity. So each man may add something to the wisdom, or comfort, or convenience, or practical charm of human life in general—be it ever so little—according to his special measure of inward and outward gift or experience ;—in a narrow or a wide circle. For this contribution, however humble, humanity, in some corner of this great globe, may yet be reasonably thankful that he has lived.

There is nothing burdensome in this suggestion. For when a man sincerely feels he has a duty to others to be performed, so long as this sense masters him he is lifted above sordidness, or mere self-gratification. The very exercise of his faculties in this direction acquires and begets, or at least cultivates, in him a spiritual impulse, that elevates his whole character to a nobler standard. Should we not teach then more assiduously our children always so to aim, by their lives and actions, that each shall strive to contribute to posterity something of value for the race ;—something which at the least shall tend in some measure toward payment of the natural debt he owes to his general ancestry ?

REFORMERS.

There are always at least two leading but widely different classes of reformers—each class being perhaps equally well-meaning, though varying in value, in respect to its way and place—but often mistakenly confounded. First there is the gradual reformer, who is thoughtful, methodical, earnest, benevolent, and a sincere lover of mankind. He observes that all the improving processes of law or nature, political and social as well as physical, by which anything great or permanent is achieved, are slow. They come by gradual accretion or reduction, each step preparing the way for the next. The thing accomplished is a coherent, consistent, homogeneous growth, that preserves the good, while discarding the evil, in whatever it displaces or modifies.

Then, there is the immediate reformer, who cannot wait. He has no faith in Time. He is an enthusiast by nature. Observation is no part of his methods, and the fruits of experience are wasted upon him. He may be a zealous lover of his race—often, however, in a rather general and abstract way—but he has no toleration for its weaknesses or errors. He is born an idealist, and is a theorist by cultivation. He does not reckon as factors in his problem men as they are, but, as it is supposed by him man might or ought to be. He takes no note of " human weakness or political necessity." He wishes to root up the old and plant the new—with little regard to climate or season and without any preparation of the soil.

The gradual reformer begins his change by introducing what is called for by general assent—does what is permitted, contemplates nothing violent—is content first to enlighten public opinion and then to progress only as keeping pace with, or a very little in advance of, it.;— leading in fact, but seeming to follow. Of him it might always be said :—Specie obsequii quieta cum industria regebat,

The immediate reformer, on the contrary, being an idealist in pursuit of perfection only, forgetful of mundane conditions, seeks to revolutionize human conduct by a *tour de force.* The result often is that he destroys all the good elements of an old system, and, in advance of events or opinion, aims to substitute something new for which no one is ready. This soon works its own destruction ;—involving all the evils of passionate and blind reaction. Ultimately too, when he has prevailed, it sometimes happens that, from sheer necessity, as a working factor in affairs, the old is rehabilitated. The reform contemplated, however meritorious, is put back for a generation or more, by his intemperate haste. For, although occasionally some reformations are best accomplished from cutting up abuses or obsolete impediments by the roots, yet, as every statesman knows, most good and permanent work of this kind creeps along by almost imperceptible degrees ;—and not without some retrogression.

HUMAN PERFECTIBILITY.

Is there satisfactory proof that civil society, as a mass, is making permanent progress toward a lasting possession of that coveted ideal perfection which so long has been the dream of religious, political, or social enthusiasts ; and which still seems relatively possible, if not practicable, in the case of an individual ? History fails to demonstrate that any whole people can be elevated to a positive approximation toward perfection in virtue and intelligence. If so elevated, could it be maintained at such a high level, for the period of time necessary to preserve society permanently pure and sweet?

Ancient annals appear to teach that, under the most favorable circumstances, long before the great mass of a community has attained the lofty ideal suggested by its early promise, first a few, then many, and finally the greater number, begin to deteriorate, and gradually to decline, until they reach, if not degradation, at least a low state of polity, manners, and morals not unlike it.

Nature almost seems to abhor a perpetuity in the best political or social results of human endeavor. The story of the Tower of Babel is typical of the fortune awaiting exaggerated human aspirations. A man, by self-discipline, and by his virtuous actions, may individually attain such a pitch of excellence, as to leave but little further to be desired in his career ;—except its continuance. Nature, however, shuts the door. His life is limited here. But that large organization of combined individuals, we call civil society, although self-perpetuating— possibly everlasting and therefore seemingly capable of indefinite progress in the right direction—no sooner attains some considerable degree of worthiness, than it appears to begin to retrograde and finally to decay.

Past civilizations have been as hopeful as ours of better things. Yet their pathways are strewn with wrecks of aspirations and enthusiasms as lofty and ardent as our own. History, as it were to moderate our conceit, lifts its warning finger and points to their common superscription :—*Hic jacet.* Still we are unwilling to believe that man does not, to some extent, progress, however irregularly—never losing quite all that is gained—toward extreme public virtue and social excellence. If it be an illusion, yet such a faith seems to be an essential element of refined human association—that it shall expect to grow wiser, nobler, better, and in all things happier, as time wears away.

Perhaps, however, if perfection were indeed accomplished—and humanity had nothing better to hope for beyond what were permanently achieved, while here— poor human nature could not long endure the dead-level of such virtuous happiness. Unless we were radically changed, perhaps there would be some sighs among us for at least a spice of wickedness, merely to break up the monotony and dispel satiety! Indeed to some skeptics the task of Sisyphus seems better adapted to develop man's largest capabilities, while in this mortal sphere, than any realization of the dreams of either the ideal philosopher or the socialistic fanatic. Nevertheless, strive as we may, the choice is apparently not with us. There seems to be no alternative but to temporize and to

> Let the great world spin forever, down the ringing grooves of change.

SOCIAL INFERIORS.

It is a peculiar misfortune to one's character to be born and bred in nominal equality among real inferiors ; —either in intellect, moral endowments, or some social circumstances. That is an especially unhealthy atmosphere for the young mind or heart to inhale, which inflates its pride into arrogance, or puffs up its vanity.

Nothing so unfits the youthful character to discover its true relations to others—to fathom itself, and to arrive at its moral equilibrium—as an engorging self-conceit. Whether exaggerated selfishness be symbolized, at its early lodgment in the human heart, as a root, or perhaps more truly as a disease, it cannot be too strongly characterized as an enemy to that real equanimity which is the spirit of all the virtues.

Happiness, moral or intellectual, can be attained only by first putting and keeping one's self in true relation to all the men and things that are the actual and unavoidable accompaniments of one's social existence. Whatever tends to place one out of harmonious relations with one's circumstances, associations, friends, and acquaintances is hostile to wise or sound development of character, and surely will make one morbid, uncertain, irregular, untrustworthy, and perhaps not unjustly, in the end, disliked and even distrusted.

The world has little toleration for merely vain eccentricity. Whenever this is harmless to society, it may go unpunished, except by others' neglect of those who indulge in its vagaries. But when it attempts to interfere recklessly with established social order or, from idle vanity, to assert itself in any way counter to the common current of things, it is buffetted, or kicked into a corner, as worthless rubbish.

When a person is born and bred among family or other relatives, who are greatly his mental or moral inferiors, this seed of misery is sometimes planted very early. The intellectual questionings of a bright mind, when put to its familiars, are liable to be met by disdain or mute despair. A juvenal, encountering such rebuffs among his near companions, soon learns to turn to books, usually miscellaneous, or injudiciously chosen. He nourishes a " youth sublime," by feeding upon what are but draff and husks to his immediate associates. This unassimilated pabulum probably soon engenders an egotism, full of self-love or self-conceit, and an arrogance that makes the youth too early self-satisfied. Besides it strongly tends to dull the edge of that intelligent curiosity, which, under more favorable circumstances, properly directed, might grow into a healthy thirst for real knowledge.

There are only a few grand characters, born in any period, whose native qualities are so vast and well-balanced, that they can rise superior to all adverse surroundings, and find their way unaided into the society of the great world of intellectual endeavor and achievement. Most men, if not absolutely controlled by unfavorable circumstances, are, at least, so handicapped or directed by them, that their real capabilities are often, even to themselves, unknown ;—at the least until the day has passed, when they might have trained such powers to secure their best development, and made them the means of accomplishing a worthy career.

CONSPICUOUSNESS.

There are obvious disadvantages, to counterbalance the charms of philosophic composure, in an isolated and obscure life. There is also some compensation, for that

20

loss of privacy and that absence of a feeling of entire independence, which are inseparable from an open career. The young man, who fancies no eye is upon him, sometimes revels in what we might call a gust of Bohemianism. He imagines he is a philosopher, when in fact he is merely a savage. The tonic influences of social ties, and self-restraint, upon his character, being relaxed or wholly withdrawn, he is liable to waste his moral substance in some unbounded license of thought, feeling, or conduct, that, like all other excess, will easily run on to satiety, even if it do not destroy the power of recuperation.

Pity it may be, but so we are made. To ignore this proverbial truth is to shut our eyes to our iron-like mortal limitations. In later life surely will come— through any over-indulgence of such private inclinations—by a natural sequence, in rapid succession if unchecked, first what might be called *cui-bono-ism ;* then indifference ; and finally, perhaps, even a sort of apathy or moral paralysis.

On the other hand he who lives in the public eye is led necessarily to keep his garments pure and white so that they may shine unspotted in the sun. The natural process of his evolution of character is, therefore, toward conventional conservatism and severe moderation in his lower impulses, with a corresponding tendency to a higher life for his better nature. In his inevitable conflict with the malignant spirits of the world he finds no armor so nearly invulnerable as this panoply of a well-recognized uprightness of personal character.

HUMAN PROGRESS.

Moral as well as political ideas seem to move in a devious track ;—neither steadily forward nor backward, nor
with a continuous deflection in the same line. Their
motion is not unlike that ascribed to pigeons ; which are
said to move by inverted cycloids, when they fly from a
height—first a descent, then a rise. Human progress
appears to be not unlike a movement of the waves of a
slowly incoming tide. Sometimes the retreat seems to
be greater than the onward movement, when considered
as separate steps ; yet when taken together headway is
visibly gained.

Perhaps, however, a still better illustration of the ordinary course of human progress may be found in its
resemblance to the motion of a cyclonic storm. Notwithstanding it contains within itself a constant rotary
motion, that makes its direction appear capricious and
variable, yet its moves steadily forward—although upon
uncertain lines, and with unequal pace—despite even an
occasional collision with a counter-storm.

The chief manifestation, by man, of his superiority in
intelligence, over that of other animals, lies not only in ac-
cumulating knowledge, but in his power first of deducing
abstract ideas from concrete facts and, then—by a higher
process of the mind—reaching another class of thoughts
that are perceptible only after the first are attained.
The most encouraging view of the matter of human advancement, and one which significantly indicates a Divine
hand, is that the firm establishment in the convictions of
mankind of one cardinal truth or virtue—however small

in itself—resembles a germinal seed. It renders another
truth or virtue, not unlike itself—sometimes superior—
possible, and sooner practicable than if the first had not
been well recognized. So men may rise, as Tennyson
says, on "stepping-stones" to "higher things."

Opinion, however, moves slowly in the right direction
and rarely can be hastened until the time—or public
mind—is ripe for its reception. But it moves. The annals of superstition, morals, political economy, and
applied science, leave no doubt of that. Its perpetuity
is another matter altogether.

THE SPIRIT OF THE AGE.

Our time is a period of disenchantment—of dispelling
illusions—of analysis and of reducing all things to first
principles. It cannot be called an age of gold or of silver ;
nor yet wholly of brass. None of these expressions
touch its leading characteristics fairly.

Disrespect for authority merely, as a power, is one of
its prominent features. The glamour of tradition neither
awes nor cajoles it. It has the simplicity—with the bold-
ness—of conscious and confessed ignorance. It wants
to know. It will not be content until it has dissected
everything. Irreverently and without fear or favor, it
traces to their source, and analyzes, facts, feelings, habits,
customs and fancies, or thoughts, together with traditions
and beliefs.

Whatever comes in its way—dead or alive—must be
taken to pieces. It might be called the Age of Atoms.
It is satisfied only by disintegration and fact. It

leaves synthesis, reconstruction, and the totality of truth to a period of broader thought, and of more reverent spirit. At all events it takes no care of the morrow ; it lives in the present—regardless of both past and future.

When it shall have destroyed all that is not based on demonstration, if there shall be no more faith nor hope left among mankind, apathy will doubtless succeed. Then, perhaps, will prevail again ignorance, and consequently, after a time, new illusions, myths, and reconstruction. Mayhap, another Golden Age will come ;— to be in its turn demolished ! So reasons the pessimistic cynic of our day.

THE PRODIGALITY OF NATURE.

The seeming wastefulness of Nature is painfully manifest in the premature death of a man, whose eminent skill and learning are the results of many years' labor in their acquisition. In statesmanship, science, invention, jurisprudence, or letters, the ripened powers of a lifetime are unexpectedly destroyed in a moment.

The loss is great to mankind ; and it is often irreparable. Not seldom, just at the time when a capacity to deal with the more difficult problems of life, or nature, has reached its acme, death comes and swallows up all. The death of even the most advanced in life—such as an Ericsson at eighty-five—sometimes seems harsh.

New men must arise, and often are obliged to work over the half-tilled field unassisted by the experience and matured judgment of their seniors, who have been cut off in the height of their usefulness,

Doubtless there is a wise compensation somewhere in such special events ; but like many others of the so-called mysteries of nature, it is at present unknown ; and is an inexplicable enigma, at least to ordinary observers.

LAW.

There appears to be a popular impression that in medicine there must be a known specific for every recognized disease, and that in law, there is a particular rule in a written code, easily applicable to every supposable case.

When, therefore, ordinary people consult a lawyer, their inclination is not to give a statement of facts, but to state a suppositious case. They prefer to put an abstract question, rather than mention details. When told that the law for which they inquire would only mislead them by its generality, and probably overwhelm and confuse them by its qualifications and exceptions, they are as much vexed as Macbeth consulting his wife's physician. They are as impatient as he to throw physic to the dogs and have none of it.

They are nettled to learn that the precise principle they seek cannot be formulated and given them in a few words. So also they reluct when requested to give particular facts which they deem non-essential. Sometimes they rebel outright when they learn that there cannot be given them a plain rule which they may readily apply for themselves.

In this dissatisfaction with the actual and intrinsic condition of such matters—which such people are prone

to consider factitious, and cunningly kept up by a profession for its own selfish gain—appears to lurk the
delusion that finds expression in the great desire and
frequent demand of the popular mind for a formulary,
of every branch of the law, which he who runs might
read.

To Do or Not to Do.

It is no easy task, at all times, for our infirm human
nature, when subjected to great temptation, to draw the
line between what is physically possible and what is
morally impossible; between what we can do with
apparent impunity, and what we feel we ought not to do,
having due regard for our own real, ultimate good
and the well-being of others. Besides in ordinary dealings the point, where the horizon of physical possibility
is cut by the line of moral impossibility, is not always
obvious to the eye of one who is under pressure of passion, or temptation of interest, or even of importunity of
others. Yet it is usually just this line—so often thin and
shadowy—which divides virtue from vice. Upon one
side of it lie all the cardinal virtues; while on the other
may be wrong, crime, sin, and shame.

Absence of Religion.

Mere men of the world, who recklessly assail a people's
faith in any religion, incur an immeasurable responsibility. They provoke also a civil problem for which
history furnishes no practical solution. Can man be
governed and kept in harmony with the well-being

of society, by simple human law? Will he not hope and expect to escape only human punishment? Can he be made to feel he must suffer for every violation of law, or of another's right—to say nothing of a neglect of clear duty—if he have neither love for, nor fear of, any supernatural, omniscient, unseen Power?

WHY SHOULD MAN LIVE?

To do good to others for the glory of his Creator, says the Christian. To do what is best for himself and his true self-evolvement, consistently with the laws of nature and society, says the pagan philosopher of antiquity. To all of these things for the perpetuation and perfection of the human race says the sublime Orientalist.

IDOLOCLASM.

However hazardous to the individual, and however dangerous to society, the occupation of idol-breaking opens the easiest door to that notoriety, the love of which is the besetting sin of the rash, or the superficial reformer. No man is ordinarily so ignorant of the remote consequences of what he is doing, as one who strives to break up the slowly-grown, or long-standing habits, laws, and customs of a people or a community.

AUTHOR AND ARTIST.

He is the greatest artist, then,
Whether of pencil or of pen,
Who follows Nature.

LONGFELLOW.

I.

VERBAL MUSIC.

My words are only words, and moved
Upon the topmost froth of thought.

TENNYSON.

POETRY may be called rightly the music of thought—imaginative or emotional thought. Some popular poems, however, appear to be, in themselves, little besides rhythmical words. Such verses give sounds evoking poetical emotions, but seem to leave the reader to supply the thought —or at least to imagine the significance and coherence of their suggestions. To consider thus is perhaps not unlike ruffling the down of a butterfly to look for its quills. Yet it may be useful to hint in what manner some exquisite bits of poetical bric-a-brac may be made to give pleasure to those who, from their indolence or dulness, find in such poets as Emerson, Browning, and Tennyson, many things obscure, incoherent, and elliptical, or only rhapsodies of inspired nonsense.

Perhaps a book of such poems could be " adapted to the use of schools," also, by a sort of prose paraphrase of the lines, or by supplying an assortment of such ideas as could be readily fitted to the words of the poet. It might furnish an edifying experiment for the young student. He could give his commentaries according to his notion of what, if anything, the poet might be imagined to have intended to say. Or he could supply what any articulate sounds of similar rhythm might be supposed to suggest to one looking for special ideas, and despairing of finding any in the text of the particular poem in hand. Such an exercise would tend at least to cultivate the poetical faculty of the pupil—aside from the value of any discoveries that might be made.

To illustrate the method proposed let us test a short popular poem of Tennyson by way of example : —

> Break, break, break,
>   On thy cold gray stones, oh sea !
>   And I would that my tongue could utter
>   The thoughts that arise in me.

The poet is watching the incoming tide upon a rocky coast—probably at Clevedon, on the British Channel. Here are heard and seen the beating and breaking of the everlasting waves of the great sea, rolling and dashing upon the resisting but motionless rocks. Melancholy sounds escape from the scattered billows, as they are driven back in myriad fragments of bubbles, foam, and spray—endlessly renewing the hopeless assault, and as often impelled by the immobility of the "cold gray stones." These monotonous sights and sounds fill the heart of the poet with sadness. He sees the untiring efforts of a great power thwarted by the mere repose of a greater one. His sympathy naturally goes with the weaker ; while the music of the rhythmical sounds stirs mournful feelings in his bosom. These emotions he shares in kind with the general mass of men and women ; although in him doubtless they are, in degree, more intense by reason of his supreme poetical temperament. So far we follow him and sympathize. His lines merely transfuse into the music of humanity the voices of the resounding sea. Thereby he claims his kinship with the whole human world—while the metrical words he employs keep time with the undulatory vibrations of the swelling waves.

But when he wishes he might "utter the thoughts that arise " in him—like many another poet before and since— he seems to mistake feelings for ideas and emotions for thoughts. If a man have a real thought, usually, somehow, he can utter or describe it. Generally men, and even poets, think either in words or in pictures, or in metaphors.

When a man tells us his feelings are too great, or too confused for his utterance, we can well believe him. But when his tongue refuses to utter what he believes he thinks ; or he brings a bill of indictment against language for insufficiency to express his thoughts, we suspect that— as in the case of other incompetent workmen who have quarrelled with their tools—the fault is elsewhere. Mayhap, however, his suggestion is more opulent to the fancy than his description could be. So that we need waste no regrets over the inability of a poet's tongue to give out more words. If they came, we may rest assured they would be as vague and obscure as the natural sounds they vainly sought to interpret. Our poet wisely leaves such practice to others. Yet, as he is filled with poetical emotions, which he is apparently conscious of sharing with all mankind, he seems to say to himself, as he says to the world elsewhere :—

> I cannot make this matter plain,
> But I will shoot, howe'er in vain,
> A random arrow from the brain.

Whereupon he proceeds to sing the sweet music of the sad sea waves, as others have sung of them before him, though seldom perhaps with such delicacy, harmony, and grace as he.

This futile travail of Euterpe has thwarted the hopes of other lyric poets, as well as Tennyson. Even our own accomplished Stoddard once sang of his grievance in this wise, with pathetic humility :—

> A thousand dreamy melodies,
>   Begot with pleasant pain,
> Like incantations float around
>   The chambers of my brain.

> But when I strive to utter one,
>   It mocks my feeble art,
> And leaves me silent, with the thorn
>   Of music in my heart !

One word more is due in behalf of the English poet. Perhaps too harsh a judgment has been given against his

opening verse. When he laments that his tongue cannot
" utter " his " thoughts," possibly he may refer to those
awful and tumultuous upheavals of the soul that sometimes are provoked by the sounds and shows of the workings of the great powers of Nature. Then the personality
of the hearer stands out, almost, as it were, palpable to
his sense of feeling. The individual is all in all to himself ; and his fellow-men are as nothing to him. All the
oppressive mysteries of existence seem to stare him in the
face, and, for the time, he knows only his relation to his
Maker ;—while he keenly feels his special responsibility
for his own peculiar identity. At such a time to " utter "
his thoughts would be to tear away the veil that hides
from the common eye the sacred penetralia, where he
keeps that part of his nature which is beyond the reach of
human sympathy.

If the poet intended to say that it would give relief to
his bosom were it permissible to " utter " thoughts of this
nature—thoughts which, purely out of respect to his
individuality, must be kept wholly to himself—then the
criticism would be unjust. Nevertheless if such had been
his meaning, the verses would be still subject to the cavil
of being a specimen of what may be called suppressed
poetry.

> O well for the fisherman's boy,
> That he shouts with his sister at play !
> O well for the sailor lad,
> That he sings in his boat on the bay !

It is " well " for youth to be deaf to the melancholy
suggestions these murmurings of the sea pour into the
hearts of those who have lost their early illusions, have

been cheated of their expectations, and have found the anticipated pleasures and gains of existence hollow and unsubstantial. Here the poet has a " thought "—although again common enough. The contrast of this happy pair of children-at-play, with his own tearful emotions, as the desolation of the past unrolls before his vision, affects him visibly.

He has no trouble with want of looseness in his " tongue " now. He thinks in a picture, and he utters a description of a scene. But, the thought being too ordinary for expansion, he puts the whole force of his idea in the simple expression " well," and, like a dainty master as he is, leaves it—as a painting of the school of *le premier coup.*

> And the stately ships go on,
>   To their haven under the hill ;
> But oh, for the touch of a vanished hand
>   And the sound of a voice that is still !

The ships (like the children-at-play) go on in their way, regardless of the roar and murmuring of these re-sistless and ever-beating sea-waves. The vessels reach their haven unaffected by such sentimental repinings as trouble disillusioned mortals. When the winds shall blow, and storms shall rage, perhaps these " stately ships " may again put forth their energy, and give battle to fierce waves. But now, unruffled and approaching port, with all their purposes accomplished—with a show of serene dignity, and a consciousness of good work done and of perils overcome—they are "stately" to the poet's eye. They now seem to have every wish most longed for accomplished. In bitter contrast, the moaning of the breaking sea still lingers in the poet's ear. The "thoughts" of his misery—as he recalls the snapping asunder of the "silver cord" of early friendship, or the breaking of the "golden bowl" of love—bring forth a sigh that touches every heart sensitive to human sympathy. His "tongue" is no longer at a loss for words. They come, tumultuous as these rushing waves, and then die away in a moan of tender regret, like the receding tide of the echoing sea itself.

> Break, break, break,
> At the foot of thy crags, oh sea !
> For the tender grace of a day that is dead,
> Will never come back to me.

As tears fill the eyes of the poet, in his dream of the past, he gives way to despair. He sees no more the children, or the ships ; or scarcely the impassive rocks. He grieves as one who will not be comforted. Joy is dead. The happiness of a former day is gone—never to return. Not even ideas now are wanting. He evolves more than mere emotion. His thought is strong and clear, and when he gives it voice the sound rings in the ear like a funeral knell. Here, too, the thought being trite, a very little dilation of it would make it impalpable or tiresome. The poet shows his skill and taste again by the delicacy of his touch ;—by leaving well-enough alone. Would that the workmen of his gentle craft might follow more frequently his example ;—instead of sometimes spinning their silken cobwebs so fine that the thread becomes invisible, or beating even gold so thin that all appreciable substance is hammered out of it.

II.

THE COMING NOVEL.

After the abundant invective poured on this class of books it is time to settle forever the controversy, by asserting that these works of fiction are among the most instructive of every polished nation, and must contain all the useful truths of human life, if composed with genius.

ISAAC D'ISRAELI.

NOT long ago one of the most enterprising of our city newspapers propounded to many men and women of letters in this country the questions : Who will write the " future novel " ? and What will it be ? None appeared to doubt that something extraordinary is coming, and is, indeed, not very far off ;—although there was a good deal of variety in their opinions as to what it will be like, and who shall write it. Of course it will be done by an American ! Not a few of either sex are assured it will be written by a woman; and, more than one, that it must be something that " will sell." As *Mr. Barnes of New York* and *Thou Shalt Not* are probably now ahead by this test, the prospect thus indicated would seem not encouraging for the classic method. Indeed, this melan-

choly view of the matter appears to be entertained by
Anthony Comstock himself. The majority however are
hopeful of better things.

Some of the respondents appear to think it will be
what is called by them a "psychological study"—or a
"sensible psychology for the idle." Others are confident it
will be "realistic." Mr. Gilder, who perhaps ought to
know as well as any one, looks for what he characterizes
as "imaginative realism"; while Mr. Howells is confident that—"when Victor Hugo died the death-knell of
romantic fiction was sounded," and that "realism will be
the style of fiction in the future." Professor Boyesen—
haud inexpertus—also thinks the "tendency of fiction is
toward a close fidelity to life and a closer adherence to
the logic of reality." Noah Brooks is clear that it will
be "realistic, not a vision"—but "highly imaginative."

Apparently conflicting opinions are expressed by many
other well-known writers, not easily reconcilable. Irrespective of what the "novel of the future" ought to be,
however, they seem to think that, while keeping in equilibrium with the sociological thought or opinion of the
progressing day, it will move probably in many of the
same channels as, and by methods not seriously different
from, those already pursued by the masters of the popular classics in this department of literature during the
latter half of this century. To our humble thinking
there is among them one hint of superior wisdom.
That is a suggestion adopted by Miss Jewett, from Flau-
bert :—L'écrire la vie ordinaire comme on écrit l' histoire.

Notwithstanding an insane oratorical outcry, now
sometimes heard, that the idea of a working rule of "sup-

ply and demand " is (like other political axioms) an exploded notion, we are conservative enough to believe that a law, obeyed or enacted at the creation of our race, as a necessity of human perpetuation, will survive the reformatory associations of our day, and continue to prevail, in literature as elsewhere, until the crack of doom. When our people assimilate and grow more homogeneous, as it is called—however far distant the day of fruition in that respect may be protracted by immigration and clannish obstinacy—and as our past social history, fading into indistinctness of detail by lapse of time, opens the door of romance—until only the elemental traits of human nature in our ancestors, and those illustrative of such events and incidents as keep the whole world akin, survive in popular memory—a more sincerely native belles-lettres literature may spring up and flourish among us.

Possibly, however, under our new copyright law, some trained English writer of genius may sooner come and squat upon our neglected patrimonial territory ;—unless some native Blackmore shall meanwhile arise among ourselves to tell more fully the romantic story of our remote past Southern social life. Here might be tested the unexhaustibleness of a mine of romance, while the realists are working the limited vein of contemporary fact.

Moreover, as our peculiar universal-suffrage civilization (by which practically the bottom governs the top) is developing, and its destiny—good or bad, for weal or woe—is working out, by actual demonstration, toward its logical end, it seems probable that, as a nation of readers, we shall meanwhile—even during our transitional period—demand that our literary appetites be consulted. Perhaps we shall be supplied with realistic literary food fit only and convenient for us in our larva state. It does not seem likely that a nascent giant—spreading out its arms to grasp and enfold all the forms of civilization with their products, and to mould them to its purposes— shall be so ignorant of its true needs as to be much longer content with literary aliment designed merely for alien appetites and a social condition widely different from its own. It never can be quite satisfied until it shall be supplied with something more in sympathy and accord with its leading tendencies, its hungriest longings, its deepest thoughts, its boldest intentions, its most earnest convictions and determinations.

It requires but little observation to perceive that the social problems of many of our political communities are steadily working toward practical solutions—whether constructive or destructive—that find but little warrant, for the merit or favor claimed for them, in the experience of the past. Demagogical lust of partisan power— with consequent class legislation and stolen wealth—is everywhere contributing some fresh impetus to the natural tendency of a newly discovered possession of strength to stimulate its possessors to exercise mere arbitrary force freely, as a sovereign cure for all possible social evils.

Conservative learning—in politics, in history, and in belles-lettres—is an apparent means of staying or directing that swelling tide of popular opinion which is now gradually undermining ancient foundations, sweeping away venerated landmarks and threatening by

revolutionary legal enactment to make every human possession subject to the caprice of an irresponsible majority,
which recognizes no restraint to its conduct, but its own
opinion of what is immediately profitable to itself. The
conflict of such elements of disorder with rights of
property and social custom, running through our daily
life, must necessarily be reflected in our current literature
if it be honest and earnest. And the modern novel seems
to have become a looking-glass in which society can best
see its full-length portrait during each passing hour.

One of the most important functions of a real and
sound native national literature is, consciously or not, to
bring into harmonious perspective—while suggesting their
true relation—the events, the social life, and the characters
that compose the national history and, as it were, manifest
the national soul. To do this, is a work of time in a
double sense. First, the component materials of the
picture must be so far developed, by their progress
toward maturity—in their interdependent relations—as to
be easy of comprehension by the common mind, when
indicated by the hand of genius. Next, the growth of
productive intellectual capacity, in the field of belles-
lettres, must be ripened by time, disciplined by study,
and trained by exercise, sufficiently to make its task easy
and genial to its possessors.

The novel is, indeed, no longer a mere romance. However romantic, it ought also to be a true transcript, in
spirit at least, of social life past or present in the country
and among the people for whom it is written. Neither is
a novel a history of public events, nor a biography, nor a
diary, nor a fable, nor an allegory, nor a parable. Nor

should it be memoirs nor letters, nor travels, nor impressions, nor speculations, nor preaching, nor moral lessons. Least of all is it a work of memory, or of simple contemplation of the lines of ordinary persons and places. Of course it must have a tale to tell, and its main purpose must be to tell it thoroughly. But it ought to be a thing of action, a drama played before the eye of the mind, an objective work of art, a presentation of practical human nature, however romantic, on its social side, as opposed to its individual or political or simple historical aspect. It is far away from the domain of science, physical, political, or moral, in the abstract. It is a mind-picture of human life—or of man as a social being, and of society as his field of conduct. True, it may involve to some extent in the hand of a great master, like Hugo or Balzac, nearly everything which in itself it is not ;— but only as secondary or incidental to its purpose ; perhaps as a background, a canvas or a frame, is necessary to a painting.

It seems to be agreed that any good novel must be a concrete representation of verisimilous men and women in their domestic and private relations with one another. In order to determine what shall be the novel of the future among us it would be well also to consider carefully what are the intrinsic nature and characteristics of the typical modern novel, as well as what features of it are non-essential, fugitive, temporary, or accidental.

The novel writer of the first class among us, whose work shall surely survive the time of its production, must be by nature a poet, an artist, and a dramatist, with a measureless spiritual inborn insight for human nature, and all its springs of action—romantic as well as practical. He must besides have an intimate acquired knowledge—apart from books or hearsay—of his countrymen in all their traditional psychical and actual social relations. He must be well informed of the motives and conduct of men and women in their personal intercourse at all times, in all places, and under all circumstances among the people of his own country. He must also have a sincere sympathy for human nature in its weakness and folly, as well as in its dignity and virtue.

It is a truism to say a novel writer of the highest order must be born with genius and practical talent to make his genius effective. Yet it is almost marvellous what a man of mere talent, by assiduous cultivation and practice, during a long life may achieve in this direction. Bulwer is a shining example. Had he possessed a little more of the divine spark that illumined the minds of such men as Fielding and Dickens his elaborate work could never grow cold.

One half the world, says the proverb, is always trying to find out how the other half lives. The novel pretends to teach them something of this in an attractive way, and will always find readers in proportion as such pretensions are verified.

There are now so many pens engaged in the same rivalry it is reasonable to suppose that somehow what is so eagerly sought will be attained ;—if there be nothing in the nature of our peculiar political or social condition to make it unattainable. They may at least learn something from one another's faults and shortcomings—of course always easily visible to each other—even if they be unteachable by their own. As our public grows more thoroughly amalgamated, and learns to manifest a common expression of what it needs and desires, the demand will probably be supplied. For, of contemporary literary fame, what can be more attractive than that of the inspired story-teller in full popularity, with fair promise of immortality? To be lovingly in everybody's mouth and heart ought to satisfy the most ambitious friend of his race.

However, novels nowadays usually are not written to satisfy a very high ideal. When they are so written, for the most part, hitherto they seem to have failed to hit their mark, or to find all the readers they covet. Practically novels are written merely so as to endeavor to entertain the public. Their aim should be to amuse, to elevate, to purify, as well as to satisfy the craving curiosity of the common mind and heart for an insight of the secret motives of men and women—past or contemporary —in their conduct, whether under ordinary circumstances or in special vicissitudes.

Moreover, all mankind likes a tale, a plot, with incidents, adventures, and the working of the natural sequence of all the romance of human affairs. This desire is born in us. It sways us very early in life—before we begin ourselves to make personal history—and it is still a resource of pleasure in our later days. A dull story may bore us; but a good one is a source of enjoyment to almost every one.

The novel that shall take and hold the American public, as that public now is or shall be constituted in any calculable future, must also be honestly home-like in spirit and in fact. It must be sincerely in touch with the essence of actual American life and ideas, past, present, and prospective. It must not be English or otherwise European. Whether it be romantic or realistic, dramatic or narrative, descriptive or psychological, historical or biographical, contemporary or archæological, or somewhat of all of these ; certainly it must be thoroughly, in all essentials, American. Probably that is the reason it is so long in its coming ;—because it must reproduce, with visible sequence, a peculiarly fragmentary life, character, sociology and ideas, which none but a genius of the highest order can blend in a harmonious picture—or even divine in its real or intrinsical spirit. A thousand brains are, however, at work upon the problem. When the time is ripe for it, doubtless it will come —although it may be a surprise to many, whensoever it shall appear.

III.

NOVELTY IN BELLES-LETTRES.

—————truth is truth
To the end of the reckoning.
Measure for Measure.

T would be hard to estimate the many difficulties overcome by a successful aspirant
for real literary honor at the present stage
of English-speaking society. Not only must
he deserve recognition and reward ; but the great reading public must have been taught by a slow process to
know his merits and thoroughly trust them. Merely to gain
the ear of that public is in itself a herculean task ;—not
unfrequently accomplished only after the writer has found
an obscure grave. Indeed it is no unusual thing—as is
too well known—for such an one to quit the world under
the conviction that both critics and successful authors
have conspired to prevent his abilities being popularly
recognized. Doubtless this fiery crucible, like some other
unprized blessings, has an incalculable value in purging
from crude ore much dross. Nevertheless the process
is easily misunderstood and readily condemned by the

329

genius that languishes with deferred hope, or dies by the stab of some literary bravo.

When a beginner, however well equipped, sets out to write upon general topics—sometimes perhaps for the mere sake of writing something to be read, unimpelled by any *furor divinus*—one formidable obstacle in his path is the apparent fact that whatever he may suppose to be worth saying, probably in some form has been said already. Nay, even if he actually shall have discovered a fairly valuable or otherwise interesting idea, the odds are that it has been well expressed before his time.

The Islamitic logic of Omar, and its fiery consequences, may perhaps somewhat contract the limits of his embarrassment. Nevertheless all written wisdom and story, he is forced to concede, did not perish in that benign conflagration. Countless crystallizations of vagrant thoughts, inspired conceptions and celestial myths persistently survive. "Gold of the dead," they are indestructible, however much they may be overlaid with the accumulated dust of centuries. Dug up from superincumbent rubbish, they are easily recognizable as the unique productions—whether discoveries or inventions— of an early day. To confront a self-conceit, born of supposititious originality, they are sedulously preserved, however obsolete—at least among cabinets devoted to rare antiques. And it may be added, their cynical collectors are not slow to invite the unwilling author—ambitious of repute for novelty—to free inspection of these sometimes unwelcome mouldy treasures.

A lack of profound originality—which is generally something far beyond mere novelty—might naturally be looked for in our own polite literature. In works of taste or imagination and all that may be called æsthetical, the American mind appears to have been largely handicapped by wide access, of author and reader, to the literary productions of all the accomplished societies of the old world. Mental indolence—positive or comparative—is a common infirmity. It is much easier to imitate and adapt than to study, or to meditate and produce original work. Hence perhaps the charge sometimes truly made of a slowness of our letters in dealing thoroughly with our own peculiar social problems or historical traits, and a tendency among us to superficialness, or flippant disdain, in handling such matters.

After Homer, Socrates, and Shakespeare; after the legion of philosophers and poets—among every people, either in the past or still existing—have explored and harvested the field of human nature, both in the abstract and in the concrete ; have studied and portrayed the character and story of man as an individual, and also as a being associated with his fellow-men in family or community—whether as a citizen or as a ruler of empire, kingdom, republic, or democracy—what can now be said or imagined by the writer of belles-lettres—partaking of the nature of either the general or the universal—that already, in some manner, has not been well enough told ? Pope seems to have felt the force of this notion as a truism when he said :—

> True wit is Nature to advantage drest,
> What oft was thought, but ne'er so well expressed.

And so too of late a popular critic has provoked the wrath of more than one genuine poet, by expressing the opinion

that there has been written already poetry enough to
supply all the legitimate wants of the present and perhaps
of a long future period.

Not very remotely akin to this want of novelty in ideas,
as a stumbling-block in the way of the class of *littérateurs*
of which we speak, may be the fact of too much novelty
—at least to the public—in the name of the writer himself. To the scientific reader in pursuit of knowledge it
matters very little what may be the source of a principle
or an idea, or even a statement of fact, that gives information or suggests a truth, provided it be trustworthy. So also
with a Bacon, a Newton, or a Franklin, the fall of an
apple, the narrative of a child, or even the cackling of a
goose, might start a train of thought leading up to the discovery of a recondite law of nature.

But with the mass of mankind what is said appears to
be of far less importance, generally, than who says it.
Despite the fact that some of the most popular books in
the world are of unknown authorship, few men can read
the expression of an idea, and take it upon its mere merits,
without first looking to see the name behind it. Seldom
opinions, of recent growth in the world, are weighed
according to their intrinsic worth. They are dependent
mostly for their current value upon the position or present
fame of those who express or endorse them.

Schopenhauer says :—" Those who, instead of studying
the thoughts of a philosopher, make themselves acquainted
with his life and history, are like the people who, instead
of occupying themselves with a picture, are rather occupied with its frame, reflecting on the taste of its carving,
or the nature of its gilding."   In political speech, such a

habit of estimating the value of another's opinion or judgment may be often judicious in order to determine the
honesty, or at least the point of view, of the speaker :—
for instance, when a debasement of the national currency
—through legal-tender paper, or a deceitful silver coinage
—is advocated by a representative of adventurous debtors,
or of owners of silver mines, or colossal speculators in the
necessaries of life.   But why should the name or fame of
an author be so commonly held to be the chief test of
merit—among the common mass of publishers and readers—in fresh belles-lettres ?   Is life too short, for us to
judge for ourselves ?

No doubt much of this condition of things is due to
our haste and indolence, since obviously it is so much easier
for most people to succumb to authority than to think
for themselves.   Almost unavoidably, amid the multitude
of affairs in our busy life, we neglect to listen to every
voice that challenges attention.   We insensibly fall into
the habit of discriminating, and letting pass unheeded
nearly all except those which, by some special claim,
arrest our attention.   Sometimes we suffer no little loss,
and perhaps deserve some self-reproach, for heedless disregard of real worth, as the habit grows upon us of turning a deaf ear to voices that are not shouted through a
trumpet.   For, as Rosalind says, even

> A jest's prosperity lies in the ear
> Of him that hears it, never in the tongue
> Of him that makes it.

To return from this apparent digression to matters
more immediately relevant, the old paradox remains that,

while "there is no new thing under the sun," yet, "of making many books there is no end." And the fact, of men and women continuing to write and to read innumerable books, that like the ever-flowing tides seem to threaten to overwhelm us, must have some explanation, other than the flippant suggestion that readers are generally foolish. It is perhaps true that not a few popular writers of our day—we refer to some of those with the largest numerical constituency of actual readers—may and do, speculate liberally upon the short memory, inattention, and ignorance of the majority of those for whom they write. Such authors may offset to the punishment, sometimes inflicted upon them by uncongenial critics, a soothing balm extracted from the sweets of revenue. In the same spirit as the Athenian miser, they may say of their critic :—

me sibilat, at mihi plaudo
Ipse domi, simul ac nummos contemplor in arca.

Among the larger mass of miscellaneous readers a great deal can be done—in the way of ministering to a gross love of apparent novelty—by a reckless author, simply through his laying vulgar hands upon subjects usually deemed sacredly exempt from profane touch—what George Eliot well calls "debasing the moral currency." Profits also may accrue sometimes by boldly trusting to the common trait, appertaining to each passing generation, of inattention to things out of sight of the current time. By this latter reliance an adroit caterer may dish up for the appetite of the common reader many a toothsome ragout. Its ingredients may be stale ; but the resources of a cunning culinary treatment may disguise their "very ancient and fish-like smell," until the literary gourmand shall cry out "delicious." The writer may change names, dates, places, or costumes, and transform situations, persons, language, or manners, until by a kind of kaleidoscopic shuffle he shall have produced odd combinations that wear all the appearance of novelty, and please the fresh reader as well as if they were pure coherent inventions, or the congruous productions of a new insight among the mysteries of things classed as unknown in nature, or society. Besides, reference should not be omitted to other familiar, but usually unconscious, resources whereby some men fancy themselves original when they are merely silly ; while others, as the proverb runs, think themselves profound when they are merely obscure.

Far beyond the scope of these tricks of charlatanry in book-making, there is, however, continually arising above the surface of the times a new world for those authors who have the keenness of perception to discover and the grasp of genius to seize and hold its marvellous possessions. Circumstances and people are always changing their relative conditions ; new inventions in the arts and sciences, as well as their application to our growing needs, are steadily modifying the social methods and moral significance of our practical every-day life. New forms of civilization ; novel experiments in local legislation ; strange vicissitudes in social intercourse involving the devolution of vast wealth upon undisciplined shoulders ; curious problems of political and communal association are continually growing up. They come also out of the opening and cultivating of new territories, the ever-broadening basis of political suffrage, the thrusting of governmental power into the hands of half-civilized or brutally ignorant men, and the commingling in forced brotherhood of remote, barbaric, or infant races with cultivated and refined older ones.

Again, as the details of our own distant past grow obsolete, and the strangeness of its contrast with the living present increases, social curiosity is easily aroused to study the old, and perhaps find delight in the retrospect or the comparison. This is eminently true in respect to the productions of semi-romantic fiction for our vast reading-loving public. By-and-by, mayhap, some new-born novelist will surprise and entertain the world, by the discovery of some Eldorado among us ;—possibly through a closer study of the lives, joys, and sorrows of our early urban colonists. For, to the sense of the rising generation, their marble records are already mossy with age, and their annals hazy with the glamour of traditional romance. Then may follow a mad rush of lesser writers to seize its now open, but almost unseen, treasures awaiting development into a coherent and characteristic basis of American belles-lettres literature.

Besides, however true it be that individual man may remain in essence the same finite, measured, weighed, and calculated entity, yet as we all know society never stands still. Its very healthfulness, like the waters of great seas, is not a little dependent upon its endless agitation, or backward and forward motion. New phases of civilization, and new social exigencies, constantly beget new dramatic situations and new ideas. The relative condition of things, temporal or perpetual, fugitive or permanent, must be constantly studied anew ; and the secret of their affinities found out and unfolded to each rising generation. The unimportant at times suddenly becomes essential ; and novel enigmas come out of the unexpected juxtaposition of current events.

Indeed, the horoscope of our future must be frequently recast, as the standpoint of the present shifts its position. Instead of the ambitious belles-lettres writer laying down his pen in despair, because there is apparently nothing new to busy it, if he rightly comprehend this modern world he lives in, he will find his energies taxed to the utmost, to keep pace with the apparently endless variety of new things, and the ever ripening harvest our period may yield to the sickle of him who shall know how to handle it.

22

IV.

AUTHORSHIP.

No author ever spared a brother,
Wits are gamecocks to one another.

GAY.

AUTHORS' RIGHTS.

UT little practical good is to be gained now, for the cause of an international copyright, among the mass of our people, by a further discussion of the mere abstract, moral right of foreign authors to the exclusive reproduction and sale of their works in this country. This condition of things arises from many causes, among which three may be enumerated. First, mankind generally are slow to acknowledge that strangers can claim anything of right, or otherwise than by privilege and comity. Second, the right to exclusive use of literary property (irrespective of legislation) is not universally recognized by civilized nations, but was denied, after a most solemn and deliberate argument, by the law of England, more than a hundred years ago, and that decision was never reversed. Third, this "right" (which, being founded upon an act of creation, apparently rests on a better basis of natural equity than most other rights of incorporeal property) is so easily disputed by appeals to cupidity, and the refutation of sophistical objections to it involves such subtle considerations and such nice distinctions, that the common mind is lost in their mazes. Through despair or indolence, it falls back the victim of bold fallacies and false analogies of those who deny altogether the right of literary property, after a first publication.

Some writers seem to think the author's right to a property in his writings, containing the expression of his original ideas, is like the right of property in animals *feræ naturæ ;*—is lost when one loses possession or control of the subject ; and that there is no right of reclamation against another who has acquired possession. Others say that ideas belong to human nature, so that no one can appropriate them, or forestall the right of every one to take them wherever he may find them, and that the notion of property is not predicable either of ideas or of any form of expressing them. Indeed, those who cannot, or will not, perceive the basis of this "right," by a conscientious instinct, are very hard to instruct or persuade. May not the subject be approached in another, if perhaps humbler, way ? Let us try.

First.—It is safe probably now to assume, that the American people recognize the fact that books must be furnished to them in large numbers to satisfy the absolute needs of the public for instruction, refinement, and amusement ; that it is well for our readers to be supplied with such books as are best suited to their condition ; and that we can well afford to incur some additional expense, if necessary, in order to accomplish this important result.

Second.—It will not be doubted that a large body of disciplined, trained, and specially educated men—to whom literature is a profession and the means of those comforts and luxuries of life which Americans so highly value—will produce more readily and more certainly the books required than *dilettanti*, or even earnest men of education, to whom literature is a mere recreation after their best powers are spent in some exhausting occupation by which they earn their daily bread—or is a refuge from mere *tædium vitæ* at a later period of life, when the freshness and energy of youth have passed irrevocably away.

Third.—It will also be conceded probably that, down to this period of time, the American people have not been supplied with miscellaneous books (of literature to say the least) particularly adapted to their special needs ; but that, on the contrary, a large number of books generally read here were written exclusively for a different people—although for the most part speaking the same language, yet of different habits and mode of government—a people whose social and political ideas, as reflected in their literature, are necessarily widely different from ours. Nay, although among these foreign people there are now some evidences of an approximation to our mode of thinking on some leading political, and consequently social, subjects, yet so irreconcilably different from ours is the fundamental basis, and, indeed, the whole structure of their society, that at least all their popular literature—which embodies manners and social ideas—

always has been, and for a generation to come, must be, better adapted to corrupt, bewilder, or mislead American readers than to enlighten, instruct, or intelligently amuse them.

Fourth.—If these propositions be admitted (and they seem almost self-evident) then those who recognize the usefulness of a body of native literature above the grade of the newspaper, and also those who feel the gross deficiency of the American people in this respect, can hardly doubt that everything should be done, if not to encourage American literary talent, at least to give it a fair opportunity to enter the field and satisfy this demand; provided always it can be done without injustice to any one's rights, and without prejudice to the interests of any one entitled to be sustained in the possession of such interests.

Fifth.—Free, unrestricted international copyright proposes to cure the great defect in our system already hinted at, and to remedy the evils resulting from it, at the same time giving Americans an opportunity to seek a livelihood in the honorable pursuit of the profession of literature. Justice demands it, and policy advocates it. Yet, I would not desire to encourage the writing of books merely to placate the men among us who wish to write. I would advocate open international copyright, not so much for the sake of doing justice to authors, either foreign or domestic, as that books might be written such as American men, women, and children ought to read. The point I would keep in view is that the minds of our whole people, ceasing to be debauched by unwholesome foreign stimulants, may, by the myriad forms of a home literature, be brought to bear intelligently upon the social and political problems of our own society ;—instead of wasting their strength and growing frivolous by becoming interested in questions and matters arising out of a social or political condition having almost nothing in common with the radical peculiarities of the American system.

Sixth.—Indeed, the clamor for impartial international copyright ought not to come from the American author. His claim is secondary in importance, though first in right. In fact, it seems to be a misfortune for the cause that so much of the cry should have come (as by the necessity of the case it has) from those who would expect to profit pecuniarily from the project. It makes men inclined to suspect their motive, while in reality, as becomes their calling, they plead not so much for themselves as for the highest interest of all Americans.

Upon these grounds, it seems an open international copyright law might be advocated. Perhaps it would be well to soar above individual interests, to advance a wide step beyond any mere hope of gain to the author (however just his claim) and to put the case, in its practical bearings, upon the ground of the greatest good to the greatest number of our whole people. That is sound American doctrine, and on that field the contest should be made henceforth. Let the watchword be : American Books for the American People.

AMATEUR WRITING.

Isaac D'Israeli, in his *Calamities of Authors*, says :— "A great author once surprised me by inquiring what I meant by 'an author by profession.' He seemed offended

at the supposition that I was creating an odious distinction between authors. I was only placing it among
their calamities."

And in that famous controversy, which most American
authors look upon as the source of all their woes, Lord
Camden's familiar and successful speech smacks of like
vintage with the thought of D'Israeli's inquisitor. Doubtless the learned nobleman uttered a sentiment popular
enough in his day, when he said : " Glory is the reward
of science, and those who deserve it, scorn all meaner
views. I speak not of the scribblers for bread who
tease the press with their wretched productions. . . .
It was not for gain that Bacon, Newton, Milton, Locke,
instructed and delighted the world ; it would be unworthy such men to traffic with a dirty bookseller for
so much as a sheet of letter-press ! "

But in this practical age successful amateurship, in
belles-lettres at least, is becoming an obsolete idea.
Literature (such as it is) has attained among us the
traits of a profession. Like most other professions it
now ranks as a business or trade—in which the spur of
pecuniary reward appears for the most part to be considered necessary to keep the faculty for work in motion,
if not to make the exercise of it respectable. Certainly
this appears to be the feeling among the guild itself.
Nay, it may be said safely that, generally speaking, the
successful writers of polite literature in our day, among
ourselves, regard its merchantable quality not merely as
one fair criterion, but as the only practical test, of its
real excellence.

Perhaps, then, it would be considered impertinent, if

not unkind, to ask the literary fraternity why that common class of so-called "cheap literature" which they hold in such contempt (next to the works of amateurs) so often brings the writer of it the largest revenue? It does seem, however, to the skeptical, a little inconsistent for the ambitious professional author to exalt the critical acumen of the purchasing public as infallible, at one breath, and to contemn it as undiscriminating, or fond of husks only, at another! Nevertheless the suggestion would be unavailing, however keen its satire or logic. The writer who can sell his manuscript to a printer, at whatever price, cannot conceal easily a self-congratulatory disdain for his brother author, whose products are found to be unmarketable with current publishers, irrespective of what may be the intrinsic worth of either. Perhaps, however, in fairness, one ought to admit the probability of better work often being produced, where an author is in need of money, and believes the best way for him to get it is by writing a really meritorious book, suitable for the needs of the public he expects will buy it.

Amateur writing usually is treated with undisguised derision and openly scoffed for crudeness, as well by the critic as by professional author. They both appear to regard such work, also, as an unauthorized invasion of the lawful territory of the latter;—an interference with vested rights and a low attempt to snatch the bread from deserving mouths. Indeed, this odium seems to affect contageously even the popular taste. The public itself does not now relish such volunteer productions because of their peculiar flavor—so unlike that of the

common supplies furnished to the regular trade for the
ordinary market.

When a man, who has given his best endeavors to
benefit others, finds his advances met with coldness, or
his beneficence rejected with scorn, his benevolence is
apt to recoil. His philanthropy begins to freeze and he
is in danger of growing cynical. Yet there may be still
a sufficient motive for authorship, even if the writer do
not expect publication. It is truer now than when Lord
Bacon said it, that writing maketh an "exact man."
And it is well for one who thinks, or even fancies he
thinks, to write much, and perhaps often, merely for the
sake of formulating his ideas. He can test their accuracy to his own eye and ear, by putting them in definite
shape ; and, by this species of self-education, give both
precision to his notions and clearness to his mode of
expression.

If, however, our amateur writer shall be found covet-
ing the spur of a pecuniary reward, as necessary to prick
the sides of his intent, let him ponder the words of one of
the "profession," who inherits, perhaps, the most honored
literary name among us, and whose own merit, as well
as experience, doubtless abundantly qualify him to speak.
Not long ago Julian Hawthorne took the public into his
confidence as follows :—

"Five hundred dollars a year for a successful
novel! How many of our authors make twice that?
How many ten times as much? How many twenty
times as much? I will engage to entertain at dinner,
at a round table five feet in diameter, all the American
novelists who make more than a thousand dollars

a year out of the royalty on any one of their novels, and to give them all they want to eat and drink, and three of the best cigars apiece afterward, and a hack to take them home in ; and I will agree to forfeit a thousand dollars to the Home for Imbeciles if twenty-five dollars does not liquidate the bill and leave enough to buy a cloth copy of each of the works in question, with the author's autograph on the fly-leaf. One hack would be sufficient, and would allow of their putting up their feet on the seat in front of them."

CONTEMPORARY REPUTATION.

Only a few authors, among poets and other writers of polite letters, can expect rightfully to achieve both contemporary reputation and enduring fame. Of course this is the ideal, and perhaps the hope, of nearly all—yet how seldom attained. Most successful literary aspirants for public recognition are compelled, either by the measure of their abilities, or by force of circumstances, to choose between the two. It will happen generally that those who possess the large capacity to produce such literary work, as appeals to a universal taste or judgment, will look beyond the factitious or accidental peculiarities of the day. Seeking only a limited contemporary audience, they will address themselves to human sympathy in its wider phases, and to such of its moods as probably will endure beyond the vicissitudes, vagaries, and special demands of the immediate time. And, although necessity may sometimes divert them from these loftier aims, to "meaner things," yet, even then truth usually vindicates herself. Such ill-begotten work will, for the most part, fail to accomplish either purpose. Good sense cannot gracefully, or even profitably, wear the fool's motley. Indeed, an author's unquestioning earnestness, sincerity, or faith in the intrinsic merit, though supposititious, of his own literary work (however flimsy or absurd in fact) appears to be the indispensable condition precedent to its popular success.

Society is always undergoing a process of change ;— whether progressing towards a higher ideal, or not. Those who glow with an invincible desire to give to the world the light they feel they possess—if that light be kindled with the spark of what men rightfully call genius —will find sometimes their prophetic eyes opened upon a horizon stretching far beyond the narrow precincts of the present day. They will see unavoidably also something, deep down in the essential nature of things about them, more than meets the common eye. If true to themselves, and honest with the real public, they will, nevertheless, speak sincerely despite the fact that the current world will not always understand, or patiently listen to, them. They may have a limited number of hearers, and perhaps a few followers ; but their works will generally prove to be a stumbling-block to most men. They will have seldom much honor in their own country, or among their own people ;—who will possibly crucify them, as they did poor Shelley.

Indeed, this victim of unpopularity knew painfully, yet prophetically, well whereof he spoke, when, in his *Defence of Poetry* he said :—" No living poet ever arrived at the fulness of his fame. The jury which sits in judgment upon a poet, belonging as he does to all time, must be composed of his peers ; it must be empanelled by time from the selectest of the wise of many generations."

There are others, however, who, either by reason of weaker wing, or less lofty aspiration, or because tempted by the seductive sweetness of popular applause, or perhaps by the desire or need of money, will prefer to seize the pleasures of the present hour, and risk the chances of finding more lasting repute without painful sacrifice. These are the popular authors of the day, whose names are in so many contemporary mouths, and whose utterances, by the contagion of imitation and iteration, become for a time household words among an undiscriminating multitude.

Thus far mention is made of only two grand classes : yet each has many subdivisions—the extremes of this division being widely asunder. It may also be added that, although members of the same guild, they often look upon each other's work as deserving of no little contempt. In which oblique view, it may sometimes fortuitously happen that neither is quite mistaken.

There are always besides, a few of the fortunate children of nature, whose capacities are so full, and so well-rounded, that they combine the merits of both classes. There are men richly endowed with the gifts of genius as well as talent, who, although sweeping up towards an illimitable empyrean with a sustained flight and tireless wing, can yet walk with easy composure upon the ground, amid the ordinary haunts of men. Such writers often speak from a sort of double consciousness. While in hearty accord with the common mind of their own day, yet, with an insight that seems more spiritual than human, they penetrate so far into the essence of things as to anticipate, seemingly, thoughts and evolutions of a later age.

This notion, in the abstract, may appear to savor of the marvellous, or at least to be purely fanciful. But the mention of the prophetic soul of Shakespeare is presumably enough to save one from the charge of absurdity in uttering it. To illustrate by a single example, among many in the same opulent author ;—where does modern psychology—whether normal or morbid—find its advanced ideas better expressed, or more fit language for its intricate discoveries, than in the soul-analysis of Macbeth or of Hamlet ?

LITERARY POPULARITY.

Whether the aim of a belles-lettres author be to instruct, or merely to amuse, in either case, of course, his prosperity will depend much upon keeping the cordial good-will of his readers. Wit can always entertain, and sometimes may teach wisely. Yet it will often bite shrewdly, and have a quality liable to put reader and writer in personal antagonism. We may admire the wit, yet hate the author. Readers, especially women, even when bad in themselves if that be possible, usually like straightforward honesty and kindness of heart in an author. Wit often, and humor sometimes, takes the form of indirect, and even malicious, slander of individuals or mankind in general. Sarcasm and irony are among the easiest attainable methods of producing the appearance of wit or humor, and therefore most tempting to those striving for the effect, or the reputation, of either. These cynical devices are so employed mostly by those to whom nature has given least original creative power in such direction.

To raise a laugh at the expense of the feelings of a fellow-being, or to shock the prejudices or sense of propriety of another, may produce the semblance of the effect of wit or humor. Yet intrinsically these may be nothing more than an insult, or a coarse offence against the common and usually well-heeded rules of social intercourse. The first result of such a breach of good manners, generally will be to tickle the ear of a thoughtless multitude. But the reaction, in reflecting minds, produces the feeling of a sort of self-degradation, and a dislike of the producer of such disturbance of our mental composure. We soon see how easy it is to be malignant, and how cheap to utter what a decent respect for the graces and proprieties of life forbids to be spoken. Surely, even if slowly, the author and his work finally will sink together, smothered by a merited contempt for both.

Infelicity of Authors.

It is an unpleasant fact—obvious in the annals of most human families—that among those who possess the highest and most susceptible capacity for social enjoyment, there is usually the least amount of real happiness. This word seems by common consent to have reference generally to such even-conditioned state of being, or content, as finds its earthly consummation in a well-balanced, well-proportioned, domestic circle ;—where affection and benevolence, self-restraint and self-respecting modera- tion are the ruling influences. It is hard to say precisely, or in particular, what each one ought to bring into such a little community, in order to contribute his proper quota to the common welfare. Yet it is quite easy to tell what every one ought to leave outside, or to keep in severe subjection, if not under total repression.

Among these latter may be named egotism, self-conscious- ness, self-pity, and morbid emotionalism or sentimentality. Perhaps, more than all, is that excess or abuse of the faculty of imagination which too rapidly, or too gloomily, forecasts the future. This dominating ideality of a certain class of persons—constantly seeking for perfection while analyz- ing character or conduct—generally overlooks what is really good in others or perhaps what is bad in them- selves. It fastidiously cavils at almost everything human, because not absolutely in keeping with its own ideal standard. All of these traits (to which, however, the world owes so much for the sweetly sad poetry and exquisite art that melt or delight the soul) although sounding, for good or evil, the deepest wells of human feeling, are among the least desirable elements of ordinary social life.

Unfortunately it happens that, among mere men-of- letters—who possess in greater or less degree the char- acteristics of genius—these barbed torments of social existence prevail to a disagreeable extent. Saddest of all too, such favorites of the gods usually have the smallest capacity for self-control or self-subjection ; and are apt to be the children of impulse, or the sport of too many irrepressible demons of social disturbance.

It is small wonder then, that this class—whose constitutions are composed of, or highly charged with, such ill-regulated and explosive ingredients as are constantly putting their possessors out of harmony with themselves as well as others—should soon reach a condition of chronic irritation. *Genus irritabile.* Whenever brought into such close social contact as to act and be acted upon by their fellow-beings—to the restraint of their fanciful code of personal liberty—they are prone, in the end, to bring reproach and misery upon themselves, either by extravagant exactions, or by outbursts of exacerbated temper, in their impotent conflict with what, after all, may be imaginary mischiefs.

When a man or woman once enters upon a crusade against fancied wrongs, in the domestic circle, the first thing usually done is to forget all past benefits and present good ; next to ignore all self-deficiencies ; then—abandoning self-restraint—to exaggerate every semblance of evil out of all proportion with its due significance even if real ; and, finally, to shut his eyes to the obvious consequence of attempting to regulate, by officious inter-meddling, the private conduct or secret opinions of others. It is not difficult to see that the bower of love soon becomes a tangled waste, where this spirit of discontent reigns supreme ; and every poisonous herb finds congenial aliment in the rank soil.

CONCERNING LIFE AND DEATH.

What 's yet in this,
That bears the name of life?
Measure for Measure.

I.

EGOISM : THE BATTLE OF LIFE.

Be thine own home and in thyself dwell;
Inn anywhere ; continuance maketh hell.
And seeing the snail, which everywhere doth roam,
Carrying his own home still, still is at home,
Follow (for he is easy-paced) this snail,
Be thine own palace or the world 's thy jail.

DONNE.

ONCE read—I know not where—these two
lines, purporting to be translated from one
of Goethe's writings :—

The art of life is easily attained ;
Trust in yourself, and you the whole have gained.

Unlike most oracular maxims they express more than a
partial truth ; but like many others this one presupposes
some practical sagacity to comprehend its full meaning.

What should be one's chief purpose in life—what the art to accomplish it? What is meant by trusting in one's self, for the pursuit of it?

When a virile man has arrived at some positive degree of nearness to maturity of his intellectual faculties, if he be self-possessed, he naturally asks himself :—" What am I? Wherefore am I here? How am I related to the rest of mankind? What are my necessities, limitations, and capabilities? What must I do, or leave undone? What can I do? What may I not do? What should be the main endeavor I ought to set before me in order to accomplish the object of my creation, so far as I can comprehend it? By what method can I best put myself in the way of most effectually exercising all my power, natural or acquired, in the pursuit of what I shall aim at?"

Inasmuch as each individual has a character and circumstances largely peculiar to himself—by the ancients often reckoned as fate—necessarily, self-study is essential to judicious self-management. A desire for self-development lies at the bottom of the primal law of intellectual being. The body ordinarily grows to its normal shape and stature without much factitious aid. Nature usually takes care of that. We shall need to do little else than follow her common promptings—giving her a fair chance, and thwarting her no more than social exigencies compel. With the mind, however, the case is different. Here the freedom of choice is greater. Although we have many limitations, natural and artificial, yet within their boundaries the area is vast, and the option to occupy is left largely to ourselves. Upon our own election, to a great degree, depends the result. The peculiar duty of each man to himself being self-evolution, from the necessity of the case, he must find within himself the chief arbiter of his destiny. Self-development is the art of life, and self-trust is the key to self-development. Position, place, power, reputation, popularity, fame, are but modes of expression of self.

The thing to do is to work out into external act one's theory of self, as one of the forces, or an atom among the forces, of the moral universe. How shall this fairly be done, if one do not trust in himself ? To do otherwise is to be a puppet. Only in this way man can be really a free agent. If he trust in himself he has a fixed centre of motion, about which always to revolve. Hence he shall have consistency of character ; and, perhaps, evolutionary, as well as expanding, growth. If he make his way, his path will be suited to his capabilities and his opportunities. His life will be simple and sincere ;— always building upon its own foundation. But if he do not trust in himself, he will be like a disabled ship that has lost her reckoning ; or the anchor and rudder of which are wanting. He will be at the mercy of the winds and waves of opinion. He will be the victim of circumstances—variable as the moon. His conduct will lack continuity or coherence. He will have no mental quietude—no repose of character. Lacking self-poise, his equilibrium will be always doubtful. Trusting in others, or drifting with the popular current, or moved by chance or by designing external influence, he may be false to himself and to every one around him. You cannot count upon him until you know from what quarter the strongest alien force shall be brought to bear upon his vacillating centre. Day by day he will grow more cowardly, more doubtful of himself—and indeed of everything else. While self-trust makes a character stronger, the want of it makes one weaker and weaker, until all manliness fades out of the composition.

When men are so feeble that they rely upon others instead of themselves, the best object of their existence, as affecting the race, is not attained. Except as slaves, to hew wood and draw water, in this view, they might as well not have been born. Besides this subserviency defeats itself. Although it be the resource of weakness, cowardice, or indolence, yet gradually it increases each one of these infirmities, until finally self-action, in thought or deed, becomes painful. Mere obedience to the will of others may bring satiety, disgust, or perhaps despair, to those worthy of superior lives.

Beware of placing unlimited confidence in others. There are sometimes—though rarely—tried men and women in whom we may trust very widely in some matters ; but one should never quite let the cord, by which to hold them in check, pass out of his hand. It is like riding on horseback ; the man who wholly trusts his horse surely sometime gets a fall. In some exigencies the most absolute confidence in others is a signal merit ; but these cases are, at the least, exceptional. They are, rather, striking instances of trusting in one's own judgment concerning the special fitness of another for helping one to encounter a particular emergency.

One likewise must avoid the mistake, and miserable policy, of distrusting others too much. As a man should be slow to distrust his own power to accomplish what he undertakes, yet may well doubt the extent of his skill and knowledge, in the choice of means; so on the contrary, while he may and should be wary of putting all his faith in the strength or will of others to aid him, still he may be justified often in thoroughly confiding in their skill or knowledge.

It is a good old practical rule to trust in others only by degrees—little by little—letting confidence, if it may, grow by proof and experience. One may treat those in whom he thus confides, as a judicious man deals with his memory. He may trust that faculty a good deal experimentally, and it will generally grow in strength by such indulgent treatment. But when it once plays him a trick, and fails him in an emergency, he learns its fallibility, and becomes cautious how he again entrusts vital matters to its keeping alone, without some artificial ally.

Assuredly one can do but little in this world without great assurance of one's ability to accomplish what is undertaken. The faint-hearted proverbially fail, notwithstanding means and opportunities. Indeed, mere physical courage often seems to lack the spirit and fire necessary for difficult achievements. Yet is nothing so sure to involve defeat of purpose, and waste of life, as excessive self-confidence, without discipline of faculties and recognition of mortal limitations, in respect to ability, resource, circumstance, and time.

To begin with, one should push his energies chiefly toward such practical aims and purposes as he may hope reasonably to accomplish. More than that is wasteful or slothful. How large a portion of life often is consumed in finding out what one may do, as well as in training the natural powers to adapt them to its performance. And even after careful examination of what is within the scope of our capacity, how comparatively little do we find it reasonable to expect we may achieve in one brief life.

A consolation of the ambitious lover of mankind lies in the fact that, as he can begin his work where his predecessors have laid it down, so his successors may take up his unfinished task, and push it on even beyond his extreme expectations. In other words, although the individual be but a temporary atom, nevertheless to great natures it is a solace that the race is a perpetuity.

Most men seem to drop into chance places in the world, do what falls to their lot, avoid what seems harmful, eat, drink, and sleep according to custom, and are happy if they may live and die peacefully. There are, however, many who feel impelled to construct their own fortunes, to create their own spheres, and to subject themselves to their surroundings only as they are modified by their own acts ;—perpetually striving to obtain the most and lose the least that the opportunities of this mortal existence afford.

The art of life—dealing, as it does, with so many elements or circumstances that are either insurmountable, or controlling unless personally mastered—still presents to each of us this double problem ;—what it is desirable to do, and what to avoid. These must be subordinated, of course, to what is possible to do, and what we may escape. In the last two propositions also lies the test of the strength, as by the first two are found the quality, of a man. By his election will be involuntarily betrayed his intrinsic and native character. As the swine goes to the mire, so the eagle soars to the skies. Yet one basely inclined, may sometimes be set on—through education and other favorable circumstances—to work toward purity and elevation, by self-discipline and virtuous emulation ; while another, of noble instincts, from bad example, or untoward events—such as early discouragement and the like —may be led to turn a deaf ear to his higher impulses, and lapse into a low condition.

A man often finds within himself two opposite tendencies ; one toward self-reliance, and another a yearning for social sympathy or support and approbation. Neither must be ignored. As he is strong or weak, unless he invoke the aid of severe discipline, the one or the other —strength or weakness—will prevail and, as either predominates, perhaps distort his character.

Before the advent of Christianity the higher education of the soul led toward self-dependence. Mythology, like the laws of nature, was relentless in visiting the consequences of error and folly upon the head of the offender. Nemesis gave no encouragement to the hope of pardon, through either a mediator or repentance for misdoing. As the tree fell so it lay. Such a system contributed doubtless to make the strong stronger ;—however it might tend to destroy or debase the weak by despair. The most fit survived and flourished, while the weaker sank in the scale of humanity to become mere servile toilers, or butterfly pleasure-seekers of the hour ;—or to join the general throng of the wretched who quickly perish.

On the other hand, Christian theology makes life more lovely by offering to the penitent believer a safe retreat from the consequences of wrong-doing. Mercy and hope become important factors in life. These gather strength from mere association of men together. Social sympathy makes many burdens more easy to carry—while waiting for the benign interference of a kind Providence to take away, or modify, the penalty of evil-doing.

The inclination of Christian civilization is, however, inevitably less toward self-reliance than that of the older theologies. The ideal man—as a self-dependent arbiter of his own destiny and fortune—was (humanly speaking) doubtless higher, stronger, and clearer than he is under our own merciful system of faith. There was a tendency to evolve more and more strength, in the habit of looking only to self as the prime force in character, and a relentless master with whom to settle for delinquencies. But faith in absolution by repentance, and a habit of leaning upon others for help, or seeking their sympathy, condolence, or charity, seem as steadily to lead toward debility of character. For however more amiable this system may make human association (except as it may elevate us, by devout aspiration, to live acceptably to our Divine Master) it inevitably tends to keep us gradually sinking to a level below what a true self-reliant manhood —aside from spiritual grace—ought to set before itself as its loftiest ideal. Happy are they who, by native force of character, can unite the hardy stoicism or heroic virtue of the pagan with the pious graces of the Christian. That, indeed, should be the sub-divine image a man of our day ought to set before himself.

True self-conduct, apart from all outside influences, should rest primarily upon the tripod of self-knowledge, self-reverence, and self-control. The first is hard to attain, as it requires study from without as well as from within—of others as well as of ourselves—to learn one's relations to his fellow-men and to acquire knowledge of a standard by which to measure one's own proportions. Time and experience alone can make such study result in anything valuable. Self-reverence will come, or delay its coming, in proportion as our higher or better nature is obeyed, or violated and abused:—wherever her promptings are high, pure, and good, and accordingly as evil inclinations are suppressed or subdued or allowed to go unchecked. It will manifest itself in many ways, both great and small ;—in an unfaltering consciousness of personal worth, as well as in a kind of fastidiousness in respect to personal surroundings, manners, and social intercourse. It will keep the heart, mind, and spirit clean and sweet by a gentle necessity ; and this will preserve the body pure, because that is the temple of the spirit dwelling within it. The notion of self-reverence will make a man careful in the choice of his company. But above all, with strong natures, stands self-control—what Lowell sweetly calls "clear-eyed self-restraint." This is the balance-wheel of a perfected character, without which all else is of little permanent worth.

If a man have neither the opportunity, nor the noble ambition, to strive to live for others, at least he ought to try to live for himself—to develop rationally the faculties and capabilities of enjoyment of which he is possessed— and to seek to reap the fruits and gather for his own gratification the flowers that grow by the wayside through life. In short he ought so to plan his journey, and methodize his time, as neither to waste material nor miss opportunity of achieving what seems to him best for himself alone. Alas, how few are even so sagaciously prudent. The mass of mankind seem to live neither for themselves, nor for others. They live by force of nature, without the intelligent direction of their human will—that is to say, unmoved by any vivifying consciousness of the possession of a soul. They live and die, as does the animal or the vegetable. They exist merely for the pleasure and business of the hour, without any method leading upward, except as may be necessary to provide for the ordinary sequence of common events. So far as respects a plan for the conduct of their interior-life, or a theory for the development of what spiritually is within the compass of human will or endeavor, they are as insensible as blocks of stone.

Amid these material, superficial, pleasure-seeking days, when I see so many young people around me, brought up at haphazard, careless of the meaning or purpose of their existence, with no habits of thrift, or prudence, I wonder how they will get through that battle of life, which their New England forefathers—with all their discipline and training by poverty, privation, self-dependence, and unstinted work—found to be so hard. For a time I am puzzled and confounded with the apprehension of disaster that seems to me sure to overtake them, when the conflict comes and they shall be found to be too poorly equipped for the task before them. But again I reflect there are divers ways of getting through the world ; and that some move smoothly and easily—although others find a more troubled transit—merely by the chances of accident. Indeed, some are pulled through, some barely struggle through, and some are apparently kicked through ; while others never reach their normal end, but drop by the wayside, seemingly born, and sent into this world, merely to keep alive the hard lesson that although death may be peace, life is war.

II.

LIFE AND DEATH.

Ampliat ætatis spatium sibi vir bonus ; hoc est
Vivere bis, vita posse priore frui.

MARTIAL.

LOVE OF LIFE.

HEN a contemplative man, in the full enjoyment of youth and health, looks upon the grand or beautiful objects of nature, in their cheerful serenity or lovely unconsciousness of human feebleness and sorrow, he clings to life, and is sometimes filled with a sense of joy that inspires the desire to live here forever. But as life passes on into age ; when one considers how much his dependence for happiness has been upon social sympathy—the ties of affection or the communion of associations with sincere friends ; when he recalls the pleasures and troubles he has shared with dear companions, and how many of those he has loved have gone before him—taking with them most of his precious moral resources—he begins to feel content soon to follow. As Willis finely says in his *Absalom :—*

How strikingly the course of nature tells,
By its light heed of human sufferings,
That it was fashioned for a happier world.

SCOPE OF LIFE.

What is the pith of a human life? Some seem to think it is enough for a man to breathe, to move, to rest, to sleep—to enjoy the pleasures of the hour and to drift aimlessly and unconsciously to the grave—gay, careless, and, if possible, joyous and happy. If every one had, and could keep, perfect health of body and mind, with wise habits—because only simple wants existed—and if society could stand still, with all human needs fully provided for, this would seem to be almost a complete response to the primal voice of nature. Such is or was nearly the happy condition of some semi-savage, and of some insular, peoples. It is the normal life too of fortunate childhood. But when the mind, impelled by civilization, has outgrown the simple demands of the body, we imperceptibly take upon us a new or other life. Mind or spirit predominates over matter; we begin to recognize a divinity within us, and truly to live. Doubtless there are many who never much outgrow the simple traits of their childish days. But most thinking people, either by native activity and increment of brain, or by sorrow, suffering, consequent introspection and self-recognition, at some time, begin to wake up and to ask themselves—who or what and why they are, whence they came, and whither they are going.

I am hemmed within a somewhat narrow circle, by the laws of nature. I cannot add one cubit to my stature.

Next there are the laws of society under which I live; and, whether right or wrong, in the abstract or under other supposable circumstances—although they be to me perhaps unwelcome as prison bars—yet I may not attempt with impunity to violate them. There are moreover, the special impediments peculiar to my individual self;—such as pertain to my social condition and my personal opportunity. Besides, are other distinctive circumstances, that make my individual self to be specifically me, and not the double of any other person whomsoever. There is, however, an almost endless variety of petty elements of environment—not unlike, in their effect, the bands the Lilliputians tied upon Gulliver—that I may either overcome, or be passively subject to accordingly as I curb, or yield to, a love of ease and pleasure, or as my energy of character, force of will, ambition, thoroughness, or persevering determination shall be strong or weak, persistent or desultory. Within my limitations, only as I develop in consciousness, power, thought, action, self-restraint, and consequent rational enjoyment of my being, do I actually live. Otherwise I only subsist;— happy perhaps as a spring-swallow, but breathing a life in all things unworthy of my opportunities.

As therefore no one is absolutely free, but all are in comparative subjection, the variance in their conditions is only a difference in degrees of constraint. Men have indeed lived alone, in caves and forests, hoping to find there the surest method of securing unalloyed freedom; but they have gained only another sort of restraint. They were so circumscribed by physical necessities—besides social isolation, which is itself a negative tyranny—they had, in some respects, really less actual freedom in their solitude than when in society.

We truly live only by virtue of thought, and reciprocity of moral, mental, and spiritual ideas. The personal ideas we most thoroughly encompass—perhaps all those we really do possess—come chiefly from what we do, and what we are, in ourselves. A man's life is to be measured by his experiences, inward as well as outward ; and he should never wholly regret them however disagreeable they may be, if he survive his wounds, and carry only their scars. These trials and proofs are soul-facts. From them alone do we derive or verify those mental, moral, and spiritual conceptions which are most thoroughly imbedded in our consciousness, and make up our intrinsic character and present identity—however, from custom or policy, we may masquerade otherwise, before the world. These atoms of vivid personal experience compose all of our very selves. Whatever maxims of self-conduct we derive purely from the thoughts and history of others— no matter how useful as guides or auxiliaries—are still exotic. They never can be trusted wholly in the critical emergencies that may be encountered, by our own special nature, in the personal conduct of our individual lives.

VALUE OF LIFE.

It is to little purpose we ask if life be worth the trouble or weariness of living. Being born without our choice, it is a law of our being that life shall be maintained by us. It is against nature, either to starve or to sicken voluntarily—or, except through superstition or other infatua-

tion, for normal physical life to take away itself. Here
we are ;—and obviously out of accord with nature do we
become when we inquire if it be worth our while to live.
Whosoever finds himself in such a state of mind, as
querulously to put that question to himself, may surely
know that he is morally incompetent to answer it for himself—either as witness or judge—by reason of his bodily
or mental infirmity, or both. If he wishes for an honest
verdict on the subject, he must seek it only outside of
himself. Health desires life. It is as natural to live—
barring hereditary disease, self-abuse, negligence, or accident—to the full ordinary duration of life, as it is to die
at the expiration of that period. The sense and sensibility
of mankind in general seem likely to continue always
sound on this subject. And the folly of those few, who
call in question the value of existence here, may be fairly
offset against the greed of those who estimate too greatly
its advantages, above either the hope of immortality, or
the nothingness of oblivion.

The true inquiry for the anxious mind on this subject
is :—What shall life accomplish? Not in a narrow, nor
merely particular and egoistic sense—for the wants and
pleasures of existence usually appear to keep an ordinary,
healthy man sufficiently occupied for the time, without
much anxiety on his part about being truly philosophical,
reasonable, or consistent. But rather, by a comprehensive
view of all this world affords, let every man consider profoundly and answer for himself. Let him take into the
calculation youth, middle-life, and old-age ; considering
man both as an isolated individual, and as a member of a
social and political organization, which in many respects

is the outgrowth of thousands of years in progressive evolutionary civilization ; as a son, a brother, perhaps a husband and a father ; as a sharer of the burdens and benefits of social and political methods appropriate to the period and country where his lot is cast, or he may choose his domicile ; as a not unimportant factor in the endless series of the generation of his race ; and as the possessor of attributes and faculties capable of producing and receiving their highest enjoyment by cultivation, prudent self-conduct and active, useful intercourse with his fellow-beings. What is his cue? If there is no higher obligation in any other direction, obviously his first object in life should be to make the most of it, without detriment to himself or others.

It is proverbially common to point to what is usually called happiness, as the chief aim of life. This should, however, rank rather as an incident than as the main object to be kept in view. To be happy is to be in accord with our circumstances and ideals ; to work under and in compliance with the laws of nature in all respects, as well as with the laws of our society—whether wise or unwise, natural or arbitrary, just or unjust—so long as we remain a part of such society. To be in conflict with these, in any material respect, will produce surely more or less unhappiness. To resist some of them may be deemed often by us necessary. Force, love, duty, interest, or pleasure may drive us into opposition, and may perhaps give us excuse, consolation, equivalent, or compensation for want of happiness ;—yet we shall lose it still the same.

But there is something richer than mere personal happiness or pleasure to be sought for in striving to achieve

24

the best uses of this life. To develop to full equable expansion all our mental and moral faculties ; to choose with our best judgment—aided by the experience and forecast of others, and all the best lights we can focalize on the subject—the most efficient mode of exercising our abilities, in doing what seems best to each of us, in order to push on the work of improving the general welfare of the race to which we belong ; these seem to be the dictates of natural instinct, of right reason, and of good sense of the best of men. The larger the capabilities the greater the true enjoyment, when capacity is so filled ; just as the ox in a broad field is believed to find more enjoyment than the canary-bird in a cage—however ignorantly contented the latter may be with its narrow lot.

PASSAGE OF LIFE.

Perhaps the best common figure of speech, used to express the ordinary notion of the passage of life, is that which calls it a journey. First, one should endeavor to provide in advance, from time to time, for such wants and emergencies as can be easily foreseen ; next, one should pursue the adventure as leading to some definite end. If one fall by the way, the casualty should be regarded with the same equanimity as an unavoidable termination of contemplated travel. The possibility of such a mis-adventure is of course a thing to be guarded against, so far as practicable, by fair precautions ;—not, however, to be exaggerated in prospect, so as to hinder one in the undertaking or the prosecution of the journey.

The object proposed should be kept always in view, as something practically certain to be reached, if length of life be granted. When we approach the end of our journey we should prepare to lay aside our baggage, and be satisfied with the completion of our travels. It is an edifying spectacle to see a great thinker, an inventor, a scientific discoverer, or a grand actor in the drama of practical life, when warned of the approaching end, withdrawing from the highway of a public career and making haste to write his autobiography—a veracious journal of the incidents of his career—to completion, while the sands of life shall hold out. Yet what a disappointment such anticipatory frank productions sometimes seem to bring to those foiled jackals of literature, whose apparent delight is to desecrate newly made graves.

APPROACH OF OLD AGE.

Passing from the extreme of middle-life to old-age usually resembles less the gradual descent over a smooth incline than it does the going down the steps of a terrace, or the series of rounds upon a ladder. We often seem to pause upon each level ; sometimes to rest or perhaps to gaze contemplatively or carelessly around about us ;— sometimes to turn toward self-introspection, or perhaps to give an absorbing attention to some external matter that may chance to interest us greatly. When we next look up, and out upon the world around us, we feel as if that world had moved on, while we had stood still. We discover that either our horizon has contracted perceptibly or our vision is impaired, and we ourselves are not what we were. We are conscious our altitude has sunken a step. We may generalize more ; but we particularize less, for old-age is coming upon us.

In youth naturally we are rising ; and so in middle-age, as life moves onward, our eyes sweep over a continually broadening expanse of the moral universe ; while we linger fondly upon each height to which we attain. We are continually gaining ground, and we rejoice in the frequent discovery of fresh acquisitions made of new territory, for the mind or heart to dwell in as their home. But when old-age is creeping over us, we are as constantly made aware of these recurring periods of slow deterioration ;—the loss, it may be, of some power or even some cherished possession of personal consciousness, upon which we always had set a value before. This latter retro-gradation of stand-point appears to be a kindly provision of nature ;—perhaps designed to give us time in which to reconcile ourselves to the misfortune of one deprivation in this mortal career, before we are called upon to bear another. In this manner our sensibilities may gradually harden ; so that when the command comes for us to yield up our all, we may have but little left that shall cause us much reluctance to part with it ;—and the more cheerfully we shall give back to exacting Nature the poor residuum of her temporary loan.

SENILITY.

When at length by wear of time and loss of mental, moral, and physical activity, a man reaches that condition of existence in which he prefers to live quite alone ; when he no longer feels the need of fellowship or human sympathy—and lacks that desire for human association, which is the significant craving of a healthy heart and brain, or the soul-ache of the involuntarily isolated, that makes the whole world akin—then he begins to die ;—if indeed he be not dead already. This impairment of the moral functions unmistakably fits him, through diminished sensibility and loss of the power of recuperation, for the great and final change that shall come when he is destined to pass out entirely from the company and sight of his fellow-men. It seems, alas, to be a necessary part of the order and complete sequence of mortal personality, in a man who lives out the full measure of his days, according to the course of nature, and who dies of extreme old-age " sans everything."

DEATH.

Although it be true, as Rowe says, that

> Death is the privilege of human nature,

certainly but few are eager to claim it. Nevertheless, it must not be overlooked, by those inclined to grieve for themselves, at the brittleness of life, and the inevitableness of the fact of death itself, that it is but a transition. For we go into the dark, as we came out of it, and when it has happened we shall know nothing more of it here ; —so surely does the antidote accompany this bane of their content. And there is this cardinal distinction, between loss of life and every other deprivation, that by death—rationally considered—both possessor and possession are extinguished at the same instant.

The end of life may come, when we are full of infirmities, when pain predominates over pleasure, or masters even philosophic passivity ; and when the catastrophe, like a welcome friend, shall put an end to intolerable evils. The actual loss of life to ourselves, merely, is in itself an immaterial concern ;—usually unpleasant to contemplate by anticipation, especially for those in health and the enjoyment of pleasure or happiness, terrible sometimes as an impending calamity—but absolutely nothing in reality when accomplished. In itself—from a rational point of view—it involves no practical harm to our mere conscious personality. The instinct for a preservation of life at all hazards and under all circumstances, however valuable, is blind and unreasoning :—although doubtless part of a wise design of nature for the preservation of the race. If, as we trust, our personal consciousness is immortal, then by death we reach the sooner that permanent state of being wherein either the eagerness of hope shall be swallowed up in fruition of enjoyment, or we may expect at least to live for some real, enduring purpose, and confidently to look forward to seeing all our aims ultimately accomplished—since the inexorable limitations of time and mortal personal environment must be forever unknown. But if, on the contrary, this life shall involve and embrace all we ever can be, as individuals, what doth it matter to our personal identity when it shall end ;—since if ourselves be not, we can neither regret, nor suffer the loss.

Nothing need now be said of a reasonable love of prolonged life for the sake of the good one may do to others ; nor of a sorrow that may afflict the man who loves his

fellow-men, when he apprehends his protecting arm, or
liberal hand, shall be snatched away from those whose
well-being may depend upon his superior strength or
resources. Such an one, however, may find some higher
consolation—as life ebbs away—through a modest consciousness of duty done, through a submissive recognition
of the unchangeableness of the laws of nature, whose
benefits he has shared, through the hope that other hands
thereafter will he outstretched to clothe the naked or feed
the hungry whom he has loved to cherish, and through a
dominating confidence in the inexhaustibleness of the
future;—or briefly in what we call the boundless providence of God.

Broadly considered, our most afflicting view of death
lies in the loss of matured intellectual power and mental
or moral resources it may inflict upon mankind, in the
world at large. Without reference to the idea of a future
state—but looked upon physically and morally as a matter purely personal—the cessation of a mere existence,
consisting of only a capacity for suffering, often may be
regarded as something to be desired by its possessor. Yet
from a wide intellectual or impersonal view, to the sur-
vivors, the death of a man has sometimes, at least, this
one aspect of immeasurable sadness.

Our whole life, if well-spent, must be an education.
That it involves the prudent employment of an ordinary
lifetime, even to learn the best method of making a wise
use of a life, has become proverbial. At threescore and
more at the least, if the higher intellectual faculties be
not impaired by disease, accident, or imprudence, they
may have become so informed and so disciplined—the

eye of the mind so keen, discriminating, comprehensive, and judicial—that it will seem to be an unmitigated misfortune to the human race for their possessor to perish at the very acme of his usefulness. Nevertheless this appears to be the course of nature in all things—lavish waste, then superabundant reproduction. Life dies: long live Life!

III.

AMENITIES OF OLD AGE.

———a good old age, released from care,
Journeying in long serenity away.

BRYANT.

 MAN is said to reach the grand climacteric at his sixty-third year—whensoever that critical period may arrive in the life of a woman. This is well enough, as a general rule. The exceptions, common though they be, are probably not numerous enough to disprove it. Nevertheless the adage, that a woman is as old as she looks and a man as old as he feels, is usually a better practical test of human vitality than the more scientific formula.

But whatever old age may be in lexicology ; every one will know unmistakably when it comes to him individually. Aside from the slackening of attention and memory, or sluggishness of brain, there are certain signs of body and members—of touch and gait, of inelasticity of joint, limb, foot, and hand—that he who can no longer run will be compelled to read too clearly ;—as his physical powers of endurance, resistance, and recuperation begin to weaken or fail.

377

The obvious question for each one to put to himself is : What shall he do with it ? Shall he endeavor to shut his eyes to the palpable fact ? Shall he repine at its inevitableness ? Shall he simply reconcile himself, with philosophical inertia, to the unwelcome predicament ? Or shall he husband his own reserves of unhackneyed feeling, borrow by companionship something of hope and joy from his younger neighbor's excess, and draw from the world's great storehouse of amenities as much as he can of whatever he may lack within himself—for his aftermath ?

Time is a sovereign test of the spontaneousness, copiousness, soundness, and savor of a man's character. Animal spirits, the natural thirst for pleasure, the excitation of the passions (whether such as rule each passing hour, or those that steadily stimulate energy to prolonged effort for remote gains, moral, intellectual, or material) and probably more than all, the ordinary exigencies of social existence, will keep most minds sound and sweet— with little heed for the prudent accumulation and storing away, for a distant future, of spiritual wealth—while youthful elasticity and strength prevail. Nevertheless, sooner or later, satiety and even disgust are likely to overtake the superficial as well as such persons as are prone to be selfish, sour, or evil-minded. And, as Cicero observes, those who have no resources within themselves for living well and happily, are liable to find every age burdensome ; while a discontented and ill-tempered disposition will always be irksome.

To be old is not necessarily to be a dotard or decrepit. Many men, now-a-days, reach even their fourscore years and sometimes more, without finding life to become a sorrow, or the grasshopper of Ecclesiastes to be a burden. Although some powers of mind, as well as of body, have become feeble, or even atrophied, the capacity for enjoyment, through many others, may continue substantially unimpaired.

Distrust and moroseness are always more or less of the nature of vices ; but they are not peculiarly the attributes of old age. Resembling the instincts of some of the lower animals, they may flourish even in the early spring of a mean disposition, and may poison the human blood at any time of life.

But that often derided caution, which is natural to elderly persons, is discriminative, rather than general, in its nature and exercise. One may hesitate to give full credence to every interested appearance of verity, or to yield up his whole heart to each new-fledged solicitation. Yet, by the cultivated tolerance of his nature, by the broad charity of judgment that experience and patience have inculcated, and, more than all, by the comprehensive sweep of ripened reason, an old man may be inclined to even greater faith than middle-age has in the permanence of human virtue, and its expansion with the growth and development of the sociology of the race. Indeed, under ordinarily favorable circumstances, optimism, rather than pessimism, is naturally the grand outlook of the healthy mind in advanced years.

Ennui, though "nameless in our language," as Byron says, is sometimes accounted among us one of the heavy-weights that oppress men as they reach the outer edge of their span of life. But that period has no monopoly of this peculiar source of misery. The difficulty that people of excessive leisure—when animated by no higher impulse than love of themselves—find in choosing interesting and pleasant employment, belongs to no particular period of life, and is a common cause of shipwreck of happiness at every date.

It is a misfortune for some to give up wholly in late years the special occupation that has engaged all their early and more energetic days. Yet many have that breadth of understanding, that versatile capacity, that elasticity of intellect, that energy of hopefulness, which will enable them, at any time, to throw off old habitudes and enter upon a new pursuit. Others, too, have through life cherished a desire that the day might come when the sordid cares of business could be laid aside with prudence and some craving taste for higher and sweeter things—perhaps long baffled and thwarted—be gratified. For such men leisure has no terrors, whenever it may arrive, or however long it may last.

But it is not necessary that even the ordinary man—when long years of useful toil have lifted him somewhat beyond the pressure of necessary care—should still be compelled to bear the irksomeness of uncongenial labor, in order to avoid a barren weariness of life. Though still engaged in practical business affairs, he may enjoy easily many of the pleasures, while escaping much of the wear and tear of the hard task-work of a younger day. He may methodize his time, and fill up his hours, so that each revolving day shall pass smoothly and happily. An old man need not worry over apprehended remote evil results. His concern with annoying details must also be less than it was formerly, for such matters, demanding accuracy and despatch, naturally fall to the share of younger men.

In the world, his place being now determined, he is no longer compelled to urge himself to make efforts merely for its establishment. Neither will any excessive exertion be expected of him. Consequently he will not suffer the dull or painful reaction from any extraordinary strain of his reserved powers. Philosophic calm may supersede irritating anxiety. By an almost divine social law, even haste is deemed unbecoming to the gravity of years. Verily herein grows a welcome hedge for an old man's graceful serenity.

It is always hard to part by death with friends we have loved early and long. Painfully obvious is it that this misfortune befalls old-age with especial burdensomeness. It is too well recognized as a portion of the price to be paid for longevity. Nay, as life passes beyond middle-age, the frequent loss of merely familiar acquaintances presses the more heavily upon us. Each one is a fibre, more or less important, in some cord of precious association. Once broken, the filaments seldom if ever reunite.

In youth, friendships of the heart grow out of a community of early associations, sympathetic inclinations, and the fellowship of unhackneyed feeling. In middle-age friendships of the mind continue to spring up from unity of interest, similarity of character, taste, or pursuit, till the number of them usually increases despite subtraction by death. But in old-age we generally lose the power to inspire, or even interest, the feelings or intelligence of our fresh acquaintances. This isolation would have been intolerable in the days of youth. It presses less heaviiy however as the sensibilities are dulled by time or the growth of comprehensiveness has made the mind more all-sufficient unto itself. Neither is it to be forgotten that while the scythe lays low the flowers, it also cuts up the noisome nettles that grow among them. Not unfrequently the tranquillity of declining years is sensibly enhanced by the loss of our enemies !

Although, with increasing years, comes a decay of that hopefulness for the result of our own highest endeavors, which is the spur of manly minds to energetic and persistent action in the world's affairs, and which gives the chief zest to noble lives ; nevertheless, the hankering love of mere existence, and the fierce desire to achieve the common prizes of the world—despite the struggle, the toil, the privation, the pain, the mental or moral anguish necessarily involved in the hot pursuit of such rewards—grow more feeble, until contentment, a crown-jewel of mortal happiness, comes more readily within our grasp.

Now also arrives that unspeakable sense of self-satisfaction, which is the heritage of him only who has earned the never-too-much lauded, most sweet, recollection of a well-spent life. Pity it is that the good fame of declining years should suffer, in popular estimation, merely from the abusive epithets, and the deserved penalties, of those who, like Dr. Faustus, have discounted their prospects ! Our English Horace had studied well old London when he wrote :—

> See how the world its veterans rewards !
> A youth of frolics, an old age of cards.

We cannot, however, afford to quarrel with the Nemesis who, presiding at the birth of human society, has governed here—punishing mortals with her Rhadamanthine severity —at all times since.

Perhaps the quality of mercy is strained enough, in these cases, by the enactment of that benign law of abused nature, which so commonly cuts off, immaturely, from the contrition of a bitter old-age, those who, in the hot gust of transitory pleasure, have wilfully violated those mental, moral, and physical obligations, which are essential to the tenure of protracted existence in normal equilibrium. For indeed, the wholly innocent, and involuntary, sufferers from mere senile infirmity are rather an exceptional minority—perhaps generally paying a debt due to the race, arising from an overdraft made by some departed spendthrift ancestor. At the least, however, we may trust that such blameless unfortunates will find their consolation through the divine promises of compensation in a future and more perfect world—where the mystery of pain shall be wholly unriddled. It would be indeed inexplicably sad if the victims of accidental misfortune should suffer also an atrophy of such a hope.

But to those of better fortune, who have lived long in harmony with nature, a cheerful retrospection at the close of life is full of charm. For it is one of the precious traits of memory—worthy of frequent iteration—that pain and misery fade from the recollection far more easily than pleasure ; and, to the healthy-minded, remembered joy becomes much more vivid than the reminiscence of sorrow, as life slips away,

True it may be, as is commonly said, that the illusions of youth have for the most part now vanished. But it must not be forgotten that the apparently providential reasons for their continued existence have also ceased. Neither is it an unmixed evil to be no longer borne along on the wings of wilful fancy, or nourished by the deceptive allurements of ill-grounded hope. Practical judgment now becomes a dominating factor in the character, and the inexplicable pleasure of being self-cheated loses its marvellous savor. One finds a solid gratification in contemplating both the lives of his fellow-men and many significant ethical subjects, as they are in reality—unmagnified by the haze of dubiety, or unillumined by the glamour of fraudulent tradition. That confidence we once too readily gave to each individual, upon his own unsupported representation concerning himself, and that eager willingness to believe, upon imperfect evidence, what we wish to be true when affecting our own interest, steadily diminish. So also that hasty or inconsiderate action—perilling the fortune, happiness, or perhaps life, of others or ourselves, and undertaken without the guarantee of prudential foresight—gives place, in most cases, to a dispassionate sagacity of conduct, which, if it sometimes lose chances in a lottery, may at the least save us from either a self-robbery, or a profitless contrition for having beguiled our best friends to their ruin.

It can scarcely be expected, however, that old age should, automatically and without some previous personal sacrifice, bring comfort to every one. Those who have played and lost, or have squandered their patrimony of health and strength—wasting it in imprudence and excess, instead of reserving and storing their forces ;—they who have nourished ill weeds in the garden of their lives until the flowers are choked and have perished ; must look into a world stretching beyond this finite period for their hope of better things. They have chosen their alternative ; and perhaps have had their reward. The hard law of discipline, necessary to preserve the continued prosperity of the race, seems to require their wretchedness here should be suffered—at the least for the sake of example to their successors.

Sad indeed, too, is the lot of those who must close their days overweighted with care, pinched by poverty, or steeped in sorrow, from no unvenial fault of their own, or in spite of a life-long effort to achieve competence and repose. The consolations of religion, or philosophy, have marvellous powers to soften the pillow of many so afflicted. With such auxiliaries we must leave them. We may be thankful that their number is not larger, and appears to be diminishing, as civilization—ameliorating civil conditions and evolving social law—gives wider scope for opportunity to individual independence, and multiplies the chances for better things.

However, for those who are ordinarily prudent and right-minded, with even a moderate share of good fortune, old age has boundless amenities. The dread of death now constantly diminishes. Although with sound health, well-nourished youthful feelings, and natural buoyancy of spirits, we may still love life greatly, yet, as it wanes, we are more readily reconciled to the suggestion that the end is near.

To some the continual dropping away of one's contem-

25

poraries effects a benumbing indifference to all surroundings, as well as to what may happen to themselves in that
way. To others, of keener sagacity and more generous
minds, the continuance of their years, beyond those of
their companions, appears rather to be the grateful boon
of an excess of opportunity for enjoyment—beyond the
lot of their general co-heirs of mortality. Noting, too, how
many of those we had loved have gone already, we are
the less inclined to fret over what is inevitable. For we
are steadily reminded that we soon must follow, only because we have not been called before.

Although we cannot longer blink the fact of the increasing nearness of the approach of death—an event so
many men are prone, blindly, to regard as the sum of all
calamities—nevertheless, in this matter, Nature usually
inclines to deal kindly with those who treat her fairly.
As time passes on, the acuteness of our sensibility to
the touch of the Destroyer is gently dulled by the
gradual loss of eagerness and avidity in those cruder
faculties of mind and heart that made us cling to life
so fondly.

Nay, infirmity sometimes so overtakes the capacities
which make ordinary life desirable, that its duration may
be less tolerable than the blow that extinguishes it. It
may indeed happen that—so far from the nearness of
death being an unalloyed evil attendant upon old age—
the apprehension of too much life will be sometimes more
dreadful than that of death. Since it is not death itself, so
much as the act of dying, that most men fear, it well may be
reckoned, among the alleviations of advancing life, that
this unavoidable transition, from here to hereafter, in so

many ways grows less and less formidable, as our years accumulate.

Many also may be the more cheerful consolations of an old man. To begin with, at the least the past is largely his own. His memory is pretty sure to cling to the stores of that treasure-house with loving tenacity, so long as the lamp of life holds out. If it be conceded possible, that an enjoyment of the retrospect of pleasure may sometimes be as great as the realization has been, perhaps here is an indestructible fund, of some amount, out of which he may always draw at sight—upon the bank of happiness— for a currency, as good as coined gold. In this spirit Lamb said : "Amid the mortifying circumstances attendant upon growing old it is something to have seen the 'School for Scandal' in its glory."

What others are still climbing mountains, or ploughing distant oceans, or circumambulating the very globe, to see, one, with closed eyes, often may summon before him, and bid await his leisure for a revision. If he miss the pleasure, so also he will avoid the shock, of ignorant surprise, over apparently new things. While his younger neighbors are startled at the seeming novelty, or amazed at the suddenness, of events in the natural, political, or social world, he calmly contrasts, or compares, them with familiar precedents in his memory ; and involuntarily smiles superior, in recognition of the similitude.

A simple minor expedient for relieving the tedium of waning days sometimes may be found in the reperusal of such books as have charmed us, or influenced our conduct, at various periods—whether of youth or later in life. They can open many hidden doors for deep self-introspection. As there will be nò itch of notoriety—to be either appeased or sold to magazines—nor any eaves-dropper to blab the secrets of one's confessional, the catalogue of favorites need not be limited to such a dreary array as has been revealed to the public by some worthy celebrities of our day. Such reminiscent explor-ations will often suggest a forgotten clue for entertaining self-study. They can tell us pretty clearly what kind of creatures we once were—what we liked or disliked, hoped for or disdained, at other times—and how widely we may have varied our very identity with changing years.

Now, too, may we look, from an advantageous point of view, at the oscillating of the civilized world, in its hoped-for progress toward our own ideal, or toward what - we have supposed to be its purpose or drift ;—while at the same time recognizing our own gradual growth of char-acter. Such a method of contemplation—even if it be shorn of some of the fascinating allurements of earlier enthusiasm—perhaps the more easily may reconcile us to the near good-bye awaiting us, and to the final change in ourselves.

Although one is no longer exhilarated by the daring and recklessness of youth, neither has he its revulsions of feeling. If we forego many of the joys of early days, yet we are no longer helpless victims of the caprice of the temporal passions that then mastered us. If one do not rise so high in the scale of pleasurable excitement, neither is he likely to sink so low in the revulsive abyss of des-pondency. Calmly we may look down, as it were from a distant height, upon the world's broad field of battle—afar from the shock, the din, the heat, the dust, and sweat of heroes contending in the common struggle for precedence, fame, or power.

The later years of a man of intellectual pursuits—who has cultivated habits of independent thought and self-contemplation—are sometimes peculiarly opulent in their sober pleasantness. By reason of experienced observation, and the extinction of some illusory cross-lights that have been an enduring source of dazzling bewilderment, the medium through which he now looks at the vista before him becomes more clear. Now countless obscurities, that have long baffled the understanding, become easily explainable.

In early life a very embarrassing impediment to the consistent conduct of one's understanding is an inability to comprehend the proper relation of things to each other —facts and ideas or principles apparently either independent or contradictory ; also what things are important or essential, what merely factitious or temporary; and more than all what are seminal ideas or pivotal facts, and what are the mere accidents of time or the frail blossoms of budding thought—what a too prodigal efflorescence, and what a truly ripened fruit, of the revolving seasons. For, alas, to the immature mind, how many of the signal events of the world's current history appear to be more or less isolated or self-dependent. Apparently they are not the parts of any system, or even the links in any chain of events, or the evolution of any reciprocating law, or indeed with any necessary coherence at all.

Even in middle life we cannot (as later we may, through knowledge and reflection) lift ourselves easily to that lofty vantage-ground necessary to enable us to view all things comprehensively. Not seeing them as the dependent parts of a necessary entirety, we are unable, oftentimes, to detect their inevitable relations to each other; or to know when one thing is found that its correlative must exist somewhere—as it were clearly bringing order and significance out of apparent confusion.

However, in life's autumn, a partial removal from the eddying whirl of the business of current affairs can give the mind that leisure, peace, and repose, undisturbed by fugitive details—which is necessary to the power of seeing things in grand masses—so as to read the meaning of the present by the clear light of the past. At such a period one may learn also, not too late, that, while in a certain abstract sense nothing is essentially new, yet in another concrete, or practical sense, almost everything—by reason of new facts, and unanticipated combinations of fact, with the consequent birth of novel suggestions—may differ in some aspects, in our day and for our needs, from what has been before. But, although the innumerable elements that make up passing events, or modify current thought, are constantly producing such new commixtures, and novel results, still, to the analytic eye of philosophic age the materials of the medley are as old as the peopled earth; and the general laws that control them, under definite circumstances, are as certain as gravitation.

Now also it grows easy to see that received opinion— whether religious, moral, political, civil, or social, be it particular or general—is commonly not spontaneous, or even always logical, but more frequently rather historical and progressive—the irregular growth of long periods of time and emergency. Sometimes, too, it is found to be the unsuspected outcome of an unapprehended concatenation of self-repeating circumstances. In this view, we may perhaps import a fresh catholicity even into such moral ideas as control our notions of right and wrong, in human affairs. We no longer close our eyes to the fact that a popular standard of rectitude is not always fixed, like an inexorable law of physical nature, but varies with shifting circumstances—appearing often to be rather modal than essential—so that what is good, right, and necessary at one social period, becomes bad, wrong or indifferent at another.

Indeed, as age creeps over us, one grows somewhat inclined to agree with that prince of stoics, Marcus Aurelius, who so often reiterates :—"All is opinion "—" life is opinion." Such views would have been unfortunate, for us in younger days ;—either as the baleful means of preventing us from fixing a rigid standard of ethics within ourselves, or as leading us to slight the cherished morals of the society in which we may have chanced to live. In age however, while we are no longer unaware that a prevailing rule of right and wrong often lacks divine authority, we calmly perceive it is the best the time permits, and its practical necessity easily justifies its rigid maintenance. In other like matters we nourish our equanimity, by a cheerful acquiescence, in an established order of things. Now we may see clearly that convenience is commonly a better test of practical wisdom, in human affairs, than a mere consistency with untried notions of some fanciful, but barren, ideal perfection.

Perhaps some of these suggestions—common though they be—may be pressed here, not unpardonably, with a little further diffuseness. In youth, and even in middle age, the mind of the intellectual man is always more or less perplexed and harassed with countless problems or apparent riddles—both mental and moral—that ignorance, inexperience, prejudice, false-education, and deficient mental, moral, or social independence, prohibit him from solving. Most men live the larger part of their lives in a hazy atmosphere, which is often thickened with doubt—if it be not darkened by despair—concerning matters of profound consequence to them, and sometimes even vital to their continuing peace of mind. Forced, by their surroundings and peculiar limitations, to look oftentimes at the most distracting questions touching their cherished hopes and aims in life, unaided—from a single and perhaps illusory point of view—they are unavoidably compelled to substitute one enigma for another;—not seldom benumbing, or puzzling, their understandings by some mere juggle of pedantic or dogmatic words.

However as one descends the downhill side of life, he, the more readily, shakes himself free from such shackles. Sweet self-deception, whose charms we have been accustomed to hug to our bosoms in a Circean embrace—as already suggested—grows unalluring. Her blandishments now vainly besiege our unwilling ears. By a knowledge of the world and its vicissitudes, acquired through a practical participation in its varied affairs; by the reading of lives and conduct of many men, and of manners, customs, and polity of numerous peoples; by the study and observation of the multiform seed-facts that time has sown in the ploughed ground of contemporaneous history, which has been opened to sunlight during our long life

—with the consequent broadening or lighting up of our mental or moral outlook and the necessary liberalizing of our views—now the medium through which we gaze out upon the vast sea of humanity is wonderfully clarified.

We read, between the lines, the elliptical story of the Book of Life. Things before insignificant now exhibit their uses. Disorder and confusion melt and fuse into regularity, until distracting problems and enigmas work out their own solution. The high colors of passion fade in the mental spectrum. The judicial faculty continues to ripen by intrinsic growth ; and gains in impartiality from the loss of some temporal anxieties that were wont to embarrass its independence. True, the once coveted sweetness of many of the delusions of life has gone—except perhaps a delicious attar that still perfumes the secret chambers of memory. Yet the turbulent passions—which made the survival of such delusions so long possible—have cooled, and halcyon days of philosophic tranquillity have supervened.

Many protracted studies in science, art, and literary entertainment, that long have been forbidden almost by pressing cares—and especially by the unavoidable but harassing interruptions of busier days—may now be pursued with delight. The great world of society also—in some of its political, civil, domestic, and even local aspects—often assumes an interest it never had for us before. For one of the highest of intellectual enjoyments is to look upon mankind as a continuing race—of which every man is a part or a significant factor—and upon the aggregate of human affairs as a perpetuating entirety.

During most of the life-time of people generally, as has

already been noted, nearly every subject or event is presented to the mind in fragments—more or less in apparent collision, if not in actual conflict, with other like or contiguous events or subjects. But with the pellucid views of these riper years the harmony of the moral universe becomes more obvious. We look now upon scenes where the parts of things are no longer apparently discordant or even segregated, but constantly blending. Unity becomes the rule, and each part suggests its complement.

The love of fresh and wide reading, whether as a mere temporary amusement, an ornamental accomplishment, or a useful resource, usually survives. In this, as in other things, we no longer swallow our food in the mass, but with a discriminating taste we select the meat that is most convenient for us. We do not run riot now over the whole field of science, history, philosophy, and belles-lettres—snatching here and there a mouthful, and ending with a surfeit of literary indigestion. Neither are we very liable to narrow our minds, or paralyze our sympathies, by riding the hobby of some impracticable specialty, in season and out of season, until boredom becomes our undisputed territory. The spur to our speed growing dull in its rowels, we naturally fall into a jog-pace, and pick our way leisurely where the road is easy and the prospect cheerful.

Now also our knowledge of human nature gives a continuing zest to the perusal of biography of men and women, who have figured in the past, influencing more or less the events of the world, or the growth of science, learning, or opinion. Long observation of the merciless greed of conflicting interests, among individuals, classes, or communities, has created a keen desire to watch the slow evolution of law in its civil or social aspects. The vicissitudes of public events, contemporary with our past lives, have shed a new, or vivid, light upon the study of politics in the Aristotelean sense of that abused word— making the story of national affairs a resource of endless interest. The opulence of a long disciplined taste brings us into the broader fields of literature—with a calm relish for the noble, the inspiring, the beautiful, or the amusing, that is neither enslaved by authority, or self-deluded by the dread of singularity. The critical judg-ment, that has survived the wreck of superstitious, childish apprehensions, or provincial maxims of a narrow environment, placidly reviews the domain of compara-tive religions or philosophies, with a divining prescience that almost glows with prophecy. But over and above all these, yet blending them into one grand, harmonious picture, the recorded history of the human race—drawn through its monuments, its laws, and its literature, civil-ized or savage, from its archæological fable to the philo-sophical or critical treatise of the present time—opens, to the contemplative faculties, that have the comprehen-sive power to consider the drama of the development of the human race as an entire story, a source of immeasur-able pleasure and satisfaction.

These resources of reading—" dukedom large enough " —with consequent reminiscence and reflective thought, may cheat infirmity of some of its pains, and can so refine or elevate the spirit, that the approach of death may come as gently as when one drops from waking dreams into dreamless sleep.

Of the limitless consolations afforded by Christian
Faith to those who are declined into the vale of years,
this is not the place to speak.   Neither is it designed in
this brief essay to open the windows of the hallowed
retreats of that vast class of men and women whose amiable superannuation adds a charm to so many a circle
purely domestic.   These thoughts and suggestions are
addressed rather to those who are sometimes inclined, as
life progresses, to look forward with dismay to the time
when their backs shall ache with those burdensome cares
of an energetic participation in the world's work that
were once carried so lightly, but which are beginning to
make their weight felt too oppressively as an irksome
load.   To such persons a timely word, from a looker-on,
may remind them of the open secret, that, when wisely
considered and sagaciously regulated, at least the major
part of the last two decades of a life of fourscore years,
or perhaps more, may, through divine philosophy, prove
to be the happiest of the whole series.

IV.

PERSONAL IMMORTALITY.

A Discursive Meditation.

Divines can say but what themselves believe ;
Strong proofs they have but not demonstrative ;
For, were all plain, then all sides must agree,
And faith itself be lost in certainty.

DRYDEN.

HE possession of that natural individual, moral consciousness, which we call a "soul," is confessedly the highest attribute claimed by man. This peculiar element of our nature distinguishes us from all others of the animal creation—however many qualities, good or bad, we may have in common with them. So far as we know, dumb animals have neither the conception of a Creator, nor the hope of a future state of existence. Typifying mere mortal life, if they have souls, they are apparently unaware of the fact. To themselves—so far as they appear to understand the matter—this life is the be-all and the end-all. Should we encounter our favorite horses, dogs, or birds in the happy-land, their surprise would be doubtless as great as our own. And we might say in passing, since happiness in this world consists so largely in a contented enjoyment of what is present, perhaps it would not be an extravagant or too cynical a conjecture (in the light of some phases of modern polemics) that they are the more happy, because of their immunity from worry over insoluble problems, inscrutable enigmas, paradoxical mysteries, or such heroic Roman dogmas, as "the infallibility of the Church, and the damnable criminality of error and doubt."

As a topic of earnest meditation, this subject can never grow stale. Speculation concerning it, however unsatisfactory, begets increasing curiosity. Necessarily, it involves personally every human being—at least from the beginning of the world to the end of time. The best evidence relating to it—be it intuitive, demonstrative, or only probable; or whether derived from Revelation, natural reason, or what is called "Christian experience" —is vague in substance, outline, and detail. The door of honest inquiry, therefore, is opened widely to the boldest thought, the profoundest reflection, and the most varied conjecture. If not concerning its verity, as a vital religious doctrine, at least this is true so far as respects its possible bearing and effect upon human nature and conduct, individual and social, here as well as hereafter.

Whence comes, and what is that "longing after immortality," which the poet takes for granted to be the instinctive wish of every human heart? Is it a real desire, for a well-defined, perpetual state of existence, belonging to the whole human race? It is not easy to understand an intelligent, or healthy longing for that which it is impossible to comprehend fairly. We can no more con-

ceive of the condition of innumerable myriads of disembodied spirits of deceased men, women, and children, in
a life that has no end—where there is neither change of
seasons, nor night, nor day, nor birth, nor marriage, nor
death ; nor want, nor care, nor pain, nor labor, nor sorrow, nor fear, nor hope, nor expectation, nor any unsatisfied desire—than we can imagine some absurd impossibility
in geometry, as a triangle with four sides. Does it not
seem idle, then, for us to speak so familiarly of a universal wish of the human race for a happiness, in a
future state, which we cannot formulate intelligently even
to ourselves ?

Yet, when a heart-friend leaves us by death, and we
feel desolate, in our personal world, without that one, we
yearn incessantly to see again the face, and to grasp the
hand, of the one so beloved. We shudder to admit to
ourselves, that we never may look again upon that form.
That thought alone wrenches the heart with pain. Nevertheless this is not so much from a desire for a definite
future state, as it is that we are pondering mournfully the
apparent fact of our being separated, from one we love,
by the impassable barrier of—"Nevermore." Even
this mere word, at such times, harrows the feelings, and,
in the freshness of profound grief, seems to chill the
blood. Only when time has steadied the nerves, when
emotion has subsided or become subordinate to the
teachings of reason, and sensibility is dulled by diversion
or routine, do we look temperately again upon a condition of things seemingly inscrutable. Then we may
remember, with Goethe, that "man is not born to solve
the problem of the universe, but to find out where the

problem begins, and then, to restrain himself within the limits of the comprehensible."

What, to our conception, is this immortality? Dumas *fils*, in his eulogy upon Victor Hugo, said :—"When a devout man dies, convinced that he shall have eternal bliss, it is as if he really had it. That moment is worth eternity—perhaps embraces it." Of course no man can expect to be able to form a sensible, precise idea of eternity, or even of perpetuity. To attempt it would be at least as absurd, as the endeavor to put a giant into the clothes of a dwarf. As Pierre Nicole says :—"L'éternité rompt toute mesure et detruit toute comparaison." But to a mind full to the measure of its capacity, it is immaterial whether any excess offered be more or less. When the soul is wrought up to such a pitch of excitement that it fully comprehends, and yields itself to, one supreme instant of ecstasy, the past and future—memory and forecast—are swallowed in the conception of that particular moment. To itself, there is only a constant—"Now." To its own instant comprehension it is as if nothing ever had been, or could be, otherwise. Analysis and comparison are not possible. If that moment be absolutely happy, it is "eternal bliss." Such has been the expiring consciousness of a martyr—sublimated beyond physical pain—floating into the everlasting. What mattered it to him then, whether that "eternity" of happiness was in fact only an instant in duration followed by oblivion, or a perpetuity? As he could look neither backward nor forward, regret was impossible, while hope and fruition of joy were one. In what respect would one such concentrated instant of time (if followed by immediate annihilation) fall below his notion of a perpetual duration of the same exaltation ? The capacity of his whole emotional, mental, and spiritual nature, being absolutely satiated, the immediate moment must s ..u to his consciousness everlasting—so far as such an idea is then, by him, conceivable. In this sense, at least, a devout believer might be allowed to win and wear his crown of immortal glory—in spite of any malign doubt engendered by an agnostic's claim to superior sagacity, learning, or wisdom in this matter.

Outside of Revelation, however—perhaps it cannot be repeated too often—"all we know is, nothing can be known" of the soul of a man—either before his mortal life began, or after his bodily death. How it comes to be born, whenever a man is created ; whether he had an ante-natal soul ; or whether that principle of life, called the soul, is anything more than a manifestation of the chief attribute of a perishable body ; or whether it is something immortal that can be transmitted to another perishable body here, or to some imperishable body hereafter—we are unable alike, without some supernatural revelation, to discover. The analogies of nature, drawn from the animating principle of the animal or vegetable world, seem to indicate it to be a temporary property of the bodily organization, and to forbid us to expect—or too confidently even to hope—anything for the individual, after the extinction of this earthly life. What sometimes is called the instinctive desire for perpetuity, appears, to the understanding, to relate to a continuity of the race alone. But, although—aside from Revelation—we may know nothing of a possible ultimate future for us, we can not dogmatically say :—"There can be none." And although we may guess only whence we came, or why we came at all, we may not doubt there is involved in the creation and conduct of the immeasurable universe, some definite plan, of which we are a significant, if not an essential, part.

Nevertheless—since man is by nature a pious-minded, or at least a superstitious creature—from the beginning of this world, imagination, fear, hope, and other willing passions and instincts of men have been played upon successfully, by religious enthusiasts and impostors, for good or evil. They have generally assumed every man to possess an imperishable soul, subject to the caprice, or to the man-like temper, of an omnipotent, humanly personified Creator of a universe, of which they have fancied this earth is at least the moral centre !

Upon bold hypotheses, as facts, they have built vast superstructures of marvels, fables, theories, ceremonials, and resonant apothegms, which, among their votaries, have been commonly called religions. Being founded generally — as respects supernatural authority — upon nothing but superstitious or fraudulent fiction, such systems have grown easily into colossal labyrinths of dogma and creed, befogged with allegorical mysticism. Puzzling and bewildering, by their rites and symbols, they have survived by inspiring men, women, and children, with alternate terror and hope. Having invented an undiscoverable *terra incognita*, their founders have opened a field where human ingenuity—unembarrassed by fact— has been free to formulate whatever chimeras or enigmas will or convenience might suggest. By the aid of power and opportunity—working upon the credulous apprehen-

sions and eager wishes of ignorant and timid people—
they have found means to establish, and sometimes
forcibly to maintain, their devices. There not being a
single affirmative fact, beyond that of apparent creation
—or of life and death—as a guide, nor evident limit to
conjectural possibility beyond the suggestion of a bare
denial, a great number of minds, for an indefinite period
in the history of mankind, hitherto have been able—
chiefly by forestalling the religious impressions of youthful or ignorant minds—to cajole, or frighten into abject
submission, vast numbers of the human race. Over a
large part of the habitable globe they have prevailed, by
at first inventing riddles, and then by exalting or tormenting human beings, with plausible endeavors to solve
them—or at least to penetrate imaginary mysteries.

Their victims do not seem to have considered that the
assumption of the personal immortality of a soul necessarily might involve the inexplicable supposition that it
never had a beginning. They seem also to have taken
for granted that an endless personal rational consciousness would be not only endurable by every one, but also
necessarily desirable. Or, even if—to make the beatitude more alluring—they sometimes counted upon a total
transubstantiation of the present consciousness of a man,
many seemed to have overlooked the fact that we may
realize an immortality superior to that, through our posterity alone ;—without subjecting ourselves to a possible
chance of intolerable weariness from an everlasting
unchangeable personal identity. No such perplexing
problems of definiteness appear to have disturbed seriously the vacuousness of their ecstatic anticipations.

Out of man's capability for conceiving this idea of the possibility that something unknown, good or bad, shall happen to his individual moral consciousness hereafter—somewhere beyond the precincts of the sphere of this mortal life—what a vast amount of the practical material of actual social existence has been contrived! The potency of this factor in the affairs of mankind cannot be exaggerated. It opens a channel for exploitation of the whole spirituality of man's nature ; always broadening and deepening—never to be closed.

From being, in the beginning—irrespective of divine Revelation—apparently a sort of random conjecture, or a loose unscientific inference from abnormal, or supposititious, experience and dubious fact, this conception of an immortal soul has been so often made use of—by sagacious men, in their desire to elevate or dominate others —that, in the course of ages, it has been, as it were, the pivot of nearly all the important motives which have controlled the highest phases, social as well as individual, of human conduct. From some points of view, it seems almost as if human nature itself had been turned topsy-turvy ;—so that, in some communities for some classes, the crown of the column has become its base. Such has been also the luxuriant growth of man's natural capacity for so-called beliefs in what he was pleased to call a perpetual state of his existence, and such varieties of suggestion swarm among its limitless possibilities, that in communities wherever such a belief has been formulated into the basis of a systematic religion, many men and women seem to have reckoned their self-absorption in reveries of a remote thought-world, apart from temporal affairs, to be their only real life—even during their mortal existence.

Among ourselves, inheritance of pious tendencies, early impressions or training, and the practical universality of a recognition of the absolute verity of our Christian theology, all have worked together, so that, when one comes to man's estate, the twisted threads of memory, association, and a tutored consciousness of what are known as spiritual ideas, form the ligamental part of his whole mental and moral history. Even practical men sometimes talk of their inner personal consciousness, its experiences or raptures, and of their anticipations of the outcome of its immortality, almost as confidently as of actualities. Indeed with some, these things seem to be more real than the fleeting reminiscence of passing occurrences, or than the substantial purposes and facts of their every-day world.

With others, whose imagination and sensibility are acutely alive to morbid impressions, such a habit of inner-self-contemplation or spiritual reverie—whether in hours of joy or sadness—becomes an inexhaustible source of exquisite emotion. In not a few persons, this peculiar exercise of self-consciousness ripens to a kind of disease ; —so abnormal does its outgrowth become, in comparison with other intellectual attitudes, and so far beyond what a plain understanding indicates to be its due proportion in a well-balanced character. With some of such people, energy, that should blossom into action, fades away, or evaporates in fruitless day-dreams. In this direction also lies the germ of much morbid melancholy, not seldom too tenderly nourished. It is a state of mind, that, when in apparent distress, however, does not deserve much sympathy ; for its root is usually an over-indulged selfishness, or at least self-pity. Not infrequently it is the flower of merely discontented indolence ;—being found to flourish most abundantly where there is the least real discomfort, and therefore called the voluptuousness of pain. But who can estimate, or characterize, the vagaries of an exaggerated, morbid self-consciousness ?

One will sometimes fancy he has within his soul a mystical susceptibility ;—not unlike that of an æolian harp giving forth sad strains of vague music, as the sighing wind passes across its chords. Another, when hope for immortal happiness seems to falter, may hear the voices of the loved and lost, crying :—" Never again." These doleful sounds he fancies resemble an echo from afar, like the moaning of the sea, when a storm is rising ; or as if such plaintive notes were a resonance of the waves of Eternity, beating against the shores of Time. Especially to persons so constituted does a lively faith in an everlasting future seem to be a necessary element of their mortal existence. Without this faith, as an anchor, they fear to drift (and perhaps, by reason of an excess of it, sometimes do drift) into the shoreless sea of moral insanity.

To the minds of most men, apparently from an incalculably remote period, some undefinable notion of future personal existence has been, somehow, not only a refuge in their hours of affliction, or depression, but also the essence of their moral subsistence. Without a conviction of its necessary verity, their individual life would seem to be, for them, a mere succession of incoherent events, leading to nothing ;—with no real purpose or significance. In the last analysis of their profoundest emotions of sorrow and anguish, the prospective compensations of a future state have enabled them to seem to solve most of the embarrassing enigmas, to reconcile the apparent inconsistencies and to clear up the mysteries, they sometimes find evolved by their theory of the divine conduct of the affairs of this world. Amid the severest trials of life, they appear to have sought and discovered a solace in the contemplation of this notion of some unformulated state of beatitude beyond the grave.

When all the resources of temporal human-nature have failed to sustain their fortitude, this faith in a personal immortality has opened for them a door to the widest conjecture concerning such a future universe of occupation and enjoyment as shall be most pleasing and satisfactory to each one's individual wishes. For, to many speculative and devout minds, there is a prodigious fascination in the vague idea, that, notwithstanding the vicissitudes of this mortal existence—however severe they may be—yet in a future state, whose duration shall extend beyond possible conception, all that is merely irksome, as well as all that is painful, shall somehow cease ; while positive joy, and unending happiness of some kind, in some indescribable manner, shall be the normal and unbroken condition of even such minds and hearts, and perhaps bodies, as we now possess.

It would be idle perhaps to suggest—at least to a pagan believer of this speculative class—that he has no faculties to appreciate such a state of things ; that every notion of which he is now capable of conceiving must be finite in its nature, deducible from his present experience and the use of his merely human powers ; since it is quite as easy for him to suppose new capacities will be given to enable him to comprehend, and take to himself all the opportunities of the new situation, as it is for him to fix his belief upon undefined resources of a fathomless future. In vain would one venture to suggest to him that his original nature, and all that embraces his present self-identity, either would be obliterated wholly by so miraculous a change from the old to the new existence he presupposes, or would be lost utterly in its infinitesimalness, amid the grandeur of his new attributes and the magnificence of the exercise of them. For his spiritual explorations are not only limitless, but untrammelled by mortal logic, or even coherent spiritual insight. He would readily imagine another miraculous variation of alleged law, by means of which the lesser, or inferior condition, would cease to suffer in comparison with the greater or superior one. All that he loved or wished for in this life, could be realized in perpetuity, without a satiety consequent upon endless repetition, and also, without in the least diminishing his fitness for an entirely new and independent state of existence ! In other words, when boundless faith in the unknown and inconceivable takes possession of the human mind, its exaltation is beyond the test of what is commonly called reason. An indefinable spirituality dominates him, and miracles become his natural food. True it is, that the majority of mankind —possibly even among Christians—do not always rise to this implicit realistic faith in the everlasting future existence of their special personal identity. Nevertheless, the substitution, in many cases, of what is considered a well-grounded hope for such things, is composed of very similar material, and carries its willing subject nearly as far; although sometimes with an unequal or hesitating pace.

Not unfrequently it is urged, at least colloquially—as a secular argument from reason alone in support of our notion of the immortality of the soul—that men always have had religions, and generally have believed in some future state as well as in the continuation in perpetuity of a direct personal relation between God and man. The fact of these almost universal, archaic, so-called beliefs, is set down as certainly persuasive evidence of a primeval revelation of some kind, far back in the ages, before the period of recorded history, when the race was new, and its relations to its Maker (perhaps directly through the heads of tribes or families) were comparatively recent and necessarily recognized. To many minds—and especially to those which are sanguine, willing, and easily credulous—this seems to be a convincing probable argument. That a thing must be true, because it is, and long has been believed commonly, is the plausible reasoning of the ordinary mind. And indeed, in general affairs, it is familiar experience that we are all prone to act, more or less, upon conclusions, with no surer basis for our understanding, or better logic for our belief, than mere probabilities to support them. However, in the common practical concerns of life, such belief rests upon apparent and well-accredited objective experience, or upon inferences from admitted facts. Besides, in ordinary matters such conclusions, if erroneous, are liable constantly to correction, by frequent recurrence of the same, or similar facts, or of like external experiences. With a belief in a future state of existence, however, and its supernatural concomitants, there is obviously always this profound distinction ; such belief must rest either upon an assumption of something not self-evident, or upon some kind of a revelation. The first at any time may be found to be gratuitous, or without deserved universal assent. The latter—except with those who are spiritually satisfied with what is now called "the evidences of Christian experience," or its unsanctified similitude—must rest finally upon ancient historical proofs, traditional or written, that are always open to be questioned. As learning, science, or the skepticism of a refined civilization advance, doubts arise ; and assertion can have but little, if any, chance of absolute verification, at this late period of time. Moreover, in any case, the value of merely probable evidence— as a basis of conviction or faith—must, of course, be somewhat measured by the magnitude, or abnormality, of the conclusion sought to be established, by such evidence.

Is there undue harshness then in the judgment that pronounces this so-called argument, from the mere fact of a general popular belief up to an absolute verity of the thing believed—however specious, or even dominant with the philosophers of pagan antiquity—to be fallacious ? Primarily, it assumes that the human mind, reasoning from the history of its own operations, is infallible. It is as if one were to say, as some often do : "I believe, because I always have believed." But the mind is necessarily controlled by its own special limitations, as well as by whatever idiosyncrasies—through birth, early impression, or education in its largest sense— are peculiar to itself. At best, such an argument—at least for all natural religion—comes only to this :—A belief in the supernatural, or in the future state, is a continuing spontaneous intuition of our nature, and therefore the thing believed must exist. This proposition assumes too much. Is not the wish father to the thought ? Would it not be much wiser, and even safer logic (if we had no specific Revelation) to say that He who made man knew that an essential element of our happiness here would be a belief of that sort ; and therefore, in order to sustain and perpetuate the race, He gave such belief to us, as a part of our nature, just as He gave us our other instincts, passions, appetites, and intellectual characteristics ? Shall it be said : "It is incredible that we would be created with so strong a desire as this so-called 'longing after immortality,' if it were wholly dependent upon a mere illusion?" But is not the happiness of our whole lives sustained by a continuous series of somewhat similar illusions ? If this belief had no other origin than what has just been suggested, how would such a source differ essentially from the ordinary sweet illusions of life, that bloom in youth, and gradually fade, as years creep over us ;—except that, perhaps, in order to justify the purpose of its existence, it might be found to endure somewhat longer than these others. But this qualification, cannot be urged with too much assurance of certainty. It is understood to be the common melancholy experience of those who limit their belief in immortality to the arguments which sustain natural religion, that their faith in the supernatural, and their hope for a happy future, grow weaker as life passes on. Indeed it is even liable to exhale altogether, when they approach the dark valley and stand most in need of the "fact" of a Christian faith as a rod and staff, to support their tottering steps.

Perhaps, it is not too much to say, that (like all other arguments outside of Christian Revelation) these popular so-called proofs rest upon plausible fallacies and fascinating self-sufficiencies, that rather tend to hurt, than to benefit the cause of a sound faith in the facts of our Divine Religion. Without this Gospel Revelation it appears to be not possible for us to know, or even to conceive coherently, aught of these things. On that basal rock we must rest or have no foundation whatever. Beyond that there is no valid rational proof ; and, moreover, we seem to be without the capacity to comprehend it if any there were. As St. Paul frankly confessed to the believers of his day : " If Christ be not risen, then is our preaching vain, and your faith vain." Indeed, some of the stoutest defenders of Christianity add another condition, and concede that the truth of this Revelation itself can be proved only to those that antecedently assume the existence of a personal God, who is the moral Governor of the world. So narrow, it would seem to the mere understanding of man, is the only plank to which we may cling, in order to escape total shipwreck of our sublime hope of a personal immortality.

.   .   .   .   .   .

My rôle in life-to-come what faith dare scan ?
How shall I claim a right to live again,
Myself to be—or yet another man ?
This light put out, will aught of me remain ?

We smile and weep through many changeful years ;
We dream ; we watch earth's phantoms come and go,
We see what manhood hopes, or age reveres,
Fade out, and vanish as an idle show.

We live and love ; we strive and hope, and pray
For what we cannot hear or see or know ;
Absorb the pleasures of the passing day,
Then drop asleep as still as falling snow.

If this be all, if death our goal and end,
Though pain and sorrow be but foils to joy,
The past, the present, and the future blend
Till Time's pure gold is lost in the alloy.

Not so. Be God or Law the primal cause,
Some purpose was, when man began to be—
Some vast design whose work will never pause
Till Cosmos reach perfectibility.

What share be mine, in vain for me to ask—
An atom in this grand economy—
To love my neighbor as myself, my task,
Not questioning divine autonomy.

V.

NIL DESPERANDUM.

——noble minds contemn despair.
MARLOWE.

NO bounds are set for star-eyed Hope ;
  The arm of God hath given her scope,
Beyond the darkness where we grope :
  None but the blind and sluggish mope ;
    Hope on, hope ever.

O Iris-tinted Dream of youth !
  Unheeding Time's corrosive tooth,
We read the gospel of thy ruth,
  Red-lettered in the Book of Truth ;
    Hope on, hope ever.

Impartial Hope ! A leveller thou,
  That stoops to kiss the humblest brow ;
E'en though thy smile illude us now,
  Still, at thy shrine, we make our vow ;
    Hope on, hope ever.

No lot is chosen ; each is drawn :
  The keenest pang is soonest gone :

The darkest hour is nearest dawn :
Some arch will span, where chasms yawn ;
Hope on, hope ever.

A hero is the world's delight :
True glory is celestial light ;
O Soldier, in the direst fight,
O Sailor, in the roughest night,
Hope on, hope ever.

While throbs this restless thing called life,
With mingled joy and sorrow rife,
Rouse all thy courage for its strife ;
War with dejection to the knife ;
Hope on, hope ever.

Though love despondent chill thy heart,
Or hatred rive twin souls apart,
Or broken faith hath left a smart,
Time hath a magic healing art ;
Hope on, hope ever.

If Fortune turn her wheel from thee,
Or Friendship prove a mockery ;
Each year is not a Jubilee,
The Future shall thy guerdon be ;
Hope on, hope ever.

When serpent-toothed Ingratitude
Would kindness from thy heart exclude,
Expand thy narrow brotherhood ;

Embrace the helpless multitude ;
   Hope on, hope ever.

Hath Slander, with envenomed tongue,
   Thy bosom nigh to madness stung ?
Live down the lie, thy foes among,
   And put to shame the babbling throng ;
     Hope on, hope ever.

Doth Pleasure's bait thy feet incline
   To sty of Epicurus' swine ?
Though all thy stars neglect to shine,
   Remember that a soul is thine ;
     Hope on, hope ever.

Is thy proud heart benumbed with shame ?
   Hast blemished a once-honored name ?
Burn pure in penitential flame ;
   Thy manhood and thy will reclaim ;
     Hope on, hope ever.

Should Death invade thy pretty fold,
   Where Love and Duty vigils hold,
And snatch thy lambs despite thy gold,
   Let not thy halting trust grow cold ;
     Hope on, hope ever.

When Faction shakes the tottering State,
   Or Parties strive with fiendish hate ;
Heed not the cry—" It is too late ; "
   Immortal Truth will pause and wait ;
     Hope on, hope ever.

Dost dread agnostic to become ;
  With blinded heart, and spirit dumb,
To measure God by rule of thumb ?
  Oh ! never to thy doubt succumb ;
    Hope on, hope ever.

Expect the mysteries, of pain
  And moral evil, to be plain,
As Law unwinds her endless chain,
  Till Faith assumes her throne again ;
    Hope on, hope ever.

Whatever portents crowd the sky,
  Look up beyond thy misery,
Nor nurse the evil in thine eye ;
  Some angel unawares is nigh ;
    Hope on, hope ever.

I am not what I seem to be,
  Nor am I bond, nor am I free ;
The Lord-of-all is Lord of me ;
  To Him I yield the victory ;
    Hope on, hope ever.

INDEX.

419

www.ingramcontent.com/pod-product-compliance
Lightning Source LLC
Chambersburg PA
CBHW021324110726
47900CB00005B/1342